PRACTICAL PHRENDONICS

Books by Douglas J. Bornemann

The Demon of Histlewick Downs (Book 1 of the Dreamweaver Chronicles). This standalone novel explores historic events that set the stage for the rest of the Heiromancer Trilogy.

The Heiromancer Trilogy:
　　Practical Phrendonics
　　A House of Cards
　　Hanged Man's Gambit

Shady Fortunes

Website: dougbornemann.com
Facebook: https://www.facebook.com/djbornemann/
X (Twitter) @DougBornemann

PRACTICAL PHRENDONICS

BOOK TWO OF
THE DREAMWEAVER
CHRONICLES

AND

VOLUME ONE OF
THE HEIROMANCER
TRILOGY

Douglas J. Bornemann

Published by SORCELERITY

First Print Edition
ISBN 978-0-9906281-3-2
Copyright © Douglas J. Bornemann, 2016

To Mom and Dad...for gifts both practical and fanciful

Table of Contents

ĐRAMATIS PERSONAE

Adam Deargard
>   *Dona's classmate at Exidgeon University*

Alexi Reysa
>   *Dona's classmate at Exidgeon University*

Alistair Nevinander
>   *Aging patriarch of the Nevinander family*

Alphonse
>   *Alexi's fencing buddy*

Amanda Merinne
>   *Dona's mother and Rayen's sister and caretaker*

Amehtan Shoruga
>   *Hathaway Professor at Exidgeon University;*
>   *Shunese defector*

Arerlo
>   *Marguerite's manservant*

Arietta Charwick
>   *Dona's gangly and unpleasant classmate*

Armand Goodkin
>   *Monsignor who arrives to investigate the distur-*
>   *bance at the University*

Aunt Olivia
 Nathalie Nevinander's sister
Jamie
 Nephew of Father Cartier, waiter at Tabalaria
Caroline Caldor
 Dona's classmate
Chancellor Wiggins
 Chancellor of Exidgeon University
Charles Danforth
 Dona's classmate
Clarke Reston
 Professor of History at Exidgeon
Constable Connelly
 Constable of Trifienne; Miranda's father
Crown Prince
 Sovereign of Trifienne, father of Princess Julienne
Crown Princess
 Wife of the Crown Prince
Damien Nevinander
 Alistair and Nathalie's eldest son
Darron Goodkin
 Primal and brother of Monsignor Armand Goodkin
Dominick Everson
 Professor of Grammar at Exidgeon
Dona Merinne
 Daughter of Henry and Amanda Merinne; student at Exidgeon University
Dorian Emolino
 Friend of Gregory Delauren, Baritone at the opera house
Dreamweaver
 Legendary niece of Phrendonian, reputed to have invented Daemonology

Francesca Harcourt
Mother of Jonas and Mathilda; they call her 'Nanna'

Father Cartier
Priest of St. Sophia's Church in Trifienne

Gregory Delauren
Dona's friend and sometimes classmate; an up-and-coming tenor at the opera

Helena Dunkirk
Dona's friend and roommate at Exidgeon

Jedidiah Nevinander
One of the twin sons of Alistair and Nathalie

Jeorg
Mathilda's hired muscle

Jonas Mapleton Harcourt
Traveling merchant dealing primarily in spirits

Marguerite Serrola
Matriarch of the Serrola family

Mathers
Librarian at Exidgeon University

Mathilda (Tilly) Harcourt
Sister to Jonas, owns and runs a brothel in Trifienne

Michlos Serrola
Son of Marguerite and Spiros Serrola

Miranda Connelly
Dona's friend and roommate at Exidgeon; Constable's daughter

Miss Maxtine
House mother of the women's dormitory at Exidgeon

Morissant
Gregory Delauren's wealthy patron

Mr. Lop Ears
Dona's childhood stuffed toy

Mrs. Caldor
Mother of Caroline, Member of the Venerable Assembly of Church Mothers

Mrs. Laverne Temrich
Hard-of-hearing member of the Venerable Assembly of Church Mothers

Mrs. Muscany
Member of the Venerable Assembly of Church Mothers

Mrs. Myra Curtsik
Member of the Venerable Assembly of Church Mothers

Mrs. Tibbleman
Senile but lovable member of the Venerable Assembly of Church Mothers

Nathalie Nevinander
Alistair's wife; Member of the Venerable Assembly of Church Mothers

Newcomb
Princess Celeste's manservant and personal guard

Ordinal Laitrech
Advisor of Primal Darron Goodkin; one of his more recently appointed Ordinals

Phrendonian
Legendary codifier of Phrendonic Heresy

Princess Celeste
Sovereign of the Island that is home to the Artist's Colony

Princess Julienne
Youngest daughter of the Crown Prince and Princess of Trifienne

Professor Amberton
Scrawny Professor at Exidgeon, confidant to Professor Reston

Professor Bartholomew Driessen
Professor of Geometry at Exidgeon University

Professor Fenton Tamry
Professor at Exidgeon, confidant to Professor Reston

Professor Rutledge
Professor of Music at Exidgeon University

Randolph Brent
Bursar at Exidgeon

Rayen the Magnificent
Dona's uncle; subject to occasional seizures, he believes they reveal the future

Reginald Nevinander
One of the twin sons of Alistair and Nathalie

Spiros Serrola
Marguerite Serrola's dead husband

Terulla Kardell
Dona's classmate at Exidgeon

Thaddeus Nevinander
Alistair and Nathalie's youngest son, younger brother to Verone

Thurman Goodkin
Armand Goodkin's son and assistant

Verone Nevinander
Daughter of Alistair and Nathalie Nevinander

Zachary Hepplewhite
Professor of Rhetoric and Theology at Exidgeon; old friend of the Monsignor

TRIFIENNE

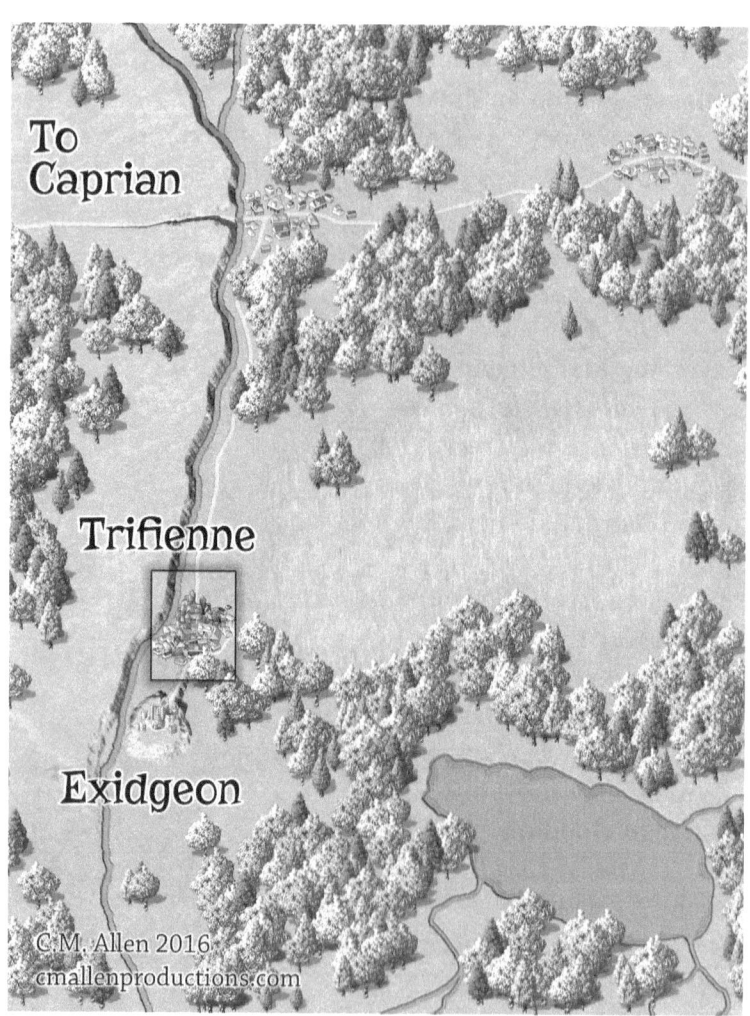

To Caprian

Trifienne

Exidgeon

C.M. Allen 2016
cmallenproductions.com

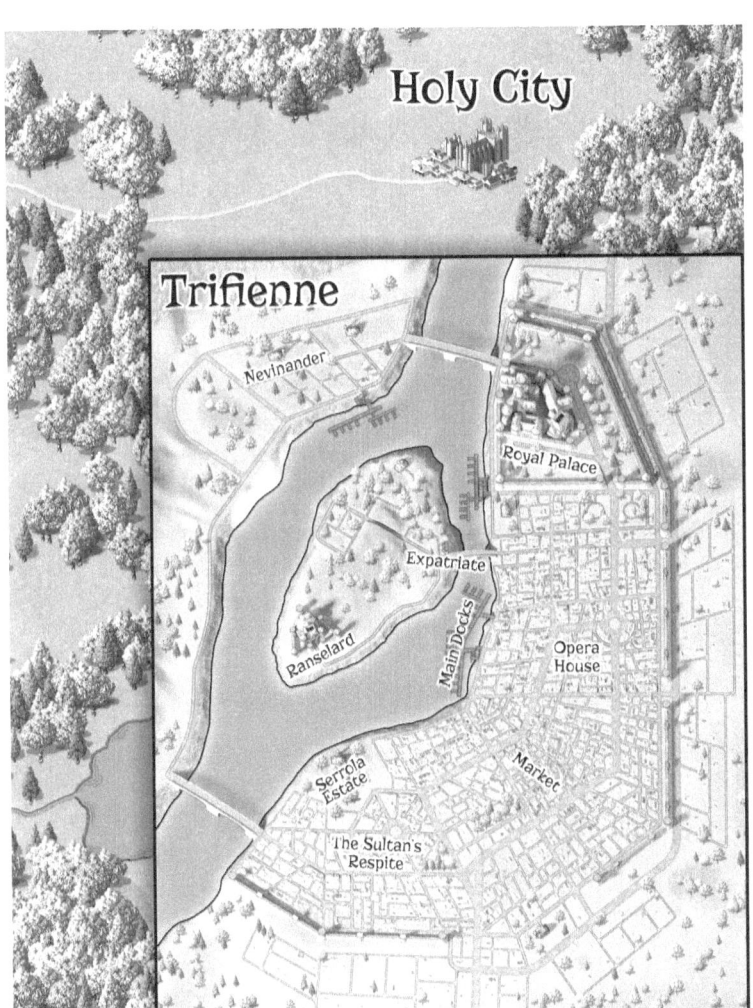

Holy City

Trifienne

Nevinander

Royal Palace

Expatriate

Ranselard

Main Docks

Opera House

Serrola Estate

Market

The Sultan's Respite

I never cease to marvel how people can ignore the overwhelming influence of fate on their daily lives. In my experience, far more turns on the "chance meeting" or the "accident of birth" than on all the best-laid plans ever devised.

~Rayen the Magnificent

FOREWORD

Forty years have passed since the Caprian Inquisition. Through unprecedented brutality, the Church achieved its purpose—to this day, Phrendonic heresy remains suppressed, the promise of its magic—and the consequences of its misuse—all but forgotten. Few alive recall the nature of that forbidden movement, and those who do, remember all too well the perils of falling under its sway. Even those who escaped found no succor, for they became pariahs—rejected by kith and kin alike, either out of disgust or for fear of falling under suspicion themselves. The Church's wrath left its imprint on the people's collective psyche. Yet, while raging flames may consume the forest, eventually the land must cool. Once it does, it takes but a single seed…

PRACTICAL PHRENDONICS

STUDIES IN DARKNESS AND LIGHT

Verone stepped from the carriage and into Trifienne's outdoor market amidst a sea of parasols and elaborate hats. Her signature gown, a study in steel grey and pinstripes, was stark against the vibrant hues that swirled about her, but it did wonders to downplay the less flattering aspects of her robust profile. Despite the brightness of the morning, she was traveling sans parasol—a conceit she'd abandoned long ago in favor of a utilitarian attaché in finely crafted leather.

A quick pat of her ginger-blonde hair, and she was off. Anticipation buoyed her every step. Today, at long last, she would topple the domino to set everything in motion.

The little patio café was every bit as crowded as the market itself. Fortunately, she'd scheduled the meeting for a time half an hour earlier than she'd intended to arrive—she'd never had much patience for such quaint plebeian pastimes as waiting in queues.

Her dining partner, Professor Dominick Everson, had claimed one of the tables scattered across the teeming cobblestone terrace, and to his credit, he'd chosen one within the dappled shade of an overhanging bough. Dominick Everson —rarely had she laid eyes on anyone so thoroughly nondescript. He was soundly middle-aged, with thinning brown hair and an academic's build—slender with a hint of paunch.

He waved to gain her attention, displaying a lack of refinement that made her cringe. Outwardly, though, her smile only broadened. The man's obliviousness to social nuance was part and parcel of what made him so well suited for the role he'd unwittingly volunteered to play for her—that, and his affiliation with a clandestine band of heretics. After all, any complex scheme could benefit from a solid fallback position. And if it should come to that, who better to take the fall for heresy than an actual, honest-to-goodness heretic?

"Dommy, darling," Verone said, as he pulled out a wrought-iron chair for her. "It's so kind of you to meet with me like this."

"It's my pleasure," Everson said, taking his seat. He eyed the surrounding tables and dropped his voice to a whisper. "I've been dying to tell someone I finally got that new spell of yours to work, and if you think about it, you're the only one I *can* tell."

"Of course it worked, hon. When brilliant teacher meets exemplary student, success is sure to follow."

Everson peered at her over his glass. "I'm so glad I managed to find you. I would never have come so far so fast working with my University group."

"And I'm so glad you're making such progress. Now that you've passed such a significant milestone, perhaps it would be a good time to discuss a little *quid pro quo?*"

"By all means. I presume you're still amenable to payment in the form of services?"

"Absolutely. In fact, you can bring your account current simply by making one tiny little delivery."

Everson leaned forward. "It's not out of town, is it? The earliest I could get away would be next summer. You weren't expecting me to cancel classes, were you?"

"My, such a worry wart. No need to panic, it's merely a delivery to someone at your very own University."

"That's it? That's all it would take?"

Verone shot him a sidelong look. "In the middle of the night." She slipped a large package out of her attaché. "And, in absolute secrecy. No one must ever know you were there."

His eye twitched. "This isn't going to be dangerous, is it?"

She patted his cheek. "You're really going to have to stop stressing like that. You'll ruin your digestion."

"Answer the question. Is this going to be dangerous?"

"I know it's a little unusual, but really, how dangerous could it be? Haven't you ever been on campus at night before? Or…would you rather talk cash?"

"I guess if you put it that way…"

Verone brightened and slid the package toward him. "So, we're agreed?"

Everson eyed the parcel and gulped. "And that will cover everything?"

Verone flashed her most reassuring smile. "Every last little thing."

"All right, I'll do it."

"Excellent. The address is on the package. The building is the third on the right past the statue of Lord Hathaway."

"It's going to a Hathaway Scholar?"

"Does it matter?"

Everson's eye gave one final twitch as he reversed the package and squinted at the label. "I suppose not."

She rummaged through her leather case. "Oh, and you might want to take this with you." She produced a lacquered stick notched halfway along its length. "If you should run into any difficulties, snap it in two."

Everson's forehead creased as he inspected it. "What's this?"

"Just a precaution, hon, and not one you should need if you're careful. And remember, the message must stay confidential. No peeking."

"I take it you're not going to tell me. Is the stick some sort of test? Am I supposed to figure it out on my own?"

Verone shrugged. "That's up to you. The circumstances shouldn't require it."

Everson pocketed the stick. "I guess you have a point—what could possibly go wrong?"

"That's my Dommy. And once this little chore is behind you, we can start discussing what to teach you next."

"I've been thinking about that—"

She cut him off with a waggling forefinger. "Oh, no you don't. That discussion doesn't start until after the delivery."

"Oh, very well. You have no idea how lucky you are coming from a family where you could learn this stuff as a matter of course."

An indignant gasp—only partially stifled—escaped Verone, but a savage effort of will instantly restored her composure. She raised an eyebrow and deliberately met his gaze. "*Oh?*"

"Don't worry, your secret is safe. I'd never have suspected if I hadn't been part of Reston's little group, and even then, putting two and two together wasn't trivial."

She fumbled for her attaché. "How lucky for us that you are such a clever student. Now, if you'll excuse me, I have a delivery of my own to make."

Everson stood. "My apologies. Had I known you were planning to leave so soon, I'd have ordered for you."

"You know I'd like nothing better than a nice leisurely lunch, but it can't be helped. Good luck, and don't forget the stick."

A glance over her shoulder confirmed Everson was waving as enthusiastically in farewell as he had in greeting.

She hadn't intended to leave in such a rush, but the subject of her family had struck a nerve, and she couldn't abide the thought of showing weakness in Everson's presence. Once well away, she found a quiet bench. From her attaché she drew forth a cream-colored document, ready for the post in all but the lack of a seal. It was addressed to Marguerite Serrola—an invitation to the 65th birthday celebration of Verone's father, Alistair. The note trembled in her hand as Everson's comment dredged up incidents she'd thought she'd locked safely away.

Steeling herself, she drove the unruly memories back into the deepest recesses of her mind. Shrouded once more in her familiar mantle of cool self-possession, she lit a lucifer, melted the wax, and dabbed some onto the invitation. The illusion of control was nearly perfect, betrayed, if at all, only by the fact that she imprinted the wax with her father's stolen seal using a bit more force than strictly necessary.

· · · · ·

Helena stopped in her tracks. "You can't be serious."

Dona set her jaw. "I've never been more."

They were taking a shortcut to class among the squat administrative buildings in the very heart of campus. Both wore simple white blouses and the plain skirts favored by the girls in their dormitory. While Dona tended to wear blues to complement her eyes, Helena favored greens and browns—today's selection was a rich cinnamon.

Tall and angular, Helena traveled with her books close to her chest, as though they concealed all her darkest secrets—not that she had all that many. Her mother was a seamstress in her father's haberdashery. The shop had done well, attracting a cadre of well-to-do clientele by virtue of her father's strong work ethic and her mother's devotion to craft. Helena would have been content help out at the shop, but her father insisted she attend the University—where all of Trifienne's most eligible bachelors would be assembled in one convenient location.

It took a few moments, but Helena worked up the courage to reply. Her goal was to show concern but not incredulity. She was afraid to say anything that would cause her friend to dig in her heels, which she just knew would happen if she implied in any way what Dona was proposing couldn't be done.

"This is rhetoric, not theology," Helena said. "You aren't expected to pick a difficult technical subject. Besides, theology is Professor Hepplewhite's specialty. Why make this harder than it needs to be?"

Dona raised an eyebrow. "You're never going to pass with an attitude like that."

Helena's brow furrowed. "I don't know what you're talking about. My brother took rhetoric with Hepplewhite last year. He passed just fine, and he wouldn't know a serious topic if it flew up his nose."

"That's exactly my point."

"Well, then I'm not following."

Dona's voice took on a note of exaggerated patience. "So, last year was the first year they combined the women and the men in the same class, right?"

"So?"

"And how do you suppose the four women in Hepplewhite's class fared?"

"How should I know?"

"Well, I found out by tracking them down and asking. Turns out one of them failed and the other three passed, but only with reservations."

"Well, maybe women are just not very good at rhetoric."

"And your brother is?"

"He's not as dumb as he sounds. I don't know why you keep singling him out."

"We're talking rhetoric here—the whole point is to grade you on how dumb you sound. I smell a rat."

"Isn't it possible those four just happened not to be very talented?"

"Yeah, and what are the chances of that?"

Helena sighed. "I imagine you'll tell me."

"I'll do better than that—I'll prove it. I'm picking a challenging topic right smack in the middle of Hepplewhite's bailiwick, and I'm going to ace it. We'll see once and for all whether it's the women or the professor who's to blame."

Helena realized then it was already too late. Dona's heels were dug in—all the way up to her kneecaps.

. . . . .

Professor Dominick Everson forced his way through the hedge behind the ivied buildings that housed the offices of the Hathaway Scholars. He suddenly received a pointed reminder that the hedge was armed with large, nasty thorns. Fortunately, the evening chill had prompted him to wear a heavy coat, or the damage would have been much worse. He emerged with a painful scratch across the back of his hand as well as several wounds in far less-convenient locations.

"Next time Verone can deliver her own bloody messages," he muttered. "I didn't sacrifice fifteen years of my life getting tenure to end up as some fat lady's errand boy."

Everything was quiet, except for the incessant chirping of crickets and the occasional hoot of a nearby owl. He wasn't himself a Hathaway Scholar, and neither did he know any. He'd always considered them an arrogant lot, what with their research being subsidized directly by the Crown and all.

He rubbed his forehead and squinted through the mists hovering over the grounds. What had she said? Third building past the statue of Lord Hathaway—yes, that was it.

How smug he'd been—open campus, tenured professor, what could possibly go wrong? *Right. Other than the bloody hedge.* Then he discovered something else. The doorknob didn't budge. Apparently buildings on this end of campus were locked at night.

After a brief search, he found an open first-floor window. By his calculations, this office was just a couple of doors down from where he needed to make the delivery. Unfortunately, years of academic pursuits had not left him particularly nimble, and by the time he hefted himself through, he was bruised and winded.

The office door was not locked and gave easy access to an utterly dark hallway. He hadn't brought a lantern because he didn't want to attract undue attention, but now that he was actually here, he realized he'd made a mistake—a man lurking alone in a locked building in the dark was far more suspicious than one carrying a lantern.

He felt his way along the walls until he finally arrived at what he believed to be his destination, but he had no way to read the nameplate. Running his hand across the plate didn't help either, as the names were painted rather than carved, but it did tell him the plate was loose. He slid out the plate and took it back to the office with the open window. The moonlight was enough: Professor Amehtan Shoruga.

"About damn time."

Slinking back to Shoruga's office, he replaced the nameplate and tried the knob. This one wasn't locked either. Eager to finally have this odious obligation out of the way, he opened the door and ducked inside, scanning for a desk upon which he could drop the package and be gone.

He was greeted by a long, low growl. Across the room, a large dog clambered to its feet, bared teeth luminous in the moonlight. Everson froze. The beast's hackles continued to rise. Ever so slowly, Everson began backing out of the office. But when the dog crouched to spring, he dropped the package and ran. He sprinted for the room with the open window. The dog lost traction at the corner and careened into the wall, giving Everson a few more precious seconds to reach the doorway. Vicious fangs snapping at his heels, he scrambled inside and flung closed the door. Too late—he'd caught the beast between the door and the jamb. It yelped in agony as the professor pressed against the door to keep it pinned. Even while struggling, the beast continued to snarl and snap. Slavering jaws edged closer with each attempt. The door wouldn't hold it much longer. Desperate, Everson pulled out Verone's notched stick and snapped it in two.

He went instantly and totally blind. Whereas before, moonlight had streamed through the office window, now the darkness was absolute, as though his eyes had been patched over with black velvet. He had little choice—he tossed away the broken stick and threw his full weight against the door. The crunch of breaking bones was followed by the dog's piteous wails. He let up on the pressure and was rewarded with the receding sound of frantic scrabbling.

Everson slammed the door and shuddered. Overwhelmed by the need to escape, he felt his way around the room for the open window. In his haste, he misjudged the ledge and pitched headfirst into the landscaping below.

His vision returned abruptly as he crawled away from the building, revealing once more the cobbled path that wended its way through the Hathaway compound. Behind him loomed a wall of impenetrable blackness. Pulling himself to his feet, he began the painful trek home.

"One day, Verone," he muttered. "One day."

.   .   .   .   .

Though the library's theology wing was endowed with comfortable chairs, ample workspace, and even the occasional masterpiece, Dona couldn't help feeling that there wasn't a creepier place on the entire campus, particularly when alone at two in the morning. All her friends were fast asleep, but then, they were content to wander aimlessly through their education as though sampling tidbits in an intellectual candy shop. Dona had plans. She'd grown up watching her mother struggle to make ends meet—supporting herself, her brother, and Dona on a dwindling inheritance at their modest country house, fully aware the money couldn't possibly last. Though they both knew they couldn't afford it, her mother insisted Dona attend college, and Dona was determined not to squander the opportunity—by hook or by crook, she would one day be a professor here. The fact that women professors at Exidgeon were nearly unheard of only spurred her on. She had the skills and determination to wear away any obstacle, but it wouldn't be easy. Such a lofty goal would take unprecedented dedication.

Despite the library-inspired flutters in her gut, she had nearly been lulled to sleep by the regular tick...tick...tick of the massive grandfather clock. Positioned near the wing's entrance, the clock was one of the priceless art pieces for which the library was known. The ancient timepiece was about to strike the hour, which would initiate a five-minute cacophony of chimes as the intricately carved wooden peasants twirled and cavorted along preset tracks, completing their chores for what might be the millionth time.

No wonder no one studies theology anymore.

Her rhetoric presentation was fast approaching, and she'd only completed a fraction of the necessary research. She wondered if any of the women from last year's class had found themselves in a similar position, and whether Helena was the type to say I told you so.

A distant crash echoed through the library just as the clock peasants began their two o'clock chores, making them seem like scurrying gapers. Dona listened intently but couldn't hear anything else over the din. Stuffing her notes into her satchel, she picked up her lantern and headed into the main library.

The usual late-night quiet had reasserted itself, and nothing seemed out of place. Several students, intent on their work, had paid the disturbance no mind. The rest never even woke up. Only two lights moved among the stacks. Dona approached the closest.

"Excuse me, did you hear that noise?"

"I did," the young man behind the light replied. "Sounded like it came from the history wing."

Although she was having trouble making out his features in the glare from his lamp, she recognized the voice. He was another student from Hepplewhite's rhetoric class.

"Care to help me investigate?"

"It's past my bedtime," he said. Then he paused. "But I suppose a few more minutes wouldn't hurt."

"Good. This place gives me chills—I'd be glad of the company."

He grinned. "Oh, I definitely have to come, then. We can't have you catching cold just before your presentation."

"I have several days yet. Don't make it sound so…imminent." She extended her hand. "I'm Dona."

To her surprise, he kissed it. "Alexi. At your service."

They picked their way toward the history wing with care. The library was mostly tidy, but oil lamps and stacks of books were a dangerous combination.

"What keeps you here so late, Alexi?"

"Likely the same as you. Hepplewhite's reputation—you know, tough, but fair."

"Oh? You're sure about that?"

"You heard otherwise?"

"Let's just say I'm reserving judgment on the 'fair' part."

The history wing was completely dark except for a shimmer at the opposite end, where one of the stacks was backlit by a golden glow.

"Not a lot of folks to interview," Dona said. "See anything out of place?"

"Not yet," Alexi replied. He held out his lamp in different directions in a futile attempt to illuminate the vastness of the wing. In the process, she finally got a good look at him. He wore his sandy hair short, with an endearingly troublesome flip in the front. His crooked smile conspired with mischievous eyes to make him look both knowing, and curious. His dark vest and starched shirt would have struck her as too formal on his lean frame if he hadn't kept his sleeves rolled up to his elbows.

"I don't see anything," he said.

"Maybe the person behind that stack saw something?"

"Possibly, but my biggest worry was that someone dropped a lamp and started a fire. That seems not to have happened. Probably no need to disturb anyone in the absence of an emergency."

"I don't know. The crash sounded pretty loud to me. Maybe someone was hurt. We should at least go check."

Dona strode toward the back-lit stack.

"Wait," Alexi said. "What's that on your left?"

"Oh, I bet that's our culprit. There's a whole cart tipped over in this aisle. Books are everywhere."

"Of course, whoever it was didn't bother to clean up after himself. Typical. Mathers isn't going to be happy tomorrow."

Dona shot him a sidelong look. "Mathers is *never* happy."

"Well, I'm not going to be happy either if I don't get some sleep. Shall we get out of here?"

"One second. I just want to check to make sure the person behind this stack is all right. He must have heard us talking, but he hasn't said a word. Maybe he's the one who tripped?"

"Haven't you already gone above the call of duty on this?" Alexi said.

Undeterred, Dona disappeared behind the stack. "Oh, my. Alexi, come look."

"Is he hurt?"

"No, no, there's no one here, but I think you should see this."

He made his way around the scattered books—and gasped.

Several more books lay strewn across a research table. One in particular attracted their attention, for unlike the rest, this one glowed with brilliant light. A single chair lay upended nearby.

"So what do you make of that?" Alexi asked.

Dona squinted at the book's cover, trying at the same time to shield her eyes against the glare. "I'm not sure yet."

"What does it say?"

"*Practical Phrendonics* I think. It's hard to read it's so bright."

"Don't touch it," Alexi said. "Probably we should tell Mathers in the morning. He'll know what to do."

"That I doubt, and in any event, we can't just leave it here."

"We can't?"

Dona raised an eyebrow. "You mean to tell me we just found a glowing book, and you don't find that the least bit interesting?"

"Well, if it weren't heading toward three in the morning, I might be more interested. But I agree—it is strange. Aren't you worried it might be dangerous?"

"Hmm, good point. I'll wear gloves." She rummaged around in her satchel and retrieved a pair of white opera gloves. After sliding one on, she lightly touched a finger to the book.

"It doesn't seem to be hot. I'm taking it."

She stuffed the book into her satchel. After some careful arranging she managed to keep almost all the light from leaking out. Then she took Alexi's arm and half escorted, half dragged him toward the library exit.

"Now that you have it, what you planning to do with it?"

"This warrants further study. I presume you agree those studies can't be undertaken here, right?"

Alexi shook his head. "I think this is a bad idea."

Dona ignored him. "I'll need to find a safe place to look this over. When I do, I'll let you know what I learn. The book's half yours after all."

They passed through the library exit just as the peasants began their quarter-hourly chores.

"Actually, I've reconsidered," he said. "I think this is a *really* bad idea."

Dona threw the satchel over her shoulder and took both his hands in hers. "I know, but thanks for coming along in spite of your reservations. You were very sweet." With that, she leaned up and kissed him on the cheek. Then, she strode off in the direction of her dormitory.

Alexi absently rubbed his face as Dona disappeared into the night. He lingered several minutes, lost in thought. "Well," he said at last, "I suppose it could be worse."

. . . . .

As she dressed for class the following morning, Dona considered her options. Since dormitory life at Exidgeon was necessarily a communal experience, finding a safe spot to open her satchel was proving to be a challenge. Students bunked a minimum of three to a room. The only privacy she could rely on happened either late at night in the library or in the garderobe. A relic of the original structure, the antiquated closet boasted twin seats that spared the dormitory's inhabitants the distasteful task of managing chamber pots. Of course, regardless of the number of seats, and despite occasionally long lines, the closet's use was strictly a private matter. After several minutes of pondering, she finally despaired of finding a better alternative and made the trip to the garderobe. When safely inside, she pried open the satchel's clasp. The dim illumination from the tiny skylight revealed nothing out of the ordinary.

Panic flared. Could she have lost it? Had it been stolen while she slept? She pawed through the satchel's contents.

That's odd.

The book was definitely there, or at least *a* book was there. Unlike the one she had seen the previous evening, however, this one was entirely ordinary. She hauled it out for a closer look.

There, emblazoned across the cover in the same ornate script she remembered, were the words *Practical Phrendonics*. It had the same heft and appeared in all other respects to be the same book. She had to assume the cover had simply stopped glowing. On one hand, that was a disappointment. On the other, that would make getting things into and out of her satchel a whole lot easier.

Insistent knocking interrupted her considerations. "What are you doing in there?"

Dona shoved the book back into the satchel.

"All done," she said, opening the door. Three students were lined up and waiting.

A sour-faced young woman stared down her nose as Dona passed. "Bout time."

"Ah, Arietta," Dona said, "I see you're all sunshine and smiles, as usual. My day is now complete. Maybe even my whole month, if I'm lucky."

Arietta merely snorted and slammed the garderobe door behind her. Her non-response left Dona gaping—it was completely out of character for Arietta to fail to be baited. Her business in the garderobe must have been pressing indeed.

CHAPTER TWO

A NOVEL METHOD

Dona always looked forward to Professor Reston's history class. His was one of those large introductory classes that everyone had to take, but Reston's approach made the class interesting. Tall, dark, and impeccably bearded, Reston was a relative newcomer to the University. As new faculty, he had not yet had time to burn out, and his lectures, when he gave lectures, were well crafted and entertaining. Usually, however, he taught Socratically—actively engaging individual members of his class in discussion on the required reading. Although his approach was formal, he was not. He often didn't bother to button his black professors' gown, which allowed his street clothes to show, and he had pretty much dispensed with the formal cap entirely. One might have expected him to look disheveled, but Dona's friends all saw him as dashing and perhaps a little reckless. He stepped up to the podium as the last few stragglers settled in their seats.

"Welcome," he said. He paused a moment to let the last-minute rustling die out. "I trust that everyone is well-rested and eager to test their mettle against what history has in store?"

He scanned the terraced rows of students, an eyebrow cocked as though waiting for a response.

"Very well, let's dive right in. Since you all did so well on last week's exam, I'm going to give you a treat and rearrange the schedule a bit—today we'll discuss the Caprian Inquisition. As a result, there will be no examination on today's material. Let's start with you, Mr. Danforth."

"Yes, sir." Charles Danforth rose to his feet directly in front of Dona's seat, but he still didn't obstruct her view. Though solidly built, he was among the shortest students in the class.

"What is an Inquisition?" Reston asked.

"A formal investigation by the Church into heresy," Charles replied.

"Very good. Miss Caldor, you're next."

"Yes, sir." Caroline Caldor rose as Charles took his seat. Dona knew Caroline from the dormitory, and they were on friendly terms. She struck Dona as reliable and well-mannered, if a bit mousy.

"Miss Caldor, do you have any ideas what the Church may have been investigating in Caprian in the year 887?

She spent a moment or two tapping her chin and staring at the walnut-paneled ceiling. At last, she shrugged. "An enclave of Chervillian death worshippers?"

"A fine guess," Reston said. "Indeed, Chervillians have long been a thorn in the Church's side, necessitating several Inquisitions over the years. However, in this case, Church records indicate the allegations were of a different nature. Thank you, Miss Caldor."

Caroline took her seat.

"Mr. Deargard."

Adam Deargard stood up.

"Does the term heresy apply only to competing religious teachings?"

Adam was blond, doughy, and terrified. Dona felt sorry for him. Wide-eyed, he struggled to stammer out a reply.

"I...um, ah, yes, Professor," he finally managed. "I think."

"So Inquisitions then, are limited only to investigations of other religious activity?"

Adam swallowed hard. "Yes, sir."

"Thank you," Reston said, as Adam took his seat. "Does everyone agree with Mr. Deargard?"

Dona raised her hand. Although her recent theological forays hadn't focused on heresy, she had nonetheless acquired some familiarity with the concepts.

"Miss Merinne."

Dona stood and cleared her throat. "Heresy is defined as any doctrine inconsistent with those of the Church. Therefore, any teachings, even those of a non-religious nature, that conflict with Church dogma can form the basis for an Inquisition. Of course, that doesn't mean that the Church hasn't used the Inquisition as leverage for political or monetary gain. For example, Inquisitions have been initiated for the sole purpose of ruining rival families, or even for confiscating works of art a Church official coveted for his private collection."

"Thank you for the definition, Miss Merinne," Reston said, his dark eyes twinkling, "as well as for the complete and unabridged set of annotations."

Dona was untroubled by the good-natured gibe, confident few others in the class could have provided such detail.

"Miss Merinne makes a valid point. Inquisitions have been initiated not only for doctrinally valid reasons, but also inappropriately for political or petty personal reasons. As with almost any action taken by an institution, often the motivations are mixed. No doubt that was also true in the year 887 when the Church initiated the Caprian Inquisition. Its stated purpose was to root out a particularly dangerous brand of heretics known as the Phrendonics."

Dona's eyes widened.

Reston pressed on. "Technically not religious, the Phrendonics were practitioners of a peculiar form of humanist mysticism. They claimed that sheer mental discipline could give them power over their surroundings, and, indeed, miraculous feats were ascribed to many in Caprian who were subsequently executed as heretics."

Dona suddenly felt exposed. That this unusual topic should come up in history class on this particular day was simply too coincidental for her to believe it could have occurred by chance. But how could Reston know? Worse still, if Reston knew, who *else* knew? She gripped her satchel and made sure the flaps were tightly closed. The Caprian Inquisition was recent history—as much as the Church might want to downplay its brutality as a thing of the past, if push came to shove, bona fide heresy might well provoke an equally ruthless response today.

Reston continued the lecture, his dark eyes revealing nothing. "You might ask how people capable of miraculous feats could be so easily captured and neutralized. Some believe the Church jealously guards its own store of mystic wisdom, and used that to overpower the Phrendonics. Still others maintain that they were victims of their own naiveté. According to the contemporary report of the Caprian historian Marius Warellus, the Phrendonics believed, as does Mr. Deargard, that they had nothing to fear. At that time, nothing in Church doctrine would have led the Phrendonics to expect they could be labeled as heretics without first espousing some sort of a religious viewpoint—a position they had been especially careful to avoid. As it turned out, the non-religious nature of the movement worked against them. Many of the accused Phrendonics were also Church members, conversant with the canons and confident they were violating no rules. They were therefore easy prey. Warellus tells us that the Church issued the Edict of Caprian to explicitly amend their laws to categorize Phrendonics as heretics. Of course, since the amendment itself appears nowhere in the Canons, to anyone reading them today, the Phrendonics might seem to always have been heretics.

"Now, would anyone care to attempt a restatement of to-day's lesson?"

A number of hands went up, but Dona's was not among them. The less attention she drew to herself and her satchel, the better.

"Mr. Reysa."

"Thank you, Professor," Alexi said. "The way I see it, the real purpose for rules that pretend to place limits on those in power is merely to allay fears that the power will be abused. Unfortunately, the instant someone in power decides such a rule has actually become an obstacle, the rule is summarily changed."

Dona started at the sound of Alexi's voice. She hadn't realized he was also in this class, nor had she caught his surname before.

Reston laughed out loud. "Clearly, Mr. Reysa, you take your politics with a healthy dash of cynicism. Does anyone believe they have a better restatement?"

This time there were no volunteers.

"Very well, then. Just to drive home the point, I'd like everyone to be ready for an examination on today's material at the beginning of class on Friday."

Groans erupted from the students, several of whom had taken this opportunity to catch up on their sleep. Arietta's hand shot up, her gangly form bursting with indignation.

"Yes, Miss Charwick?"

"I thought you said there wouldn't be an exam on today's material."

Reston's eyes glittered. "Were I you, Miss Charwick, I would study Mr. Reysa's restatement with particular care. Class dismissed."

As she and her satchel jostled their way out of the classroom, Dona could have sworn Reston's inscrutable gaze was tracking her. She hoped her paranoid mind was simply playing tricks on her.

. . . . .

The peasants had just finished their enthusiastic celebration of midnight when the last person in the theology wing finally left Dona alone with her research. Reston's class had made her aware in no uncertain terms that this strange book had the potential to get her into serious trouble, and she was taking no chances. After one last careful look around the wing, she finally opened the satchel, half expecting a burst of light to betray her secret to prying eyes. With relief and regret in equal measure, she saw nothing of the sort. The book was still merely a book: well crafted, a bit oversized, and emblazoned with a title that, to her newly educated sensibilities, reeked of heresy. She wrestled it out of the satchel and onto the tabletop near her lantern. Although the book appeared little worn, its scent intimated a work of some age. Slowly she lifted open the cover—and gasped. The book was entirely hand-illuminated.

Practical Phrendonics: A Roadmap for the Journey to Enlightenment.

My friend,

Knowledge is a heady mistress during the ardor of youth, but she can leave one cold and destitute once she has yielded up her secrets. For me, the hardest lesson was learning that for every truth, there are a thousand who will misunderstand it, a hundred who will abuse it, and ten who will fight to the death to suppress it, but only one who will embrace it. I pray you are that one.

I dedicate this work to my niece, without whose keen intellect, many sections would have been muddled or incomplete. May she live to realize her potential.

Phrendonian

Dona hadn't really known what to expect from a text that had been responsible for so much carnage. To her surprise the contents resembled a run-of-the-mill academic text. There were the obligatory sections on various philosophical, theological, and physical theories and how they were interrelated, as well as sections on practical applications of the theories. At first glance, the substance was altogether unremarkable. Upon closer inspection, however, differences from her familiar academic texts became apparent. The non-theoretical segments contained a compendium of "spells" discussed in depth and seemingly in all seriousness. She could find no indication anywhere that the work was intended as some sort of allegory or parody. The overall impression was bizarre. The work was clearly written in a careful academic format by a mind capable of superb technical writing, but the subject matter was absurd. It was like reading a treatise that attempted to derive the laws of the universe using nursery rhymes as primary source material. She flipped over to the table of contents and picked a subtopic at random.

"*A Spell to Induce Sleep*," she muttered. Really? Why the Church would have been worried about such nonsense was even more puzzling…that is, unless they actually *believed* it.

"Read any good books lately?"

Dona slammed the book shut so fast she almost extinguished her lamp. She turned to see Alexi, hazel eyes sparkling, pretending to wait as though he really expected an answer.

"Very funny," she snapped. "Say, pretty coincidental how Reston chose today to lecture on the Caprian Inquisition, wasn't it?"

"You noticed that too?"

"I had assumed we were going to keep the book a secret."

"You don't think I had anything to do with that?"

"The subject matter was just a little too convenient, don't you think? I suppose now you're going to tell me you came up with that little 'restatement' of yours entirely off the cuff?"

Alexi gaped in indignation. "If we are to start basing thinly veiled accusations on suspiciously over-prepared classroom oratory, I think we need look no further than a certain overblown set of annotations."

Dona stood and drew herself up to her full height. "And just what do you mean by that, Mr. Reysa?"

"Just this—if you continue to behave as though you are the only student at Exidgeon with the skill to turn a phrase or structure a brilliant answer, not only will you discover you are sadly mistaken, but you'll be doing it alone."

"At least if I were alone, I wouldn't have to worry about someone betraying my confidences. I felt like Reston's whole lecture was a cautionary tale directed squarely at me. How else do you explain that?"

His jaw clenched, Alexi re-rolled his cuffs. "If you had thought for even one second instead of jumping to conclusions, you'd have realized Reston could have chosen that topic for any number of reasons. First of all, there is at least one other person who knew about the book. You remember him, don't you? The person who actually left it there? Maybe he talked to Reston. Second, we don't know for sure that we were the only ones to see the book before you ran off with it. Third, Reston is himself a historian, and the book was in the history wing on the night before his lecture. Did you ever stop to consider that he might have left it there? Did it ever even cross your mind that Reston might actually want to prepare for his lectures? Or did you just presume that since you are standing by with such a wealth of information at your disposal, professors no longer need to do that?"

Dona regarded him coolly. "So are you telling me I *am* wrong then, or simply that I might be?"

Alexi shook his head. "I was going to offer to help you hide the book, but I'm sure you won't want to risk associating with someone guilty of such clumsy attempts at treachery. Lady, if you ever come down from your high horse, drop me a line."

He stalked out of the wing.

Dona sank into her chair, staring pensively after him. After a moment, she smiled. "I think he just implied my answer was brilliant."

Out on the library steps, Alexi paused to catch his breath. "Why, that self-centered egotistical prima donna."

He sat and tried to fathom what had just happened. After he'd gone over the exchange several times, a subtle smile stole across his face. "She remembered my name."

. . . . .

Chancellor Wiggins hailed the approaching carriage. "Monsignor," he cried. "Welcome."

Monsignor Armand Goodkin's round face appeared in the open carriage window as the horses drew to a stop.

"Harald," he exclaimed. "How good to see you again."

The Monsignor wrestled the carriage door open, and the Chancellor extended a hand to assist him. Despite his salt and pepper pate, the stocky Monsignor was clearly still a man of irrepressible energy. Nonetheless, he was grateful for the help—his right knee had not yet calmed itself from predicting last night's showers, and his cane was not particularly useful for disembarking.

Like the Monsignor, the driver wore a black cassock and a heavily embroidered Inquisitorial stole, but his garb lacked the Monsignor's azure fascia and trim. He hopped down from his seat intending to help, but arrived a moment too late.

"Have you met my son Thurman? He's been helping me get around."

A consummate gladhander, the wispy-haired Chancellor pumped Thurman's arm. "Very pleased to meet you."

"Likewise, Chancellor," Thurman replied. "I'll see to the carriage."

The Monsignor nodded. "Thank you, Thurman."

The Chancellor held out his arm to indicate a cobbled path leading past a lordly statue through a tidy cluster of low buildings.

"After you."

The two men started off, the Monsignor relying heavily on his cane.

"The old injury is still giving you trouble?"

"Let's just say it was insistent I bring my umbrella, and that I was glad of the advice."

The Chancellor's bearing became somber. "Thank you for coming. I was terrified they would send someone with less appreciation for the importance of discretion."

"That's very kind of you to say, Harald. As you might expect, it's pretty rare for anyone to actually look forward to my arrival nowadays, much less toss a compliment my way."

"Life of the Inquisitor not all it's cracked up to be?"

"Well, there are days."

The Chancellor paused. "I think we might have an opening on the faculty for a master theologian..."

"I am flattered, as always, but I think I am more needed where I am. Do keep trying though. Perhaps one day you will wear me down."

The two men arrived at a building cordoned off from the rest.

"This is the scene?" the Monsignor asked.

"Indeed. I had it roped off as soon as I found out."

"Very good. And what do we know so far?"

"Not much, really. I didn't witness the event myself, but several of my faculty reported seeing a large black mass or cloud concealing the side of this building."

"Solid?"

"Seemingly not. One of them tried poking with a stick. It passed through without resistance."

"Did the mass have a defined shape?"

"I heard it described as hemispherical, if that helps."

The Monsignor nodded. "In fact, that does help. And where is this mass now?"

The Chancellor shrugged. "Gone. Vanished sometime around mid-morning. Several of the faculty said they saw it go."

The Monsignor nodded and jotted a few notes. "What are these buildings? Is there a reason they're separated from the rest of the University?"

"As a matter of fact, there is. These are the offices and laboratories of the Hathaway scholars. Their research is specifically funded by the Crown and often involves sensitive topics."

"Military research?"

"Why, some of it, yes. Do you think that might be important?"

"I hope not. Whose offices did you say had been disturbed?"

"Professor Broadmore's and Professor Shoruga's. Shoruga's was two doors down from Broadmore's. Shoruga's dog was killed."

"He kept his dog in his office?"

"He did. He's pretty broken up, poor man. He defected some years ago from Shune to have more freedom to work on his research. Incredibly talented fellow, but he hasn't adapted well to the cultural change. A while back, a few of the Hathaways felt sorry for him and got him a puppy. He kept the dog in his office because he spent so little time at home. I suppose he may also have intended for the animal to guard his work."

"Are the offices occupied?"

"Not at the moment. As soon as I heard, I declared the building off-limits. Of course, some faculty entered before I was aware of the problem. That was how Shoruga retrieved his dog. Apparently much of the inside was darkened as well, but he managed to get to the animal anyway."

"He ventured into the blackness?"

"That's what some of the other faculty told me. The dog wasn't dead at that point, and when Shoruga heard the whimpering, he made a mad dash inside. Poor thing died in his arms not half an hour later. He's been a wreck ever since."

The Chancellor unhooked the rope barricade. "Why don't you poke around and see what you can find? You can fill me in at lunch. In the meantime, since we're trying to keep this incident low-key, would you mind helping create the impression that the purpose of your visit is primarily academic? You know, sit in on a few classes, visit the library, interview some of the faculty—that sort of thing. I'm sure Zachary in particular would be glad to have you stop in."

"That sounds perfect."

"I really appreciate your efforts here. See you at lunch then?"

"I'll be there."

The Monsignor made his way into the front door of the building, pausing a few minutes to examine the lock. Once inside, he opened each door he passed, and popped his head in for a quick look. When he came to Broadmore's office, he was a bit less casual. He carefully inspected the door and took note of tufts of coarse fur stuck to its edge. He found fur stuck to the jamb as well. He ran his finger across a dark smear that trailed along the hallway between this office and Shoruga's.

Apparently Broadmore was a neatnik, because the space was immaculate. He glanced through several tidy stacks of papers on the desk. They consisted primarily either of technical notes or papers in the process of being graded. Then something odd caught his attention. Lying on the floor just behind the door were two sticks. He squatted for a closer look. Reaching into his pocket, he retrieved a ball of string. Laying one end next to the stick, he unrolled the string as he moved toward the window. He poked his head out the window and checked the ledge and the ground below.

"Thurman," he called.

Thurman looked up from his work on the carriage. "Yes, Father?"

"Could you unravel the rest of this string for me?"

"I'll be right there." He jogged over, grabbed the string, and unrolled it out into the yard.

"Could you put a mark where the string ends?"

"Already doing it." He inserted a tiny wooden stake into the ground.

Thank you." With a salute, the Monsignior retrieved the string and ducked back into the office. Donning gloves, he wrapped the sticks in cloth and affixed a label. Next, he moved down the hall to Shoruga's office. Unlike Broadmore, Shoruga was not a tidy man. In the end, he collected only one item there—an unopened package he found lying on the floor.

Thurman was waiting for him at the carriage. "Find anything interesting?"

"I'm not certain yet. I still have to talk to the witnesses, but I did find a few things that I'll need to inspect more carefully."

"So what are your famous instincts telling you so far?"

The Monsignor's brow furrowed. "It's heresy."

CHAPTER THREE

RULES AND REGULATIONS

Early morning thundershowers had washed the ivy-laden stone of the campus buildings clean and left the air brisk and fresh, but negotiating the saturated cobbles without soaking a foot or spattering a stocking proved to be a challenge. Three young women were picking their way to the dining hall from geometry class, and it was slow going. Normally that wouldn't have been a problem, but there had been a last-minute menu change. Since that happened only when the University was hosting an honored guest, it often meant the food would actually be good, and that, in turn, meant lunch would be crowded. Getting caught at the back of a long line could make them late for their next class.

"So, are you ready for the big presentation?" Helena asked.

"I'm getting there," Dona said.

"Ooh, what's your topic?" asked the third young woman. Rampant enthusiasm, a porcelain complexion, and striking blonde ringlets all conspired to give Miranda Connelly a beatific quality that made her easy to be around. Since her father was Trifienne's Constable, she had a reputation for leading a charmed life. Only her closest friends realized that, for her, a good day consisted of curling up around a book—which, depending on her mood, had even odds of being a literary masterpiece or a tawdry serial. She loved a good story, and was eager to find out whether Dona might be up to something controversial—Dona had a knack for that sort of thing. "From what I could pry out of Helena," Miranda said, "it sounds like it will be quite the challenge."

Dona's nose wrinkled. "Yes, it's turning out to be a little more difficult than I expected. Don't tell Helena, but I'm starting to think she may have been right."

Helena's lips pursed in a self-satisfied grin. "You aren't actually admitting you were wrong, are you? If you're not careful, you could end up ruining a perfectly good 'I told you so.'"

"Heaven forbid. So which of my other secrets have you seen fit to share with Miranda?"

"You know I'd never betray a confidence. Not only did I not tell her what your rhetoric topic was, even under brutal questioning, I even managed to avoid mentioning your new infatuation."

Miranda's eyebrows disappeared beneath her curls. "Infatuation? Forget rhetoric, this sounds much more interesting."

"Well, don't just stand there, tell Dona how you didn't hear it from me."

"Not a single word," Miranda said, taking Dona by the arm, "but we'll have to fix that, won't we? So tell me, what's all this I haven't heard about your new infatuation?"

Dona blinked a few times, genuinely nonplussed. "I don't know what she's talking about."

"Oh, come now. Surely we can do better than that. Perhaps Helena can jog your memory?"

"Oh no, I really couldn't," Helena said. "All of Dona's secrets, especially how she has been spending the last several days making moon-eyes at Alexi Reysa, are completely confidential."

"Ooh," Miranda cooed. "Alexi Reysa is it? So she fancies the cute ones. And here I thought she'd go for the smart ones."

"He is smart," Dona protested.

Miranda smiled in triumph. "Good to know I was right, then."

"Wait," Dona said. "I never said—"

"You didn't have to."

Dona, to her dismay, felt color creeping into her features. "But I'm not—"

"Of course you aren't, dear." Miranda winked at Helena, who could barely contain her laughter. "And don't you worry. The secret of the gentleman whom you are most definitely not infatuated with is absolutely safe with the two of us. Isn't it, Helena?"

Before Helena could answer, a horse-drawn carriage draped with a cloth banner bearing the Church symbol of two intertwined serpents swept past them, nearly clipping Helena's shoulder and raising a sheet of mud-laden water that soaked the three of them head to toe.

Miranda sighed. "So much for keeping our stockings clean,"

"They aren't supposed to be driving carriages on this path," Dona said, fuming.

Helena shrugged. "I doubt University rules apply to Church officials."

"We can't be seen in public like this," Dona said. "I'm going to go change."

"There's no time," Helena pointed out. "By the time you got back and ate, class would be half over."

Dona sighed. As much as she fancied the prospect of a really good meal, the thought of eating it in soggy, mud-covered clothes left her cold. "You two go ahead. I guess I'll just grab an apple or something before class."

"Hmmm," Helena said. "I think it's my turn to admit that there's a chance, however slim, that Dona may have the right idea here. No way could I sit through class in these wet things."

Miranda gaped in mock amazement. "Don't tell me you two actually agree on something? And just my luck, it happens to involve skipping a good meal. Fine. I know when I've been outvoted. To the dormitory it is. I just hope one of you has an apple or two to spare."

· · · · ·

Despite her usual enthusiasm for Reston's history class, Dona had a hard time dragging herself out of bed the next morning. She had worked late into the night to put the finishing touches on her rhetoric project, and although she was satisfied with the results, the effort had taken its toll. She hoped she would recover enough by the afternoon to present the project with a modicum of enthusiasm, but either way, at least it would be done. Finally, she'd have time for other things, chief among them, the mysterious book. Curiosity had been eating away at her. Once she was convinced it wasn't going to light up again, it had been a simple matter to place it with some other books in her hope chest. Of course, there was no longer enough room inside for Mr. Lop Ears, her favorite stuffed toy, but his presence stirred so many pleasant memories she was happy to give him a cozy spot on top of the chest where she could keep an eye on him.

She had skipped breakfast in exchange for a few more minutes of sleep, but she swung by the dining hall to grab a cup of warm tea and an oatmeal cookie to quell the growling of her stomach. She plodded into Reston's class and collapsed in the seat next to Miranda, hoping her recent theology studies would be sufficient to rescue her if Reston made good on his threat to give an exam.

Miranda interrupted Dona's yawn with a nudge. "Hey, sleepyhead. Notice anything unusual?"

Dona didn't have to look hard. Reston's professorial gown was freshly pressed and buttoned completely to the top. He was even wearing the cap—something Dona had never seen him do before. She raised an eyebrow, and in return, Miranda inclined her head. Down in front sat a stocky older man in a black cassock with an azure sash. He rested his hands before him on a cane, smiling benignly at the students as they entered.

"I think we've found our mud-slinger," Miranda whispered.

"What's he doing here?"

Miranda barely had time to shrug before Reston called them to order.

"Good morning, all. Permit me to begin by introducing our esteemed guest, Monsignor Armand Goodkin."

The Monsignor rose to his feet with assistance from his cane and smiled broadly. "Thank you, Professor Reston. It's a pleasure to be here." He nodded first to the class, and then to Reston, and resumed his seat.

Once the Monsignor was settled, Reston continued. "Many of you expressed concerns about Wednesday's lecture. Let's clear those up before introducing any new material. Does anyone care to speculate on why we might have focused on the Caprian Inquisition even though it changed the order of the syllabus?" Reston scanned the room, then his gaze settled. "Mr. Reysa."

Some three rows behind Dona, Alexi rose to his feet. Miranda gave her a sly nudge, and Dona felt her face coloring once again. In spite of herself, she turned in her chair for a look.

"Thank you, Professor," Alexi said. "Did it have anything to with Monsignor Goodkin's visit?"

Reston's eyes narrowed. "Care to elaborate?"

"If I recall correctly, the name of the lead Inquisitor at Caprian was Roman Goodkin. Assuming they are related, you may have chosen to discuss the Caprian Inquisition out of deference to the Monsignor."

It was Reston's turn to smile. "Clearly some of our students are not afraid to do a little background reading. You are precisely on point, Mr. Reysa. The Monsignor is his son: a most astute inference."

"Ooh," Miranda whispered. "He *is* a smart one."

As he took his seat, Alexi shot Dona a significant look that bordered on smug. In spite of her exhaustion, she took the point at once—her accusations had been unfounded. Her face colored again, but this time in shame. Her mind was so busy trying to work out how she could possibly make it up to him that it took several more minutes for her to realize her predicament—not only did she possess a heretical text, she was sitting in the same room with someone likely to be expert at rooting out heresy. Could the book be the real reason for the Monsignor's visit? But, if not through Alexi, how could the Monsignor have tracked it here? What would become of her if she were caught with it? Expulsion at the very least—and quite possibly worse, if she recalled her history correctly. She shrank back into her seat praying this was all just a huge coincidence.

Reston surveyed the class. "Now that you've all had time to consider our discussion and to do the assigned readings, are there any additional questions or comments regarding the Caprian Inquisition?

"Miss Charwick?"

Arietta rose to her feet. "Thank you, Professor. I was wondering about the comment you made about that historian, Warellus I think he was, who said that the Church amended the Canons to redefine the term heresy to include non-religious activities like what the Phrendonic heretics were doing. I think you said that current Church records made no mention of the change. Did you mean to say the Church had something to hide?"

Reston did not immediately answer. A murmur rippled through the class.

Dona knew Arietta was a vengeful little snit, but she'd never thought the girl would be so shortsighted as to try to embarrass Reston publicly.

The Monsignor's eyes drifted from Arietta to Reston. His look was one of amused anticipation.

At last, Reston spoke. "Very good, Miss Charwick," he said. "Your question clearly demonstrates your preparation for today's discussion. I must say I am impressed by your retention of the content. Can anyone speculate for Miss Charwick whether such an omission should be more properly viewed as innocuous oversight or as evidence of a pernicious conspiracy to conceal the truth?"

The tension in the room was thick.

"Anyone?"

After what seemed an eternity, the Monsignor raised his hand. "With your permission, Professor Reston."

"Of course, Monsignor."

With effort, the Monsignor rose to his feet. "There we go," he said, laying his cane across a desktop. "Miss Charwick's point is well-taken. After all, who wants to devote his life to an institution that is less than scrupulously honest? The difficulty is that the question assumes that the Canons are a repository of historical knowledge when they're not. Rather, they're intended to be a compendium of what the law is, not what the law used to be. As a result, when the Canons are periodically reprinted to reflect the current doctrine, they generally don't mention the Edicts that made the changes. Out-of-date doctrines are systematically eliminated, not to deceive or obscure, but for the sake of clarity. I can say from some experience that even trimmed down in this way, there is more than enough to study. The Church has, quite reasonably I think, made a deliberate decision to leave the intricacies of history to trained historians, such as Professor Reston here. Indeed, it seems he and Warellus have done an admirable job of highlighting the relevant distinctions, with Miss Charwick's help, of course."

Reston's expression was unreadable. "Thank you, Monsignor."

As she resumed her seat, Arietta looked as though she'd sucked a lemon, but then, that's how she always looked.

In the meantime, a number of hands had gone up.

"Miss Kardell?"

Terulla Kardell stood next. She was a short, dark woman with snappy eyes and a ready smile. "Thank you, Professor. I was wondering where the Church gets the authority to suppress heresy, and what governs the tactics used to do it. After all, some of the accounts of things done to the Phrendonic heretics in the name of the Church seemed pretty dreadful, especially if they didn't know what they were doing was wrong."

No one answered when Reston turned the question over to the class. It seemed everyone was curious to see if the Monsignor would respond, and it didn't take the Monsignor long to figure it out. After a few awkward moments, he raised his hand.

"By all means, Monsignor," Reston said.

"If you don't mind, Professor, I think I may field this one sitting down."

Reston nodded.

The Monsignor leaned forward with both hands on his cane. "The issue of authority is, of course, central to any enforcement action. The Church shares responsibility with the State for the welfare of its citizens—the State for the secular welfare and the Church for the spiritual welfare. The use of force can only be justified when the greater good is threatened. Such threats can be either to the Church itself, to other individuals, or even to prevent individuals from harming themselves. For secular analogies, one need only look to the crimes of treason, theft, murder or suicide. As for some of the things that happened in Caprian being 'dreadful,' I cannot agree more. That's why in recent years, the Church has taken great pains to ensure the vast majority of Inquisitions are resolved quickly and equitably."

"Monsignor," Reston said, "perhaps you could illustrate for the class how the Church would respond today if they were to discover heresy of the sort that caused such suffering in Caprian?"

"Certainly, Professor. Nowadays such situations can usually be resolved quietly if the heretics are willing to renounce the heresy and perhaps to perform a small penance. Only in that tiny fraction of cases where heretics muster organized resistance do we run the risk of the types of unfortunate outcomes we saw in Caprian. Before you judge the Church too harshly, consider that when the State faces organized resistance in the form of rebellion, the result can be pretty dreadful as well."

As the class continued, Dona reconsidered her initial impression. This man seemed so affable and thoughtful it was hard to believe that just moments before she had been sinking back into her seat to avoid being seen. She suddenly found herself tempted to ask his views on the nature of Phrendonic heresy, but kept pulling back her hand. In the end, unable to justify drawing unnecessary attention, she didn't ask.

That didn't stop Arietta from asking a final question, however.

"Miss Charwick?"

"Thank you, Professor. Weren't we supposed to have an examination today?"

"Actually, Miss Charwick, I believe I made it clear that you would not be tested on this material."

Arietta's confusion was palpable. "But, you said to be ready for an exam today."

"And clearly, Miss Charwick, you were."

A number of snickers could be heard throughout the class, Dona's among them, as Arietta slowly registered that she had studied for nothing.

Reston lectured on new material until the appointed time and then addressed the class. "Everyone should have the next chapter read by Monday, when we'll discuss the First Drewor Incursion. I'd also like to thank our guest, Monsignor Goodkin, for his indulgence and some most stimulating discussions. Class dismissed."

As the classroom emptied, Dona tried to catch Alexi's eye. She managed it for a moment, but even though she flashed her most sheepish smile, he looked away again, as if he hadn't noticed.

. . . . .

Most days Dona's music class was a pleasant diversion from the drier intellectual rigors, but not today. Her rhetoric presentation was coming up in a few hours, and she couldn't stop worrying. Not only did she possess a heretical text, she had also wrongly accused her co-conspirator of betraying her confidence. Under the circumstances, she did what any girl in her position would do—she poured her heart out. She did, however, retain enough presence of mind not to reveal anything that was particularly sensitive heresy-wise.

"I don't think he's even speaking to me," she said to the raven-haired young man sitting next to her. "How can I apologize if he won't even acknowledge I exist?"

In the background, Professor Rutledge's booming voice could be heard correcting the bass section on subtle matters of timing. Ostensibly, Dona was cleaning her violin, and her companion, Gregory Delauren, was committing the new score to memory. They were seated in a corner of the auditorium far enough from the chorus that if they were quiet, they could still hear each other, but not themselves be heard.

Though he didn't take his eyes from his music, the young man's mouth turned up at the corners in a sardonic smile. "In my experience, apologizing doesn't require audience participation. Are you certain, Bella-Dona, that the difficulty isn't so much one of '*how* can you apologize,' as it is of 'how can *you* apologize?' In apologies, as in music, emphasis is everything."

Dona looked stricken. "I don't know why everyone has this impression that I can't say I'm sorry."

"Could it be because no one in living memory has heard you do it?"

"That's ridiculous."

"Is it? Humor me. Regale me with examples."

Once again, Dona felt unaccustomed color blossoming.

"Well, I so rarely do anything that would require one—"

"That you aren't really sure how to go about it?"

"I have a better idea. Why don't you humor me instead? Tell me—how would the expert do it?"

Gregory snapped his fingers. "Simplicity itself. Start by throwing your arms around his neck and weeping bitterly. Men are suckers for weeping women. Then, collapse to the ground, put the back of your hand to your forehead, and throw yourself on his mercy, offering him anything, *anything*, if only he'll consider forgiving your terrible transgression, whatever it was."

To demonstrate, Gregory put the back of his hand to his forehead and assumed his best look of utter despair.

Dona risked a sidelong look away from her violin. "Mightn't that be just a tad melodramatic?"

"Not now," Gregory stage-whispered. "I'm taken by the muse."

Dona stole a covert glance to verify Rutledge was still occupied berating the basses. Then her bow lashed out—the tip found its mark in Gregory's ribs.

"Hey," he yelped, rubbing his side. "I'm only trying to help."

The music stopped, and Dona felt the heat of Rutledge's disapproving glare. After a long pause, he cleared his throat, and the basses resumed their work.

"You have him so wrapped around your finger," she whispered.

"Most transcendent voice in a generation. It's in all the reviews."

"Morissant paid to have those printed."

"That's what patrons are for."

"Spoiled brat."

"Well, for that too, of course. Normally I make no apologies for my excessive talent, but in your case, Bella-Dona, I'll make an exception." He raised the back of his hand to his forehead, but before he could pretend to weep bitterly, Dona leveled the bow at the base of his ribcage. "Do it and die."

Gregory shrugged. "As you wish. I'm not surprised, though. I've long suspected the practical effect of excessive talent is that one need never apologize. Hey, maybe that's it. Maybe you're excessively talented too."

Dona sighed. "So very true, but since I don't have a patron, the world may never know."

"Oh, that reminds me," Gregory said. "Morissant gave me tickets to *Amoretorium* for tonight. Interested?"

Dona's eyes got big. "*Amoretorium?* It's supposed to be brilliant, and Badalore is singing the part of Franco-Marro. Now *there* is the most transcendent voice in a generation."

Gregory's voice dripped disappointment. "Oh? And here I was so hoping I could take you with me."

Dona giggled. "Second only to yours, of course."

Gregory beamed. "Great. I'll come calling at six, then?"

"I'll be waiting."

· · · · ·

Professor Dominick Everson pointedly ignored the rap on his office door. If he interrupted his grading every time a student wanted to wrestle another point out of him, he'd never finish anything. He could almost see the bottom of the pile, and he wanted to be certain he was done with this stack by no later than dinnertime. The thought of having to resume this drudgery over the weekend was one he didn't care to contemplate. After all, he had far better uses for his talents than spoon-feeding glaze-eyed grammar students the finer points of constructing sentences. Even on the off chance he succeeded, the likelihood they'd ever use those sentences to say anything of consequence was far too small to justify the effort. For his latest obsession, he would be eternally grateful to his distinguished colleague, Professor Reston.

Such a shame, he thought. *He's so perceptive on some levels, but so naïve on others. But then, he's new. And, after all, the opportunity was one that even I might have overlooked if I hadn't been raised here.*

Another knock, this one more insistent.

Everson didn't look up. "Office hours are over for today. Come back Monday at eleven."

The knock came again, louder still.

Everson closed his eyes and sighed. Then, unable to suppress a snarl, he stalked to the door and yanked the knob. "If you expect to not fail outright, you'd better have a compelling reason for this impertinence."

He gaped in surprise. Before him stood a tall heavyset woman in gray pinstripes.

"Dommy, darling," she said, patting his cheek. "When you get to know me better, you'll realize my reasons are always compelling and that I never fail. Are you going to invite me in, or shall we discuss our business in the hallway?"

"Verone?"

"Impressive. Usually my beauty renders men speechless for at least a full minute."

"Uh, come in."

"Thought you'd never ask." She swept past him and settled soundly in his desk chair. "Close the door, sweetie, this should only take a minute."

Everson closed the door but made no move to sit. "What's the meaning of this?"

"Oh, Dommy, don't be so naïve. Surely you didn't think my services were provided with no additional strings attached?" She ruffled through the papers on his desk. "Do these students train for free?"

"They pay tuition, of course. What I meant is what are you doing here? I had thought our little relationship to be strictly confidential."

"Well, hon, the true nature of our relationship *is* confidential, but fortunately, since no one here knows me, they'll merely jump to the obvious tawdry conclusion. Luckily you aren't married or that could have been considerably more awkward for you. But enough about us, dear, let's talk about you."

"I don't know what you mean by 'strings.' I've already delivered on my part of the bargain. As far as I'm concerned, we're even."

Verone smiled brightly. "Consider this barter then—my ongoing services in return for yours. You would like to continue your training, no?"

"What do you mean by services? Are you saying you need someone tutored?"

"In a manner of speaking." She opened the leather case to reveal a neatly folded set of priest's vestments. "And, by the way, you'll need to dress the part."

CHAPTER FOUR

PRESENTATIONS

Buoyed by the prospect of box seats at the new opera, Dona was finding it much easier than she had expected to climb the steep hill to Hepplewhite's classroom—easier, but not easy. She wished she felt as confident now as she had when she'd first decided on her topic. *Oh well. What's the worst that can happen?*

She stepped through the doorway and stopped short. There, in the front row among the assembling students, smiling benignly and resting his hands on his cane, sat the Monsignor.

The extra color she'd been accumulating at various points throughout the day drained away. This was way more than she'd bargained for. The heat of the room was suddenly oppressive. She felt faint.

Hepplewhite, a stolid man of medium build, carried himself with the dignity and bearing one might expect from a proper gentleman. Dona had never known him to raise his voice, but his command of the language was such that she couldn't imagine he would ever need to. He stood at the podium, stroking a scrupulously waxed mustache as his pale blue eyes scanned the classroom. He noticed her immediately.

"Ah, there you are, Miss Merinne. Please, come in. I'd like to introduce you to my old friend, Monsignor Goodkin. He's doing a survey of the educational experience we offer here at Exidgeon and has asked to sit in on today's class. Since you are presenting, I took the liberty of accepting on your behalf. The Monsignor is a gifted rhetorician, and it would be a rare opportunity for you and the rest of the class to benefit from his expertise. We studied, for a time, under the same mentor."

In a daze, Dona somehow made her way to Hepplewhite, whereupon he turned to address the Monsignor.

"Monsignor Goodkin, may I present Miss Dona Merinne. She will be giving today's presentation."

Over the Monsignor's head, Dona glimpsed Alexi. He was sitting near the back, scowling.

Setting his cane aside, the Monsignor smiled warmly and took Dona's hand in his. "The pleasure is all mine. Thank you so much for the opportunity to sit in today. I find that these student interactions do wonders for keeping the old brain nimble. Come to think of it, at my age, I should probably just enroll. But pray, don't let the ranting of an old man interrupt. I'd love to hear what you've prepared."

Although the Monsignor's friendly words were comforting, her gut still roiled. Determined to do her best, she stood tall and feigned an enthusiastic smile. With a nod to the Monsignor, she took her place at the podium. Polite applause greeted her arrival.

She began.

"In the year 858, Antoine Barget began studies at the Seminary of Saint Sophia in Coscus. Possessed of a slight build, Antoine avoided athletic activities, instead, focusing intense effort on the curriculum."

The Monsignor shifted uncomfortably, and for a moment, Dona's concentration wavered. She took a deep breath, steadied herself, and forged ahead.

"By the end of the third year, Antoine was the darling of the Seminary. Faculty competed with each other for the honor of having Antoine in their classes. One evaluation, from no less than the Abbot, reported that Antoine possessed the keenest theological mind he had ever encountered. As graduation approached, seminaries and monasteries competed to bring Antoine in as a scholar, coveting the prestige that landing this inspired theological thinker would accrue for them. However, despite the keen mind, despite all the accolades, and despite all the achievements, St. Sophia's refused to go through with Antoine's ordination. Can anyone guess why?"

Helena raised her hand.

"Yes, Miss Dunkirk?"

"He committed a crime?"

"You might say that. At least in the eyes of the Church, Antoine had committed a most heinous crime indeed. One for which the punishment extended far beyond merely denying ordination. For this crime, Antoine was condemned to a life of shame and ridicule. You see, Antoine had violated the unwritten Canon against the use of nicknames."

An undercurrent of puzzlement rippled through the class. Clearly this wasn't the crime they had been expecting.

Finally, Hepplewhite intervened. "Miss Merinne, do you seriously expect the class to accept your proposition that the Church had a Canon against the use of nicknames?"

"There must have been, Professor. What else could explain it? Can anyone guess what nickname the Church found so offensive?"

The Monsignor was watching Dona intently. The benign smile had vanished.

Charles Danforth raised his hand.

"Mr. Danforth."

Charles stood. "Did he call himself something with religious significance, like the death-god Chervil?"

"A great guess, but no religious significance was involved." Charles took his seat.

"In fact, as far as the Church was concerned, the nickname Antoine used must have been even more offensive. Just look at the punishment. Does anyone else have a guess?"

After a long pause, the Monsignor raised his hand.

Dona's stomach did a little leap, but she maintained composure. "Yes, Monsignor?"

"I presume 'Antoine' was itself the nickname in question?"

"Indeed it was." She addressed the class once more. "Thus, the Church denied the ordination just because Antoine had the temerity to use a nickname, even after four years of admittedly brilliant work. Who thinks justice was served?"

While such a question would normally have inspired lively debate, the room remained silent. Many eyes were on the Monsignor, who shifted in his seat once more.

Finally, Alexi raised his hand.

"Mr. Reysa."

Alexi rose to his feet. "Before we can pass judgment, it might be useful to know what you are so obviously leaving out. If Antoine was only his nickname, what was his real name?"

Dona smiled broadly. "An interesting question, Mr. Reysa, but is it really relevant? What about Antoine's real name could possibly justify such outrageous treatment?"

Alexi's eyes narrowed. "Well, the fact that we've gone this long without finding out, in addition to your evasion of my question, suggests to me that you might consider it to be a matter of some importance."

"Not, I, Mr. Reysa, but rather, the Church. It turns out they considered it of vital importance…so important, in fact, that they denied this 'finest of theological minds' ordination once they discovered it. What name could be so heinous?"

There were no more volunteers.

Dona paused for dramatic effect. "It was…Antoinette."

A number of reactions rippled through the class. Some laughed at the surprise, some frowned in moral outrage, but most looked to the Monsignor, hungry for some indication of what response would be appropriate.

Alexi raised his voice over the background rustle. "Miss Merinne, didn't you just deceive us there? Surely this Antoinette character was denied ordination, not for her name, but rather for violating some Canon against ordaining women?"

"If that's true, Mr. Reysa, then they have since changed the rule, because there is no mention of it in the current Canons."

Alexi pondered that for a moment. "In that case, if called upon to pass judgment, assuming you're not withholding any other relevant facts, I'd find in favor of Antoinette."

Eyes leapt nervously between Dona and the obviously uncomfortable Monsignor. Even Hepplewhite's brow had something of a crease to it. He raised his hand.

"Yes, Professor?"

"Miss Merinne, aren't you unduly minimizing the dishonesty issue? The Church may have found it difficult to overlook the fact that Antoinette had misled them about her gender for almost four years. Shouldn't that play some role in your analysis? Perhaps the ordination was denied on the basis of a lack of integrity rather than, as you seem to imply, gender discrimination."

"Professor, with all due respect, how many women have been ordained since that day?"

Hepplewhite considered that for a second. "Well, none that I know of, but neither am I aware of any other women who have completed the required course of study."

"And how many women has the seminary accepted?"

"I doubt any applied."

"Professor, seriously, what woman in her right mind would bother, after the brutal treatment the admittedly brilliant Antoinette received? And even if one did, what do you suppose her chances of acceptance would be?"

Hepplewhite tried another tack. "Miss Merinne, how would you address the position held by a substantial number of the clergy that women are better suited to serve as sisters rather than as priests?"

Dona didn't even pause. "I would ask how the greatest theological mind the abbot had ever encountered could possibly achieve the greatest good playing a subordinate role to a collection of almost certainly lesser minds. Consider— this fiasco took place at the Seminary of Saint Sophia. If we acknowledge that women can achieve the revered status of sainthood, how can we maintain they are not suited, solely by virtue of their gender, to the clearly lesser station of priest?"

Hepplewhite thought a moment and tried again. "Might it not be simply a consequence of the culture in which we live? Is there any validity to the fear that churchgoers may simply be unlikely to take a woman priest seriously? What is the point, if in the end the woman would be ineffective in the role, not for inability, but purely because of prevailing social mores?"

"How could you be certain a woman would be ineffective in the role if you have never given even one the chance to try?"

Nonplussed, Hepplewhite opened the floor to discussion. Given the visible change in the Monsignor's demeanor, however, the ensuing lack of participation was not surprising.

Hepplewhite addressed the class. "Very well, then. Remember that Mr. Danforth will take the podium next week, and make sure you stay up to date on the readings. Dismissed."

Dona was still light-headed, but she wanted to be sure to catch Alexi before he left. Politically, however, she could not ignore the Monsignor. Dona gulped when she realized he was still watching her, but he seemed somehow more pensive than angry. After an awkward moment spent staring at each other, she finally approached him.

"Monsignor, I apologize if you found my talk offensive or inappropriate, but I was looking for a challenging topic and I had no idea you were going to be here."

"Miss Merinne, did you wonder how I happened to know Antoinette's nickname?"

"I admit to having been a little surprised, but I presumed the event caused quite a stir, and perhaps you remembered hearing about it."

A hint of a smile returned to the Monsignor's face. "Oh yes, I definitely heard about it. Did you by chance follow what happened to Antoinette after she was denied ordination?"

"There really wasn't much in the library to find after that," Dona said. "I presumed the shame of the ordeal drove her into hiding, or perhaps to the sanctuary of a convent somewhere."

"Actually, she did neither. She pursued a longer-term approach to meaningful participation in the Church she loved so much—she married my father."

Dona's eyes went wide. "Oh, Monsignor, I sincerely apologize. I meant no disrespect."

The Monsignor flashed a kindly smile. "Miss Merinne, I was proud, honored, and a little embarrassed by your presentation. Proud that my mother's story could still spawn such impassioned arguments in support of her cause, honored that I was able to be here in person to hear you deliver it, and a little embarrassed that in my long career I have managed to achieve so little to address this inequity."

"I don't know what to say."

"Believe me, you've already given me plenty to think about. I just thought you should know you have made an old man's day. I shall remember this visit for a very long time."

Dona remembered her manners enough to curtsey. "It was my pleasure."

The Monsignor struggled to his feet. "Well, it seems Professor Hepplewhite is eager to usher me off to some meeting or other. Do be careful, my child. You will find that nothing generates resentment like ability."

"I shall, Monsignor. Thank you for coming."

As she left, she scanned the classroom half hoping Alexi had remained behind. He hadn't.

"Great," she muttered. "Now I'll never catch up to him."

She stepped outside the classroom to squeals of delight. Unlike Alexi, Helena and Miranda had waited for her.

Helena could barely contain herself. "That was wonderful—Hepplewhite was nearly speechless."

Miranda stepped forward and gave Dona a warm hug. "Well done. And under very trying circumstances, too."

Together, the three of them strolled down the hill toward the main campus.

"What did the Monsignor say?" Helena whispered. "Was he angry?"

Dona shook her head, still finding it difficult to believe. "He told me Antoinette was his mother."

Helena clapped both hands to her mouth. "No, really?"

"It's true. Apparently, he's sympathetic to the issue. I wonder if Hepplewhite has any idea his friend has a soft spot for gender equity. No doubt that would give them endless opportunities to practice their rhetoric on each other."

"How did you ever have the nerve to continue when you saw the Monsignor sitting there?" Miranda asked.

"I had no choice. I couldn't very well decline to give a talk, and I certainly didn't have anything else prepared. I was not willing to fail the class on the off chance I might offend the Monsignor."

"You had everyone on pins and needles," Helena said.

Miranda's mien turned playful. "I notice you even managed to get Alexi Reysa's attention."

"So I saw," Dona said. "This morning he refused to acknowledge my existence, and this afternoon, he's suddenly Mr. Class Participation. And now that I think about it, did he actually accuse me of lying?"

"I thought he set up your next point quite nicely," Miranda said. After a slight pause, she added, "you two seem to work so well together."

Helena smirked. "You noticed that too?"

"It's so obvious, isn't it?"

Stress and lack of sleep were taking their toll. "All right," Dona said. "Have your fun—I deserve it. I can't believe I was so stupid. Here I worried myself silly trying to apologize, and then he tries to sabotage my grade."

Miranda and Helena came to an abrupt halt. "Apologize? *You?*"

Once again Dona colored. "Hey, I say I'm sorry when I'm wrong."

Helena snorted. "You mean when you *think* you're wrong."

"Maybe I'm just not wrong all that often. It's not like it's a game where you take turns."

As they rounded a curve in the path, their dormitory came into sight. Looking ahead, Helena noticed something the others hadn't yet seen. "Speaking of games," she said, "I can't wait to see how this one plays out."

At the dormitory entrance, leaning casually against a pillar, was a clearly spruced-up Alexi Reysa, absently sniffing a single red rose. His face lit up as they approached.

He presented the rose to Dona with a deep bow. "Allow me to congratulate you on an extraordinary performance."

Dona's jaw had dropped when she'd first seen him and still hadn't recovered. She eyed him dubiously, but she took the flower.

Miranda tapped Helena's shoulder. "Weren't you going to show me those new earrings you beaded?"

Helena, who was watching Dona and Alexi with rapt attention, resisted the hint. "In a moment."

Miranda took her by the arm. "I want to see them *now.*"

Helena sighed. "Oh, very well. Has anyone ever told you that you have absolutely no sense of fun?"

"Not and lived to tell the tale. Earrings. Now." She marched up the dormitory steps, practically dragging Helena behind her.

Alexi chuckled as the door closed behind them. "Those two seem pretty entertaining."

Dona breathed in the flower's sweet scent. "Yes, they're a little crazy."

Alexi nodded. "But then, aren't we all?"

"True…Alexi, I…um… I wanted to apologize for my behavior the other night. I totally jumped to conclusions. I guess being a heretic makes me a little paranoid."

"No, it's my fault. Of course you must be careful. And I overreacted and made things worse instead of offering to help, like I should have."

"No, I should have asked instead of accused. The evidence was circumstantial and clearly didn't justify my assumptions. That's not careful—far from it. Can you forgive me?"

He grinned. "No, I always give roses when I'm holding a grudge."

"Why the change of heart? I thought you were glaring at me as recently as this morning."

"Actually, I was. Sometimes it takes me a while to figure out when I'm wrong. I was still angry when I started grilling you in class. But in the end, you really did sway me, and I think everyone else in the room, too. You're a tough one to figure out, you know. One minute you are the most exasperating person ever, and the next, you are the most brilliant. Faced with that brilliance, I started to wonder if maybe I could actually be wrong. When I thought about it again, I started to see where you were coming from."

Dona finally permitted herself to smile. "We women work very hard to preserve our mystery. If we allowed men to figure us out on the first attempt, we'd lose one of our most potent weapons."

"Still, you can't blame us for trying."

Dona's grin turned coy. "It's futile, of course, but we patiently acknowledge that each man will have to come to that realization in his own time."

"Perhaps you'd be so kind as to tutor me over dinner tonight? Clearly I have much to learn."

Dona was about to say she'd be delighted when she realized that she already had plans for the evening and precious little time to get ready.

"Oh, Alexi, I'd love to, I really would, but I told Gregory I'd go to the opera with him tonight."

Alexi's face fell. "I see. Well, if you need help with the book, let me know."

"I'm so sorry. Maybe we can go another night?"

"Of course," Alexi said. "Congratulations again on your presentation—it really was first-rate."

"Thank you. That means a lot coming from you."

"Well, I suppose I should let you get ready. You probably don't have much time if you are traveling into town yet tonight."

"You really are very sweet," Dona said. For the second time, she leaned up and kissed him on the cheek. "I hope you'll call again soon."

CHAPTER FIVE

PERFORMANCE ANXIETIES

At three minutes to six, a black carriage rounded the bend in front of the dormitory. The horses pulled to a restless stop as Dona appeared at the top of the stairs. The midnight blue of the one formal gown she owned lay resplendent against her fair skin, and her treasured opera gloves provided elegant contrast. Miranda had somehow cajoled her dark tresses into a stylish coiled chignon. Her little black hat was a perfect accent, complete with a flurry of blue and white feathers and just enough black tulle to make it formal. She looked every inch the lady, and no one seeing her descending the stairs would ever have suspected the extent of Helena's frenzied last-minute adjustments.

Gregory leapt from the carriage, dashing in his black coat and tails. As Dona approached, he held his hand aloft. She smiled and took it in hers. The coachman gave a short bow and opened the carriage door. Gregory assisted her in, and then followed her as the coachman resumed his spot atop the vehicle. A shake of the reins and an encouraging shout to the horses, and the carriage shot forward.

In an upper window, elbows resting on the sill and chin resting in her hands, Helena sighed wistfully as the carriage faded from view.

"Dona has all the luck. Do you suppose once the ball is over, she and her prince charming will live happily ever after?"

Miranda looked up from her book with a wry smile. "She'd have a better chance kissing frogs."

. . . . .

Opening night at the opera was a society event in Trifienne, and nothing showed that more clearly than the tangle of pedestrians and carriages gathered in the city's central square. Dona delighted in the chaos. A veteran of several operas, this was her first opening night, and the thrill had given her a second wind. She peered eagerly out of the carriage and pointed at the most interesting passersby, while Gregory obligingly put names on the faces of Trifienne's *crème de la crème*.

"That's Judge Remmelford and his wife," he said.

"But she's so young."

"At least 20 years his junior. The first Mrs. Remmelford was less than thrilled by the new addition to the family. You'll find her over there—she's the one in green. Unfortunately for His Honor, her two sons followed in their father's footsteps and are expert solicitors. A result, she's able to boast that gown, those jewels, and that young man she's sporting on her arm. She's not much for opera, but she'll jump at any opportunity to rub it in."

"And who's that?" Dona asked, pointing out a slender young woman in a deep scarlet gown that teetered on edge of modesty. Crimson jewels glittered at her throat. She was accompanied not by a young man, but by an entourage.

"That would be Princess Julienne, the Crown Prince's third-born. He's said to refer to her as 'the Royal Pain.' She's not exactly known for her self-restraint."

"She's gorgeous."

"By all accounts. No doubt that adds considerably to her father's discomfort."

"Oh look, it's Hepplewhite and the Monsignor."

"What luck, Maybe during intermission, you can sneak over and get your grade."

Dona gave his arm a playful tap. "Don't be silly. After the presentation I gave today, he'll be sneaking over to see me—for my autograph. But I won't play favorites. He'll have to wait in line like everyone else."

Gregory grinned. "Word of your 'excessive talent' must be getting out."

"Speaking of getting out, we're close enough. Why don't we just walk the rest of the way?"

"Good point—I think that would be faster."

Gregory pounded on the roof of the carriage, which slowed from a crawl to a stop. He and Dona hopped out and pushed their way through the crowd. Fortunately, he had played this venue before and knew the shortcut. Dona took his arm, and he escorted her down a narrow alley. Coming upon a heavy door, he rapped smartly three times. After a pause, he rapped two more times. The door swung inward.

"Gregory!"

"Dorian, how wonderful to see you. I didn't think you were in this one."

"I'm not, really," Dorian said. "I was going to take a break, but they begged. I'm helping with make-up."

Dona followed Gregory in, and the door fell closed behind her.

"And who have we here?" Dorian asked.

"Allow me to introduce my good friend, Miss Dona Merinne."

Dorian raised an eyebrow.

As her eyes adjusted, Dona caught her breath. "You're Dorian Emolino."

Dorian bowed low. "The very same."

"I absolutely adored you in *Hesperia.*"

"I was good, wasn't I?"

Gregory shook his head. "Baritones are such preeners."

"We have to be," Dorian protested. "You tenors keep stealing all our thunder. Anyone with the emotional range of a dishrag can pull off a lovesick hero. The real talent lies in portraying the villain."

"He has a point," Dona said.

"Oh, I like this one, Gregory."

"She makes a fair first impression," Gregory said, "but trust me, it's fleeting."

"Hey!" Dona said.

A voice called out from backstage. "Thirty minutes to curtain. We could use a little help in here."

"Coming," Dorian called back. "Well, I'd love to stay and chat, but it seems there's a dishrag in need of pressing. Soooo needy. Pleased to meet you, young lady."

Dona curtseyed. "The pleasure was all mine."

As Dorian retreated backstage, Gregory led Dona off through a passage that bypassed the lobby in favor of a side stairwell. Upstairs they found a lavish corridor lined with arches, each draped with velvet curtains. Gregory counted them until he found the one he was looking for, drew back the curtain, and ushered her through.

"My heavens. This box is exquisite."

Gregory grinned. "Not bad, eh?"

"This can't be more than three away from the Crown Prince's. Oh look," she said, pointing. "There's the Princess."

Gregory gently pushed Dona's arm down out of sight. "Um, sort of considered bad form to point."

Dona was mortified. "Oh no—I'm such a boor."

The Princess, who'd been fanning herself with a program amidst her entourage, must have caught the movement, for Dona could swear she was now looking her way. Trying her best to fade into the woodwork, she forced herself to watch the orchestra in the midst of its warm-up. After what seemed an eternity, she let her eye wander back to the Princess. To her horror, the Princess still seemed to be staring directly at her. For an instant, their eyes met.

Dona turned and nudged her date. "I think the Princess is watching us."

"Really?" He shot a quick glance in Julienne's direction. She responded by turning sultry, pursing her lips as though secretly blowing a kiss.

Gregory forced his gaze back to the orchestra. "Oh, that doesn't bode well."

"Was it something I did?"

"It's not so much what you did as what you're going to do."

"What do you mean?"

"This." He leaned over and planted a kiss—right on her lips.

Startled, Dona snapped her head back. Her hat tumbled to the floor. Several curls came undone in the process.

"Bella, humor me," he whispered.

Dona froze, her eyes wide, as Gregory came in for another. After a moment, he leaned back and took her hand, his eyes fixed on hers as though mesmerized.

"What on earth was *that?*" she hissed.

"None other than your stage debut as a lovesick dishrag. You really should try for more emotional range next time."

Her eyes narrowed. "What do you mean, *next time?*"

"Our Princess has a reputation for being, shall we say, persistent. She may find one heartfelt, if stilted, display a tad unconvincing."

"You want me to play the role of your *girlfriend?* Are you serious?"

Gregory assumed his best hurt-puppy look. "Would that really be so awful?"

"Oh, stop it," she said. "No, no of course not. It's just, well…a little unexpected. So, all this time you were just using me to fend off the unsolicited affections of your admirers?"

"Cheap and tawdry of me, I know. In my defense, I only just thought of it now."

"You leave me no choice," Dona said.

"I do?"

This time her kiss caught *him* unawares. Fortunately, given his dramatic training, he recovered quickly. In the middle of it, the orchestra began playing the overture, and shortly thereafter, the curtain rose.

The awkwardness of their arrival was soon forgotten as they were swept away by the operatic spectacle unfolding on the stage below. Rhyven Badalore had a range that made even Gregory a little envious, and a presence borne of years of experience that seized his audience and never let go.

Captivated by the first act, Dona hadn't given the Princess another thought. But as the lights came up for intermission, she snuck a glance in her direction. Julienne was still paying their box undue attention, but now her expression was one of amusement, and perhaps a little pity. At the edge of her vision, Dona caught sight of a wayward curl—no doubt displaced by her overture activities. Belatedly she noticed her hat lying off to one side. After snatching it up, she leaned down to give Gregory another lingering kiss.

"She's still watching?" he asked.

"Like a vulture. Excuse me a moment."

As she made her way down the curtained corridor, Dona found herself praying that Princesses didn't use the common powder room. To her relief, she recognized no one there, and by the time she'd repaired her damaged coif the room was nearly empty. Judging herself once again presentable, she assumed her most dignified air and strolled back toward Morissant's box.

To her dismay, all the curtained archways seemed identical. While backtracking to make certain she had the right one, a familiar voice made her pause.

Was that Professor Hepplewhite? Knowing it was foolishness, she loitered a bit longer on the off chance they were discussing her presentation. Pretending to adjust her hat, she edged nearer the curtain.

"Surely you must be mistaken," Hepplewhite said.

"I wish I were," the Monsignor replied, "but the evidence is quite convincing to one who knows how to interpret it. A pernicious brand of heresy has taken root at Exidgeon."

A chill went up Dona's spine.

"Surely that label doesn't apply to what goes on at the University," Heppelwhite said. "The Church has long recognized the exemption for academic freedom."

"Exempt to discuss," the Monsignor said. "Not practice."

"Practice? Why would you suspect someone at Exidgeon of that?"

"As I said, Phrendonic heresy is particularly seductive. Few who have studied it are content to merely leave it at that. That is why it is especially important that we get to the bottom of this quickly. We certainly don't want another Caprian on our hands."

At the mention of the word "Phrendonic," Dona's throat tightened. The Monsignor was pursuing heresy at the University after all—and he'd shown up in *two* of her classes. That couldn't possibly be a coincidence. And when the Monsignor finally tracked her down and proved she possessed the book, she would be expelled—possibly even imprisoned, but certainly expelled. Drawing back in shock, she retreated to her box and pulled back the curtain. Several people she didn't know craned their necks and frowned in annoyance.

"Oh, pardon me," she croaked, letting the curtain fall.

She found Gregory on the next try. He smiled expectantly as she approached, tilted back his head, and pursed his lips. Dona sank into her seat and ignored him.

"She's still watching," he whispered.

"I have bigger problems than a petulant princess at the moment. How soon can we get out of here?"

"Whoa," Gregory said. "We have half an opera left—Ravenna hasn't even sung her first aria."

Dona thought for a moment. "I suppose you're right. It would look odd if we left early. Best not to draw attention."

"What's gotten into you?"

"I can't talk about it right now. Let's just get through this and get out of here before someone else notices us."

"It must be pretty serious to make you eager to abandon an opera on opening night."

"It could well become that. Let's pray it doesn't."

As the performance resumed, Dona sat wide-eyed in her seat. Gregory favored her with frequent perplexed glances, but said nothing further.

At last, she began to calm down. Not only was the second half of Amoretorium even more entrancing than the first, but the Monsignor's words had finally begun to sink in—if universities had the academic freedom to study heresy without thereby committing it, the mere possession of a book on the topic shouldn't be problematic. The Monsignor had to be looking for someone else.

By the curtain call, she was fully enjoying herself again and was among the first on her feet for the standing ovation. Her renewed enthusiasm had quieted Gregory's concerns, and when he offered his arm to leave, he was back to his usual flippant self.

"Apparently the Princess was so overwrought with jealousy that she couldn't stand it anymore," he said. "Poor dear had to leave before the performance was even over."

Dona had pretty much forgotten the Princess after the little scare from the Monsignor. A glance in the direction of the Crown Prince's box confirmed it now sat empty.

"Don't get your hopes up, dear boy. Believe me, once the Princess left, the 'performance' was definitely over."

"But it seemed so real. I'd have never dreamed such passion could be faked."

Dona's tone was smug. "Must be yet another of my excessive talents—I'm heartened to see my reviews are positive."

"I'll be sure to have them printed up straight away—just as soon as I uncurl my toes."

. . . . .

The curtained corridor was no longer crowded, but as Gregory escorted Dona down to the lobby, they found the throngs had yet to thin. Actors, still in costume, mingled with star-struck fans. Patrons gathered in groups, discussing the show, commenting on current events, or sharing society gossip. It was all a bit of a blur to Gregory, who was luxuriating in the comfortable daze that always gripped him after a particularly spectacular debut. Apparently Dona's mind was elsewhere as well, since neither of them noticed the Princess as they passed.

She, however, noticed them. "Why, if it isn't Gregory Delauren."

Gregory froze.

Julienne's entourage parted, leaving a clear path between them.

"You're looking as handsome as ever."

Gregory fancied himself a master of 'polite, but distant,' and he used it now to full effect. "Thank you, your Highness."

She sauntered over, looking him up and down as though he were prized livestock "Have I mentioned how impressed I was with your performance in *Ghost Pirates?*"

"You are too kind, Highness."

As she spoke, she circled him. "I think I did mention it once before. Wasn't it in this very lobby? Oh yes, I remember now. I think I even invited you to a little gala we were having, didn't I?"

He could feel sweat beading on his forehead.

She paused directly before him, mere inches from the tip of his nose. "I must say, I was deeply disappointed you didn't show."

Gregory replied through clenched teeth. "I offer my sincerest apologies."

Julienne adjusted his cravat. "How inconsiderate of me to have bothered you like that during the run of the show. No doubt the rigors of stage life make it difficult to fraternize with mere members of the audience, regardless of how devoted. So you can imagine my delight at finding you here as a patron of the arts rather than as a performer."

Gregory gulped at the sight of Dona's narrowed eyes and folded arms.

"Surely now," Julienne continued, "freed from the onerous burden imposed by your art, you will be able to accept my humble invitation to dine with me this evening."

Dona cleared her throat. "Your Highness, I don't believe we've met."

"I've been remiss," Gregory said. "Allow me to introduce Miss Dona Merinne."

Dona curtseyed. "I'm so very pleased to make your acquaintance."

Julienne ignored her. "Shall we adjourn to my carriage? I have a perfect little spot in mind."

"My apologies, Your Highness," Gregory said. "But I am with Miss Merinne this evening."

Julienne waved dismissively. "Oh, bring the servant as well, if you must."

Dona's eyes became saucers. After a moment, they narrowed again, and she stalked off into the crowd.

Gregory wavered between honor and fear. He felt obliged to rush after Dona and beg her forgiveness, but he feared Julienne's wrath if he were to ditch her mid-invitation. Fear won out.

"Miss Merinne has had a very busy day, and to entice her to accompany me, I promised I would have her home at a reasonable hour. I'm sure you understand."

Julienne flashed a crooked little smile "It looks as though Miss Merinne has decided to find her own way home." She slid her arm into Gregory's. "Poor thing looked exhausted. I do hope she makes it there all right. Now, where were we?"

"I, um—"

"Ah yes, I remember. We were about to adjourn to my carriage."

The Princess applied enough force that Gregory actually took a step in the direction of the entrance.

Suddenly, Dona's voice echoed over the din of the crowd. "She's an absolute delight, Monsignor. I know she would be ecstatic to meet you."

The crowd parted, revealing Dona, arm in arm with Monsignor Goodkin. Hepplewhite trailed behind, looking every bit the fifth wheel.

"Well, Miss Merinne," the Monsignor said, "seeing as how you recommend her so highly, I would be honored."

They approached Julienne, who had frozen mid-stride at the sight of them.

"And here she is," Dona said. "Your Highness, may I introduce Monsignor Armand Goodkin."

The Monsignor, leaning on his cane, bowed slightly and said, "So very pleased to make your acquaintance."

Reluctantly, Julienne relinquished Gregory's arm to extend her hand. "The pleasure is all mine, Monsignor."

"I trust you enjoyed tonight's performance? The critics are already hailing it as a *tour de force.*"

The Princess shot Gregory a subtle but pointed glance. "Indeed, I have been looking forward to tonight's performance for quite some time."

"So Your Highness is an opera fan?"

"I enjoy a good performance, if that's what you mean."

"Oh, I'm forgetting myself. Allow me to introduce Zachary Hepplewhite. He's one of the distinguished professors up at the University."

Julienne forced a smile. "Delighted."

The Monsignor maneuvered in close. "I'm so very pleased to see our young people taking such an interest in the arts. I recall speaking once with your father about the importance of fostering art appreciation in our youth, but at the time, he had seemed dubious."

Dona sidled up to Gregory, took his arm, and nudged him toward the exit. Oblivious, the Monsignor droned on. "Apparently your father was more receptive to the advice than he seemed. It's good to know an old man can still have some influence on the things that really matter…."

The next thing Gregory knew, they were dashing across the square for Morissant's carriage. Once inside, he knocked on the ceiling.

"Exidgeon, Roberts, and hurry."

The carriage lurched forward. Moments later, they'd disappeared into the relative safety of the night.

· · · · ·

As the two of them settled in for the ride, Dona burst out laughing.

"What?" Gregory asked. "I can't help it I'm irresistible."

"Maybe if you hadn't insisted on being so ridiculously polite…"

"Easy for you to say. You weren't the slab of meat on the auction block."

Dona stripped off her opera gloves. "No, as you may recall, I was the slab's domestic."

Now it was Gregory's turn to chuckle.

"What?"

"Nothing. I just had this mental image of you wielding a feather duster. Most unsettling."

Dona shot him a sidelong look. "Oh really? And I suppose you always laugh when you're unsettled?"

Gregory rubbed his chin in thought. "Yes, I suppose I do—when it also happens to be funny. In all seriousness, though, thanks for rescuing me back there. That Monsignor ploy was inspired."

The carriage suddenly careened hard to the left, throwing both Dona and Gregory off balance. The initial lurch was followed by a series of bumps and jostles that made it plain the vehicle had left the road.

Gregory pounded on the roof. "Roberts, what's going on out there?"

There was no response, and after a few more minutes of bouncing, the carriage finally came to rest.

"Roberts?"

The door to the carriage flew open. Moonlight limned a figure draped in priestly vestments, his face obscured in darkness.

"Roberts has taken the rest of the night off. Perhaps I can help?"

"Who are you?" Gregory demanded.

"What do you want?" Dona chimed in. Though badly rattled and aware she held very few cards, she was determined not to show it.

"I'm here for your confession, Miss Merinne."

He was after the book. That much was clear—but if the Church were truly aware she possessed it, why hadn't the Monsignor simply taken her into custody? It didn't add up. Despite the vestments, there was no way this man was acting on behalf of the Church—which meant he was probably a heretic, perhaps the one who'd lost the book in the first place. Had he been able to prove that and simply asked her nicely to return it, she might have complied, if for no other reason than to end having watch over her shoulder. But to kidnap and corner her? Now there was no way she was giving up that book without a fight.

"You really shouldn't have gone to so much trouble," Dona said. "But since you have, allow me to oblige you. I confess— to being puzzled as to why a priest would risk kidnapping innocent people and then waste time pretending to want to help them."

Gregory chimed in. "I daresay Morissant is not going to be pleased by the theft of his carriage, either."

The man laughed softly. "Let's just say, Miss Merinne, that your recent activities have made me…inquisitive."

Dona took a risk she might not have dared had the man brandished a weapon. "Father Whoever-you-are," she said, "it's late, I'm tired, and it has been a very long day. If you want something from me, ask. If you plan to rob us, just do it and get it over with. If, however, you want to play twenty questions, I suggest you find a partner who isn't half asleep."

The man laughed softly. "My hat is off to you, Miss Merinne. Most of my clients show far less spunk. I'll be plain. Surrender the book and you can be on your way."

"I'd be happy to. Obviously, though, I don't have it with me. I'll just head home and deliver it to the Monsignor personally first thing in the morning."

For a fleeting moment, the man's confidence wavered. It was just the sign Dona had been hoping for.

"Unacceptable," he said

"Don't worry, you'll still get credit. I'll be happy to tell the Monsignor you sent me. What was your name again?"

"That book is unspeakably evil. I can't risk it being outside Church custody even one more night."

Dona shrugged. "Fine. We'll find the Monsignor tonight and get this all out of the way. Surely his friend Professor Hepplewhite will know where he is staying. In fact, he may even be staying *with* Professor Hepplewhite. Why don't we go see?"

Again, the man hesitated. Then he seemed to make a decision. "Get me that book, or I swear I will set the Inquisition on you."

"And risk losing your precious book forever?"

After a long pause, he shook his head. "That's it. I've had it. I did not sign on for this."

He turned and fled into the wood.

Gregory shot Dona a puzzled look. "What was that all about?"

"It's a long story, and we don't have time for it right now—we have to make sure Roberts isn't hurt. Have you ever driven one of these things?"

Gregory eyed the carriage. "Not really."

Dona climbed out and put her hands on her hips. "If we can turn it around, I think I could probably manage. I must warn you, though, I have never driven one at night."

It took a while, but they finally got the carriage back on track. Both of them hopped up top, and Dona took the reins. The initial forward jolt nearly knocked Gregory off, but before long, they were making good progress. Fortunately, the horses seemed inclined to keep to the road.

"So," Gregory said. "Now that we have a little time to chat, why don't we discuss something interesting, like, oh, say, how your day was, the chance of rain tomorrow, or maybe why that man dressed as a priest kidnapped us?"

"My day was mostly just peachy," Dona said. "How about yours?"

"Pretty good, up until the last few hours, particularly that bit where the man dressed as a priest kidnapped us. You wouldn't happen to know anything about that, would you?"

"Shhhh," Dona said, pulling back the reins.

Once the noise from the carriage quieted, the sound of galloping hooves was unmistakable.

"Now what?" Gregory asked. "You don't suppose he's bringing friends?"

"I only hear one horse," she said. "If he's coming back, he's coming alone."

"Well, since I still don't have the slightest idea what's going on, do we run away, ignore him, or invite him in for tea?"

"Run away? I'm not running anywhere in these shoes. If our errant priest is after us again, he's going to have to jump a moving carriage to get to us."

"In case you haven't noticed, these things don't really move all that fast."

"Well, here he comes. If that's our priest, he's changed clothes."

The horseman reined in his horse, waved his hat, and whooped.

"Roberts!" Gregory cried.

Dona heaved a sigh of relief. "Thank goodness you're safe."

"Good to see your smiling faces too, m'lord and m'lady. I'd have felt horrible if anything bad had happened to you."

Roberts dismounted and did a quick check on the wagon. Then he tied his horse to the back and jumped into his customary spot. It was crowded, but neither Dona nor Gregory was eager to get back into the coach.

"What happened back there?" Gregory asked. "Why weren't you with the carriage?"

Roberts scratched his bald spot. "And here I was about to ask why you left without me. All I know is once I parked the carriage, I hopped down to give the old legs a stretch. I strolled over to the fountain and sat to watch the water for a bit, and the next thing I knew, I was waking up and all the carriages were gone. Odd thing is I didn't even think I was tired. Age sure creeps up on a man in strange ways. So I grabbed me one of the Master's horses and high-tailed it up here towards the school, and what do I find but the two of you on the road headed the wrong way."

"Was there a priest hanging around by the carriages?" Dona asked.

"I'm sorry, m'lady. There might have been, but I wasn't really paying folks there any mind. Most of them wouldn't have had any use for the likes of me anyways."

Despite a queue of unanswered questions, Dona felt her eyelids drooping.

"Why don't we stop and put you in the carriage?" Gregory said.

She tried unsuccessfully to suppress a yawn. "That's all right. It isn't that far."

"Will you be safe in the dormitory? Why don't you stay with me tonight?"

She shook her head. "I'll be fine. If our 'priest' had trouble facing down a slab of meat and a domestic, he wouldn't stand a chance against our house mother."

"All kidding aside, are you sure?"

"That place is like a fortress. In fact, I think it used to be one."

"Well, if you change your mind, you'd be more than welcome."

"Very sweet of you, but if I'm going to have any chance of catching up on my sleep, I'll need my own bed."

A little while later, after Dona had sent Miranda and Helena off to sleep with promises she'd tell all come the morning, she snuck out from beneath her coverlet and lifted the lid on her hope chest just enough to slip her hand inside. Feeling the unmistakable texture of the book's cover, she silently closed and locked the chest. After secreting the key in a hidden cleft beneath the windowsill, she climbed back into bed. She was asleep before her head touched the pillow.

CHAPTER SIX

SNEAKING SUSPICIONS

It was late morning before Dona finally woke to sunshine streaming through the window. She'd slept through the normal bustle of Miranda's and Helena's Saturday-morning rituals. She'd also slept through breakfast. That sacrifice she considered a small price to pay for a little privacy. Rifling through her wardrobe, she found a faded red dress. Borrowing Helena's shears and a needle and thread, she measured, cut and sewed until she had a passable cover for the book. Several of the other women in her classes had covered their texts with fabric, and although Dona had thought it unnecessary and pretentious, in this case she was willing to sacrifice her aesthetic sensibilities for the practical benefits of masking the book's distinctive look and controversial title. At least then she'd be able to rummage through her satchel without fear of discovery—even take the book out, if need be.

But now what? All the recent hullabaloo had made her more determined than ever to get a closer look at this book, but given the events of the previous evening, finding a truly private spot might be unwise. There was no one she could safely tell about it either. As far as she knew, the only people who were aware of it were Alexi, Gregory—who had probably at least gotten an inkling from the kidnapper—and the kidnapper himself.

That of course raised the question of how the kidnapper had known. She could envision two possibilities: either Alexi told someone or, more likely, the kidnapper was the book's original owner, and he had seen her leave the library with it. Given how she had treated Alexi before, she was loath to jump to conclusions, but even so, she really needed to know whether he was somehow involved.

She once again locked away the book, put the key in its hiding spot under the windowsill, and carefully placed Mr. Lop Ears atop the chest. Then she paused—she couldn't shake the feeling he was staring at her.

"What? I'll only study, not practice, I promise."

Still, he stared.

Finally, she faced him the other way and left to find Alexi.

An hour and a half later, after walking nearly the entire campus, she finally tracked him down. The school gymnasium was divided into sections for a variety of activities on Saturday mornings. Alexi, she was told, should be in the fencing section.

It was easy to find—no one else wore outfits like that. Two opponents were squaring off as she approached. The coach gave the signal, which instigated a flurry of blades. One masked man, who moved like a practiced dancer, instantly landed a barrage of blows on the other, despite frantic attempts to fend them off. In a matter of seconds, the loser was forced off the *piste*, and the coach called the match.

The two men bowed to each other and removed their masks. Alexi congratulated his opponent.

"I don't know how you do that. I can't even see your blade it moves so fast."

The dancer pulled his hand through his long dark hair. "Practice. It's all about practice. You need to spend many more hours here than you do if you want to pick up the subtleties."

"Can't, my friend, I have too many other responsibilities. I guess I'll just have to settle for being second-rate."

Turning, Alexi saw Dona standing patiently to one side. Mopping his face with a towel, he started toward her. She couldn't help noticing he had lit up when he'd seen her, and his smile seemed genuine.

"In my defense, I don't lose that badly *all* the time."

"Glad to hear it," Dona said. "The bruises would make it pretty hard to sit through lecture."

"Alphonse is the best in the class, but he's a fanatic. He lives for this stuff."

"Did I hear my name?"

"Alphonse," Alexi said. "This is Dona."

"Ahh, you must be the lucky young lady who received the rose. I am enchanted, but disappointed. Had I not already known, I would be sorely tempted to present you with one myself."

"I see your tongue is as mighty as your sword," she said— and immediately regretted it. She smiled sweetly, as if unaware of the heat rising in her cheeks.

Alphonse chuckled softly. "Indeed, that is a matter of some pride." He shot a sidelong look at Alexi, who was trying his best not to burst out laughing. "Alexi, my friend, you are a lucky man. I hope you'll both excuse me. I have another match." He bowed to Dona. "Charmed to meet you."

"Likewise," Dona said, playing it safe this time.

Alphonse headed back toward the other fencers.

"Well, that could have gone better," she said.

Alexi grinned. "I'm not sure how. How was the Opera?"

"Spectacular! Amoretorium is destined to become a classic."

Alexi's smile faded a bit.

"Listen," she said. "I wanted to tell you once more how sorry I was that I couldn't accept your invitation last night. Are you free for lunch? I haven't eaten yet, and I'm famished."

"You're sure Gregory won't mind?"

Dona laughed. "Why, if I didn't know better, Mr. Reysa, I'd say you're jealous."

"No, just respectful."

"Believe me," Dona said, taking his arm. "Gregory will get over it."

"All right, but I'll need to drop these things off at the house and change first."

. . . . .

She gawked in surprise as they approached Alexi's residence. "I didn't know you were with a fraternity."

"There are some advantages over dormitory life," he said, "chief among them is that, fraternities have some control over who can join. That alone can make it worthwhile, unless of course, you prefer to share space with the Arietta Charwicks of the world."

"I'm not sure they even have such things for women."

"Not at Exidgeon, anyway. Several universities in other cities are starting them up though. Let me show you around."

The common areas were spacious and almost luxurious compared to her spartan dormitory. They had study areas, meeting rooms, and recreational areas set aside for the members. In one of these, they came upon Professor Reston, who was in the midst of a lively poker game.

"Professor Reston?" Dona asked.

Reston stood up. "Miss Merinne, welcome to our humble abode."

"You live here?"

"Only temporarily. They offered to take me on as an advisor until I find a place of my own. It's a great opportunity to meet students, and it gives me time to check out the area."

"I was just giving Dona the tour, Professor," Alexi said.

"By all means. You'll skip the messy parts?"

"As per standing orders."

"Then carry on."

"It was good to see you, Professor," Dona said.

"And you, Miss Merinne. I'll see you in class."

"I look forward to it."

When the tour took him near his room, Alexi ducked in for a quick change, while Dona waited in a nearby lounge. Something struck her as wrong that Alexi hadn't mentioned Reston living in the same house, but before she could put her finger on it, he was back and ready to go.

"Why didn't you ever mention Reston lived with you?"

Alexi shrugged. "You don't say much about your house mother either."

"Yes, but as far as I know, you don't know her."

He shrugged. "I guess it just never seemed like it was worth mentioning. After all, we've only ever had a few conversations. So, where would you like to eat?"

Dona's stomach was happy to let him change the subject. "The cafeteria?"

Alexi grimaced. "Surely we can do better than that."

"Well, that's what's on campus."

"Let's go into town."

Dona had to remind herself why she was here in the first place. In light of that, a trip to town didn't seem a very good idea. "I think I'm too hungry to wait. Besides, it's a very long walk."

"Ah, but this is a fraternity. I'm sure a brother would lend me a horse or two for the afternoon."

"It's very kind of you to offer, but I think immediacy is winning out over quality just now. Besides, if I get used to good food, I'll starve, since I'll never want to go to the cafeteria again."

"Well, if you insist," Alexi said, "but in all fairness, taking you there would be like Gregory taking you to a puppet show. How can a guy compete?"

"I guess you'll just have to work that much harder. Say, I have a question. You haven't told anyone else about the book, have you?"

"You aren't still worried about the Monsignor, are you?"

Dona raised an eyebrow. "Let's just say I've developed some additional concerns. So, have you told anyone?"

"Why do you mistrust me so much?"

"And why are you evading the question? Don't try to deny it, either. After all, you're the one who taught me to watch for that."

Alexi stopped walking. "What additional concerns?"

Dona took a deep breath. "Our carriage was hijacked last night. Turns out the gentleman wanted to retrieve a certain book from me, which was a bit odd, given that as far as I know, we are the only two who know I have it."

"Damn it!"

"Oh, so you do know something about this?"

"Are you all right? He didn't hurt you, did he?"

"Does this 'he' have a name?"

"I'm not sure, but I have my suspicions."

Her jaw dropped. "Um, so just how many possibilities are there?"

"Look," he said. "I feel awful about this, but I really can't tell you."

Dona folded her arms and tapped her toe. "Just so you know, Gregory is comparing rather favorably at the moment."

"It's not that I don't want to tell you, it's that I can't. It would put everyone in a lot more danger, including you."

"I fail to see how knowing the name of my assailant could possibly put me in more danger."

"This charade has gone on long enough. It's time you knew the truth. Come with me." He started back the way they had come.

"Where are we going?"

"I can't tell you, but I know someone who can."

"At the fraternity?"

"Yes."

"No offense, but under the circumstances that doesn't seem like such a good idea."

Alexi stopped short. "Hmm, I see what you mean. Would it make you feel safer if someone knew you were going there with me?"

"Not if I'm thereby endangering someone else."

"Tell you what. You go tell whomever you like that you are meeting me at the fraternity. That way you don't endanger anyone, and you can still find out the truth."

"And have you simply deny I ever got there?"

Alexi sighed. "Let me think a minute."

Dona tapped her toe a bit faster.

"All right, how about this. In the park across from the cafeteria, near the big oak tree, there's a garden shed. Next to the shed there's a bench. The bench and the shed are in plain sight of the cafeteria. If you want an explanation, be in that shed in twenty minutes."

Alexi turned and ran back down the path.

Dona shrugged and decided to go see this shed for herself. As she passed the cafeteria, cold hands suddenly covered her eyes.

"Guess who?"

Dona sighed in relief. She turned to see Helena's smiling face. Miranda was with her.

"What's wrong?" Helena asked.

"Nothing, you just startled me."

"We missed you at breakfast," Miranda said. "And we were so looking forward to an update. How did it go?"

Dona thought fast. She really didn't want to get her friends involved, at least until she knew it wouldn't endanger them. Neither did she want to lie.

"It was fabulous. I'd love to tell you all about it, but I'm supposed to meet Alexi in just a few minutes, and I don't want to be late. Can we chat later?"

Helena's nose wrinkled in confusion. "Your night with Gregory was so fabulous you are rushing off to meet... Alexi?"

"Of course, you should go," Miranda said, "but we'll need to hear all these additional details just as soon as you get back."

"I'll see you tonight."

Dona was already in sight of the shed, but she didn't want her friends to see where she was going, so she continued along the path past the cafeteria and circled back. As with many of the buildings on the campus, the shed had no lock. The gardening tools were well organized, but the shed itself was old and rickety. Shafts of sunlight illuminated the space through numerous holes in the walls. Since the floor was dirt, Dona waited standing up.

She didn't wait long. After a few moments, Alexi's voice filtered through the cracks between the boards. "Let's stop here. You may want to be sitting when you hear this."

"Fine," Reston replied.

The bench creaked.

"Now what was so sensitive that you couldn't tell me in the fraternity?"

"Dona Merinne was attacked last night."

"Attacked? She wasn't hurt, was she?"

"No."

"Thank goodness for that. Well, I concede that's terrible news, but why couldn't you have told me at the fraternity?"

"Her attacker demanded the book."

There was a long pause.

"No one outside knew, correct?"

"Not as far as we know."

Reston sighed. "I see why you didn't want anyone in the fraternity to hear. I think it's time to retrieve the book from Miss Merinne. The whole point of letting her keep it was that she had no obvious connection to the rest of us and could claim the academic freedom exemption if things went awry. If she's now in danger from within, then it's only right for us to reassume the risk while we try to remedy the problem. Will she give the book to you, do you think?"

"I can ask, but she has a mind of her own."

"Try to convince her. Meanwhile, I will see if I can come up with some way of neutralizing our miscreant, but it may take a while to be certain who it was. I can't afford to be wrong about this."

"Isn't it obvious?"

"Patience, Alexi. To a man, this is a clever group. Indeed, they were selected for just that trait. It seems oaths can only bind clever men to a very limited degree. Under these circumstances, the most obvious choice may be obvious for reasons that have nothing to do with fact. I must be certain. Does her friend know?"

"Delauren? He must know the attacker demanded a book. Beyond that I don't know."

"And what's this I've been hearing about a rose?"

Alexi paused.

Reston sighed again. "Once you lost custody of the book, the idea was to allow it to reside somewhere with no close connection with anyone in the group until the threat had passed. Public displays of affection don't foster that illusion. You know what's at stake."

"I'm sorry, Professor. I didn't think."

"It's all right. I was young once too, and it wasn't even that long ago. And maybe it will help with what you have to do now. Is there anything else?"

"There is one more thing...."

"Yes?"

"I think she should be offered the option to join us."

"Impossible. Not only would that put her at increased risk, but it would be very difficult to maintain our cover within the fraternity."

"Professor," Alexi said evenly, "not all our members live at the fraternity. And Dona's already had the book for a week. By now, she is probably well acquainted with its contents. Because of our poor decisions, she's now in danger. As for the Inquisition, if they figure out what we've been up to, they're not going to consider a claim of academic freedom from anyone they catch with that book, whether legitimate or not. If she joined, at least we'd be able to keep her apprised."

"You have a point about keeping her apprised, but I don't think admitting a woman would sit well with the other members."

Dona felt her hackles rising.

"You must admit she's qualified intellectually."

"I'm not saying she's not, but there's the group dynamic to consider."

"No offense, but the present group dynamic hasn't exactly served us well—need I remind you you're about to run off to figure out who among us needs neutralizing?"

"Keep this up Alexi, and I'll see to it that Hepplewhite drops you from his course."

"You aren't confusing rhetoric with common sense, are you, Professor?"

"My biggest concern with your suggestion is precisely its *lack* of common sense. The last thing we should be doing when under threat of Inquisition is adding new members."

"As I said, if the Inquisition discovers us, she'll likely be treated as a member whether she is or not."

"And if she decides to report us to the Inquisition?"

"We take that same chance with every new member."

"Ah, but the pressure to report to the Inquisition is much greater during an investigation, lest the candidate believe himself to be a target just for having been asked."

"She already has plenty of ammunition to damn us," Alexi countered. "She has the book, and she has the story of how she was abducted by someone demanding it. Those two facts alone would be sufficient to compel a full-scale investigation. And other than curiosity about the book's contents, she has no reason not to report it. She can do most of the damage we fear unwittingly."

"I'll have to think about it."

"Consider quickly please, Professor. Were I in her shoes, I would already have reported the kidnapping."

"Perhaps I can be of some assistance," Dona said, stepping around the side of the shed. Once in full view, she waved at Helena and Miranda, who were still having lunch together outside the cafeteria.

"A very clever group indeed," Reston muttered. "You heard everything, of course."

"Every last word," Dona said.

"And what's your feeling on the matter?"

"That's a little simplistic, isn't it Professor? There are actually several issues here. If you are asking how I feel about the willingness of your little organization to use me to hide your precious book—about that I feel betrayed. If you are asking me how I feel about the threat this situation poses to my education, I would say I'm angry. If you are asking how I feel about your feeble excuses for excluding women, I'm outraged. I think I've made it pretty clear what I think of the Church's track record on the issues of abuse of power and equality. So far, you're making them look pretty good."

Reston bowed his head. "You're absolutely right, Miss Merinne. Although we never expected things to progress to this stage, I admit that by taking the easy way out and not reclaiming the book sooner, we unfairly put you at risk, and for that I am truly sorry. I offer my total cooperation in trying to make things right. However, what I meant to ask was your feeling on membership."

Dona's jaw dropped. "Are you serious?"

"Indeed I am."

"I thought you needed to consider it."

"I needed to consider the risks to you. However, since you are now apprised of the situation, I no longer think it fair for me to presume to make the decision for you. My judgment on your behalf has been something less than infallible of late. The main advantage to you is that we would then be free to keep you informed, whereas as things stand, certain oaths make that difficult."

"I would need to know a whole lot more about what I would be getting myself into. It's not at all clear to me why you people put yourself at such risk over this."

"Why, knowing the book contained heresy, did you choose to keep it?"

Dona offered no explanation. In retrospect, she wasn't sure herself.

"The reason no doubt differs for each member," Reston said. "Some intentions are more noble than others. I, for one, take umbrage at the hubris of a single entity claiming to know the nature of truth and seeking to impose it universally. The potential for abuse of that kind of power is simply too great to go unchallenged."

"The ten versus the one?" Dona asked.

"Ah, I see you have done your reading. We at least try to exclude those we think would abuse the knowledge. However, recent evidence suggests I'm finding that more difficult to predict than I thought."

"What kind of oaths are we talking about?"

"Alexi can provide more details."

"So you swear you had nothing to do with our abduction?"

"I only found out about it moments ago, and I was horrified. Can you describe your attacker?"

"He was a man of average height, dressed in priestly vestments." Dona said. "His face was in shadow the entire time, so I never got a good look, but his voice was distinctive… sort of low and gravelly. Unless he was deliberately trying to mask it, I think I would recognize it again."

"He dressed as a priest?"

"He did. He was pretending to be with the Inquisition, but when I told him I'd turn myself and the book in—but only to the Monsignor—he gave up and fled."

"If the Church gets wind that someone is impersonating a priest, they'll react all the more fervently. Can I ask that you keep that information secret at least until I've had a chance to investigate?"

"I'm not the only one who saw it, Professor. A friend was with me, and I can't vouch for what he's already told people."

"Gregory Delauren?"

Dona shot Alexi an exasperated glance. "Is there anything you didn't share?"

Alexi shrugged.

"Yes, it was Gregory. For all I know, he may have told dozens of people by now. Since I was in the dark, I had no reason to ask him to keep it quiet."

"Keep what quiet?" Helena asked.

The three of them had been so engrossed they hadn't seen Miranda and Helena approaching.

"Why the surprise party, of course," Dona said.

Helena clapped. "Oh, I love a good surprise party."

"Good day, Professor, Alexi," Miranda said, nodding to each in turn.

Reston nodded back, "Ladies," he said, "I'd love to stay and chat, but I'm pressed for time at the moment. Miss Merinne, I trust Alexi can help you with your other questions. He's a very capable student."

"Thank you, Professor."

Reston started off at a brisk pace toward the fraternity.

Helena sighed. "Dona, can't you stop being the model student for even a few minutes on Saturday? You're making the rest of us look like slackers."

Dona merely shrugged.

Alexi targeted Dona with that crooked smile of his. "How about I answer some of those questions over dinner tonight?"

"Um…" Dona said.

"I won't take no for an answer. I'll come calling at 4:30 at the dormitory. I know a great little spot."

Helena's jaw tightened.

"I'm sure it will be marvelous," Miranda said. "And we'd be delighted to help Dona get ready, wouldn't we, Helena?"

Helena frowned, and then sighed. "Oh, I suppose."

"Great, I'll see you then," Alexi said. "In the meantime, I've got a few things I need to do."

He took off in the same direction as Reston.

Miranda took Dona's arm and escorted her toward the dormitory. "Thought you were going to get out of giving us our details, didn't you? Lucky we were here to remedy that. Oh, and whom is the surprise party for?"

A few feet behind, Helena shook her head and muttered. "Oh, I know where this is headed. Helena, can you help with this? Helena, can you help with that? Figures, doesn't it? Good old 'ever-the-bridesmaid' Helena—never too busy to help."

By the time they made it back to the dormitory, Dona had filled them in on the escapades of the previous evening, with the exception of the hijacking and the discussion she'd overheard between Hepplewhite and the Monsignor.

Helena gasped. "You used the Monsignor as a diversion?"

"Well, I'm not sure 'used' is the word I would have picked. I prefer to think of his appearance at that moment as opportune."

"Oh yes, most opportune," Miranda said. "Almost makes one believe in miracles."

"Speaking of miracles," Dona said. "What am I going to wear to this little dinner engagement you volunteered me for?

I only have one formal dress, and I don't think it was designed with horseback riding in mind."

Helena's eyes widened. "Did she just use the word *engagement*?"

"Why, I do believe she did," Miranda said. "You don't suppose?"

"I'm afraid so," Helena replied.

"Hmm. What does one wear to an engagement?"

Helena tapped her chin. "Something elegant, yet suitable for riding, perhaps?"

Miranda shook her head. "In general, I've found 'horses' and 'elegant' to be mutually exclusive."

Helena grinned wickedly. "Who said anything about horses?"

"Very funny," Dona said. "You don't suppose we could fit some actual brainstorming into the comedy routine do you? I have a tight deadline here."

"Relax," Helena said. "We've got you covered."

"Or we will, anyway," Miranda said. "And in time, too."

Dona shook her head. "It's a good thing you guys can make dresses. It will keep you from starving as traveling performers, unless, of course, you think you could survive on all the rotten tomatoes."

Helena shrugged. "Couldn't be worse than dormitory food."

. . . . .

"Professor Shoruga, please, take a moment to compose yourself," the Monsignor said gently. "I was merely going to ask if you take sugar with your tea."

The little workroom the Chancellor had provided as a base for the Monsignor's investigations was bare and cramped, but it did have the advantage of being close to the Hathaway compound.

Shoruga was trembling and dripping sweat.

"I do my work and I go home. I teach when asked. I am simple man who is victim," Shoruga said.

"Of course, Professor," the Monsignor said. "We were saddened to hear of your loss. It was a dreadful thing for them to do. Do you have any idea who may have wanted to hurt you this way?"

"I am simple man," Shoruga said again, shrugging. "Who wants to hurt simple man?"

"That's exactly what we'd like to know, Professor. Can you think of anyone?"

"I am lucky to come to great University in fine city. I try to be friend to everyone."

"So there haven't been any recent arguments or disagreements that could have led to someone wanting revenge?"

Shoruga shrugged. "No one other than maybe former employer, but I am here now for many years."

"Perhaps we can start with your research, then, Professor. Can you describe your latest projects?"

Shoruga, if possible, paled even more. "I am permitted to say only that it is state secret."

The Monsignor raised an eyebrow. "You were specifically instructed not to tell me?"

"I have liberties to tell no one."

"Can you tell me who gave you these instructions?"

"It is condition of funding."

"Let me try this another way. Can you think of anyone, other than your Hathaway funding source, who would be interested in obtaining your research?"

Shoruga looked uncomfortable. "I do not know what I am to do. I want only to be helpful, but think I am permitted only to say it is state secret."

Thurman, who had been pacing the small expanse of floor behind the Monsignor, slammed a package on the table. "I suppose that's the same thing you told *these* people, isn't it?"

Shoruga shrank back.

The Monsignor held up his hand. "Patience, Thurman. We'll get to that presently."

Fuming, Thurman backed off.

Shoruga stared at the package uncomprehendingly.

"Professor," the Monsignor said. "As long as the topic has been raised, have you ever seen this package before?"

Shoruga shook his head.

"Can you read this inscription?"

Shoruga leaned over and squinted. "It is written in Shunese. It says, 'In accordance with our agreement.'"

"Any idea what might be inside?"

"I do not know. I have not before seen this package."

Thurman reached over to the package and flopped it open, revealing large stacks of cash. "So I take it you deny you've been selling your precious state secrets to the highest bidder?"

"Thurman, *please.*"

"I'm sorry, father. I have no patience for traitors."

"That has yet to be established."

"How much more evidence do you need?"

The Monsignor met his son's glare and held it. "Enough to be confident of the truth. No more, and absolutely no less."

Thurman snorted.

The Monsignor turned back to Shoruga. "Professor, would it surprise you to know that this package was discovered on your office floor?"

Shoruga rocked anxiously in his seat, pausing every so often to mop his brow. "I know nothing of this. I am simple man."

A sharp rap at the door echoed off the bare walls.

The Monsignor exchanged a glance with his son, eyebrows raised. "You instructed we were not to be disturbed?"

"I did," Thurman replied. "I'll attend to it." He opened the door and stepped out into the hallway. He returned a moment later. "It's a sealed missive."

"Couldn't it have waited?"

"It's from His Primacy."

The Monsignor broke the seal. "Let's have a look." Engrossed in the document, he absently addressed Shoruga.

"Thank you, Professor. We will be in contact as we know more."

Shoruga backed out of the room, bowing repeatedly.

The Monsignor turned to his son. "Thurman, could I ask you to take charge of this investigation for a few weeks?"

"Of course, Father. Are you going somewhere?"

The Monsignor nodded. "It seems His Primacy has requested my presence."

CHAPTER SEVEN

A TAD OVERDONE

True to their word, Helena and Miranda soon had Dona before a mirror admiring her new outfit. Helena hovered, making a few last-minute adjustments to the skirt. With Miranda's vision and Helena's technical expertise, they cobbled together a passable riding outfit in hues of brown and olive by begging various articles from the other girls on the floor. They'd even managed to find a smart riding hat boasting several pheasant feathers. Dona felt quite the sportswoman as the sound of horses drifted through the open window.

Miranda, who was seated near the window, glanced out over her shoulder and did a double take. "Who on earth is *that?*"

Helena rushed for a look, with Dona not far behind. There were two horses near the front steps of the dormitory. Alexi was riding one, but Miranda was gawking at the man astride the other.

"Oh, that's Alphonse," Dona said. "He's Alexi's fencing partner."

"And I thought Alexi was good-looking."

"Is he seeing anyone?" Helena asked.

"Back off, vixen." Miranda said. "I saw him first."

Dona admired herself in the mirror one last time. "I have no idea," she said. "But since you have proven yourselves to be such excellent tailors, you have earned the right to be introduced. After that, though, you're on your own. Follow me."

As Dona made her debut, Alexi's face lit up. "You look stunning."

Miranda and Helena exchanged self-satisfied glances.

Dona regarded him coolly. "I'd be flattered if I thought I could trust anything you said, Mr. Reysa."

Now the glances exchanged were puzzled and alarmed.

"But I'm forgetting my manners. Alphonse, it's a pleasure to see you again so soon."

Alphonse stood at attention, then bowed deeply. "The pleasure is all mine."

"What an honor to be in the presence of a true gentleman. Allow me to introduce my very good friends Miranda and Helena."

As their names were mentioned, they curtseyed, even though curtseying had fallen out of favor for all but the most formal of occasions.

Alphonse bowed again. "I am indeed most fortunate to have gained the acquaintance in a single day of not one great beauty, but three. When Alexi said he'd make helping him worth my while, I had no idea he'd make good on his promise so soon."

Miranda favored him with one of her angelic smiles. Helena giggled, blushing.

"Shall we be on our way then?" Alexi asked.

"May as well get it over with," Dona said.

"You know," he whispered as he assisted her onto Alphonse's horse, "I'm going to make it my business to see you smile at least once before the evening is out. I really can be quite engaging when I put my mind to it."

"Do your worst."

In a moment he'd mounted his own horse, and with a shake of the reins, they were off. Dona waved in farewell, but her friends were too distracted to notice—Alphonse, an adoring young lady on each arm, was strolling off toward campus.

. . . . .

The heat of the day was fading, and a whispered suggestion of a breeze carried with it the distant songs of cicadas and the pungent scents of the autumn harvest. Dona didn't often get to ride since she'd started at Exidgeon, and the joy of it almost made her forget herself and smile. Almost.

On reaching town, Alexi targeted streets off the main thoroughfares that led to sections of the city that made her uncomfortable, but by the time she thought to voice an objection, he'd stopped and dismounted.

She found herself in a large cobbled circle surrounded by dilapidated buildings whose purposes were difficult to discern. Carriages were parked haphazardly, and horses were hitched to almost anything available. Unlike the more commercial areas of town, there were no brightly colored signs to direct the attention of potential customers, nor were the usual street vendors hawking their wares. Despite the day's warmth, the place had an oppressive feel that made her shiver.

Alexi smiled broadly and extended his hand.

She did not take it. "I presume this is some sort of joke? If so, you'll notice I am not laughing."

For a second he seemed taken aback. "Oh," he said. "I suppose the outside *is* a little off-putting. I guess you'll just have to trust me on this one."

"I trust the irony does not escape you."

Alexi grinned. "Nope. As it happens, I'm a particular fan of irony."

"You can't be serious. Look around you. Who in their right mind takes a lady to—"

One of the nearby carriages looked familiar. She probably wouldn't have noticed except this particular carriage had once nearly run her over. It no longer flew the banners of the Church, but its distinctive shape was burned into her memory. It was unmistakably the Monsignor's.

"—a place like this?"

His eyebrows knit in puzzlement, he tried to follow her gaze. He turned back and shrugged. "You'd be surprised."

She set her jaw and took his hand. "I think I already am. Let's go."

Alexi led her to one of the more run-down buildings. As he reached out to knock, the door opened. The doorway framed an enormous man, who by the look of him spent the bulk of his days lifting heavy things.

He scowled. "And just what might the two of you be wanting?"

"I, uh," Alexi said. "I understand 913 was a vintage year."

The man eyed Alexi, and then glanced suspiciously at Dona. Just as the moment got unbearably awkward, he beckoned.

"Aye, that it was. Well, don't just stand there. Come on in."

Alexi led her into a small, spartan apartment. Dona followed grudgingly, uncertain where this was leading, and not liking it one bit.

Once they were inside, their musclebound host slammed the door shut behind them. Almost immediately another door opened, and a dapper gentleman with a white cloth draped over one arm greeted them. Strains of chamber music filtered through the open doorway.

"Good evening, and welcome to the Sultan's Respite. May I presume a table for two, or will additional members be joining your party this evening?"

"A table for two would be perfect," Alexi said.

"Very good, sir. Right this way."

The gentleman led them into a wonderland of lights and brilliant colors. The building must have taken up several blocks, for there seemed no end to it. There were areas devoted to dining, bars, wine tasting, and games of chance. There was even a small stage on which the chamber group was performing an updated arrangement of a Shunese folk tune. The landscape was dotted with large canopies resembling tents and punctuated with artifacts that, to Dona's unsophisticated eye, looked authentic to Shune. Dazzling fabrics were suspended from the ceiling and from numerous balconies, making it difficult to know where the actual walls were. Despite the bewildering array of sights and sounds, everything inside managed to appear as tasteful and exotic as the outside had appeared dreary and derelict. To her delight, the dapper man escorted them to one of the canopies suspended above a table for two.

As they were seated on jewel-toned floor pillows at a low table situated beneath silk draperies, Dona felt every inch the Shunese princess. She was so taken with her surroundings it took her a few minutes to realize that Alexi was beaming at her.

"What?"

"I got my smile."

His delight seemed so genuine she felt her anger melt away.

"Well, so you did. You should be more careful, though. If this is how you insist on winning fights, I may be inclined to throw down the gauntlet more often."

"If you always smile like this when you lose, I shall gladly take it up."

"So this is the Sultan's Respite? I've heard the name whispered, but I don't think I know anyone who's ever actually been here—or even knew where to find it, for that matter."

Alexi raised a dubious eyebrow. "Not even Gregory?"

"You *are* jealous."

"Just like to know how I compare to the competition."

"How many times do I have to tell you? You aren't competing."

"You may want to reserve judgment until you've sampled the cuisine. Music may be food for the soul, but it's the gut that makes all the really important decisions."

"No, I mean…. Oh never mind. So, where is the menu?"

As if by magic, the canopy walls parted, revealing their waiter. "Good evening. Is there anything you desire before we discuss the house specialties?"

Dinner was nothing short of sumptuous. It began with a savory mushroom appetizer, progressed to melt-in-your-mouth spiced lamb flavored with a garlicky white sauce, and finished with dessert, which burst into flames as it was served. Everything was an absolute delight. Dona was not normally a wine drinker, but she was beginning to think that might be because she'd never before had the good stuff. The bottle Alexi chose was light and fruity, with a hint of sparkle. Despite all her misgivings, he was proving to be the perfect complement to a perfect meal. All the stresses of the week faded away as he regaled her with stories, told sly jokes, and smiled that crooked smile of his.

As the waiter took away the dessert dish, he suggested that they were welcome to linger at their leisure and without interruption, but that they should signal him if there was anything further they required. With that, the curtains fell closed.

"How very strange," Dona said.

Alexi shrugged. "Not really. This establishment is famous for being the place where power is brokered and deals are made. Privacy is its most valuable commodity. That's why there are canopies, background music, and the ability to see the floor all the way around your table. No one can stand nearby and listen in without being noticed. It's precisely why I wanted to come here tonight."

Dona's heart sank. Throughout dinner she'd flirted with a fantasy of Alexi as an incurable romantic wooing the woman of his dreams, knowing that despite incredible odds, any heart could be unlocked with patience and the proper key. Apparently in this case, that key turned out to be little more than a suitable business purpose.

Must have been the wine. In retrospect, the whole notion was silly. She couldn't envision herself ever being comfortable as the object of such mindless infatuation. She shuddered at the realization that even bright little girls began their wifely indoctrination at an early age.

She folded her arms. "I suppose you'll want to be discussing what to do with a certain book, then?"

He nodded and lowered his voice. "Indeed. There are some incredibly important things you should know about that book…"

Dona leaned in to hear him over the background noise. "Yes?"

He glanced at the edges of the canopy to be certain no one was nearby, and then leaned in closer still.

He continued in a whisper. "But I think it can wait." And he leaned in the rest of the way.

Their lips met, and Dona, to her surprise, did not resist. After all that practice with Gregory, she had developed an idle curiosity as to how Alexi might compare. Or at least that's what she determined in hindsight must have been the reason. Somewhere in there, she decided "favorably" might be the correct term. She also decided, for the moment at least, that she just might be able to find it in her heart to forgive him.

The conversation found its way back to the book.

"Perhaps everyone would be better off if I were to just give it back to you."

He eyed her dubiously. "Are you sure?"

"All right, it was a dumb suggestion. I guess you'd better tell me what I'm getting myself into."

"Maybe it would be easier if I showed you." From his pocket, he produced a wooden box. Keeping his eyes on hers, he flicked back the lid to reveal a swathe of black velvet upon which rested a gold locket in the shape of a leaf. The base of the leaf sported a small gem that glinted green in the lantern light.

She lifted the locket off the velvet for a better look. "Oh, Alexi, it's lovely."

"I'd like for you to have it. It's like it was made for your outfit."

"More like the outfit was made for it—but I couldn't possibly accept. It looks frightfully expensive."

He smiled his crooked smile. "Green really isn't my color. Besides, not only will it be much more flattering on you, it's the least I can do for all the trouble I've caused."

"Well, you shouldn't have—on both counts."

If Alexi caught the implied reproof, he made no sign. "Go ahead, try it on."

"All right, if you insist." She turned so that Alexi could clasp it around her neck.

"It really is gorgeous," she said. "But I must have missed something somewhere. I thought you were going to show me what I was getting myself into."

"Behold." He passed his hand over the locket. As he did so, his eyes narrowed in intense concentration and his jaw moved, as though he was muttering under his breath. Tiny beads of sweat formed across his brow, so much so that she grew concerned. As she was about to say something, sparkling rays of light burst forth from beneath his hand. When he drew it back, the locket was glowing, its gemstone shooting glittering rainbows about the canopy.

At first she was startled, but when it proved cool to the touch, she laughed with delight.

"That's amazing. How does it do that?"

"Are you prepared to face the everlasting wrath of the Church?"

Try as she might, Dona had trouble believing him. Her eyes narrowed.

"Are you trying to tell me those so-called spells from that ridiculous book actually work?"

Alexi smiled and shrugged.

"I'm not that gullible. What's the trick?"

"You have a better explanation? You saw the book glow, and now you're looking at the locket. How do you fake a thing like that?"

"So, the book—the night in the library—that was *you,* wasn't it?"

"My first success, actually. Just reading about it, you'd never believe Phrendonic magic could be real, and even if you did, you'd never think the book's spells would work for you. I was so surprised, I literally fell out of my chair, and to make matters worse, while trying to recover, I tripped over the book cart."

"So that's what caused the crash?"

He nodded. "I didn't have the slightest idea how to douse the light, and I was worried someone would come investigate.

You can see how inconvenient that could have been. My only sane option was to leave it behind. Fortunately, you brought your satchel with you."

Dona sipped her wine. "That must have gone over well with Reston. I'm surprised he didn't expel you on the spot."

"That probably would have been one of the nicer things that crossed his mind. You can imagine that, as Reston's primary source material for working Phrendonic magic, the book was never to leave the fraternity, but there was a party going on and I couldn't concentrate. Luckily, the Professor's pretty pragmatic."

A disagreement escalating at a nearby table drew Dona's attention, and she stole a peek past the curtains. Just across from them, a tall wiry man, his dark hair shot with strands of silver, was lifting back the fabric of the next canopy and peering inside. An irate voice emanated from within. "I very much *would* mind. This is a private occasion in a private venue. Leave at once, or I'll have you forcibly evicted."

Heavy footsteps approached. Large men in the formal dress of the restaurant staff converged on the scene.

The wiry man spoke softly. Even poking her head out of the canopy, Dona could just barely make out what he was saying.

"You are, of course, free to attempt that, but you might first consider the notoriety that deed would attract. Are you certain your father would approve?"

The indignant man's voice became incredulous. "Are you threatening me?"

At this, the large men advanced as one. The wiry man didn't even look at them. He raised a bejeweled hand, snapped his fingers, and the bouncers collapsed. From the canopy, there came a shriek. Its side billowed outward, and with a shredding sound, much of the fabric pulled away from the framework. The wiry man stepped aside as the tattered canopy flew past. Dona barely managed to roll out of the way. There was a thud as shins connected with the low table and the figure fell forward, collapsing their own canopy and entangling Alexi.

Dona felt suddenly exposed. Dangling about her neck, the locket illuminated the unfolding chaos with an eerie green light. The wiry man faced her with an appraising look. Near him, another man, athletically built, with a prominent jaw and a look of contemptuous indignation, stood revealed as well. He now stared at her with an open-mouthed gaze of obvious alarm. He seemed familiar, but before she could place him, he pointed and let out a bloodcurdling bellow.

"Heretics!"

The wiry man sighed and waved his hand. The room went utterly dark. Dona instinctively reached out and grabbed something solid to steady herself, grateful, for the moment at least, to be out of the spotlight.

Then she remembered Alexi.

She could make out the sound of his cursing over the din. Her relief was short-lived, however, once she smelled smoke.

"Oh, dear lord—Alexi, this way. Hurry."

"Keep calling," he cried. "I can't see."

"Over here. Take my hand."

As the smell of smoke became stronger, the confusion gave way to terror. Others screamed and scrambled for exits. Dona lost the ability to make out Alexi's cries over the din. Miraculously, a hand finally clasped hers in the darkness. The smoke burned her eyes and throat, but she kept her bearings. Holding on with all her might, she made a beeline for the exit. Fortunately, the rest of the patrons had not yet made it that far, and her path was clear.

As abruptly as the darkness had descended, it dissipated, revealing an inferno. Fire leapt from one canopy to the next, enveloping everything in its path. Screams punctuated the roar of the flames, goading Dona toward the exit. Weeping from the smoke and the horror, she burst through the door and away from the building. Only then did she turn to embrace her precious Alexi.

She found herself in the arms of a short, middle-aged man with close-cropped brown hair sporting about four days' growth of stubble. He returned the hug a bit more enthusiastically than was strictly proper for a total stranger.

She slapped him.

He regarded her with playful blue eyes. "Aww, is that any way to treat the man you just rescued from certain death?"

"Out of my way." She pushed him aside and raced back toward the burning building just as Alexi emerged, doubled over and coughing. One of his sleeves was smoldering. She patted it out as she urged him farther away from the scene.

"Put it…" he tried to say, but then he succumbed to a bout of coughing.

"What? Are you hurt?"

"Lock…" he coughed.

"Oh, of course." She doused the light from the locket by dropping it down the front of her dress. Fortunately, in all the turmoil and the light from the flames, which were now beginning to shoot out through the slats of shuttered windows, no one seemed to have noticed.

Dona tried to help Alexi, but he waved her away.

"Give me a minute," he said. Then he started coughing again.

Since Alexi seemed to be safe for the moment, Dona cast about for something she could do to help. A knot of people had formed in the center of the circle. One man barked orders, and some of the others actually seemed to be listening instead of gawking.

She made her way toward them, but as she got close, she heard a shout. One of the carriages that had littered the circle shot straight toward her, its horses wild-eyed and frothing. She dodged aside, barely in time. Once again, the Monsignor's carriage had narrowly missed her—and now she knew where she had seen the thick-jawed man before. He had been driving the carriage the first time as well.

An earsplitting shriek followed by a slow thunderous rumble signaled the collapse of a large section of the roof. Flames swirled upward through the resulting chasm, washing the landscape in eerie tones of red and orange. Nearby church bells sounded the alarm as the town woke to the threat. The group in the circle had arranged itself into a double line and passed water-filled buckets. Citizens arrived with additional buckets. Others made for the church to retrieve fire-fighting equipment. Dona and Alexi added their hands to the brigade, passing buckets toward the burning building. Despite the efficiency of the collective effort, Dona had a queasy feeling it would not suffice.

As mobs of citizens responded to the pealing bells, the lines lengthened and the pace of the bucket-passing increased. Still, the fire gained ground, and nearby buildings smoldered, threatening to ignite. Though the helpers increased in number, so also did the spectators, whose wide-eyed presence hampered the firefighting efforts. When another building burst into flames, Alexi was forced to leave the line to move their horses. While he was gone, Dona witnessed a new commotion among the milling spectators.

The militia forced its way through the crowd. At its head rode an imposing figure on a black stallion, a host of medals flashing on the chest of his crisp scarlet jacket. Next to him on a white mare was a lithe woman wrapped in a white cloak. From his livery and bearing, Dona had little doubt as to the man's identity—the Crown Prince had arrived. The militia took charge of the situation, pressing the spectators into service. The Crown Prince dismounted and conferred with the man who had taken charge early on. The lady had not left his side and seemed fully engaged in the discussion. The Crown Prince even seemed to be seeking her counsel, a sight so unexpected that Dona dropped her bucket and thoroughly soaked her shoes.

"Did I miss anything?" Alexi asked.

"Only the arrival of the Crown Prince."

"And the Crown Princess as well, by the looks of it."

The lady in white pointed out some of the surrounding buildings, and the Crown Prince nodded thoughtfully. Then he barked orders, and the militia attacked the nearby buildings with oversized hooks, ladders, and axes.

"What are they doing?" Dona asked.

"I think they're creating a firebreak. They'll want to make some open space to keep the fire from spreading."

But their progress was too slow. Soon a third building was shooting flames.

Finally, the militia formed a line around the area and forced back both helpers and gapers alike.

"Now what?" Dona asked.

"We'd better head back," Alexi said. "I don't want to be caught in the crowd if this thing spreads any farther."

Together they headed for the horses, but leaving the scene was fraught with difficulties. Enough gapers had accumulated that forcing their way through on horseback proved difficult, especially given the close quarters and twisty street. A large covered cart bedecked with garish signs extolling the virtues of various elixirs, tonics, and concoctions sat in the roadway just ahead, making their progress slower still. After several frustrating minutes, Dona found an opening and urged her horse around the right side. Pressing her advantage, she soon found herself even with the driver. When their eyes met, she was shocked to recognize the playful blue eyes of the man she had so recently 'rescued.'

He winked and doffed his hat.

At that instant, a deafening boom battered the crowd. Its nerves already frayed by the fire and the throngs, Dona's horse reared, and she felt the reins slip through her fingers. As her head struck the ground, she briefly saw bright lights, and then, darkness.

. . . . .

The wiry man paced the parlor. The fire roaring in the fireplace did little to relieve the chill he always felt there. The furnishings were exquisite, the silver first-rate, the accessories sumptuous, but nothing in the room had changed in his memory. Even as a child growing up in this house, he had felt imprisoned in some bygone age in which he could gaze upon wonders, but never touch. It was the way Mother wanted it, and Mother always got what she wanted.

A shriveled fossil of a man with a bare wisp of white hair appeared in the doorway.

"Master Michlos," he said. "The mistress will see you now."

"Thank you, Arerio."

Arerio was an institution. Michlos would have sworn he looked the same today as he had in his earliest memories, perhaps slightly more bowed, maybe his tuft a bit thinner. It was hard to tell.

"The mistress is receiving in the dining room today." It was about as conversational as he ever got, but Michlos was fond of the old man. Although rigorous in his adherence to protocol, Arerio cared deeply for his charges. It was a trait rarely present in the newer staff.

"Thank you, I can find my way."

"Very good, sir."

"Oh, and Arerio?"

"Yes, sir?"

"It's good to see you."

Arerio would not, of course, permit himself to smile, but his eyes brightened.

"You as well, sir."

As Michlos entered the dining room, Marguerite Serrola looked up from pouring tea. Her black hair, which showed less gray even than her son's, was pulled back from her broad face in a style Michlos had long thought was too severe for her. The dark background of her gown lent her a somber air that even the fabric's subtle pattern of pale pink roses couldn't dispel. She was seated at the end of the long table in an ornate high-backed chair that made her look shorter than she was.

"How good to see you, my son."

"Likewise, Mother." He bent to kiss her cheek, and she tilted her face to receive it. He took the seat she indicated.

"So, how fares the project?"

Michlos swallowed. "It went less well than we had hoped."

Her lips pursed. She studied the teapot as she poured. "Oh? How so?"

Michlos should have been hardened to it by now, but his mother's disapproval still had the power to affect him. At least he was practiced at not letting it show.

"I followed the spirits merchant. As you predicted, he had set up a meeting with the Inquisitor."

"Go on."

"Unfortunately, they chose the Respite for their meeting."

"I see."

"When I approached them, the Inquisitor became indignant."

Marguerite stirred in a teaspoon of sugar. "You mentioned his father?"

"I did, but that only seemed to agitate him further. Still, the situation might have been managed if not for the actions of the merchant himself, who unaccountably threw himself into the next canopy."

She passed him the cup. "Thereby starting the fire, I suppose."

"Yes."

"You did not see fit to douse the flames?"

"There was an additional complication."

"Oh?"

"A young woman. She was revealed when the adjacent canopy was torn away. She was wearing a locket."

"A locket? I take it that detail is important?"

He took a sip of his tea. "It was glowing."

For the first time, her eyes met his. "Sorcel or talis?"

"I can't say. I saw it for only an instant. I should mention the Inquisitor saw her as well. He called her out as a heretic. Given that, and since she was an unknown quantity, I decided to leave under cover of darkness. I therefore didn't see the fire until I was too far away to manage it."

Marguerite sighed. "So we have even less bargaining power and greater risk of an Inquisition than we started with."

Michlos looked away. "It would seem so."

"Who is this woman?"

"I have no idea, but I intend to find out."

"Do so. We can't afford to approach this blindly—the situation is too volatile. I trust it shall be treated as such in the future."

Michlos did not reply. Instead, he set his cup on the table and pushed back his chair.

"Will you not stay for lunch?"

"I have much to account for, and time is not our friend."

"True enough. Be safe."

"Thank you, Mother."

She took another sip of tea as he took his leave.

· · · · ·

Dona's eyes burned and her throat squeezed closed in protest as acrid vapors assaulted her. She coughed and tried to pull away, but immediately regretted the movement. Her head was pounding, and a spot right in the back throbbed with particular intensity. Nearby, someone was talking.

"What did I tell you? A miracle for every occasion."

Another voice, somehow familiar: "She didn't seem to like it much."

"The best medicines are often the nastiest. I don't make the rules."

"Dona, are you all right?"

A face came slowly into focus. Dimly she made out Alexi leaning over her, his forehead furrowed. She couldn't place where she was—a confined space lined with shelves and cubbies, lit by a sputtering oil lamp. There was barely enough room for Alexi and someone she could see only in silhouette over his shoulder.

Then the tiny room lurched, and she cried out as stabbing pains shot through her head.

"What *is* this place? Is the room spinning?"

"What a relief to hear your voice," Alexi said. "You had us worried sick."

Dona winced as she fingered the goose egg on her scalp. "What are you talking about?"

"The only thing louder than the explosion was the sound of your head hitting the cobbles. Luckily Jonas saw it happen and stopped so we could toss you in the back of his wagon. Without him, we might well have been trampled."

Things were still not entirely in register. "What explosion?"

"I think they were destroying more buildings to make a firebreak."

Dona wrinkled her nose as she tried to remember. "Who is Jonas?"

The figure reached past Alexi to thrust a small blue vial toward her face. "I think she needs another dose."

Dona caught a whiff and turned her head…and immediately regretted it. "Get that thing away from me."

"Or not," he said, withdrawing the vial.

"Who *is* this person?"

"Oh, we've met, but I don't think we were formally introduced. I'm Jonas Mapleton Harcourt, humble merchant of spirits, totems, and elixirs, at your service."

Dona squinted at him. "Aren't you the man who groped me after I accidentally pulled you out of the fire?"

"An unfortunate misunderstanding, to be sure, but who would not have been emotional after being rescued from certain death? Who would not wish to repay his brave rescuer with a grateful hug?"

Alexi scowled a little at that but rose to the man's defense anyway.

"Well, he did save us from a pretty difficult situation back there. And he was able to revive you after you bumped your head."

"Yes, by trying to poison me."

Jonas bowed. "A service I am providing free of charge, I might add. By the way, I couldn't help but notice your remarkable necklace. Would you mind if I had a closer look?"

Panic danced in Alexi's eyes.

Dona's hand strayed toward her chest. "Perhaps I lost it in the fall."

"A pity," Jonas said. "I'm sure the right buyer would have paid a pretty penny for something like that, assuming it was a talisman, of course. Was it?"

Under other circumstances Dona might have been more civil, but the pounding in her skull was a constant distraction. "Talisman? What on earth are you talking about?"

Jonas shook his head. "You honestly don't know, do you?"

Dona felt herself coloring. The only thing worse than ignorance was ignorance accompanied by an expectation that she should have known better. "I don't see where it is any business of yours."

Jonas laughed. "Oh, it's absolutely not, but whether you intended to or no, you probably saved my life back there. The least I can do is return the favor. So where did you get it, anyway? Family heirloom? Please tell me you didn't steal it."

"Why such interest in a silly locket?"

"It's not the locket so much as the light streaming from it that caught my eye. Not that my interest that matters, mind you. Now, *theirs*, on the other hand..."

"Whose?" Alexi asked. "The Inquisition's?"

Jonas snorted. "They'd be the least of your worries. The way I see it, you either inherited it from a rogue nouncer, or stole it from one of the families."

Alexi's forehead furrowed. "What if we made it ourselves?"

"Bloody unlikely. There aren't that many sources for that kind of know-how, and you can bet they are all jealously guarded. No way they'd let some novices prance around town flaunting their ignorance so openly, at least unless they wanted them dead—and even if they did, there are much more subtle ways to manage that."

Dona and Alexi exchanged alarmed glances. There was a long awkward pause.

Finally, Jonas spoke again. "Look, you are right—it's none of my business. But if I were you, I'd keep that thing well-hidden and hope like hell no one else saw you with it."

Dona's mouth went dry. "I think they may have seen it."

"Who do you mean by *they*?"

"The Monsignor's driver. And the thin man with all the rings."

Jonas's expression was grim. "In that case, it's already too late."

CHAPTER EIGHT

houses of ill repute

Professor Dominick Everson drew his pen across the page with a flourish. Though he was reticent to fail a student, at least since he had discovered it usually resulted in extra work for him, this student had been particularly annoying. Students rarely came to him for assistance outside of class, but this one kept showing up at every opportunity, diverting precious time from his new pet project. Not only that, but the dullard couldn't seem to grasp a concept even when it had been clearly explained several times. How he managed to get passing grades in other classes was a complete mystery.

What little pleasure he had garnered from failing his gadfly drained away at the sound of a knock on his office door. Telling himself it must be a student, he started marking up the next paper on the stack, hoping whoever it was would mistake silence for absence and leave. He continued grading silently, but the knock came again, a bit louder. By the third knock he felt his eye twitch—he was no longer convinced it was a student. By the fourth knock, he could take it no longer. He strode to the door and threw it wide.

"For crying out loud, haven't I done enough already?"

Startled, Professor Reston took a step back. "That depends, I would guess, on what you've done so far."

Everson froze.

Reston raised an eyebrow. "Expecting someone else, were we?"

"Ah, Reston, it's you. Why yes—yes I was. I, ah, I have a particularly tenacious student. You know the type. Can never get enough attention from the professor."

Reston nodded knowingly. "I'd like to grab some of that attention for myself, if I may."

Everson's eye twitched again. "Um, certainly. Have a seat."

Reston stepped into the office and closed the door. "Dominick, where were you Friday night?"

"What possible interest could you have in that?"

Reston fixed him with a steady gaze. "I need to know."

"I think you'll need to tell me why, then. You make it sound like you're interrogating a criminal."

"Am I?"

Everson snorted. "If that's the tone you're going to take, this conversation is over."

"For your sake, I hope it isn't."

"Is that some sort of threat?"

"The oaths bind you."

"And just what oaths are we referring to? I take it you're implying I've violated one. Or is this just a courtesy visit?"

"Very well, I'll be direct. Did you, or did you not, steal a certain carriage away from the opera on Friday night?"

Everson rubbed at his eye. "Aside from the outrageous nature of that accusation, even if we assumed that I *had* done such a thing, just how do you propose that would violate any oaths?"

"Most obviously, by risking exposure."

Everson laughed incredulously. "That is one heaping help-ing of irony you are doling out there, professor. You recall my strenuous objections to permitting the Merinne girl to keep the book you so negligently allowed to fall into her hands? They were based on similar concerns. How dare you accuse *me* of risking exposure?"

"Maybe in retrospect you were correct, but Dominick—stealing carriages? Kidnapping? Impersonating an Inquisitor? Are you mad? You'll bring the Inquisition down on us all."

"Don't try to pin that on me. This situation resulted entirely from your poor judgment—"

"Compounded by your poor judgment in taking the matter into your own hands."

Everson sniffed. "An unsubstantiated accusation, at best."

"I need your word that in the future, you'll leave Miss Merinne well enough alone."

Everson spat. "Another oath you can use as a threat? I think I'll continue to use my own judgment in deciding what's best both for me and for our secret society. It's time someone with a little foresight and maturity gave it a shot."

Both men started at a knock on the door.

Everson rose from his chair. "I think we've said all that bears saying on the matter."

Reston's eyes narrowed. "Miss Merinne is under my pro-tection. Remember that when you're deciding what's best."

Everson opened the door for him. "I'll keep that in mind."

Verone's dulcet voice wafted in. "Why, Dommy, darling, what took you so long? You know how madly I miss you." Leaning forward, she planted a kiss squarely on his cheek.

Turning to Reston she said, "I swear, the man is such a tease. Don't worry, hon, he'll get around to introducing us eventually." Leaning closer, she added, "He's a little slow socially."

"Uh, Verone Nevinander," Everson said, "may I present Professor Reston."

"The pleasure is all mine," Verone said. "I hope I didn't interrupt anything."

Reston inclined his head. "Not at all, Miss Nevinander. I was just leaving."

"Well, don't be a stranger, now."

Once Reston stepped out, Everson opened his mouth to speak, but Verone silenced him with a shake of her head.

"Now Dommy, honey," she said. "The air is taking on quite a chill. I took the liberty of bringing you your favorite sweater for your walk home. I can't have my Dommy catching the sniffles on me, now can I?"

Only then did Everson hear Reston's footsteps recede down the hall. He felt a sudden urge to call him back, but Verone nudged the door with her elbow, and it creaked closed. That sound was followed by the *snick* of the deadbolt sliding into place.

. . . . .

Once Dona finally succumbed to the sedative offered by the insistent spirits merchant, Alexi hopped atop the wagon alongside Jonas. Jonas gave the reins a shake, and the horses lurched forward.

"Does your University have an infirmary?" Jonas asked.

"It does. The Sisters of Solace run it."

"Should we head there?"

Alexi considered for a moment before shaking his head. "I'm not sure that's such a great idea."

"Why not? It's a nasty bump. She should have it checked out."

"I think she would prefer to recover someplace less public."

"I take it you're worried about the Inquisitor and the man with the rings?"

"The thought had crossed my mind."

"Well, I know a place you could stay for a few days. It's not much, but I imagine the little lady would be hard to find there."

"What place is that?"

"My sister runs a shop in town, and she likes it if I drop in when I am in the neighborhood—or at least she tells me she does."

"We wouldn't want to intrude."

"Oh, it's quite all right. She is fond of visitors. She's always saying 'the more guests, the better.' And it gives me a chance to give something back. After all, the young lady did save my life back there."

Alexi was torn. Accepting Jonas's offer implied a level of trust that was greater than he'd had time to establish, but taking Dona back to Exidgeon was fraught with risks, particularly if Reston hadn't neutralized the kidnapper. Not only that, but the Inquisitor had seen the glowing locket, and there was no telling whether he'd also recognized her. The man with the rings was even more troubling.

"All right," Alexi said. "Maybe it wouldn't hurt to stop there for a little while."

Jonas gave him a wide smile. "Splendid."

At Jonas's suggestion, Alexi rode the rest of the way inside the wagon. That way fewer people would be able to connect the two of them, and he could keep an eye on Dona. Despite the bump and sway of the wagon over the cobbles, Alexi found himself fighting to keep from nodding off. In the end, exhaustion won out.

He opened his eyes in alarm. He couldn't move his hands or legs. A thick wad of fabric prevented him from crying out. Men in embroidered vestments surrounded him, poking, prodding, and grinning wickedly. They drew back as a square-jawed Inquisitor approached, garbed completely in white. Intertwined snakes were emblazoned in silver across his chest. His hand wielded a poker, its cherry-red tip fresh from the furnace. Alexi tried to pull away, but the bonds held fast. Smirking, the man plunged the smoldering end into Alexi's side.

He screamed…and awoke.

Jonas hovered over him, shaking him in the lantern light. "We're there. You all right?"

Alexi grinned sheepishly. "Bad dream."

Dona was still in the thrall of Jonas's elixir. Though they could rouse her, she was only half-awake. They emerged from the wagon into a cavernous space. If there was a ceiling, it was out of sight in darkness. A single guttering lantern in the distance lit a doorway. Alexi could barely make out several carriages and wagons surrounding him. From another part of the darkness he heard a horse snuffle.

"What is this place?"

"We call it the carriage house," Jonas said. "It used to be a warehouse, but my sister bought it some years back."

Dona snagged her toe on the uneven floor, and Alexi barely caught her in time. "That does it," he said. In one swift movement, he swept Dona up into his arms. "This place isn't far, I hope."

Jonas pointed. "Just through yonder door."

Despite the late hour, the door opened onto a scene awash with light, color, and activity. A number of elegantly dressed women populated the room, reclining on couches or playing games of chance. Several of them paused to regard the newcomers. Though expansive, the room felt intimate due to the soft light of the lanterns and the dark blue walls. The furniture was upholstered in burgundy velvet. Gold accents and an impressive chandelier gave the place a look of garish opulence.

Alexi stopped in his tracks. "Um, I thought you said it wasn't much."

Jonas shrugged. "I guess she's been doing better lately."

"Jonas!"

Jonas held out his arms. "Tilly."

Tilly strode over to embrace him. She was a substantial woman, only a little past her prime. Her emerald gown sported enough feathers to stuff several pillows, but the effect was oddly impressive. Her blue eyes twinkled. "Nanna will be thrilled."

"How is she doing?"

"She's not as young as she was. You need to visit more. But I'm forgetting my manners. Who are our guests?"

"Dona and Alexi," Jonas said, "I'd like you to meet my sister, Mathilda."

"Oh, she's not well." Tilly said.

Alexi gently laid Dona on the sofa.

Tilly clapped her hands. "Norene, Shelby—ready some rooms for our guests."

Two of the women who had been playing dice scurried off.

"Dona, here, saved my life from a fire at the Respite," Jonas said. "I told them they'd be welcome to stay a few days until they work out some issues."

"Of course they can," Tilly said. "What happened at the Respite?"

"It's a long story…."

"Very well. Let's get you all situated for the evening, and we can discuss it over breakfast."

· · · · ·

Breakfast at Tilly's turned out to be a chaotic affair. Alexi had no trouble finding it—both his nose and the noise led him in the right direction. A large round table dominated the dining area, and Jonas and Tilly sat near each other catching up, Jonas in his usual threadbare jacket and waistcoat, and Tilly in a lavender housecoat belted at the waist with a twisted purple cord. An older woman hovered near the oven and fireplace, effortlessly managing multiple dishes. Numerous young women flitted into and out of the room, some stopping to gobble down a meal, others pausing only long enough to say 'good morning' and grab a cup of tea before dashing out again. It reminded him a little of breakfast at the fraternity.

Jonas waved him over. "Good morning, I trust you slept well?"

"Like a log," Alexi said. "The bed was really comfortable."

Tilly beamed with satisfaction. "It's the goose feathers. They're not cheap, but nothing's too good for my girls. Now let's see about getting you some breakfast."

"That's very generous of you, Miss Harcourt."

"Please, call me Tilly. Everybody does. Now grab a plate and help yourself. I do recommend the sausages. Nanna makes a mean sausage."

The older woman smiled but didn't interrupt her intricate dance among the pots.

"Tilly tells me they finally got the fire at the Respite under control," Jonas said. "Burned three full blocks, but the firebreaks did the trick. If the Crown Prince hadn't acted so quickly, it could have—"

"Ooh the sausages *are* good." Alexi said. Then he noticed Jonas gaping at something behind him. He turned.

Dona stood in the middle of the stairway, her once smart riding outfit disheveled and filthy. Dark circles had appeared beneath her eyes, her hair was a tangled mess, and judging by the way she gingerly touched the back of her head, she was still in some pain.

"Alexi," she said, "might I have a word with you?"

. . . . .

Thurman rose to greet Chancellor Wiggins. "Thank you for coming, Chancellor."

"I came as soon as I got your message. What have you found?"

"The situation is dire. Our investigation shows that heretic spies have hatched a plot to obtain military research conducted at Exidgeon."

Wiggins blanched. "How serious is it? Can it be contained?"

Thurman snorted. "We are well beyond the point of containment."

"What are your recommendations?"

"First and foremost, the traitor Shoruga must be taken into custody. He's in this up to his eyeballs."

"Shoruga? Are you sure?"

"Exhibit A." Thurman tossed the incriminating package on the desk. "We found this Shoruga's office. Next, we will require more expansive accommodations. I'm sending to the Church for backup. There's no telling how deep this thing goes."

"But won't an increased presence cause a stir?"

"Unfortunately, that's unavoidable. I'm sure I don't need to emphasize the need to root out this heresy as quickly as possible, particularly if the heretics are acquiring a military presence."

"Isn't there a less obtrusive way to go about this? Your father said—"

"My father had to leave suddenly."

"Where did he go? I'm sure if I could draft an appropriate letter to re-emphasize the need for discretion—"

"He will be unreachable for some time. In the meantime, perhaps you can explain why you feel such an overwhelming need to conceal the presence of a dangerous conspiracy between heretics and traitors at your University."

The Chancellor stiffened as the implications of Thurman's statement sank in. "Of course, Exidgeon will do everything possible to assist in your investigation," he said at last.

Thurman smiled. "I knew I could count on you, Chancellor."

. . . . .

Back in the privacy of her room, Dona drew herself up like an indignant thunderhead. "Are you utterly out of your mind? What on earth were you thinking? Way deep down, wasn't there even a tiny shred of brain that whispered, 'golly, Alexi, maybe this isn't such a great idea?'"

"Well, I just thought—"

"No, no you didn't. When I agreed drink that vile potion, I expected you'd at least have the presence of mind to get us back to Exidgeon. Instead, of all places, I wake up here."

"I didn't think it was so bad."

"So once again you didn't think. At least you're consistent."

"If nothing else," Alexi said, "the beds are nice. And no one would ever think to look for us here."

Dona huffed. "Alexi, it's a *brothel*."

Alexi's eyes widened in mock horror. "It *is?* Well, then I stand corrected—at least no one would think to look for *me* here."

He dodged a shoe in the nick of time.

"Look," Alexi said, "I know you are still aren't feeling one hundred percent, and I know you have reservations about Jonas, but you can't ignore the fact that only a few hours ago, the Inquisition pronounced you a heretic. If the Monsignor's driver recognized you, he could have all of Exidgeon searching for you. Not only that, but that other man got a good look at you as well, and Jonas was none too optimistic about him either. Finally, your kidnapper is still at large. I know coming here was a risk, but it was only one risk."

"Not true. Your friend Jonas could sell us out to any of those people, and maybe some others you haven't thought of yet."

"That's unfair. So far, he's only been helpful."

Dona harrumphed. "Helped himself to a bit more than he was entitled to, as I recall."

"All right, my plan was terrible, and I'm an idiot. What does the resident genius suggest?"

"That depends." Dona said. "Do we trust Exidgeon or don't we?"

"I defer to your superior intellect."

"Fine, be that way. Even if we don't trust the University anymore, they would be looking for me, not you. I propose we distance ourselves from our hosts as soon as possible and find a safe place where I can hide out while you check on the University."

Alexi folded his arms. "And, just what places do you consider safe?"

Dona bit her lip. "I'll have to think about that."

"This decision-making thing is not as easy as it seemed, is it?"

"Oh, shut up and take me down to breakfast. Smugness interrupts my creative flow."

. . . . .

Her anger spent, Dona was the picture of decorum arriving to breakfast, at least as far as her behavior went. Her outfit was another matter.

Jonas rose as they approached. "How's the headache?"

Dona felt the spot on her head and winced. "Still making its presence known, but with bells rather than trumpets."

"That's good to hear. You're certainly looking far better than you did last night. Do you recall meeting my sister Mathilda?"

Tilly held out her hand. "I am in your debt. Jonas tells me that, but for your quick thinking, he might not have made it out of the Respite."

Dona blushed. "Oh, it was nothing, really."

"Well it was a very great thing to me. Please, make yourself at home, and help yourself to some breakfast. It's simple fare, but Nanna has a way with simple fare."

"That's very kind of you," Dona said. "This really does smell wonderful."

"When you've eaten, perhaps we can see about finding you a change of clothes. I am mortified the girls let you sleep in that outfit. It's a wonder you got any sleep at all."

"We don't want to be a bother," Dona said. "We should be getting back to Exidgeon as soon as possible anyway. We both have plenty of studying left to do for class tomorrow, given that the weekend has been kind of busy."

"You are students?"

"We are," Dona said. "Alexi and I have several of the same classes."

Jonas spoke through a mouthful of sausage. "Is it true what they say about Exidgeon?"

Dona looked to Alexi, but he only shrugged. "Is what true?"

"Was it really originally built as a Chervillian stronghold?"

"You mean as in the death-worshippers?"

"I suppose that would be the official Church view," Jonas said. "I suspect, like many Church-cultivated definitions, it approaches reality a bit myopically."

"Pardon my asking," Dona said. "But where do you get your vocabulary? I don't think half my professors would know that word."

Jonas laughed. "Seems a little incongruous on a traveling salesman?"

"For example."

It was Tilly who answered. "Our family has always placed a high value on education. Jonas and I were schooled by our Aunt Jennala, since we could not get into the University ourselves.

"I know what you mean—I don't know how my mother affords it."

Jonas and Tilly exchanged looks. After a moment, Jonas nodded and Tilly continued.

"It wasn't simply a matter of money, though at the time we had precious little. It was the Inquisition."

The unmistakable clang of cast-iron hitting brick forestalled Dona's reply. Over by the fireplace, Nanna focused on cleaning up the eggs scattered by her accident. Jonas went to help.

Once it was clear Nanna wasn't hurt, Dona turned her attention back to Tilly. "You mean the Caprian Inquisition?"

"You could tell by our accent?"

"Well no," Dona admitted, "but I'm not that familiar with many other Inquisitions."

"We were young when we fled Caprian to Aunt Jennala's farm," Tilly said. "Most can't tell the accent. Aunt Jennala insisted we lose it."

Jonas whispered to Nanna. She nodded and went upstairs. He finished cleaning up.

Dona's brow furrowed. "Why would the Inquisition keep you from going to school?"

Still chewing his biscuit, Alexi looked up from his plate. "Isn't it obvious?"

Dona's eyes went wide. "You're heretics."

Jonas snorted. "To the extent that children under the age of ten can be heretics, perhaps we were."

"We were lucky," Tilly said. "At the first hint of trouble, our father had the foresight to send us here to Trifienne to stay at his sister's farm. We never saw him again. Only later did we discover that the Inquisition had executed him. It was even worse for Nanna, though. As the wife of a heretic, her lands and property were forfeit. It was common for relatives to be forced to renounce the heresy publicly. Often, they were pilloried for weeks at a time in the town square until their renunciation was sufficiently 'heartfelt.' And then, as if that weren't bad enough, they were branded on the palm of the left hand with the letter R."

Dona was incredulous. "They knowingly punished the innocent?"

"Oh yes. It sent a message to heretics that their families would suffer. Some may be willing to martyr themselves for a cause, but few are willing to martyr their families. The renouncers became outcasts. Many of them starved to death right under the noses of their former friends and neighbors. Nanna lived on the streets of Caprian for several months before our uncle was able to find her and bring her back to the farm."

"How did she survive?"

Tilly shook her head. "We'll probably never know. Nanna hasn't spoken a word since." Tears welled in her eyes. "I remember she used to sing us to sleep at night. What I wouldn't give to hear her sing again."

Dona placed her hand over Tilly's. "I'm so sorry."

Tilly dabbed her eyes with a kerchief. "I don't know what's gotten into me. I am not usually this maudlin." She stood and started gathering the dirty dishes.

"Oh, let me help you with those," Dona said, grabbing Alexi's plate while he was still in mid-bite.

Jonas smirked, but said nothing.

. . . . .

As the women bustled off with the dishes, Alexi leaned forward. "I have a question, if you don't mind."

"Shoot," Jonas said. He sucked air through his pipe in small puffs to stoke the flame.

"Yesterday you said the Inquisition would be the least of our worries. Did you mean that?"

Jonas leaned back. "I did."

"Well, by Tilly's account, it seems to me they should be a pretty major worry, at least if they still operate that way."

"They are, and I expect they still do."

"Forgive me for being dense, but what threat would be worse than that?"

Jonas regarded Alexi for a long time. At last he spoke. "Where did you get the locket?"

"I got it at an estate sale last year, but I broke up with the girl before I gave it to her. Why does it matter?"

Jonas choked, coughing out a small white cloud before he recovered. "You bought a glowing locket at an estate sale? Whose estate was it?"

"It wasn't glowing when I bought it."

"So, there's a switch or a clasp to light it up?"

"No, no, it's nothing like that." Alexi said. "Why is that important?"

"So, you expect me to believe *you* made it glow?"

"So what if I did?"

"Tell me how."

"I think it would take a long time to teach," Alexi said, "and anyway, I couldn't tell you if I wanted to."

"No, I mean what were the steps?"

"Steps?"

"Yes, if you were going to explain casually to someone how you did it, how many steps would there be?"

"Oh, two, I suppose."

Jonas's eyes narrowed. "Which two? And in what order?"

"If I answer that, will you answer my questions?"

Jonas paused, considering. "Deal."

"All right, Light first, and then Charge."

"Why in that order?"

"That wasn't part of the agreement. It's supposed to be your turn to answer *my* question, but I expect the answer you're looking for is that if you cast the Charge first and there's nothing there to charge, it dissipates. And then when you cast the Light, there's nothing to charge it, and without a charge, the Light spell doesn't have any fuel."

"How can you know this and yet know nothing about the families?"

"What families?"

Jonas sighed. "All right, fine. Have you at least heard the name Phrendonian?"

Alexi considered his already tattered oaths. "I'm not sure I can say."

"Very well, I'll start there. Phrendonian was the author of a work called *Practical Phrendonics*. In it he described a methodology for using rigorous mental discipline to channel natural forces to produce fantastic effects."

"A book of spells."

"Of a sort. But it wasn't magic in the way many folks use that term. He also described, to some extent, his theories of the underlying mechanics—and its limitations. It turns out the limitations were pretty substantial."

"What does all this have to do with these families?"

"As you can imagine, once it became clear he was not a total fraud, this Phrendonian character attracted quite a following. Some of his apprentices went on to amass wealth and power. In some ways, the implied threat of their unknown talents gave them more power than the talents themselves. They soon discovered there was great incentive to let people know they could do things that others could not, but there was no incentive to let them know what those 'things' actually were. In most cases, they kept their secrets within the family. Over time, that had the effect of establishing a *de facto* aristocracy—the 'haves' versus the 'have-nots.'"

"Even if such families still exist," Alexi asked, "why would they care about Dona's locket?"

Jonas took a long draw on his pipe. "Caprian, I suppose."

"Oh, of course. They would be terrified of another Inquisition."

Jonas nodded. "The Church turned out to be more effective at suppressing heresy than they knew. Caprian changed everything. Petrified that any Phrendonic display within their city would bring the Inquisition down on them, the families became zealous anti-heresy enforcers, preventing any Phrendonic displays where they could, and eradicating all evidence of the event where they could not."

Alexi's frown deepened as he considered the implications. "And unlike the Church, which at least pretends to provide a hearing for the accused, I don't suppose these families give their targets any sort of warning, much less an opportunity to exonerate themselves?"

"And thereby risk exposure?"

Alexi's stomach clenched as another implication became clear.

"And you and Tilly must be members of one of these families, or you wouldn't know all these things."

Jonas laughed out loud. "Afraid you're going to disappear without warning, are you?"

The question hung in the air like pipe smoke.

At last, Jonas spoke. "If you'd been listening before instead of chewing, you'd have heard that our family hails from Caprian, not Trifienne, and that Caprian was cleansed of its heresy. We were children when it happened. Our father was killed, and our mother has not spoken since. Our Aunt, who raised us, was a farmer, not a heretic. While she was a forceful woman, she had essentially avoided any Phrendonic entanglements when as a young woman she chose to marry my Uncle. No doubt Nanna, for the terrible sin of associating with my father, was forced to renounce them as well. I, for one, am not willing to risk going back on that promise. No, lad, we are nouncers through and through, as pure of spirit as we are polluted of reputation. You have little to fear from us."

Tilly and Dona emerged from the next room and headed upstairs.

"I don't know what they were thinking when they left you in those clothes," Tilly said, "but we'll have you fixed up and presentable straight away."

"I'm fine, really I am," Dona said, but she followed Tilly upstairs just the same.

Drawing on his pipe, Jonas followed them with his eyes all the way up.

. . . . .

Tilly opened the wardrobe to reveal gowns in a wide array of colors and styles. "We have quite a selection up here. Is there something that strikes your fancy?"

"Anything that is clean and fits would be a great relief," Dona replied.

Tilly pulled one out for a closer look. "How about something in a chocolate brown?"

"How about this red one instead?" Dona asked, stroking the velvety fabric. "Or would it be too much?"

"I think it would be lovely on you, but it's hardly a color in which to keep a low profile."

Dona frowned. "I suppose that's true."

"Perhaps this wine-colored one would be a good compromise. It's still a beautiful color, but not quite so eye-catching, and I think the lines will do your figure justice."

"Oh that *is* nice," Dona said. "Are sure you don't mind?"

"Not at all."

"Could you give me a hand with these clasps and pins in the back? I'm afraid this outfit was a bit of a rush job."

"Surely."

Dona turned her back and Tilly started in.

"I've never seen so many pins in a skirt. It's a wonder you didn't puncture yourself." After a moment of fussing, she paused. "What on earth is this?"

"What is what?"

"I'm not sure," Tilly said. She held a small disc up to the light. It looks like a medallion."

"A medallion? Was it a pin or some kind of clip? Helena can be pretty creative when the need arises."

"I don't think so. It looks like ivory or bone. And look here. It's been etched with something, maybe a snake. A Church symbol, perhaps?"

"Let me see that."

Dona had never before seen its ilk. "I don't think Helena would have had anything like this, and if she had, I doubt she would have used it."

"Maybe someone left it on your seat at the Respite?"

Dona shook her head. "I think I'd have seen it."

"It's a puzzle, isn't it? All right, I think I have the worst of this unpinned. I'll let you freshen up while I go check on the boys."

"You don't think they'll be all right by themselves?"

Tilly snorted. They get bigger as they get older, but that's it. You know the saying: 'Boys will be boys...always.'"

Dona chuckled. "Strange, I'd never heard the full quote before."

Tilly winked. "I'm not surprised. We've had to shorten so many things to accommodate their attention spans. Come down and join us when you are feeling more yourself."

"I will."

. . . . .

"I've never seen anything like that," Alexi said.

"Like what?" Tilly asked as she came down the stairs.

"Any skull symbols or the like. Jonas seems to think the University was built on the ruins of a Chervillian stronghold."

Tilly shot Jonas one of her best 'oh, not *this* again' looks. "I seem to recall one of our Aunt's textbooks did hint at that, but it was one entry in one book. Anyway, I'm happy to report Dona seems to be recovering nicely from her bump on the head."

"I'm glad to hear it," Jonas said. "I'm surprised she's up and around at all, given the sound she made when she hit."

"Nothing rivals the healing properties of a new outfit."

"She's changed, has she?"

"She's in the process. I expect she'll be down shortly. What are your plans, Alexi? If you'll still be around, perhaps Dona can accompany Nanna and me to the market this afternoon."

"We haven't talked about it," Alexi said. "I had hoped to check on a few things at the University. I suppose I could come back for her after that."

"Let's plan on that. I think I'll be able to twist her arm."

Alexi gave a brief nod. "I'll go ready the horse."

. . . . .

"You're sure this outfit isn't a little much for a trip to the market?" Dona asked.

Tilly grinned. "Depends what you are shopping for. I don't think it's ever a bad thing to put your best foot forward. Just because you're a student, doesn't mean you must always look like one. Remember, regardless of what you *do*, you also *are* a young lady. No one else will fail to notice. To the extent you can, make that a strength, not a weakness."

Dona held up her arms and spun in a slow twirl. "Well, then, is this strong enough do you think?"

Tilly took a long look. "Not bad, but you'll need a hat. I'll be right back." She headed up the stairs.

As she approached Dona's room, Tilly heard the floorboards squeak. She gently pushed the door inward.

Jonas looked up. He was leaning over the pile of Dona's cast-off clothing.

Tilly placed her fists squarely on her hips. "Looking for something?"

"This isn't what it looks like."

"Really? And just what does it look like?"

"I swear I've given that up. I haven't stolen anything in years."

"You mean I haven't caught you in years."

"No, I mean I haven't done it."

"So I presume you have a better explanation?"

"I do."

Tilly tapped her foot. "I'm all ears."

"I lost something, and I merely wondered if Dona had happened across it."

Tilly snorted. "I presume you are aware the accepted way to address an issue like that is to ask."

"All right, fine. I was wrong, but I thought this way would be harmless and far less complicated."

Dona called up the stairs. "Is everything all right up there?"

Tilly gave Jonas a significant look.

After a long pause, Tilly called back, "I'm just trying to decide. I'll be down in a second."

"Thank you," Jonas whispered.

Tilly strode to the wardrobe, grabbed two hats, and headed back across the room. She paused momentarily at the door. "You've got some explaining to do when I get back."

She called out to Dona on the way down. "I couldn't decide between these two. What do you think?"

CHAPTER NINE

BEST-LAID PLANS

Two men plodded along a great hallway. Scintillating color splashed across the polished marble floor, the result of autumn sunlight streaming through stained glass. Their footsteps were barely audible over the trickling water of fountains in nearby gardens and the songs of the birds they attracted.

The older man, his face gaunt, his skin as papery pale as his starched vestments, paused for breath. "How I shall miss these quiet times in the rectory. You're certain there is no mistake?"

The younger man's gold-trimmed vestments were no less ornate than those of his companion. Handsome and clean-shaven, with close-cropped dark hair and piercing eyes, he absently fingered a silver pendant in the shape of two inter-twined snakes that dangled from a cord about his neck.

"I performed the diagnosis thrice, Your Primacy, but if you have doubts, I would be happy to perform a fourth."

The Primal sighed. "It's funny. I had always imagined when my time came, I would be resolute."

"You have been heroic. You have no cause to be ashamed."

The Primal chuckled. "Oh, I'm not ashamed, but neither am I resolute. Instead, I feel…incomplete. I guess no matter where the finish line gets drawn, one still longs to know what lurks beyond."

A cloud passed over the Primal's face. The younger man rushed to support him.

The Primal held up his hand. "Just a twinge, it will pass."

"You should be more careful. A fall could be disastrous."

The Primal eyed Laitrech sidelong. "You realize if you hadn't been such a gifted Ordinal, you would have made a respectable nanny."

"You are too kind. Now, are you going to sit, or must I take you over my knee."

"All right, fine. I'll have a seat in the garden. Maybe I should take a cue from Armand and start using a cane."

"A cane won't protect you from fainting."

"No, but it could come in very handy for beating insolent subordinates."

Laitrech snorted. "Need I remind you that naughty Primals go to bed without supper?"

"Do they also get to avoid taking their medicine? If so, I expect I could find ways to be very naughty, indeed."

"*They* get a double dose."

"In that case, I'll be good. Speaking of Armand, what's his status?"

"The last I heard, he had been sent for. If he was in Trifienne, he should be on his way."

"I wish he'd hurry. It's so frustrating trying to accomplish everything in so short a time."

"Is there something I can do to help?"

"Not unless you have more pull with him than I do."

"You don't mean to tell me he refused a direct request?"

"Oh, many times now."

"Then you have only to ask, and I shall see that it is done."

"It's too late for that—you already have. Armand has been my first choice for Ordinal on four separate occasions. He has steadfastly refused me every time. I always thought I'd get him to say yes next time, but now it seems there may not be a next time."

Laitrech nodded. "It's a pity there aren't any vacancies."

The old man waved dismissively. "A technicality. Armand has studied the Canons as thoroughly as anyone. I'm sure he can come up with something to get around that."

"Might that not offend the other Ordinals?"

"I hope it does. I've done many things in this position of which I am immensely proud, but sadly, my Ordinal appointments, with the exception of yours, have been, at best, unremarkable. It turns out the most politically expedient appointment is not always the best one. Maybe if I can finally twist Armand's arm, I can leave a legacy in which I can take some modicum of pride."

"You aren't thinking to revoke a previous appointment in favor of Armand, are you?"

"I haven't thought about it that carefully. I know what I want, and I'm prepared to do what it takes. If Armand feels he needs to justify it under the Canons, I'll leave that up to him."

"And if he refuses again?"

The Primal smiled. "I guess I will just have to make sure it's an offer he can't refuse."

. . . . .

Professor Reston shook his head. "I'm fairly certain he did it, or was at least involved, but I still can't for the life of me figure out why."

The first of the Professor's companions, a skinny blond man with an air of aggrieved entitlement, raised his eyebrow.

"*Fairly* certain, or certain? We can't risk acting on mere supposition, don't you agree, Tamry?"

The mountain of man that was Fenton Tamry was propped in his chair with his head lolling forward, seemingly asleep. At the mention of his name, he opened an eye and fixed it on the blond man. "Amberton, when you finally manage to say something of substance, I'll be happy to chime in to oppose it, but until then, could you please keep it down? You're giving me a headache." The eye snapped back shut.

"Reston," Amberton sniffed, "I don't know why you continue to put up with this mockery of a human being. If snores were advice, I'm sure you would be well served. Since they are not, however…"

"Gentlemen," Reston said, "could we please save the bickering for another time? This situation is serious. We had best manage it soon and manage it well."

Amberton snorted. "Surely you're overreacting. So what if Everson donned a few vestments and briefly waylaid the girl? By your own account, she didn't come to any harm. And not only did he fail to get the book, she doesn't even know who he was. What kind of disaster could possibly arise from that?"

An urgent voice carried into the chamber. "Professor Reston, are you there?" The double doors swung slowly inward, revealing Alexi, gasping from exertion. "They've posted Inquisitors at the front gates. No one is allowed in or out without identifying themselves and their business."

The room fell silent. Even the usually indolent Tamry seemed suddenly attentive.

At last, Reston started to speak, but Amberton cut him off.

"Don't even," he said, folding his arms. "Don't even."

Tamry stirred. "So, I take it the Merinne girl has reported the incident to the Church after all?"

"She must have given them the book," Amberton said. "They wouldn't dare take such a step just on the hearsay of the girl. They'd need proof."

"Alexi, close the doors, and have a seat," Reston said. "You look worn out."

Alexi collapsed in a chair. "It can't have been Dona."

Reston raised an eyebrow. "Your loyalty to Miss Merinne is admirable, but you must admit the evidence is mounting against her."

"Professor, I don't mean to say that I don't believe Dona didn't do it, I mean to say that I *know* she didn't. We were together the entire weekend."

"Well, then it must have been the Delauren boy," Amberton said. "Who else knew?"

With all due respect, Professors," Alexi said, "instead of pointing fingers based on what you think might have happened, wouldn't it make more sense to find out what *has* happened?"

Reston clapped the young man on the back. "Well said. Amberton, check with your sources in administration. No doubt someone there was consulted. Tamry, you've known Hepplewhite as long as anyone, and as the Monsignor's friend, he's surely the best source we have on the faculty. Pay him a visit and feel him out."

"Bah," Tamry said. "I can try, but Hepplewhite is not one to betray a confidence. Nor is he likely to give up anything accidentally. The best I'm going to get is the official line."

"That's more than we have now. Let's meet again here tomorrow at noon."

Moments later, Alexi and Reston were alone in the chamber.

"There's one more thing, Professor."

"Why do I have a feeling it's not a good thing?"

"It's not. The Monsignor's carriage driver spotted Dona wearing a locket at the Sultan's Respite."

"The place that burned yesterday? What was she doing there?"

"It was my idea. I thought it would be a good private place to explain what she needed to know about joining."

"So the Monsignor followed you there? That sounds ominous, indeed."

"No, nothing like that. It was only the Monsignor's carriage driver, and he was there before we were, so he couldn't have been following us."

"Well that's a relief anyway. So, why do we care if he saw Dona's locket?"

Alexi shifted uncomfortably. "Um, it was glowing."

Reston winced. "I suppose there's an excellent reason for that, but I'm just missing it?"

Alexi studied his shoes. "I thought it might be a good recruitment tool."

"So I take it she's now in Church custody?"

"No, it's really much more complicated."

Reston sighed and sat down. "All right, I'm listening."

"So, the Monsignor's driver was at a tented table near ours, when a man wearing a bunch of rings interrupted them, at least according to Dona, who saw it happen. The driver got annoyed and started getting noisy, which drew the attention of the bouncers. Now here's where it gets weird. Dona said the guy with the rings made some sort of gesture, and at least five bouncers dropped to the floor."

Reston gasped. "A Phrendonic?"

"I don't know. I didn't even see him, but it sure sounds that way."

"That doesn't make sense. He'd have to target one at a time, not five at once. Vesting theory is very clear on that point."

"Well, maybe he bought them off. Regardless, once that happened, the man who was with the Monsignor's driver went crazy. He screeched and launched himself through his own curtain and right into Dona's and mine. It was then the driver saw the locket, since our curtains were torn free. He never saw me, though—I ended up covered in fabric."

"How do you know he even saw the locket, then? Maybe he missed it?"

Alexi grimaced. "I think he saw it. Dona says he pointed right at her and screamed 'heretic.'"

"And *then* he took her into custody?"

"Well, no, actually. That's when the lights went out."

"You just lost me."

"I presume someone cast a Darkness spell. There's one just like it in the book."

Reston gasped. "In the middle of the Sultan's Respite?"

Alexi shrugged. "All I know is that I could feel the heat and smell the smoke as everything around me burst into flames, but I couldn't see a thing."

Reston's eyes widened. "How did you get out?"

"It was Dona, actually. She had her bearings and kept calling to me until I untangled myself from the curtain and got pointed in the right direction. It was blind crawling from there. By the time I got outside, the darkness was gone, and the fire was out of control."

"So the posting of Inquisitors at the University could actually be due to the presence of this other Phrendonic, and not Miss Merinne?"

"There's no doubt she was seen. I suppose it's possible they're searching primarily for the other Phrendonic, but then why look at the University?"

"Where is Miss Merinne now?"

"I'd rather not say, just in case things go badly here."

"She's safe, though?"

"As far as I know, but she has no idea what's waiting for her if she comes back here. I had better go warn her, or it could go badly for all of us."

"And the book?"

"I have no idea. She didn't have it with her."

"All right, off with you. Check in with us tomorrow if you can, I hope to know more by then."

"I will. And Professor?"

"Yes?"

"I'm sorry."

Reston sighed. "So am I, Alexi. So am I."

. . . . .

The air was autumn-brittle but the sun still warm as Dona, Tilly, and Nanna wandered among the market booths. Tilly was in her glory, greeting the vendors by name, expressing appreciation for the weather, and clucking about the terrible fire and the dreadful loss of life. Dona couldn't help noticing that while the men seemed open and friendly, the women were most often standoffish or even frosty. Tilly greeted them all with equanimity, taking any rudeness in stride. The fruit vendor had cleverly placed out a few fresh-baked pies, and the scent had Tilly and Nanna examining apples and contemplating a similar fate for them. Dona hovered nearby, captivated by a vendor distilling oil from a vat of rose petals.

"Try a sample, Miss?"

Dona nodded. The woman swirled a little stick in the collection dish and touched it to Dona's wrist. The scent was light and sweet. Dona decided she simply had to take a vial home.

"Roses suit you." The voice was soft and oddly familiar. "What do you think? Would it work for an older woman as well? It's my mother's birthday on Thursday."

She turned to find herself staring directly into the intense green eyes of the wiry man from the Sultan's Respite.

Dona froze, but the man made no threatening moves. She pulled her eyes away from his and focused deliberately on completing her transaction.

"What do you want?"

"My name is Michlos. I'd like to buy you lunch. I know some things you may find interesting."

"I hope you'll forgive my reticence. The last time we dined under the same roof, quite a few people died."

There was a long pause.

"I am deeply sorry for that," Michlos said at last. "I hadn't realized your friend had caused a fire until it was beyond my ability to remedy."

"*My* friend?" Dona asked. "He started out in your canopy."

"My apologies if I jumped to conclusions. I had presumed the assumption reasonable from the fact of your accompanying his sister to the market. And as you could no doubt see, I was less than welcome in his canopy."

Dona turned to face him. "Wait a minute, are you trying to tell me that *Jonas* was the one in the canopy with the Monsignor's carriage driver?"

"Not at all. I had presumed you already knew."

"That's ridiculous. What business could a spirits merchant have with the Monsignor's carriage driver?"

"I would have posed the question differently" Michlos said. "I would have asked what an inveterate nouncer like Jonas Mapleton Harcourt was doing in the cozy company of Armand Goodkin's son."

Dona's jaw dropped. "That's his son?"

"I thought you might find that interesting."

Dona tucked away her purchase. "I have a better question. What would a Phrendonic heretic want with the two of them?"

Michlos cocked his head. "What a coincidence. I was about to ask you the same question. But mightn't this discussion be better held in a more private venue?"

"Where would you suggest?"

"My usual spot is still smoldering. I'm open to suggestions."

"You'd really let me pick?"

Michlos shrugged. "Of course. Why wouldn't I?"

"Just not what I expected," Dona said. Over Michlos's shoulder she noticed Tilly and Nanna working their way toward her. "Let me think about it. Where can I get in touch with you?"

"You can leave a message at the Expatriate Hotel."

"It's Michlos, right?"

He nodded. "Out of curiosity, whom will you say has left the message?"

"Oh, forgive me. I'm Dona."

"Charmed," Michlos said.

Dona smiled. "Likewise. Now if you'll excuse me, my friends are almost here."

"Be safe, Dona."

In a matter of moments, he'd melted into the crowd.

"Who was that?" Tilly asked.

"Oh him? Just some gentleman asking my advice on a birthday present for his mother."

Tilly raised an eyebrow. "Really?" Then she sighed. "I remember when I used to get those kinds of requests. Apparently my advice isn't what it used to be. Ah, the good old days."

"Poor dears. They don't know what they're missing."

"So true," Tilly said. "Still, one can wish young men would be more inclined to seek out a mature perspective now and again." She gave Dona a sly wink. "You know, for their own good."

. . . . .

"So, tell me, Father Cartier," Thurman said, addressing his new assistant, "what did the Chancellor have to say? I trust he was…cooperative?"

Cartier looked up from his clipboard. The good father was fastidious and clean-shaven. His cassock was neatly pressed, his manner, efficient. When he'd heard of the arrival of the Inquisition at Exidgeon, he'd made the difficult decision to take time away from his flock at St. Sophia's Church to offer his aid, and Thurman had eagerly accepted.

Although the room where they now stood was the same one in which the Monsignor had interrogated Shoruga, the spare furniture had been replaced with a heavy cherrywood desk and a comfortable leather desk chair. Additional chairs were also now available for visitors. Thurman leaned back against the leather and knitted his fingers behind his head. "Have a seat."

Cartier availed himself of one of the new chairs. "The Chancellor was kind enough to assign us an entire floor in Dexter Hall," he said. "Looked pretty nice to me."

"Dexter Hall? Is that near the front gates?"

"A stone's throw away. We should be able to keep a pretty close eye on all traffic in and out of the University."

"Excellent. What about Shoruga?"

"Locked in an office on the third floor with three guards round the clock."

"Any confessions?"

"None yet, just a lot of whimpering and weeping."

Thurman nodded. "Keep at him. He's obviously guilty, and what he knows could save lives. Pity the dog died. It might have been useful. What about my request for assistance?"

"I've dispatched two separate couriers and offered a reward to the one who arrives first."

"Inspired," Thurman said. "I'd also like you to look into another matter, if you would."

"Of course, Father."

"I need to know the whereabouts of a traveling salesman by the name of Jonas Harcourt. He shouldn't be hard to find—his wagon is covered with all sorts of signs advertising his wares. Can I ask you to do that?"

"Any idea where I should start?"

"As of last night, he was in Trifienne. If he's traveling in his wagon, he probably hasn't gotten far."

"I'll see to it," Cartier said. "May I ask why this vendor is important?"

"You don't need to know."

"Understood. I'll also get the move underway."

"No, don't. Delegate that. Make the vendor your top priority. Without him, all the rest of this may not matter."

"As you wish, Father."

. . . . .

"Dommy, darling," Verone said, breezing into Everson's office without bothering to knock. "I'm so glad you're still in. We need to talk."

"For crying out loud, Verone, we just talked this morning."

She patted his cheek. "Why, you lucky man. I'm so proud of me. Despite being a very busy woman, I clearly still take the time to dote."

Everson dropped his quill and sighed. "What is it this time?"

"Now, Dommy, don't get cross with me. After all, if only you had finished your chores in the first place, we wouldn't be in this position."

"Don't start with me. I have done everything you've asked, to the letter."

"Well, there's no doubt you've been an eager little plugger for the cause, but unlike you, we just don't have the luxury to be able to give an A for effort. Fortunately, though, you can always sneak by on the makeup."

"I told you, I did everything you asked already."

"Oh, goodness me, then it must be my mistake. You must have already gotten that pesky book from Miss Merinne and already given it to me, and I just didn't notice. Here, let me look." She opened the case she carried and peeped quickly inside. "Hmmm, nope. Not here."

"Wait right there. You didn't say I had to *get* the book, you just said I had to ask for it."

"Dommy…sweetie, why would we want you to ask for it if we didn't expect you to get it?"

"That does it. Get out. Get out of my office. Nothing you can teach me is worth this."

"Temper, temper, dearest. I'm only trying to help."

"Now!" Everson roared. He grabbed her arm and shoved her toward the open doorway.

Her hand shot out like lightning, backhanding him across the face. He dropped to the floor senseless, blood dripping from a jagged slash across his cheek left by her ring.

She closed the door, returned to where he lay motionless, and straightened her bodice. "Well, what couple doesn't have their little spats? But on the brighter side, I'm so glad we have this opportunity to review the ground rules. Rule number one: Don't touch me…*ever*. Listen carefully to rule number one, because even if I am very fond of you—and you know that I am—I do not give second chances on rule number one. Rule number two: Do as you are told. I trust that rule is simple enough even you can understand it. Rule number three: There is no quitting, not now, not ever. Let's just say I don't take rejection well."

She nudged him with her toe. He was unresponsive.

"Now," she said. "Assuming you survive this, we would be most appreciative if you could do your best to retrieve that book from Miss Merinne. If you fail, we just might have to consider it a violation of rule number two, and we certainly wouldn't want that, would we? And if you don't survive it... well, please *do* try to survive it. I look terrible in black. Oh, and if I don't see you again, do try to have a nice rest of the day."

When the door closed behind her, Everson still hadn't moved.

. . . . .

"Stay here again tonight?" Dona cried. "I couldn't possibly. I have class in the morning."

"I don't see where you have a choice," Alexi said. "They've posted Inquisitors at the gates."

A mostly dressed young lady hobbled past on one high heel. "Has anyone seen my boot?" A moment later she'd disappeared into the vestibule.

"Was the Monsignor or his carriage driver there?" Dona asked.

Alexi shook his head. "Not that I saw. But that doesn't mean—"

"So they don't have any way to even recognize me, then."

"They may well have your description."

Dona shrugged. "So all I have to do is make sure I don't look much like me. How hard can that be?"

"This is crazy. The Inquisition is looking for a heretic who fits your description, and you're worried about missing class?"

"Stop blowing this out of proportion. Worst-case scenario—"

A young woman wearing a red sequined gown appeared on the stairway carrying an empty makeup case. "Who used up all the rouge? Shelby, hon, do you got any rouge?"

"No, hon," came a voice from the vestibule. "Do without. It's almost time, and you use too much anyway."

"Dammit," she said, scooting back upstairs.

"As I was saying," Dona said. "The worst-case scenario is that they recognize me, take me into custody, and burn me at the stake, right?"

"This is serious."

"True, but not *that* serious. The chances he recognized me are really low. I'm not prepared to throw away my entire education on the off chance the Inquisition has mobilized a small army to catch one little girl heretic who, for all they know, burned to death in the fire. Don't you see? This whole thing has got to be about something else. It's the only thing that makes sense. In fact the Monsignor said as much."

"You asked him?"

"Not exactly," Dona said. "But—"

The back door to the kitchen flew open, slamming the wall. A half-undressed blonde rushed through the kitchen and up the stairs, throwing off additional articles of clothing as she ran by.

After a moment of silence, Dona reached over and gently closed Alexi's mouth. He had the grace to blush. Then she burst out laughing. Alexi joined in.

It took several moments for Alexi to finally catch his breath. "It's too bad we don't laugh more than we argue. I love it when you laugh."

Dona brightened, and took his hand. "That's so sweet. Let's promise to laugh more than we argue, then."

"I promise."

"Well," she said after a long pause, "maybe I could stay one more night."

"No, no. You were right—the risk isn't really that great. We'll find a way to get you back tonight. And I really can't imagine the Monsignor doing the kinds of things Tilly described. Those things happened a generation ago. We've come a long way since then."

"All right, if you say so, but we'll need a plan."

"About that," Alexi said. "I think—"

"Excuse me?" A stocky man stepped into the kitchen, wringing his hat. "Can you tell me where—"

"In there," Alexi and Dona said in unison, pointing toward the vestibule.

"Thank you." The man edged his way hesitantly in that direction, took a deep breath, and finally stepped inside.

Dona and Alexi looked at each other and laughed all over again.

. . . . .

Exidgeon University is situated on a low plateau overlooking the Scandus River as it meanders south to the sea. The plateau's origin has been a matter of long-standing debate. Professor Gottfried Klouch made a career of insisting it rested on the remnant of an extinct volcano, while Professor Flaxton Pierce debated fiercely that it was produced by a prehistoric earthquake. The two men agreed, however, that the long earthen ramp leading up to the front gates must have been constructed in antiquity by some long-dead culture. That, however, was where all agreement ended.

Standing at those gates afforded the two Inquisitors a magnificent view of the sun as it set over the western hills, but they barely noticed, so intent were they on their new duties. They were on the hunt for heresy, and they knew that the first to find it would not escape the notice of the new Grand Inquisitor. Each was determined to find it first, and even if his only reward were reassignment, it would be worth it.

Today Inquisitor Travis was in charge of the gate log, which recorded the names and business of everyone entering or leaving the University, while Inquisitor Renrick was in charge of searching clothing and cargo. Neither of them knew exactly what they were looking for, but both had faith they would know it when they saw it.

"When are they sending in the night crew, anyway?" Travis asked. "It's getting kinda cold out here."

"It's not the cold, but the bugs that'll get you," Renrick said. "Be glad you aren't on night duty, I bet that ain't any fun."

"That, and you'd have no chance of finding anything at all. This place gets as dead as the inside of a coffin at night."

A low moan punctuated his declaration.

Travis cocked an ear. "What was that?"

"I'm not sure," Renrick replied. "Do you see anything?"

"It's pretty dark, I'm not sure."

"Do you hear that?"

Once the two men were quiet, they could hear the unmistakable clippity-clop of horses on the ramp.

Then the moan came again, louder this time.

"What *is* that?" Renrick asked.

"I dunno, but it's getting closer."

At last, the two men could make out a lone figure leading two horses, his head bowed. One of the horses dragged a makeshift litter; little more than three stout sticks lashed together with rawhide and ragged strips of fabric.

"State your business," Travis said as the man approached. The horses came to a halt, but as the man began to speak, a bloodcurdling wail pierced the twilight."

The man dropped to his knees. "Please," he said. "Is there a midwife here? The baby, it's been trying to come, but it's not coming."

The two Inquisitors looked at each other, at a loss.

"I don't know anything about any midwives," Travis said. "Do you know, Willard?"

Renrick shrugged. "I'm not sure, but I think there's supposed to be Sisters in there somewhere."

The form on the litter thrashed and moaned.

"Oh, bless you, sirs!" The man stood and began leading the horses toward the gate.

"Just a minute," Renrick said.

The man froze.

"I have to search everyone who goes into or out of that place. No offense. It's my job."

Another wail shattered the night calm.

The man nodded. "Please be quick about it, good sir. I'm not sure how much longer she can last."

Renrick hastily searched the ragged man but found nothing of interest. He then approached the litter. A woman lay there, wrapped in blankets and writhing in obvious pain. Judging by her outline, she was very near to term. As he got closer, he hesitated.

"I ain't never searched an expecting lady before."

"Please hurry, sir, I beg you."

The woman, breathing in ragged gasps, bit down hard on one of the rawhide straps and moaned between her teeth.

Renrick extended his hand, and just as he touched the woman in the litter, he noticed something he'd missed before. The litter seemed to be dripping.

"Uggh. She's soaking wet."

"Maybe her water broke," Travis suggested.

Renrick snatched his hand away. "Go on," he said. "Get her in there. She needs help straight away."

"Bless you, good sirs," the ragged man said. "Bless you."

He led the horses through the gate as the Inquisitors looked on.

"You don't see that every day," Travis said.

Renrick wiped his hand on his vestments "Or stick your hand in it neither. I sure do hope that baby's gonna be all right."

"If the Sisters can't help her, nobody can. They're lucky they came this way. They'd have never made it all the way to town."

. . . . .

Once well inside the gate, Alexi helped Dona out of the litter, and she fell giggling into his arms.

"Oh, Alexi, that was marvelous."

"My hat's off to you. You almost had *me* convinced."

"Shhh," she said, "You'll wake the baby." From the front of her rough blouse she pulled the bits and pieces of the riding outfit Helena had crafted for her, as well as the wine-colored gown Tilly had given her. Finally, she pulled out one last thing—a goatskin, now-empty. As she did so, something else dropped to the ground, where it clattered on the cobbles and lay still.

Alexi retrieved it for her. "What's this?"

"Oh that. I'm not sure. Tilly found it stuck in the back of my riding outfit. I have no idea how it got there."

"Strange. Well, I better get these horses back, or I won't be allowed to borrow them anymore."

"Thanks, Alexi. You were very sweet to help me."

"You know me—I'll do almost anything for one of those smiles."

"I'll hold you to that, you know." Standing on her toes, she kissed him, and this time, not on the cheek. "See you in class."

He waited a few minutes for her to disappear into the dormitory and held up his hand in farewell. As he did so, he noticed he was still holding the item she had dropped. He shrugged and slipped it into his pocket.

CHAPTER TEN

NOTABLE ABSENCES

Nothing rattled Dona more than arriving to class unprepared. She'd taken a seat near the back, and was skimming furiously, hoping to catch up before class started.

"Hey there."

She looked up to see Alexi smiling down at her.

"Good morning, handsome."

Alexi's smile broadened. "I bet you say that to all the guys."

Dona considered a moment and nodded. "To all the handsome ones, anyway. So, what's wrong with Reston—is he sick?"

The professor was seated at the front of the lecture hall looking even more disheveled than usual.

"Probably hasn't gotten much sleep. This whole situation has really thrown him."

Dona sniffed. "I'm not surprised."

"I think he's worried primarily on your behalf."

"How very considerate."

"You shouldn't be so hard on him. After all, it was my mistake."

"I remember full well. And don't think you're off the hook just because in a moment of weakness I mentioned you were handsome."

"Perish the thought."

"Good morning, class," Reston said. "Let's get started."

At that instant, Helena and Miranda slipped in and took seats near the door. Reston paused momentarily, but the gentle chiding he usually visited upon the tardy never came.

Neither was Reston himself throughout the lecture. Although he competently described the first skirmishes between civilized folk and the tattooed Drewor, whom he painted as vicious barbarians from the North, he did so with none of his usual flair. Nor did he call on anyone to recite. At one point, Dona elbowed Alexi to stop him from snoring. The only good thing about the entire class was that it finished fifteen minutes early.

Dona saw Helena and Miranda waiting for her outside the classroom, but she never made it that far.

"Miss Merinne," Reston said. "Do you have a moment?"

"Of course, Professor."

Alexi hung back as the rest of the class filed out.

"If you are planning to stay, Mr. Reysa, would you mind getting the door?"

"Not at all, Professor." With a shrug at Helena and Miranda, he closed off their only chance of listening in.

"I apologize for keeping you, Miss Merinne," Reston said, "but I thought you should know—I am disbanding our little group."

Alexi's mouth fell open. "You can't mean that."

"I don't like it any better than you do, but the events of the last few days make it painfully clear that Trifienne simply isn't ready. I can't justify endangering people this way, even in the name of truth."

Dona was unexpectedly shaken. Although she hadn't realized it before, she was starting to view Reston's group as a source of strength. Perhaps it was Alexi's influence, but she now saw them as a network of like-minded people committed to knowledge for its own sake, who, if pressed, were willing to take a stand against wrong-headed Church dogma, even if only from behind the scenes. Without their implicit support, she doubted she'd have the resolve to keep from turning the book over to the Monsignor. And that would be tragic, not only from the perspective of knowledge irretrievably lost, but also for the harm to those who would thereby be implicated.

"I don't follow, Professor. What do you hope to gain by disbanding?"

Reston bowed his head. "We are still in our infancy, and already the Church is on our doorstep. I never dreamed they would sniff us out so quickly."

"But they might not be aware of you at all—they might be investigating something else entirely. It's not like you are the only Phrendonics in town."

"Yes, I heard about your mysterious encounter at the Respite. If we're lucky, the Inquisition will focus their efforts there. That way we can all just fade into the background."

"But what if that's not their focus? What if the Inquisition really is after someone in your group? How does disbanding help then?"

"Isolation," Reston said. "If there is no active network, maybe the Church would be content with catching whomever they are looking for and ending the Inquisition there."

"Forgive me, Professor, but that's not a strategy, that's cowardice."

For the first time during their conversation, Reston fully met her gaze. Anger blazed where previously there had been only resignation.

"Cowardice? Perhaps someday, Miss Merinne, if you ever find yourself facing inevitable defeat while being responsible for someone other than yourself, you will realize there is no cowardice in salvaging what you can."

"In fact," Dona said, "it's worse than cowardice. Your noble plan to stand idly by while the Inquisition seizes your co-conspirators and then pray they don't come for you is downright stupid. Who in that position wouldn't point the finger directly at you, and everyone else who abandoned him?"

"They took oaths."

"I'm sure they did. No doubt that will heighten their sense of betrayal. I bet they won't even have to be threatened to give you up, much less tortured. Look, I don't know where you get your ideas of loyalty, but where I come from, a person is loyal only when he feels a part of something bigger and when he knows his comrades have his back. Without that, your silly oaths are merely so many words."

Alexi gently took her arm. "Come on, we should go." He tugged several times before Dona finally shook her head and let him pull her away.

Reston watched them go with haunted eyes.

Miranda and Helena pounced the moment Alexi opened the door.

"Where have you two been?" Helena asked.

"We've been worried sick," Miranda added. "When you didn't come home, we started to think maybe you were caught in that fire at the Sultan's Respite."

"We were," Dona said. She didn't elaborate. She was still fuming.

"Really?" Helena exclaimed. "Are you all right?"

Miranda chimed in, too. "You were at the Sultan's Respite? What was it like? Did you see anyone famous? Was it as exotic as everybody says?"

Dona held up her hands. "Whoa there. All will be answered in due course, but I was up early this morning, and I'm starving. Lunch anyone?"

"Oh, I can't right now," Alexi said. "I need to get going. Maybe I'll see you for dinner?"

He leaned down and gave Dona an innocuous peck on the cheek. Her heart leapt, but she had enough presence of mind to treat it as though it had been expected.

Miranda waited barely long enough for Alexi to get out of earshot. "Looks like the building wasn't the only thing that caught fire at the Sultan's Respite."

Dona ignored her. "The place was fabulous."

As they made their way to the cafeteria, Dona told them her tale, except for the events surrounding the locket and Reston's society. She wove her story with exquisite detail, describing at length the extravagant canopies that probably explained why she hadn't seen anyone famous, the cuisine itself, which was the most sumptuous she had ever experienced, and the terrifying circumstances surrounding the outbreak of the fire. She was particularly gratified by Helena's scandalized reaction to their stay at Tilly's.

"You spent the night in a *brothel?*"

"I was mortified. But the owner turned out to be the world's sweetest woman. Since my clothes were a wreck, she even gave me a new dress. I can't wait to show you."

"Quite a story," Miranda said. "Ours sounds pretty tame by comparison."

Dona's ears perked up. "Oh? There's a story?"

"Well, maybe not a story so much as an interesting event. Did you know there was some sort of crime committed over on the Hathaway campus?"

"What were you doing over there?"

"Nothing really," Helena said. "We were just taking a little walk with Alphonse."

Dona eyed them sidelong. "*Both* of you? And here I thought my story was scandalous."

Miranda waved dismissively. "Oh, hush, you."

"Anyway," Helena said, "we're not sure what the crime was, but they had a whole area roped off, and one of the buildings was closed."

"Here's where it gets interesting," Miranda said. "So Alphonse asks one of the gardeners what's going on, and he says he doesn't know, but that there were—get this—*church folk* checking out the place, and one of them was an old guy with a cane."

"The Monsignor?" Dona asked.

"So it would seem. Apparently, he didn't visit our fine school solely for academic reasons. I wonder if he's after your mysterious bejeweled arsonist?"

"Oh, I don't think he's the one who started the fire."

"Regardless, it sure sounds like he did a few things that would have gotten the Monsignor's attention. But if the Monsignor was after this guy, it seems sort of strange that he'd approach the carriage driver—did you say he was the Monsignor's son?"

Dona's heart raced as she realized she'd let that detail slip. "Oh, I'm only assuming that."

"Based on?"

"Family resemblance, maybe? I don't know."

"Regardless. I think I'll press Professor Reston for a few more details about what the heretics did to incite the Caprian Inquisition. Maybe that will shed some light on the cause of the fire. By the way, what did he want with you after class, anyway?"

Dona momentarily froze. "Um, an extra credit project. But you're absolutely right—he might know things that could help. You needn't bother him, though. I'll be sure to ask him about Caprian next time we talk about my project."

"I might have guessed," Miranda said. "Ever the over-achiever. But I don't mind asking. I love a good puzzle. Besides, I prefer my information to be as first-hand as possible—I intend to let Daddy know about this, and he's a stickler for sources."

Dona fought down panic. Things were complicated enough without getting the secular authorities involved, and Miranda's father was the constable. "I'm sure that's not necessary. The Monsignor seems to be pretty capable, and if he's involved, I bet things are under control."

"That's not the point. Daddy says every time the Church gets involved in a secular matter, they overstep their authority and try to take full control. Maybe everything is just fine, but I think he should at least be made aware that the Church is poking around up here."

Their chat had taken them to the cafeteria, only sparsely populated, where the students had erected a corkboard near the entrance to facilitate student communication. Helena paused to check for messages on the way in.

"Note for you, Dona," she said. Unlike most of the notes, which were merely folded over, this one was sealed in an envelope.

"For me? No one leaves messages here for me."

"Who's it from?" Miranda asked.

"I'm not sure," Dona said, breaking the seal. She stiffened as she scanned it.

Miranda's brow furrowed. "What's wrong?"

Dona skimmed it again to be sure there was no mistake:

If you want to see Gregory Delauren alive again, wander the market with the book at noon on Tuesday. Tell no one, and come alone.

Beneath, in a different hand, was written:

Bella, please do as they ask.

"It's nothing. Look, I've got to go. I just remembered something I forgot to do."

"But you haven't eaten yet," Miranda said.

Dona grabbed an apple. "Don't worry about me, I'll get by. See you tonight."

Miranda's mouth fell open. "You're skipping Hepplewhite's class? Don't you want to know your grade?"

"And find out I failed, like all the women last year?"

"Don't be ridiculous. You gave the best presentation so far."

"Kind of you to say, but I've really got to go."

Miranda harrumphed as she watched Dona leave.

"What?" Helena asked.

"She's hiding something."

"How do you know?"

"I wasn't sure before, but I am now. Nothing short of the apocalypse would keep Dona from finding out a grade."

. . . . .

The basement chamber that served as the meeting hall for Reston's secret society could hold up to twenty, but today, only three were present. In light of recent events, Reston was keeping only his most trustworthy associates informed.

"As I was saying," Tamry said, "Hepplewhite swears the Monsignor has left Trifienne entirely."

Reston shook his head. "That makes no sense—then who is running the Inquisition?"

Tamry shrugged. "I'm not sure. Hepplewhite seemed unaware of the situation at the gate. Apparently he hasn't left campus for a few days."

"I wasn't able to find out much either," Amberton said. "My sources in administration were tight-lipped, even when I pressed them. If I didn't know better, I'd say they were frightened."

"Frightened?" Tamry said. "Why should the administration be frightened? Surely not everyone can be a heretic."

"You'd be surprised," Reston said. "In Caprian, scores of people were rounded up and tortured on suspicion of heresy for mere association with suspected heretics, or more insidiously, for reasons that had nothing to do with heresy at all. It was a dangerous time to be inconvenient to the Church."

"Apparently my sources have gotten the message." Amberton said. "The best I got was this, and it isn't much." He held out a scrap of paper on which was scrawled a single word: *Shoruga*.

"What's this?"

Amberton shook his head. "I have no idea. My source kept saying he didn't know anything, but at the same time he wrote this out and handed it to me. I couldn't get anything else out of him."

A loud thud reverberated through the chamber. Something heavy had hit the doors.

A muffled voice cried out on the other side. "Open these doors. *Now.*"

Amberton sat up in his chair. "Was that a woman's voice?"

"Sounded female to me," Tamry said.

Reston was already there, turning the key in the lock. As he threw open the doors, only Alexi's quick reflexes prevented Dona from launching another chair.

"Miss Merinne?" Reston asked.

"Oh, what luck—I see the little boys' club is in session."

Tamry craned his neck for a better view. "Reston, isn't this the young lady who made off with your book?"

"She shouldn't be here at all," Amberton sniffed. "These meetings are private for a reason."

"On the contrary," Reston said, "she has every reason to be here."

She tossed the ransom note on the table. "You bet I do. Take a look at that. How about first we talk about who's responsible for this? And then, we can chat about exactly what you plan to do about it."

Reston snatched up the note and read it aloud.

Alexi quietly closed the doors.

"This matter certainly bears discussing," Amberton said. "Let's clear the room of non-members, and then we can address it."

"I agree completely," Reston said.

"Professor," Alexi said, "you can't mean that."

"Oh, I surely do. And to accomplish it, I hereby nominate Miss Merinne for membership in our Society. All in favor?"

Alexi broke into a wide grin and raised his hand. "Aye."

"Aye," Reston said.

Tamry shifted his bulk and gave Dona a good hard look. "Aye," he said finally. "After all, she seems to be considerably more on top of this than we are."

They all eyed Amberton expectantly.

"Oh, for goodness' sake, aye. Not that it matters anyway, since we don't have anything even remotely approaching a quorum."

Dona snorted. "Not that it matters anyway for anything other than branding me a heretic, you mean. What an honor it would be to join just in time for you to disband. Thanks, but no."

Tamry opened both eyes wide in surprise. "Disband? What's this about?"

Reston pulled up a stool. "Don't sell yourself short, Miss Merinne. You gave me quite a lot to think about this morning, and after I did, I made some decisions. You should know I've reconsidered."

Alexi's whole face lit up. "You mean we aren't disbanding?"

"No, but we *are* restructuring. This democratic model has been nothing but trouble. Under the new regime, not only will I be dispensing with the plethora of pointless oaths, I will be taking charge of the decision-making as well. We need a leader here, not a council. Let's see if our conspirators are easier to lead than they were to squeeze a consensus from."

Tamry pounded the table. "Hear, hear, Reston. It's about time you took charge."

Amberton looked as if he'd eaten something that disagreed with him. "I daresay I don't think this new plan is going to go over very well with the council."

"Then they are free to make their own society," Reston replied. "They may find advancement difficult without any of the materials, however."

Amberton swallowed hard. "I see your point."

"So what say you, Miss Merinne?" Reston asked. "Will you do me the honor of joining my new regime? I could really use your insights."

"If it will help us focus on rescuing Gregory, then fine, whatever. Now can we please get down to business?"

· · · · ·

Going over it again in her mind, Dona decided she was pleased with the plan. Initially they'd discussed simply giving up the book in return for Gregory, but the very idea galled her. First, there was no way to tell whether Gregory was already dead, or, for that matter, whether he'd even been abducted at all. They'd looked all over campus, but he wasn't in any of his usual haunts. That, however, was not unexpected, since he had a full performance schedule—even his music class he managed to attend only sporadically.

Given that uncertainty, they had finally come to agreement. The goal was to capture the kidnapper at the point of exchange and force Gregory's location out of him. They were all agreed that the kidnapper would most likely expect Dona to comply with the ransom note and arrive at the market alone, trusting that the heretical nature of the book would prevent her from seeking aid from either the constable or the Inquisition. To capitalize on that expectation, Reston and Alexi would have to keep some distance as she wandered the market, but still be close enough to help when the time came. While it would be useful for Tamry and Amberton to be stationed nearby, they would keep to a predetermined location—too many people might become obvious and scare the kidnapper off.

The discussion about whether Dona should take the book with her had been interminable. Overruling Alexi's suggestion, they agreed that Dona should carry a decoy rather than the real thing. If by chance the authorities got involved, the book would only be a liability. Reston also suggested that Dona and Alexi stay the night in town. An evening escape from Exidgeon would be much simpler to arrange.

Reston still believed Everson to be the most likely suspect. The man had clearly been chafing under Reston's *de facto* leadership. But even as he suggested it, Reston shook his head. He just couldn't see Everson as willing to go to these extremes, even for all the advantages the book would grant. Regardless, Dona found having a name to pin on the man who had probably hijacked their carriage oddly comforting. Being suspicious of everyone was getting old.

The sun had been down for the better part of half an hour as Dona, Alexi, and Reston approached the Exidgeon gate. Dona and Alexi were mounted, while Reston was on foot.

"Stay here until I give the signal," Reston said. "Then head through the gate and down the ramp as fast as the horses will carry you."

"Wait," Dona said. "Won't we run a risk of trampling the Inquisitors?"

"I'll take care of that."

"And how can we be sure they won't recognize us?"

"Dona," Alexi said, holding a finger to his lips. "Shhh." Then he nodded to Reston. "We're ready."

Reston moved toward the gates and found a good vantage point. The Inquisitors were busy with a straggler—a wagon draped with strings of sausages and wheels of cheese clearly destined for the cafeteria. He settled down and waited. After about ten minutes, the wagon rolled past Dona and Alexi into the college.

The Inquisitors resumed their dice game at a small wooden table obviously confiscated from a nearby classroom.

"Slow night," Renrick said, stretching and taking his seat.

Travis threw the dice. "Yeah, for you."

Renrick chuckled as the dice settled. "Oh, I don't know about that—looks like your streak just ended." He grabbed the dice and gave them a toss. One of them shot off the table.

"Oh bother, not again." He got down on his knees in search of it. "I'm starting to think dice are a bad choice out here. How do you feel about checkers?" He finally located the cube and climbed back to his feet.

"Travis?"

Travis was still sitting in his chair, but his head now rested on the table.

Renrick shook him gently. "Hey, are you sick?"

Travis began to snore.

"Wow, now that's boredom. It's a good thing at least one of us has the stamina to actually get the job done."

A moment later, he was snoring too.

Reston stepped out, waved, and then melted back into the shadows. Dona and Alexi charged past. The Inquisitors didn't even stir.

. . . . .

Miranda lay on her bed trying to prepare for her geometry quiz. Geometry wasn't her strength on the best of days, but tonight she couldn't focus at all. Not only had Dona failed to return yet again, but now Helena was gone too, and neither had bothered to breathe so much as a whisper about where they were going. She was not accustomed to feeling like the odd man out, and she didn't like it one bit. With a sigh, she closed the textbook. It was no use—geometry was just not going to happen tonight. Instead she pulled out her journal, thinking she might feel better if she wrote a little about her frustration. Sitting on her bed with her knees pulled up, she began detailing her growing sense of abandonment, but the exercise only made her feel guilty for feeling that way.

There's probably a perfectly rational explanation that has nothing to do with me. Her eyes fell on Dona's stuffed bunny.

"All right, Mr. Lop Ears, what would I have to do to get you to tell me Dona's secret?"

Then she noticed the hope chest beneath the rabbit.

She had often wondered whether Dona kept a journal. She knew Helena did not, but most of the girls on the floor did.

She had never actually seen Dona writing in one, but then, Dona spent so much time at the library—maybe she wrote in it there.

Of course, she couldn't look. It would be an unpardonable breach of trust.

She closed her journal and opened the geometry text. Another half an hour passed before she slammed it closed in frustration. It was easily past ten o'clock, and there was still no sign of either roommate.

But what if Dona's in trouble? If I knew, maybe I could help, and if she's not, I could just forget I ever saw it—no harm done.

The stuffed rabbit seemed to mock her.

"That does it. Time for lights out." She reached up and turned the knob on the lamp.

Fifteen minutes later, the lamp was burning again. Dona's and Helena's beds were still empty.

Still arguing with herself, she retrieved the key from beneath the windowsill, tossed the rabbit on the bed, and turned the lock.

Mr. Lop Ears stared at her. She paused, but only long enough to throw a blanket over him.

She rummaged through the chest searching for anything remotely journal-like. At the top were several textbooks, including a large one wrapped in red fabric. Moving them out of her way, she spotted something that caught her attention. She peered through Dona's prized opera glasses with delight, recalling fondly the occasion of Gregory's gift. Digging deeper, she found a stash of old letters, which she set aside. Snooping through a journal was one thing, but reading private letters was another thing entirely. Deeper still, she found a mahogany box with a golden clasp. Undoing the clasp revealed an interior of black velvet, against which rested a stunning gold necklace set with crimson stones. Matching earrings were recessed into the velvet on either side.

"Pretty," she said, latching the box again, "but woefully out of fashion. No wonder she never wears those."

Next, she came upon the obligatory stacks of fabric, kerchiefs, doilies, cross stitch, and crochet work, bearing a variety of initials that no doubt identified several generations of needle workers. Beneath the fabric, she felt something solid—a small antique picture frame with a lifelike portrait of a woman with dark hair and fine features wearing the jewelry from the mahogany box. There was a distinct family resemblance.

At the bottom of the chest she discovered a stack of small books. Eagerly she pulled them out, but to her disappointment, they turned out to be a collection of fairy tales. Miranda smiled to herself. Of course Dona would never have let on about this collection, even to her. It seemed somehow too girly—an adjective Dona did her best to avoid in all things, with, perhaps, the solitary exception of Mr. Lop Ears.

Just to be sure she hadn't missed anything, she went back and inspected the textbooks. Most were the same ones Miranda had. The largest, however, the one in the red fabric cover, was entirely unfamiliar. She picked it up and peeked inside.

Practical Phrendonics?

"Oh," she said. "This must be the extra-credit project."

She paged through the book with increasing interest. After a few minutes, her position on the floor became uncomfortable, so she closed the chest and had a seat on top.

She started at the sound of Helena's voice drifting up through the open window:

"I had a wonderful time. I'm so glad you were free tonight."

Miranda leapt to her feet, opened the chest and stuffed the books back inside.

"I almost never get to go dancing," Helena said, "particularly not with someone who really can."

Miranda struggled to lock the trunk lid, only to find that the contents were piled a little too high. She tried sitting on it and *then* using the key, but still it didn't quite close.

"You are too kind, my lady. If I seemed accomplished, it was merely a faint reflection of your own elegance."

That voice. Miranda paused, trying to place it. "Alphonse?" Then her eyes widened. "*Alphonse?*"

She scrambled to the window.

Helena tittered. "You always know just the right thing to say."

"With such a muse, what man would not be inspired?"

"Oh, please," Miranda muttered.

"I would like nothing better than to stay and inspire you all night," Helena said, "but I have class early tomorrow. I hope we can do this again soon."

"The honor would be mine."

"Until then." She turned to enter the dormitory.

In a panic, Miranda rushed to the chest, threw it open, and frantically rearranged, but still, the lid would not close. She could hear Helena humming a waltz as she climbed the stairs.

Miranda attempted another hasty rearrangement, to no avail. In desperation, she removed the red-swathed book from the chest and stuffed it in her book bag. At last, the lid fell shut. She tucked the key back under the windowsill, climbed into bed, and reached for her journal. Then she noticed Mr. Lop Ears still hiding under the blanket on Dona's bed. She dashed over, plopped him in his usual spot on the hope chest, and then leapt back into bed, letting the extra blanket billow down over her. Just as the blanket settled, the door opened.

"Oh, you're still awake?" Helena asked.

"Just jotting a few notes in my journal. You're out late."

"Oh it *is* late, isn't it? I must have lost track of time."

"Out studying?"

"No, just ran into a friend."

"Oh? Anyone I know?"

Helena yawned and stretched. "Let's talk in the morning. I'd better get some sleep, or I'll never make it through geometry."

"Yes, let's *do* talk in the morning," Miranda said through clenched teeth.

Either Helena missed that nuance or she deliberately chose to ignore it.

hunting to distraction

Clattering plates, the sizzle of frying sausages, and the bawdy banter of young men seeking to one-up each other made sleeping in at the fraternity virtually impossible. Not by nature an early riser, Reston generally relied on that commotion to keep him punctual. Today, however, despite a restless night, he was wide-awake long before breakfast started. For an academic, few decisions were life-or-death, and the stress of Gregory's situation was taking its toll. In the end, he reasoned that an early morning was just the thing if he wanted to meet up with Dona and Alexi by eleven o'clock—and he wanted to be there even earlier if possible.

Alphonse wandered into the kitchen carrying a basket of eggs and whistling cheerily, prompting Reston to reflect, not for the first time, on just how annoying a true early bird could be.

"Good morning Professor," Alphonse said. "Package for you." He reached under his arm and tossed the package on the table. Still whistling, he set about stoking up the cooking fire. "Over easy, like usual?"

"Yes, thank you," Reston said as he examined the package. Labeled "Professor Clarke Reston, Urgent," there was nothing to indicate who had sent it or what it might contain. *Odd.* He couldn't recall ever having received anything at the fraternity before—all his correspondence generally went directly to his office.

He shook the package. It was small and light, but something solid slipped around inside. He shrugged, ripped open a corner, and immediately slammed it down on the table, covering the tear with his hand.

Alphonse looked over in alarm. "Are you all right, Professor?"

"Oh, I'm fine," Reston said, still awkwardly clamping his hand over the package, "but if these roaches get any worse, we'll have to start cleaning this kitchen more often."

"Eew," Alphonse said, though it was unclear if he was reacting to the idea of the roach or the cleaning.

Once Alphonse had gone back to cooking, Reston carefully slid the package inside his jacket. "I'll be back in a bit."

Alphonse nodded, still whistling.

Inside his room with the door safely closed, Reston pulled the package back out of his jacket. Bright golden light gleamed from the tear. Carefully he slipped the contents (a six-inch ruler and a note) out onto his bed. Only the ruler was glowing. He picked up the note.

> *Dear Professor,*
>
> *I seem to have misplaced several items similar to the one enclosed, and I was wondering if you could help me find them. They are:*
>
> > *A Blackboard Eraser*
> > *An Inkwell*

A Pointer
A Professor's Cap
A copy of Hargraf's 'A Brief History of Trifienne.'

They shouldn't be too hard to find, as I tend to lose things in plain sight. You may want to start with the inkwell. Last time I saw it was payday.

Sincerely,

Your secret admirer

P.S. You were right, passive charges are very useful. They become a bit unpredictable when combined with reservoirs though—which just goes to show, you never know when you are going to find something illuminating…

Reston reread the note with a growing sense of alarm. If he understood correctly, his 'admirer' was sending him on some sort of high-stakes scavenger hunt. Apparently, the writer had rigged specific plain-sight items so they could start glowing at any time—a result no doubt intended to attract the attention of the Inquisition. Not only that, but the items that would glow were those likely to be used by a professor—the inclusion of Hargraf's work pointing directly to a *history* professor. The ruler was no doubt included to prove his 'admirer' was making no idle threat.

Reston groaned. "Great. Just great."

He paced, considering his options. If he ignored the scavenger hunt to help Dona, and the note's author made good on the threat to "brighten" his day, the Inquisition would have a roadmap leading directly to his doorstep. On the other hand, if he embarked on this scavenger hunt and tried to neutralize all the items before they lit up, he might not make it into town in time to help Dona—no doubt the whole point.

After several minutes of wracking his brain, he still saw no way out—the trap was airtight. He grabbed pen and parchment and jotted a quick note:

> *Complications. May be late. If I am, start without me.*

> *Reston*

Perhaps he could get one of the fraternity members to deliver it to Tamry, assuming he hadn't already left. He had a sinking feeling he might not get the chance to deliver it personally.

. . . . .

Miranda had slept almost not at all. The more she thought about Helena pursuing Alphonse behind her back, the more she smoldered. To make matters worse, Dona could show up at any moment to start work on her extra credit project, only to find that it had gone missing. She really didn't relish having to explain how it happened to find its way into her book bag.

When Helena asked if she was going to geometry class, Miranda merely grunted and put her pillow over her head. Not only was Helena the last person she wanted to go to class with today, she needed her to leave so she could sneak Dona's book back into its usual spot.

Having a plan in place made her feel better, at least with respect to Dona's project. What she didn't count on was falling asleep waiting for Helena to leave. The sun was much higher in the sky by the time she woke.

She leapt out of bed. "Oh no," she cried, "the quiz." She threw on some clothes, grabbed her book bag, and rushed out the door.

"Morning, Miss Maxtine," she said to her house mother as she hurtled past her down the stairs.

. . . . .

"Gracious!" Miss Maxtine said as she side-stepped Miranda. By the time she recovered enough to greet her in return, the girl had already disappeared out the front door.

"I suspect that one may be late for class. Now, as I was saying, Mr. Mathers, this whole procedure strikes me as unnecessarily severe. If Dona's library book is overdue, why not just assess a fine and wait for her to return it?"

The man, who had paused to watch as Miranda flew past, turned to face Miss Maxtine, revealing a painful-looking gash on his cheek still in the early stages of healing.

"Under normal circumstances, that's exactly what we would do," he said, "but these are not normal circumstances. This book is incredibly rare and should never have been loaned out in the first place. That's what we get for employing students instead of hiring trained professionals to operate our library. The student librarian has been disciplined, and a library-wide meeting held to ensure this sort of thing does not happen again."

They arrived at Dona's room, and Miss Maxtine turned the key in the lock. "But why not just ask her to return the book?"

"Oh, believe me, I tried to reason with her, but she apparently feels entitled to keep it. It's been over a week now. I assure you, obtaining the warrant from Chancellor Wiggins was a last resort."

"Well, if it's still not technically overdue, I can see where you might have run into trouble. Dona can be stubborn if she feels she's in the right. Still, couldn't you just wait until this book *is* overdue? She might not feel entitled to keep it then."

The man shook his head. "Unfortunately, this book is irreplaceable. You'll see from the documentation that Chancellor Wiggins agrees."

"If it's all the same to you, I'd like to remain present during the search."

"Of course. This should only take a few minutes."

. . . . .

The small stone structure that was the Bursar's Office dated from the earliest days of the University. It was obscured by a layer of ivy so thick it looked more like a hedge than a building. Reston was praying this was the right place—the clue was far from conclusive. Randolph Brent was responsible both for collecting fees from students and for paying Exidgeon's debts, including the salaries of the professors. Brent, a prim gentleman, whose high forehead was framed by a receding gray hairline and an incongruous pair of jet-black eyebrows, was almost as much an institution as the building itself. Although now bowed with age, he was sharp as ever. In fact, he was so reliable, most people didn't even bother to check the amount of their pay. From long experience, they simply assumed it would be correct.

Brent spent much of his time going over the books at a tall table with a tilted top. It was high enough that it allowed him to do much of his work standing, though in recent years, it was more common for him to use a tall stool. He was perched on the stool as Reston entered.

Brent stopped moving his quill to peer at Reston over his reading glasses. "Good morning, Professor. What can I do for you?"

A quick scan of the office confirmed what Reston had remembered about the place—the room contained multiple desks to accommodate Brent's assistants, and each held its own inkwell. Today only Brent's desk was occupied. Unfortunately, if the inkwell he needed was here, as suggested by the 'payday' clue, he had no way to identify which one it was. But maybe there was another way…

"Good morning," Reston said. "I'm trying to track down Professor Everson. Have you by chance seen him?"

"As a matter of fact, I have. He was in half an hour ago. He mentioned someone might be looking for him. Even left a note."

"May I see it?"

Brent reached under his desk. "Sure thing,"

"I appreciate it." Reston said. He started to open the note, but then he remembered what happened when he'd opened the package. Instead he stepped outside and scanned the area first to be sure no one was nearby.

Fortunately, the note displayed no special properties.

> *Dear Professor,*
>
> *Congratulations! I trust you have located that pesky inkwell and are now ready to move on to the next item. Sadly, the details of our lives are written in ink, not in chalk. I suspect by now you may be wishing the mistakes of your life could be as easily erased as the mistakes in your lectures…*

Reston frowned. This note gave him no clues for identifying the problematic inkwell. If he were Everson, which one would he pick? Brent's own inkwell would likely pose the greatest challenge. In any case, it was the only one that stood out.

He popped back into the Bursar's office.

Brent looked up. "Back so soon?"

"I was wondering if I might leave a note for Professor Everson, in case he comes back."

"Of course."

Reston approached his desk and indicated the quill. "May I?"

Brent looked at him for a long moment, as if he were a child asking a question he didn't know was rude.

"If you must." He grudgingly handed it over.

"You wouldn't happen to have any paper I could borrow?"

Brent sighed and handed Reston a blank piece of parchment from a stack on the far side of the desk.

"Thank you so much."

Brent waited patiently as Reston wrote.

After scrawling a few words, Reston stopped and looked at him askance. "Would you mind? This is private."

Brent shook his head and closed the book he had been working on. "I was due for a break anyway." He left his desk and rummaged in the back portion of the office, quietly bemoaning the lack of social awareness so prevalent in younger generations.

Reston didn't waste his opportunity. Now that he'd narrowed the inkwell to a single candidate, he focused all his attention on it, muttering beneath his breath. Nothing happened—it wasn't the right one.

"Oh, I'm so sorry," Reston called out. "How rude of me. I bet Professor Everson had the manners to write his note somewhere other than at your desk."

"As a matter of fact, he did."

"I can certainly do the same, then. Where did he write his note?"

Brent stood blinking in disbelief.

"Which table? Where did Professor Everson write his note?"

"If you must know, it was that one there. Not that it actually helps me if you move, since you are still in possession of my quill."

Reston took a seat at the indicated table. "Oh, so I am. Sorry about that. I'll just be one minute more." He positioned himself to block Brent's view and concentrated on the inkwell. For an instant, almost too brief to notice, the inkwell flashed a dark shade of violet.

Eureka. Reston slipped the inkwell into his pocket.

Brent had resumed his perch atop the stool and was waiting, arms folded. Reston handed him the quill. "Thanks so much for all your help." He turned to leave.

"Just a minute, Professor."

Reston halted mid-stride. "Yes?"

"Didn't you want to leave the note?"

"Thanks, but I've just thought of an even quicker way to contact him."

Brent stared openmouthed as Reston headed for the door.

Once outside, Reston pulled out Everson's note. Presumably he was intended to locate the eraser next. Unfortunately, this note was even less clear about where to start than the first had been. Reading it again, he felt his hackles rise at the implication that his lectures were error-prone. In fact, since he favored a Socratic approach, he rarely even used the blackboard, which Everson knew full well.

That must be it. He started for his next destination at a jog, just as the Exidgeon clock tower struck nine.

He was relieved to find the classroom empty. Obviously,

though, he'd come to the right place. It wasn't merely the overabundance of erasers on the chalkboard ledges that tipped him off—it was the next clue scrawled in chalk on the room's central board:

> *Dear Professor,*
>
> *I have complete faith in your ability to determine that one of these things is not like the others. However, your ability is not at issue—it's your propensity for flagrant disregard of time-honored tradition. Loyalty, sir, like the heart, shows to best advantage on one's sleeve—but only when it's neatly pressed. Contempt for the uniform is contempt for the institution. Once permitted to take root, such institutional disrespect multiplies geometrically. Before it's too late, save both yourself and our way of life—consult the expert.*

Reston scanned the room to be sure he'd spotted all the erasers. Scratching his head, he considered his options. All of them were standard university issue. He really didn't want to expend the time or effort it would take to test each one, and he didn't know of an easy way to test them as a group. He picked one at random and erased the message. Next, he took a seat to examine the eraser carefully and to ponder a bit more how to tell what might set one apart from the others.

After a minute or so, he burst out laughing. He was going to have to take pains to not let Everson misdirect him in the future—he had almost wasted valuable time solving a pointless puzzle. Still chuckling, he went about the room collecting up all the erasers. Carrying all eight proved to be too awkward. Setting them on the podium, he grabbed the Exidgeon banner and yanked it off the wall.

Maybe Everson is right about me after all.

He piled the erasers in the middle of the banner and tied the corners to make a crude bag. Since he was making good time, he decided to risk dropping the items off at his office. He didn't trust anywhere else to be safe.

Besides, he now had a good idea where he was going next, and his office was on the way. The clues hadn't been all that difficult—at least so far. Likely, Everson intended only to delay him, since, by exposing the Society, he also ran the risk of exposing himself. That made it a race—so long as Reston solved the puzzles quickly, there was a chance he could still make the rendezvous.

Arriving at his office, Reston stuffed the bag of erasers in a cabinet. As he pulled out the inkwell, he noticed a sizable stain had appeared near his pocket. While he inspected the stain, the inkwell, of its own accord, began emitting a soft golden glow.

Reston blinked in shock. *He really did it. Thank heavens I took him seriously.* With the threat confirmed, there was no time to lose. He tossed the inkwell into a drawer and headed for his next destination.

Geometry professor Bartholomew Driessen was well known as a stickler for detail. The joke around the University was that Driessen wasn't satisfied with merely dotting every 'i' and crossing every 't'—he wasn't happy until he'd gone back and dotted the 't's and crossed the 'i's as well.

Reston and Driessen were oil and water. Driessen was vocal in his disdain for Reston's casual approach to both classroom attire and University policy. Reston, for his part, made no secret of his opinions on Driessen's inflexibility and inability to connect with students on any level.

Everson's rant had immediately brought Driessen to mind. It was entirely possible he'd been quoting Driessen directly. Although that made it easier to decide where to look next, Reston shuddered at the hopelessness of gaining any meaningful cooperation, particularly if, as he suspected, the clues were pointing to Driessen's professor's cap.

Finding Driessen's office wasn't difficult—all the mathematicians were housed in the same building. Unfortunately, Driessen wasn't in. After several inquiries, he learned Driessen was teaching class. Several more inquiries, and he had a classroom location as well. On the way, the clock tower chimed ten. He had to hurry.

The door to the classroom was open as Reston approached, likely due to the unseasonable warmth. To his relief, Driessen wasn't actively lecturing, but instead seemed to be proctoring an examination. Predictably, he was pacing the aisles in full Exidgeon regalia, including both the robe and the hat. Despite the heat, the robe was buttoned up tight against the man's double chin. It made him look like he was choking. Little rivulets of sweat only added to the effect.

Reston had no interest in interacting with the man unless it was absolutely necessary. Since all the students were agonizing over the examination, and Driessen himself couldn't see his own hat, he decided to risk a test. When Driessen's hat turned fleetingly violet, Reston was the only one to see it.

He was in the right place, but he still had no plan for getting Driessen's hat away from him. He spent several minutes trying to devise clever ways to encourage him to part with the thing. He considered simply asking to borrow it, but given their relationship, his chances were slim at best. Since he wasn't wearing his own academic garb, Driessen was unlikely to believe he needed to use the hat for an important meeting.

And then he had it. Everson had done it to him again—he didn't actually need to *collect* the hat—all he had to do was make certain it didn't glow. Since he had identified the proper target, he could instead Dispel Everson's handiwork. It would be hard to tell whether such a Dispel had succeeded, but in this case, he need only repeat his test and look for a negative result, like the one he'd gotten with Brent's inkwell.

He could think of no reason it shouldn't work. He waited for Driessen to come into sight and concentrated, working through the complicated mnemonics under his breath.

Unfortunately, while he was doing so, Driessen spotted him and pulled the door closed, leaving Reston unable to confirm his handiwork. Even more problematic—he still hadn't found the clue to lead him to the next item.

Of course, he could go outside and check whether the window was open, but that would be pretty obvious to both Driessen and the class. If only he had gotten the next clue—then if the hat lit up, Driessen could experience firsthand the rapture of his precious university protocols—as exacted by relentlessly efficient Inquisitors. Tempting, but he couldn't do it. Not even Driessen deserved that.

He had no choice—he was going to have to engage the man. He steeled himself to knock on the classroom door, but before he had a chance, the door burst open. Students rushed out in a steady stream. To his surprise, not a single student remained seated. He should have guessed. There was no explicit provision in the university protocols for allowing students extra time, so of course Driessen would never think to permit it.

Reston worked his way upstream through grim-faced students. Driessen was at the front of the room, straightening stacks of exams.

"Ahh, Reston," he said, fixing him with his tiny wide-set eyes. "I noticed you lurking outside. To what do I owe the honor?"

"I'm trying to track down Professor Everson. Have you seen him this morning?"

"Briefly. He blindsided me at breakfast, or I might have managed to avoid him. Effective technique, blindsiding, though perhaps not as effective as cornering someone in a classroom."

Reston bit back bile. "I apologize for the inconvenience, but did he happen to leave a message with you?"

Driessen snorted. "He tried to. Of course, I refused. I have plenty of legitimate things to occupy my time without becoming a delivery service for ne'er-do-well faculty."

"What happened to the note, then?"

"I have no idea. After observing that both his legs appeared intact, I suggested he might consider delivering it himself."

"Did he say anything else?"

"He said something like 'you'll do nicely,' and then, he laughed—impertinently, I might add. You'd think the junior faculty would show a little respect for their superiors."

"Professor Everson does have tenure, you know. Shouldn't that bump him out of the 'junior faculty' category?"

Driessen grimaced. "Don't remind me. The shoddiness in tenure decisions of late is surpassed only by the committee's utter ineptitude in making recent hires–oh, no offense, there, Reston."

Reston bit his tongue. "So you think granting Everson tenure was ill-advised?"

"Obviously. Precious few of these junior faculty show any loyalty at all to the institution that pays their salaries. I wrote a note opposing his tenure, but the committee ignored me.

Just you wait. I'll be vindicated one of these days, same as I was with Shoruga."

Reston struggled to recall where he'd heard that name before. "Shoruga?"

"Yes, the committee awarded him tenure as well, once again over my strenuous objections. Can you imagine? They gave him tenure, and he could barely even speak the language. I bet they're all kicking themselves now."

"Why's that?"

"Because he's a traitor of course. Haven't you heard? The Inquisition took him into custody for selling military secrets to heretics. It's a total fiasco for the Hathaways. People are saying the Crown may pull their funding over this. And it was completely preventable, if only they had exercised an iota of judgment in making their tenure decisions. But I'm not one to say 'I told you so.'"

"Do we know anything about the identities of these heretics?"

"Nothing," Driessen said. "But I'm sure it's just a matter of time before the Inquisition gets it out of him. Thank goodness they nabbed him when they did."

As unexpectedly fascinating as the conversation had become, Reston was running out of time. He would have to pick Driessen's brain later. Now, he needed that next clue.

"Did Everson say anything else?"

"Only that perhaps he could get someone at the library to deliver his message. I wished him luck with that, seeing as how, since Mathers isn't blind, he's likely to be able to spot two functional legs as well as the next man."

"Thank you for your time, Professor, you've been very helpful."

Driessen smiled. It was something Reston had never seen before. He found it more than a little unsettling.

"You know, there still might be hope for you, Reston."

"Why, thank you, Professor."

"But not if you insist on wearing rags like that to work. Good lord, is that an ink stain?"

Reston backed toward the door. "You are absolutely right, Professor. It *is* an ink stain. I'll have it laundered straight away."

Once safely in the hallway, he pulled the door closed.

Behind him someone spoke his name. "Professor Reston? Do you have a moment?"

He turned to see Miranda Connelly, nervously clutching her book bag. The morning light bouncing off her golden curls combined with her melancholy expression made her look remarkably like one of those martyr statues he'd seen in churches.

"As it turns out, I am in a bit of a hurry."

"Just one quick question?"

She looked so plaintive Reston couldn't refuse.

"Very well, Miss Connelly, what is it?"

"It's about Dona's extra credit project. I was wondering, if for some reason she didn't finish it, how much would it affect her grade?"

"Excuse me, Reston," Driessen said, emerging from the classroom carrying the bundled exams.

"Oh, pardon me," Reston said, stepping out of his way. "I'm sorry, Miss Connelly, what extra credit project?"

Reston stole glances at Driessen's hat as it bobbed off, painfully aware he was losing his opportunity to check whether it still posed a threat.

"You know—the one she's doing on *Practical Phrendonics*."

Miranda now had his full attention. He couldn't imagine why Dona would have told Miranda about the book, much less fabricated a story about an extra credit project. Even more disturbing was the fact that Dona had not told him that she'd done so. How many others had she told this?

"May I ask why you ask?"

"I…I was just trying to decide if I should do an extra credit project too. How much do they affect your grade?"

"That depends on the project."

"One like Dona's, then."

Reston heard the door at the end of the hallway slam as Driessen, and his hat, left the building. His gut told him something important was happening here, but now was not the time to figure it out.

"I'm not at liberty to discuss Miss Merinne's grade, but if you'd like to do a similar project, we can certainly explore that. Can we discuss it after class tomorrow?"

Miranda's face fell. "Of course, Professor. Thank you for your time."

Reston smiled reassuringly. "I'll see you tomorrow then."

He scurried after Driessen as quickly as he could without drawing undue attention. It took fifteen minutes to track Driessen to a place where he could safely confirm the hat had indeed been deactivated. The pressure was mounting. It was almost eleven, and he still had two items remaining. His only clue was that Everson had mentioned the library. As clues go, it wasn't much, but when he stopped to consider one of the remaining items on his list was the Hargraf history text, checking the library made perfect sense.

The library was bustling. Reston was no stranger to these halls. Indeed, the history wing was fast becoming a second home. He needed no assistance locating the shelves bearing tomes on local history, and it took him only a few minutes more to find the Hargraf work, present in three copies on a shelf at eye level. He had a feeling that he'd be able to identify the correct one easily, since, if Everson were true to form, it should contain the next clue. He pulled the first one off the shelf, cracked it open, and breathed a sigh of relief. It held a folded piece of parchment:

> *Well done, Professor!*
>
> *I certainly hope that unpleasant things have not come to light during your investigations. What things, you ask? Aren't they obvious? No? Well, perhaps not yet, but soon you may find that at least one of those things will come home to roost. I sincerely hope you see my point before it is too late..."*
>
> *1 of 4*

He huffed. No doubt Everson thought the 'light' wordplay very clever, but on the whole, the clue was less than illuminating. Then he noticed something he'd missed on the first read-through. He pulled out the previous notes to compare. None of them had page numbers. Was the clue unclear because he only had a fragment? But if there were other fragments, why weren't they in the book? Then his eyes lit on the other copies still remaining on the shelf.

"Oh, I don't believe this."

He pulled down the second copy and threw open the cover. A second piece of parchment fell out and drifted to the floor. The third book held a third parchment. He scooped up the second note:

> *...and speaking of roosts, Professor, whatever was the point of letting that little girl make off with a priceless piece of history? Imagine the damage if the wrong people found where 'that'*

had gone home to roost? I hope you finally see
this point as well…

2 of 4

Reston unfolded the third parchment:

…and while we're at it, Professor, have you
given any thought to where this whole ugly
business will ultimately come home to roost?
Bigger heads than yours are on the block—a
final point that certainly bears illuminating…

3 of 4

Reston scanned the shelf again, but there was no sign of a fourth Hargraf book. He quickly leafed through the other books on the shelf, but no additional parchments revealed themselves. He rubbed his eyes in frustration, trying to decide his next move.

Did these clues suggest there were four pointers as well as four books? If so, Reston decided that not all of them could be rigged to light up. Each would require a light spell and a passive charge, with each spell taking substantial effort to generate. At his level of expertise, even if Everson had done only the minimum on each item, by the time he managed three or four, he should have been completely drained. So far, only the ruler and the inkwell had actually glowed. The hat had tested positive, but that didn't necessarily mean it would light up—only that it had at least one spell from the proper category. Either Everson was taking shortcuts, or at most, only one of each of the items could possibly be a risk. Indeed, once Everson established he was able to carry through on his threat, there was no longer any reason to do so. If even one of the Hargraf books might light, he'd be forced to check out all of them. In that way, Everson could maximize the time Reston spent delayed, while minimizing his own effort.

Knowing Everson, Reston expected only the barest minimum. That suggested none of the rest of the items was a threat. He was sorely tempted to abandon this diversion entirely, but he couldn't quite muster the confidence to carry through. He gathered up the three copies of Hargraf's history and rushed off.

Mathers raised an eyebrow at checking out three copies of the same book, but Reston's status prevented any arguments. It took another ten minutes, but Mathers was able to confirm the library only stocked three copies of the Hargraf books. Unless Everson had supplied his own copy, it was looking like the fourth page was simply another misdirection. That meshed well with the third clue stating it was making a 'final point.' As he stepped out of the library, the clock tower chimed eleven. He had thirty minutes to complete the hunt for there to be any chance of meeting Dona as promised.

The note made mention of three locations. The first was his home, currently the fraternity. The second was Dona's home, presumably her dormitory. The third was a little more nebulous. In a broad sense, if the heresy were discovered, those who ran the University would likely take some heat, with the Chancellor foremost among them. He wasn't certain, however, whether the difficulty would "come home to roost" for the Chancellor at his office or at his home, and he definitely didn't have time to check out both. In fact, he didn't think he'd have time to check out either.

Although he would have preferred to check the dormitory first, the fact that he was carrying three books, any of which could draw unwanted attention at any moment, was strong incentive to make the fraternity his first stop. He started off in that direction at a brisk walk. If he could just keep up this pace a little longer, he might still finish in time. As the fraternity came into sight, however, Reston noticed a small crowd of students gathered in the front yard under an ancient oak, staring up into its gnarled branches. On closer inspection, Reston made out a student climbing among those branches, while the others shouted encouragement. Just out of the climber's reach, a wooden pointer dangled, of the sort normally used by professors while teaching. It was in every way a standard pointer—except that it glowed with a pale golden light.

Reston sighed. *Looks like I'm going to be a little late.*

CHAPTER TWELVE

A SHOW OF FORCE

Dona paced the plush red carpet of the brothel's vestibule with a growing sense of desperation.

"Where is he? It's almost time to leave."

"He'll be here," Tamry said. "Reston is a man of his word."

"Perhaps he was detained at the gate?" Amberton suggested. "All it would take is a large group arriving there before he tried to get through."

"It doesn't matter why he's not here," Alexi said. "He's not, and we'll just have to make do. Professor Tamry, would you be willing to take his place?"

Tamry looked ill-at-ease. "I will if I must, but I don't pretend to have Reston's expertise. The best I could do is take Everson down and sit on him, but that's only if I get hold of him. I wouldn't have a prayer of catching him if he saw me coming, and I'm unlikely to go unnoticed."

Alexi turned to Amberton. "How about you, Professor?"

"Don't look at me—I can't manage most of Reston's little tricks yet either, and I'm certainly not equipped to play the part of hired muscle."

"Well then, how do you geniuses suggest we capture him?" Dona asked. "I can't just wander out there, hand him a fake, and wave goodbye as he goes on his merry way. There's no telling what he'd do to Gregory then."

Alexi shook his head. "I told you we should have brought the real thing with us."

"We could try to follow him once he has the fake," Tamry suggested.

"That plan is great, as long as we don't lose him," Alexi said, "which is no doubt why he wanted to meet in the market. Plus, if he sees us, he might not lead us back to Gregory at all."

Tilly appeared in the doorway. "Is it just muscle you need?"

Alexi shrugged. "I don't think we have a plan without it."

"Let me ask Jeorg if he's game. I think he will be. It's been pretty tame around here lately, and he's easily bored."

Dona threw her arms around her. "Thank you so much. You're a lifesaver."

"You're most welcome, dear. I only hope it's enough."

. . . . .

Dona adjusted her satchel over her arm and moved to the next booth to check out the selection of herbs. The sweet scent of basil made her nostalgic for home, where she had been free to experiment with new recipes. That wasn't possible in the dormitory, and the cafeteria couldn't compare. She often wondered whether the cafeteria cooks had ever even seen an herb.

Jeorg shadowed her expertly. He somehow managed it in a way that wasn't obvious, even to her. Despite that, she was beginning to wonder whether Everson had discovered them, though if he had, she had no idea how. It was already twenty-five minutes past noon, and there was still no sign of him. With the addition of Jeorg to the plan, it had been agreed that even Alexi should keep a fair distance on the off chance Everson might recognize him. Dona resolved to find a way to properly thank Tilly once this was all over. She had no idea what they would have done without her help.

Dona checked out the wares at several more booths, but still there was no sign of Everson. She took a seat on a bench to examine the ransom note yet another time. She looked for double meanings, held the note up to the light for hidden messages, even tried reading it backwards, all to no avail. Was this whole thing some sort of mean-spirited joke?

Pounding hooves in the distance caught her attention. Although horses in the market were not particularly unusual, riding the animals at a gallop was. People started exchanging nervous glances as the horse drew closer.

Jeorg seemed to suspect something as well and drifted closer. Still the hoofbeats rumbled. In the distance, the sea of market-goers parted as horse and rider bore down on them. He seemed to be keeping to one of the major thoroughfares. If it was Everson, he would have no chance of knowing where she was. She glanced around again for accomplices, but no one seemed to have the slightest interest in her—everyone was fixated on the horseman.

He was close enough now that she could make out he wore some sort of sheet or bag over his head. Other than that, his clothing was nondescript—he could have been anyone else in the crowd. Two young boys startled her by jumping on her bench for a better look, prompting a scolding from their mother.

The horseman approached his closest point, keeping to a trajectory that would take him right on past. Just as Dona sighed in relief, her satchel lofted itself off the bench and flew through the air towards the horseman. It knocked one woman to the ground and grazed several others before it finally plastered itself against the horseman's saddle. As Dona stood gaping, the horseman disappeared into the distance, taking her satchel with him.

By the time Dona had established that the woman wasn't hurt, Alexi had found her.

His face was a mask of concern. "Are you all right? Did he hurt you?"

"I'm fine," she said. "How did he *do* that?"

Alexi shook his head. "I don't know. We had better find Reston."

"No, not Reston, we need to find Gregory. There's no telling what Everson will do when he discovers the fake."

"I'd like nothing better, but I have no idea where to look. At least I know where to look for Reston, and maybe he can figure out what we're up against."

"Yeah," Dona said. "He's been such a big help so far."

"He must have gotten waylaid."

"Yes, and no doubt if he kicked you in the teeth, he'd only be doing it for your own good."

"At least hear him out."

"No offense, but the hero worship is getting a little ridiculous. You go ahead and run crying to Reston every time you need to sneeze if that's what makes you happy, but I'm going to get to the bottom of this."

"We're more effective if we stay together."

"Then by all means, come along. Who knows? It might do you good to take a step on your own for a change."

Alexi shook his head. "I have a bad feeling about this."

"It can't possibly be worse than the one you should have had about our last plan."

Alexi sighed. "Let me talk to Tamry and Amberton first. They can find Reston and fill him in."

"You have five minutes."

. . . . .

The Monsignor paused at the rectory door. The old man seated on the garden bench beside the fountain looked serene enough, his eyes closed, drinking in the garden sounds. But the man's restful exterior didn't fool him. The Monsignor knew perhaps better than anyone that this man's mind was never at rest. Never. And while his goals were generally laudable, his methods frequently were not.

The Primal spoke without opening his eyes. "Armand, is that you?"

The Monsignor stepped into the courtyard. "I'm here, Your Primacy."

"Thank you for coming so quickly."

"I don't often get an urgent summons from the Primal. I thought it best to take it seriously."

"The summons wasn't professional. It was personal."

"Oh?"

The Primal finally opened his eyes. "Well, mostly personal anyway." He stood and opened his arms. "It's good to see you."

The Monsignor returned the embrace. "It's good to see you too, Darron."

"I've been doing some thinking. It's time we put our differences behind us."

"I'm all for that," the Monsignor said. "Forgive me for asking, but why the sudden change of heart?"

The Primal became somber. "Because I don't have much time left."

"Oh, stop being melodramatic. You're sixty three."

"I'm not saying I'm old. I'm telling you I'm dying."

The Monsignor paled. "Dying?"

"Something is eating away at my brain. Laitrech can give you the details if you want them, but the important thing is that I probably only have a few months left."

The Monsignor's brow knitted. "Is there nothing Laitrech can do?"

"He's trying, but he ascended to Ordinal not that long ago. Apparently, even for an Ordinal, this kind of healing is a complicated business—it takes years of training and practice, not to mention aptitude. Unfortunately, these were not traits I considered when making Ordinal appointments. So you see, you could say it's at least partially my fault that I find myself in this situation, which brings me to my next topic…"

The Monsignor sighed. "Oh, here it comes."

"…I'd like to raise you to Ordinal."

"Oh Darron, please. Not this again."

"This time, I'm determined. I won't get another chance."

"You say that as though you have one now, and you don't. Last I heard all the Ordinal positions were filled."

"Since when have I let minor technicalities keep me from achieving my vision?"

"You can't just dismiss an Ordinal. They're appointed for life."

"You never know when one might resign, though."

"You can't possibly think I'd condone such an outrageous abuse of authority."

Darron sighed. "No, of course not. You always did insist on doing things the hard way."

"When the hard way happens also to be the right way, I did and do."

"Sometimes the difference between right and wrong is not so clear-cut. Wouldn't what you are calling the wrong way suddenly become the right way if said Ordinal were abusing his position?"

"One of the Ordinals is abusing his position?"

Darron winked. "I don't know, but we could certainly check."

"Um, I think that would still be the wrong way."

"Where is it written that an investigation must only be undertaken when it's inconvenient? Would you seriously forgo one of your little Inquisitions just because the suspect happened to be a political rival?"

"I would refer the investigation to someone who didn't have a conflict of interest."

"An easy out, since we have an abundance of Inquisitors. As it happens, there's only one Primal."

Armand snorted. "Believe me, one is plenty."

"Fine, I'll grant you your concerns about a conflict of interest, and I'm in no condition to conduct an investigation anyway. Would you be more amenable if I assigned the investigation to someone with impeccable credentials, if you could be certain he didn't have a conflict of interest?"

"And who could you possibly think would fill that bill?"

Darron grinned. "Why, you, of course. Think about it—you're perfect. You run investigations all the time, and since you adamantly don't want the position, if anything, you'd have incentive to *not* find corruption."

"That doesn't work either. What if I turned a blind eye to the corruption just to avoid the having to take the position?"

"That's why you're perfect. We both know that if you found any corruption, you'd have to report it—it's one of those little inconveniences that goes along with insisting on doing things the hard way."

"You mean the right way."

"Whatever."

The Monsignor let out a long, exasperated sigh. "All right, now you're just baiting me. We both know how it would look if I initiated an investigation that resulted in the resignation of an Ordinal, only to take his place. I want no part of it."

"Hmph, I expected as much. Allow me, then, to suggest a slightly more radical alternative."

"*More* radical?"

"I thought you'd never ask. Since I expected you might be a little reluctant to replace a sitting Ordinal, I looked into whether I could simply appoint a new one. As it turns out, there's nothing in the Canons that specifically forbids it."

"That's absurd. Everything in the Canons concerning Ordinals refers to them as 'the Nine.' It's implicit."

"Won't the scribes be pleased. 'The Ten' is fully one letter shorter."

"You can't just change the Canons on a whim. You'll only end up undercutting your own authority."

"The good news is I probably won't live to see it."

"Why do you want this so badly, anyway?"

Darron paused. "It's funny. You don't actually pay much attention to your legacy until you realize it's all you have left. As Primals go, I was a good one. But I appointed Ordinals out of expedience. I'll even admit that in the past, when I twisted your arm, I did it more because you were my brother than for your strength of character. And now, when I am gone, this same group of shiftless, self-absorbed miscreants will select my replacement, in all likelihood, using the same flawed, self-serving criteria that I used in selecting them. Once that happens, all my accomplishments are moot."

"Aren't you being a little hard on yourself? I thought you were happy with Laitrech."

The old man shook his head. "I was merely lucky with Laitrech. Even he, I chose for political reasons."

"You only appointed five out of the nine. It's not like if they choose poorly, it's entirely your fault."

"You're not following. It's not about blame, it's about keeping the Church on the course I, or rather *we,* have charted. You saw what things were like in our father's time. We're by no means perfect, but we've come a long way since then. I'm not so naïve to think I can undo all the damage I've done, but with your appointment, I can at least give the body of Ordinals a conscience."

The Monsignor nodded. "I do feel for you. But your calling is not my calling. This appointment adds only one voice to the nine already there. If what you say is true, a 'conscience' will only serve to annoy them, not sway them, and it's an empty life whose sole purpose is to annoy others. Not only that, but if my 'strength of character' did have any persuasive effect, it would be nullified by the circumstance of inventing a new position that reeks of nepotism. No one listens to a dirty conscience."

"I think you underestimate your powers of persuasion. And no one in his right mind would question your qualifications, regardless of the circumstances of your appointment."

"You're not listening," the Monsignor said. "I'm not interested."

"Armand, don't force my hand. I'm desperate."

"You're too late. The damage is already done, and I can't fix it this time."

"I was hoping it wouldn't come to this."

The Monsignor sighed. "It's just like we never grew up, isn't it? Here's the part where you get petulant and start threatening me."

"Don't be silly. I was merely going to point out how fortunate you were, given that there are positions open that are far less desirable than that of Ordinal. For example, the Abbot at the monastery of Saint Sophia of the Triad has a position open for an assistant. It seems the last one went missing. They are hoping he simply had a change of heart about his calling, and that his disappearance has nothing whatsoever to do with a local band of marauding Drewors."

The Monsignor shook his head. "If you want to send me there, then send me there."

"Actually, I was thinking perhaps it might be a better fit for Thurman."

CHAPTER THIRTEEN

Lost and Found

Alexi had to hurry to keep up. "Where are we going again?"

He was convinced Dona was at her most exasperating when she got into these dictatorial moods. She'd asked directions that were leading them into sections of town with which he was increasingly unfamiliar.

"For the third time, the Expatriate Hotel."

"Let me rephrase. *Why* are we going there?"

"To find someone who might actually be able to help."

"And who might that be?"

"Someone who might actually be able to keep an appointment."

"So, you're not going to tell me?"

"No."

"Why not?"

"Because I have no interest in arguing about it."

"Which can only mean you think this is a bad idea, and you just don't want me to point it out."

"No. It's because no matter what the decision is, you'd still insist on debating it."

"And that's a bad thing?"

"It is when time is of the essence…ah, there it is."

They had come over a rise in a rough neighborhood near the riverfront. Below them, wooden ships docked at long piers extending out into the deeper parts of the river. Burly longshoremen bustled about like ants, moving the merchants' cargoes. A stunning marble-faced span reached out across the water. In its center, a raised drawbridge allowed passage of a high-masted ship. The far end prodded a behemoth mound, an island that rose from the depths, looking for all the world like the shell of some great prehistoric tortoise. Where bridge and island met, a charming stone building stood, its castle-like towers draped in scarlet banners that proclaimed "The Expatriate."

"Is that the Artists' Colony?" Alexi asked.

"I think it must be."

"How do we get down there?"

Dona shrugged. "Trial and error, I suppose. It doesn't look straightforward, does it?"

After several false starts, they happened across a path that took them down to the wharf. From there it was easy to reach the bridge. By then, the drawbridge had closed, granting them passage. The bridge was an artistic delight. Sculptures in bronze and marble of nearly anything imaginable were displayed along its length, from realistic pigeons, to human torsos, to completely abstract forms. Leaning a little out over the marble parapet, Dona discovered a series of bas-relief panels sporting mythological themes. She was already captivated, and she hadn't even set foot on the island.

The Expatriate loomed before them, looking much larger in person than it had from across the river. Dona suddenly felt underdressed. Apparently, patrons viewed searching for artists as a formal event. When she thought about it, it made sense—to some extent, the artists here would have their pick of patrons, and, for many artists, that meant the richer the better. A slovenly patron wouldn't stand as much chance of landing a worthy artist.

From where they stood, the island seemed little more than a great expanse of parks, ponds, gardens and fountains. A cluster of buildings resembling a village perched atop a hill, likely housing galleries, shops, and studios. The landscape was dotted with paint-spattered artists, their easels and canvases in tow, supposedly intent on capturing the island's essence. While a few focused on their work, most seemed more preoccupied with catching the eye of a wandering patron.

"This is all very interesting," Alexi said, "but what does it have to do with Gregory?"

Dona pushed open a set of polished teak doors. "Just bear with me."

A rococo fountain dominated the hotel lobby, its waters shimmering in the light of crystal chandeliers. Dona almost slipped on the slick marble floor, but Alexi caught her in time.

"Whoops, thanks."

He grinned. "Ever at your service."

The dapper man behind the desk raised an eyebrow. "Can I be of assistance?"

"I'd like to leave a message for someone." Dona said.

"Room number?"

"I don't have a room number. The gentleman just said he sometimes gets messages here."

"I'm sorry, Miss, but as you can no doubt surmise, we are not a delivery service."

"I'm not asking you to deliver it. I'm just asking you to keep it here in case he stops by."

"Assuming we did provide such a service, without a room number, just how would you propose we keep track of these messages?"

"Might I suggest alphabetically by name? It's all the rage in polite establishments."

Alexi gave her hand a cautionary squeeze.

"We don't want to be any bother," Alexi said. "Could you bend the rules this once and let us leave a message for this gentleman, in case he shows up?" He turned to Dona. "What was his name again?"

"Michlos. His name was Michlos."

They turned to see the tall, wiry man standing behind them.

The clerk's tone slipped effortlessly from snide to obsequious. "Oh, good afternoon, sir. Are these good people with you?"

"They are," Michlos said.

"Well, why didn't they just say so? There, now, any messages can be delivered directly, and everything is as it should be. Is there anything else we here at The Expatriate can provide for you today?"

Alexi squeezed Dona's hand hard to cut her off. "No thank you," he said. "I think we're fine now."

"Then you have a great day."

Michlos ushered them toward the door. "I don't suppose you two care to take a walk?"

"We'd love to," Dona said, glancing at the clerk. "It's a little cold in here."

"Why don't we have a look at the gardens?" Michlos said. "They're only a touch past their peak."

"That would be wonderful. Did your mother like her gift?"

"Ahh, the rose oil. I won't know until she opens it. Her birthday isn't until Thursday."

"Oh, that's right."

"Now, perhaps you would do me the honor of introducing your friend?"

"Oh, I'm sorry. I forgot he hadn't seen you at the Respite. Alexi, this is Michlos, the man I saw talking to the Monsignor's carriage driver just before the fire started."

Alexi eyed Dona and gulped. After an awkward moment, he finally extended his hand. "Uh, pleased to meet you."

"Likewise," Michlos said. Then he turned to Dona. "You've decided you'd like to chat?"

"Not exactly. I mean I would, but I have an urgent situation I was hoping you could help us with."

"Does it involve the theft of your bag?"

"How do you know about that?"

Michlos raised his eyebrows. "After our last conversation, I presumed you knew we were watching the brothel. You'll recall that's how I found you in the first place."

"So when we showed up there, you followed us?"

"Not personally, but yes, you were followed. In fact, the reason I was able to make such a timely entrance is because you asked one of my people for directions."

"I don't suppose your people also followed the man on the horse?"

"Unfortunately, no. They were on foot."

"Do you think you can find him?"

"I'm not certain. Would you care to fill me in? Perhaps I can be of greater assistance if I understand the situation."

"Just one second," Alexi said. "Dona, can we talk for a minute— in private?"

"I'm sorry, Alexi. I already know what you're going to say, and I already know I'm going to do this anyway. Our decisions got Gregory into this. If we have to take risks to get him out again, that's the price we pay."

"Could we at least find out who he is and why he follows people?" He favored Michlos with a self-conscious smile. "No offense."

Michlos's eyes twinkled. "None taken. You know, you could just ask me."

Alexi looked to Dona.

"Go ahead," she said.

"Very well, then. Who are you, and why are you watching the brothel?"

"I am Michlos Serrola, and I am trying to determine what business Jonas Harcourt has with Thurman Goodkin, who, as you may know, has implemented the first stages of an Inquisition at Exidgeon University."

Alexi blinked. "Why would you think Jonas has anything to do with the Inquisition?"

"Because he's had several meetings with Thurman, the latest of which took place at the Sultan's Respite. Dona was a witness."

"Not really," Dona said, "I didn't see Jonas until after we got out of the Respite, but I can believe it—he must have been pretty close when the darkness fell, since he was able to grab my hand."

Alexi's brow furrowed. "You mean it was *Jonas* who knocked over our canopy?"

"Indeed it was," Michlos said. "That, I saw quite clearly, although I didn't know for certain that you were the other person in Dona's canopy until just now."

"And you care about the Inquisition because…?"

Dona nudged him and shook her head.

Michlos smiled. "As you could probably tell from your experience at the Respite, I have a vested interest in preventing the Inquisition."

"So you belong to one of the heretic families?"

"I can trace my line back to one of the students of Phrendonian, if that's what you mean."

Alexi backed away. "Dona, I think this is a really bad idea."

"I don't see why. He's answered all your questions. What's the problem?"

"Didn't he see your locket?"

"I did," Michlos replied. "And I'll be honest. That's the main reason we are having this conversation. It marked you as someone with potentially as much to lose as I have from an Inquisition"

"Don't you see," Alexi said. "He's going to get what information he can out of us, and then we'll just disappear. We're a risk he can't afford to take."

Dona let out a long sigh. "That's some pretty ironic paranoia you're peddling. What makes you think he's any greater threat to me than you are?"

"Ask the people who didn't make it out of the Respite."

"Haven't you been paying attention? Jonas started the fire, not Michlos, and it was an accident."

"How do you know? Once the darkness fell, he could have been doing anything. You heard him say he wanted to prevent the Inquisition. What better way than if the Monsignor's son burns to death in a tragic accident?"

"Alexi, please. You saw what he did to those bouncers, or at least you heard. If he had wanted the Monsignor's son to stay in the burning building, I think he could have managed it."

Alexi opened his mouth, and then closed it when he realized he couldn't really argue with that.

"Alexi is correct to be cautious," Michlos said. "There are others you could have met with fewer scruples. They can be dangerous indeed, and they are no strangers to deception."

Dona held out the ransom note. "We don't have time for caution. Take a look at this."

Michlos skimmed it. "Gregory Delauren—the tenor?"

"That's him."

"He's a Phrendonic?"

"No," Dona replied. "He's only involved by association, since he took me to the opera last week."

"And what is this book?"

"It's called *Practical Phrendonics*."

Michlos did a double take. "An original?"

"I don't know. It's a well-crafted book, and it's pretty old."

"Was this book in your bag when it was taken?"

"No, all he got was a copy of Driessen's geometry text."

Alexi snorted. "Well, he certainly won't be learning anything from *that*."

"That's why I'm so worried," Dona said. "Now that he didn't get his book, there's no telling what he'll do to Gregory."

"Do you have any idea who the kidnapper is?" Michlos asked.

Dona nodded. "Our best guess is that he's a professor from Exidgeon. His name is Dominick Everson, but the evidence is circumstantial. The only hard evidence is this note."

"This Everson—is he a Phrendonic?"

"He is," Alexi said, "though not very far along."

"Well, whoever he is, the kidnapper, or someone working with him, is at least far enough along to work multiple Kinesis spells."

"Kinesis spells?" Dona asked.

Michlos smiled. "They're in the book. I'm pretty sure it would have taken more than one to snatch away Dona's bag like that. Probably he cast a Tag on the bag, and the Attraction spells on the horse's saddle to make sure he had enough counterweight. He was taking an awful risk that something else along the way wasn't Tagged as well."

"What would the chances of that be?" Alexi asked.

Michlos shrugged. "Probably not high, but there have been Phrendonics in Trifienne for a very long time.

"But the Tag would, at most, last only a day, right?"

Michlos frowned. "Not necessarily. All it would have taken is for a Tag spell to have gotten Patterned on something. It's not likely, but it's certainly within the realm of possibility."

"Patterned?"

"Made integral to the item. It's sort of like making the spell permanent."

"You can do that?"

"A few can. It's pretty advanced stuff—you won't find it in your basic book."

Dona crossed her arms. "I'm sure this technical jargon is all very fascinating, but we are in a bit of a hurry.

"Have you checked with his friends?" Michlos asked. "When was the last time anyone saw him?"

"We checked at the University, but not in town."

"Fine," Michlos said. "Why don't you check there, and I'll follow up on whether my people have tracked down your horseman. Shall we meet back at the rose oil by six o'clock?"

"Agreed," Dona said. "I just pray we aren't too late."

. . . . .

"*Now* where are we going?" Alexi asked. Dona had led him across the sculpture bridge and was headed toward Trifienne proper.

"I can think of three obvious places to get news of Gregory," Dona said. "I have no idea where his parents live, so that leaves the opera house or his patron's estate. Take your pick."

"Which is closer?"

"The opera, I think. That's in the town square. I've never actually been to Morissant's estate, but I think we could probably find it."

"Seems like the opera house makes the most sense, then."

"All right, we'll try there first."

After getting lost twice in the winding streets above the harbor, they made good time to the square. On arriving, Dona wished they had chosen Morissant's estate instead. When last she had seen it, the opera house had been glamorous and exciting, with lanterns casting tall shadows in the dusk, their flickering light bouncing off the jewels of society dames and illuminating the eager faces of debonair escorts. It was drama personified. By the stark light of day, however, the opera house showed her age. Shutters on the upper windows hung askew, with several missing outright. In some places, worms had infested the great timbers, and many of the gray slate shingles were cracked or crumbling. Under the cover of night, she had been a grand dame, but daylight robbed her of her mysteries to reveal a pathetic creature, well past her prime, clinging to dim memories of greatness past.

Alexi started up the front steps, but Dona stopped him. "It's not open yet. This way." She led him down the side alley to the heavy door. Once there, she rapped three times, paused and then rapped twice more.

After a few moments, the door swung open, revealing the impish face of Dorian Emolino. "Well, well, if it isn't Gregory's young lady friend. I'm not so much for names, but I never forget a fan."

"It's Dona," she said. "And what a delight to see you again, Mr. Emolino."

"Please, call me Dorian. Formality gives me hives. What can I do for you?"

"We're concerned about Gregory. When was the last time you saw him?"

"Just a second, I'll get him." He turned and shouted back into the darkness. "Hey Gregory, you have visitors."

Dona's jaw dropped. "He's here?"

"Yes ma'am," Dorian said. "I asked him to help out with the makeup, since he's not in a run at the moment."

Gregory emerged from the darkness "Who is it?" Then his face lit up. "Bella!"

Dona threw her arms around him. "I was worried sick."

Gregory's eyebrows shot upward. "You were?"

"I had visions of you being tortured."

"Huh?"

"And here you are, safe and sound…"

"Uh, I do my best."

Dona's initial relief gave way to a rush of resentment. "Hiding yourself away while I run myself ragged trying to save you."

Gregory sent Alexi a questioning look, but he only shrugged.

"I suppose you thought it was all very funny, making me skip class for this."

"Bella, what are you talking about?"

She threw the ransom note at him. "Don't you 'Bella' me. Fool me twice? I don't think so. And if you ever pull a stunt like this again, you'll wish you *had* been kidnapped." Turning on her heel, she stomped off down the alley. Alexi scampered after her.

Once Gregory read the note, he stepped into the alley and called after them. "Hey, I didn't write this. This isn't even my handwriting."

He turned to Dorian. "I didn't do anything. I swear."

Dorian crossed his arms and clucked. "I never did like her much."

· · · · ·

By the time Alexi caught up, Dona was sitting by the fountain in the square staring at her reflection in the basin. "You don't really think he had something to do with the ransom note, do you?" he asked.

Dona didn't answer for a long while. "I don't know what to think anymore."

"Hey, those aren't tears, are they?"

Dona turned away, wiping her eyes with the back of her hand.

Alexi took a seat next to her and wrapped her in his arms. "There's no need to be upset. You found him and he's fine, and you didn't even have to give up the book to do it. I'd call that one big fat success."

She leaned her head against his chest. "Things have spun so far out of control. On the one hand, I'm so relieved he's safe, but on the other, I'm furious. I don't see how he couldn't have had a hand in it. No one else knew he called me Bella—no one. And yet, I just can't think he would knowingly have tried to hurt me. I must seem like such a fool."

Alexi rocked her, gently. "No one thinks that."

"I don't see how they can't. Reston probably thinks I'm a spiteful little harridan, Hepplewhite thinks me irresponsible for skipping class, my friends think I'm giving them the cold shoulder, and now Gregory probably hates me too."

"He doesn't hate you."

"And against your advice, I've stupidly involved this Michlos character, exposing us both to who knows what kind of danger—all for nothing. And now I have to go tell him it was all just a false alarm."

"It wasn't a false alarm—you were attacked."

She shook her head. "But no one was ever really at risk."

"You were. When you thought your friend was in trouble, you dropped what you were doing and risked everything, including your own safety, to save him. That doesn't seem foolish to me. I'm proud of you."

"Really?"

He lifted her chin to look into her eyes. "Really."

"You aren't angry that I ignored your advice and dragged you on a wild-goose chase?"

He gently brushed away her remaining tears. "Are you kidding? I wouldn't trade the time we spend together for anything in the world."

She smiled. "Some parts of it weren't so bad, were they? The Artists' Colony was amazing."

"And who can forget how we snuck back into the college?"

"Oh, that *was* fun, wasn't it? And you should have seen the look on Helena's face when I told her we stayed at a brothel."

Alexi chuckled. "I'm sorry I missed that."

"Alexi?"

"Yes?"

"Thanks."

"Like I said—ever at your service."

Dona pulled herself to her feet. "Well, I suppose we should think about telling Michlos no one was actually kidnapped after all."

"We have time, and we're right here. Are you sure you don't want to patch things up with Gregory first?"

"He's probably busy," Dona said. "It's not that long until show time."

"It would only take a second."

"But what if Michlos gets back early? We don't want to keep him waiting."

"He picked the time. He can hardly complain as long as we arrive when he said."

"But if he's found out anything about Everson, we'll want to know as soon as possible."

"I'm sure five minutes either way won't matter."

Her eyes narrowed then. "You're enjoying this, aren't you?"

Alexi broke into a wide grin. "A little."

She planted both hands firmly on her hips. "I will work things out with Gregory *later*."

"Suit yourself," he said, still grinning.

She harrumphed and marched off in the direction of the market. *"Men!"*

.   .   .   .   .

Jonas furtively scanned the office for escape routes but saw nothing promising. Thurman sat behind a large wood desk with his back to a wall, allowing him unrestricted view of both the sole door to the office and the window that faced the cobbled courtyard that lay before the immense Exidgeon gates. The two goons standing near the door, who had none-too-politely escorted him here in the first place, discouraged escape in that direction, while the window looked sturdy enough to block an attempt in that direction as well.

"Jonas," Thurman said, his smile smug. "I'm so glad we have this opportunity to revisit our negotiations. I've been having some difficulties reconnecting with you after our last discussion was so rudely interrupted. Please, have a seat."

Jonas plopped himself down in the proffered chair. "Don't mind if I do."

"As you can see, my circumstances have changed since our last discussion."

"Does that mean you'll be able to offer a more reasonable price?"

"In a way, perhaps. My original offer, which as I recall, you have already accepted, still stands. However, if the goods check out, additional items might be able to command a higher price."

"Additional items? I thought this was a one-time deal."

Thurman shrugged. "Plans have changed. In the end, we may require quite a few."

"In that case, the price may increase significantly. It's not like they grow on trees."

"We can discuss that once our first purchase has passed inspection."

"Inspection? You seemed satisfied enough when I showed it to you at dinner."

"I'm not qualified to perform the appropriate tests, but someone will be arriving shortly who possesses the requisite skills. You would be ill-advised to disappoint him."

"All my wares are sold as is. Guarantees are bad for business. If you don't like what you see, don't buy."

"That's fine, assuming the item you sold us is everything you represented it would be. If it isn't, well then, I'm afraid the Church takes a very dim view of grave robbers."

"I did exactly as you asked—the item didn't come from a consecrated grave."

"And I'm sure you'd have every opportunity to present your case, if it came to that. But let's hope it doesn't, shall we? Now, if you could just turn over the item that I've already paid for, we can conclude this business and I can get on with other pressing matters."

"That would be nice," Jonas said, "except I don't have it with me."

Thurman sighed. "How unfortunate. Well, no matter. Just tell me where it is, and I'll send someone to retrieve it."

"It's not quite that simple. I seem to have misplaced it. I've been looking, but so far, no luck. I certainly hope it didn't get lost in the fire."

Thurman took a deep breath and exhaled slowly. "All right then, you have eight hours. By that time, you will have completed your end of the bargain, or the consequences will be dire. Do I make myself clear?"

"Clear as crystal," Jonas said. "That's why it's always such a joy to work with you."

"Two of my men will accompany you. And let me remind you once more that subsequent transactions could prove very lucrative."

Jonas smiled. "Like my daddy always said, that which does not kill you will only make you richer."

"You would do well to heed his advice."

"It always worked for him."

"Eight hours."

Jonas saluted in farewell. "Wouldn't miss it for the world."

. . . . .

Michlos hummed merrily as he pounded the heavy metal spikes deep into the gnarled trunk of a massive maple tree strategically located close, but not too close, to the road.

"Six should do it. No, let's do seven just to be sure."

A quick stop at the market had given him an ample supply of spikes and a hammer, along with a burlap shoulder bag for carrying them. He put additional spikes in each of two nearby trees and strung a hammock between them. In a few moments, he was relaxing in the hammock, which faced down the road toward Trifienne. His spot was mostly obscured by encroaching vegetation, but his own view of the road was clear. Once he'd made himself comfortable, he pulled out a small wooden stick, which he placed in the hammock next to him. Finally, he produced a book, and settled in to read.

His reading was interrupted several times by traffic. In one case, a sharp-eyed young lady spotted him through the underbrush. She and her escort paused and exchanged puzzled glances. Michlos merely nodded politely and resumed his reading. Several hours elapsed, and Michlos was beginning to doubt his plan when he heard the tell-tale clippity clop of an approaching horse. The rider was a middle-aged man and otherwise unremarkable, save perhaps for the large scratch across the side of his face. Michlos resumed his reading until the horse was about even with the maple tree, at which point he set down his book, took up the stick, and snapped it in two.

The horse jerked strangely to one side. Startled, it reared up, then fell sideways, throwing the rider. The saddle burst its bindings and shot toward the maple tree, its edge biting deep into the ancient bark among the spikes. The horse rolled, recovered, and ran off down the road, the remnants of its tack trailing behind it.

Michlos stepped out from the bushes. "Are you all right?"

Everson lay on his back in the middle of the road and moaned.

"Can you move?"

He moaned again.

"You can't stay there in the road. What if someone comes galloping through? Here, let me help you up."

Everson yelped at his touch. "No—my shoulder!"

"Oh, that does look nasty. Can you get up if I assist with the other arm?"

With Michlos's help, Everson managed to get to his feet.

"Let's get you off the road, and then we'll see about getting you some help. Just a bit farther, now…there."

Everson gritted his teeth. "Can you flag down a carriage or something?"

Michlos pointed toward the hammock. "Here, why don't you have a seat? Careful, now."

Everson was lowering himself into the hammock when he

caught sight of the saddle with its edge wedged into the tree bark. Michlos followed his gaze.

"Ooh, I better take care of that," Michlos said. After a few minutes, he managed to retrieve the saddle.

Everson's eyes brimmed with suspicion. "Who are you?"

"A friend," Michlos said, rummaging through the saddle-bags. "Maybe there's something in here that would help."

Everson's eye twitched. "What do you want? There's a little money in there, not much, but it's yours if you want it."

Michlos pulled a book from one of the bags. "I think I might prefer this."

"It's yours." Everson said. "Just help me get back to the University."

"There is just one other thing."

"Name it."

"I'm trying to find a tenor by the name of Gregory Delauren. Perhaps you've heard of him?"

Everson's eye twitched again. "He's at the opera house."

Michlos arched an eyebrow. "Really? I've heard rumors he was being held somewhere against his will."

"I swear. He told me he was going to be at the opera house."

"You aren't going to make me resort to harsher measures, are you?"

"Honest, he's there."

"Guess I'll just have to go check it out myself. Lie down."

"I can't. Look at my shoulder—I'd never be able to get out again."

"Of course you will. It will just hurt more, that's all. Now do it."

As Everson dropped painfully back into to the hammock, his good hand came across a piece of the broken stick. As he held it up for a closer look, his eye twitched violently.

"Verone put you up to this, didn't she?"

Just as he said it, he went limp, and his breathing became deep and regular.

Michlos scratched his head and sighed. "Oh, now that was bad timing, wasn't it."

· · · · ·

For the second time that day, Dona and Alexi found themselves wandering among the colorful booths and wagons of the Trifienne marketplace. They had been back to the rose oil vendor on three separate occasions, but Michlos had yet to materialize. Dona was intently comparing bolts of colorful silks offered by a Shunese merchant, while Alexi was making a heroic attempt to master his boredom.

"Which do you like better? The seafoam or the aquamarine?"

"Um, they're both nice."

"Yes, but which one do you think would make a better gown for Helena? She and Miranda have been so helpful this week that I really should do something nice for them. I've already picked the cranberry for Miranda, but I could use some help with Helena's."

"Either one would be great."

"You're no help. Don't you have any opinion at all?"

Finally, he pointed to the aquamarine bolt. "I like the seafoam."

"I might have known," Dona muttered. She handed the aquamarine bolt to the merchant. "I'll take this one."

Alexi was grateful for an excuse to change the subject. "I expect it's getting close to six."

"Yes, let's head back to the distiller."

Michlos was waiting for them.

"Did you track him down?" Dona asked.

Michlos held up the geometry text.

"You got it back."

"All in a day's work," Michlos said. "Did you learn anything?"

"We learned that Gregory was never actually kidnapped. It turns out he was helping out on the new opera."

"So you found him?"

"We did. He didn't even know he was supposed to be in trouble."

"Well that's a relief."

"So where's Everson? And how did you find him?"

"He's probably still in a carriage on its way to the University, perhaps a little worse for wear. I doubt he'll cause any more trouble for a while."

Dona gaped at Michlos. "You let him go?"

"What was I supposed to do with him?"

"Shouldn't he be locked away or something?"

"For what? For *not* kidnapping Delauren?"

"For extortion. You saw the note."

"Would you care to be the one to explain to the constable exactly what he was trying to extort from you?"

"It's no crime to simply have the book."

"So, you'd be willing to risk having the constable turn the matter over to the Inquisition for investigation?"

"If you put it that way, I suppose not, but what's to stop him from biding his time and trying again?"

"After today's experience, I'm guessing he may be a bit less motivated than he was."

"This was his second attempt. I just *know* he's going to try again."

"Then perhaps you should consider getting rid of the book."

"I shouldn't have to."

Michlos chuckled. "In life, the principled and the practical often diverge. In the end, whether you choose the principled path usually comes down to whether you are willing to pay the toll."

"There must be other options than just those two," Alexi said. "What if he merely thought you gave it up?"

"For that matter," Michlos said, "you could always address the reason he wants it in the first place. By the way, why does he want it?"

"I'm not sure," Alexi said. "He already had access of a sort. Maybe he wanted unrestricted access? Or maybe he wanted to prevent other people from having access? Or maybe he thought Dona's having it was too risky, but none of those reasons really explain the lengths he's gone to. It doesn't really make sense."

"Well, what kind of access did he have?"

Alexi blushed furiously. "I'm not sure I can really say."

"No matter," Michlos said. "I didn't mean to pry."

"You've been so generous," Dona said. "Is there some way we can repay you for your kindness?"

"You may already have. Speaking of which, you might want to go easy on the good professor. I have a feeling he may not be entirely responsible for his actions."

"How could he not be responsible?" Alexi asked.

Dona scowled. "You mean he's losing his mind?"

Michlos considered that. "If he's lucky. Anyway, I should be going. This little adventure has taken me away from some other things that need my attention. If you care to chat more, leave me a note at the Expatriate, and I'll do my best to reply. And don't worry—unless I miss my guess, your welcome there is likely to be warmer next time."

"Thank you again," Dona said.

"My pleasure." With a wave of farewell, he disappeared into the bustle of the marketplace.

CHAPTER FOURTEEN

RELICS, LULLABIES AND FATALISMS

Although Nanna's cooking was as tasty as ever, breakfast in Tilly's kitchen was not the same without Jonas, particularly with Tilly periodically checking the windows and looking fretfully toward the door at the slightest noise.

"It's not like him to disappear without his wagon," she said. "He said he was just going out for tobacco."

"I'm sure there's a good explanation," Dona said.

Alexi gulped a mouthful of scrambled egg. "Is there anything we can do?"

"Absolutely. You can stay far away from whatever he's gotten himself into."

"But we'd like to help," Dona said. "And what makes you think he's in trouble? Did he say something?"

Tilly shook her head. "He never does. And then I have to pick up the pieces without any idea of how they fit back together."

"He's done this before?" Alexi asked.

"More times than I can count. Like the time a few years back when he sold front-row tickets to the hanging of that mass murderer, what was his name...Chenforth, I think. People got pretty upset when they found out the execution was actually public—no tickets required."

Dona couldn't decide whether to be horrified or amused. "What did they do?"

"Those who didn't get into a fight with people already occupying the front row tried to hunt him down. He barely got away and almost led the lynch mob back here."

Dona gaped. "Oh, how awful."

"Or the time he went up and down the businesses along the riverfront telling them he was there to collect their protection money."

"Do they pay protection money?"

"Apparently some of them do. You can imagine their dismay when someone else showed up asking them to pay it again. He ended up leaving town for almost a year after that one."

"Did he even know who was supposed to be doing the collecting?"

"Not that he told me," Tilly said, "but then, he did leave town in a hurry."

"No wonder you're worried."

Tilly wrung her hands. "As usual, I'm torn between needing to know what he's up to and wanting nothing to do with it."

"Could his absence have anything to do with the Inquisition?" Alexi asked.

All the usual cooking sounds suddenly stopped. "I don't know," she said, lowering her voice. "Why do you ask?"

"Well, as I understand it, Jonas was at the Respite having dinner with an Inquisitor when the fire started."

"That can't be true. Jonas would never have anything to do with the Inquisition."

"Well, I didn't see it myself, so I can't be certain, but they were both there at the same time."

"But so were you, and you didn't have anything to do with the Inquisition, did you?"

Dona shot Alexi an exasperated look. "No, of course not," she said. "I'm sure it was just a coincidence."

At that moment, Jonas barged through the kitchen door, sweat-drenched and covered in filth. "I think I've lost them."

Tilly leapt from her seat. "Lost *whom*? What have you done this time?"

Jonas ignored her, instead focusing all his attention on Dona. He dropped to one knee and placed a filthy hand on her shoulder. "Dona, I need your help. Did you ever find a little ivory-looking medallion with snakes on it? It was about so big." He made a circle with his thumb and forefinger.

"Oh, that must be the thing we found tucked in the back of my dress."

Jonas relaxed visibly. "Thank heavens. Can you get it for me?"

"I would love to, but, I have no idea where it is."

Jonas buried his face in his hands. "Oh no."

"What is it?" Tilly said. "What have you dragged me into?"

"Try to remember," Jonas said. "Did you leave it here or did you take it back to the college?"

"I don't know," Dona said. Jonas's urgency was making it difficult to concentrate.

"Think. Where was it the last time you saw it?"

"Jonas, for the last time, what is going on here?" Tilly cried. "What have you done?"

"Tilly, will you shut up. If I don't get this thing to Goodkin like I promised, I'm a dead man, and I don't have much time."

Tilly stared at Jonas, aghast.

Alexi rubbed his chin. "You know, I think I remember seeing something like that."

Dona brightened. "That's right. We saw it right after we snuck back into the University."

Nanna, tears brimming in her tired old eyes, slipped past them and slowly made her way up the stairs.

"Where is it now?" Jonas asked.

Alexi's hand strayed to his pocket, but it wasn't there. "I don't know. Maybe back at the University?"

"The University?" Jonas cried. Before he could say more, there was a crash like thunder from the vestibule, followed by the sound of multiple feet scrambling in.

"This is the Inquisition," a deep voice boomed. "You are all under arrest. Hands over your heads."

Everyone at the breakfast table froze.

For a long moment, silence reigned. It was broken at last by the strains of a lullaby, ethereal and bell-like, drifting down from above.

> *Hush my little one, life has just begun, there*
> *is time to learn its wonder.*
> *Put your faith in me, I can help you see, there's*
> *no need to fear the thunder.*

Tilly stared at Jonas, her eyes the size of saucers. Jonas sat blinking in disbelief.

"Nanna?" He mouthed the word.

Alexi grabbed Dona's hand and pulled her gently beneath the tablecloth. He motioned for Tilly and Jonas to do likewise.

"You. Upstairs. Come down here slowly, hands over your head."

The singing only became stronger.

When the sky is clear, I will still be here, a
knowing guide if you should falter.
As you learn and grow, you shall always know,
a love no force on earth can alter.

Since Tilly wasn't moving, Jonas gently pushed her under the table, and then dove beneath it himself.

The tablecloth was still swaying when a man brandishing a blade poked his head around the corner and scanned the kitchen. He was clearly more concerned with the eerie music from the stairwell behind him, and his scan was brief.

"All clear."

"Right. Everyone upstairs."

Three armed thugs followed by two men in embroidered vestments rushed up the stairs.

"Now's our chance," Jonas whispered. "We can make it to the horses."

Tilly was on the verge of hysteria. "We can't leave her—it will kill her."

"We don't have a choice. It's that, or they kill us all. Don't you see? She's giving us this chance. We can't waste it."

Every few moments, a loud crash resonated from the upstairs. Still the singing reverberated.

When I'm old and gray, and we have had our
day, there will be no cause for sorrow.

"Now!" Jonas said, flipping the tablecloth out of the way.

Dona and Alexi made a break through the arch and across the vestibule to the side door leading to the warehouse where their horses waited. At first, Tilly and Jonas were right behind, but at the stairway, Tilly paused. Jonas screeched to a halt and turned back for her.

*For from my time with you, you'll know what
to do, to love the children of tomorrow.*

"Hands over your head," the booming voice bellowed.

Abruptly the singing stopped.

Tilly made a sudden dash up the stairwell. "Let her *be!*"

Jonas spat. "Oh, bloody hell."

But before Tilly made it to the top, a blinding flash of light and heat pushed her back. The Inquisitors and their men screamed in anguish, their bodies seared by the firestorm erupting in the hallway.

"*Nanna!*" Tilly wailed.

Then there was another flash.

Over the cries of the burning ruffians, Nanna's quavering voice rose a final time.

Love the children of tomorrow.

There was another flash, and another, and then, finally, all that remained was the rustle of the flames.

Jonas reached Tilly where she lay weeping on the landing. Tears streaming down his face, he lifted her into his arms, carried her through the vestibule, and out to the waiting horses.

. . . . .

The Monsignor was beginning to chafe under the ministrations of the tailor, who after seemingly having measured every inch of his anatomy three times, was having yet another go.

"Try to be patient," Laitrech said. "It's not every day he outfits an Ordinal."

"Outfits? At this rate, he couldn't even *measure* one every day."

Laitrech chuckled. "There are quite a few pieces to prepare. Cassock, mozzetta, rochet, et cetera. And don't forget the miter. You aren't really considered an Ordinal until you've weathered an outdoor ceremony without losing your miter."

"I had always imagined staying put was a natural function of the hat. Just put it on, and your head swells."

Laitrech handed him his cane. "I can see you're going to fit right in. This august group is so well known for enjoying humor at its own expense. Oh, speaking of regalia, has His Primacy decided what he wants to do about the Relic?"

"What do you mean?"

"The Relic." Laitrech said. "Every Ordinal carries one. It's why there have traditionally been only nine Ordinals—there are only nine Relics."

"I'm well aware, but surely another Relic can be found? Not to minimize their contributions in any way, but the Church has had its fair share of martyrs."

"It's not that simple. If it were, there would have been more Ordinals than nine long before now."

The tailor signaled that he was finished and withdrew, bowing.

The Monsignor frowned. "This Ordinal thing could take some getting used to. So what's the complication?"

"Perhaps it would be easier to just show you. Are you up for a walk?"

"I'll be fine."

"We'll take it slowly."

Though the Monsignor had wandered these halls many times, he still felt a sense of awe at their grandeur. Gothic arches soared above them. Massive ceilings sporting vibrant frescos topped chambers dripping rococo detail. Intricate mosaics spread out beneath their feet in all directions. Fresco, mosaic, painting, and sculpture all paid homage to some tenet of the faith, running the gamut from the purely historical to the most-likely mythical. It was a spectacle unlike any other.

Laitrech smiled. "Incredible, isn't it?"

"I find it humbling. It always serves to remind me that the contributions of any one man are insignificant compared to the capabilities of an inspired team working in concert with a single shared vision."

"Not necessarily," Laitrech said. "Wouldn't it be naïve to presume all contributions are equal? After all, a single man might well contribute the entire vision."

"Perhaps, if you presume such vision is not divinely inspired."

"Touché. If you're trying to loosen my hat, it's working."

The Monsignor touched Laitrech's shoulder. "I hope, when necessary, that you will return the favor."

They entered a small hallway that led to the oldest parts of the palace. Laitrech lifted a lantern off a post on the wall and lit it. In the sputtering lamplight, the Monsignor saw that the hallway, though still scrupulously clean, lacked the opulence of the newer additions.

"Holding up all right?"

"So far, so good," the Monsignor said. "I'm not sure I've ever been down this way."

"I'm not surprised. You're approaching the Chapel Ordinalis."

"Ah, the celebrated Chapel. Odd that it's so deserted, then—I had presumed it would be guarded."

"There's no need for guards," Laitrech said. "And no one else is permitted in."

The Monsignor paused. "I'm not an Ordinal yet. Am I allowed to proceed?"

Laitrech shrugged. "You're only a few days away. And if I don't object, who will?"

"If you're sure it's all right…"

Ahead in the distance, the hallway ended abruptly at a brass-bound door. Unlike the rest of the architecture, there was nothing the least bit artistic about it.

Laitrech brandished a brass key. "We'll have to see about having another of these made, too, I suppose."

Despite its age, the lock's tumblers turned easily, and the door swung open. Beyond the door, a thick layer of dust carpeted the hallway, except for a clear path down the center. The Monsignor moved forward with deliberate steps to be certain he didn't lose his footing in the dust. Even at that pace, when he struck what felt like a barricade he nearly fell over backward.

"Hello, what's this?"

Looking ahead, he could see nothing that should have impeded his progress. When he extended his cane, it met with no resistance. Yet, when he tried again to step forward, his way was barred. Reaching out, his hand encountered nothing solid–only pressure. As he pushed harder, it yielded slightly, like forcing two opposing lodestones together, but stronger.

"The Bastion of Bethany, I presume?"

Laitrech's eyebrow arched. "I see someone's been reading apocryphal accounts."

The Monsignor shrugged. "It's possible my literary tastes have, on rare occasions, meandered beyond the list of approved texts. Is this what we came to see?"

"Not entirely."

Laitrech clutched the silver snake pendant suspended around his neck. Closing his eyes, he recited a short prayer in a commanding voice.

"There. Try again."

The Monsignor reached again, but this time his hand encountered no resistance. "Hence, no need for guards?"

"Quite so," Laitrech replied. He strode down the corridor toward yet another heavily fortified door. "Stay close. Only my proximity protects you from the Bastion."

"I'm right behind you."

Laitrech reached the door and threw it open. "Behold, the Chapel Ordinalis."

The Monsignor was momentarily blinded. As his eyes adjusted, he looked about in awe. After the long walk through the confined corridor, he had envisioned the Chapel would be small and sepulchral. Instead, the chamber seemed to go on forever. Glowing sconces threw twisted shadows against the walls, but the bulk of the illumination emanated from ornate scrollwork panels set into the ceiling that the Monsignor at first mistook for skylights. A gleaming altar dominated one section. Another area was devoted to a great circular table. Although the space clearly held a functional chapel, the bulk of the chamber bore more resemblance to a vast library. Shelves and cabinets of scrolls, texts, and documents filled much of the remainder of the space.

"Well, what do you think?"

"Very impressive. I'm particularly curious about the sources of light." He hefted a glowing candlestick.

"Yes, they are remarkable, aren't they? "And ancient. The secret of their manufacture has been lost."

The Monsignor frowned. "Lost? Are you certain? I have occasionally come across items resembling these in my work."

"Yes, lost. These items were produced by Ordinals, not heretics."

The Monsignor raised an eyebrow. "Are you suggesting an Ordinal cannot also be a heretic?"

"Not at all. Anyone can fall prey to heresy. But an Ordinal need not resort to heresy for results of this sort."

"I'm not sure I see the distinction."

"Observe, then." Once again clasping his pendant, Laitrech began a series of commanding recitations. After a few moments, the Monsignor's cane flared alight.

"I thought you said the making of these was lost."

"Oh, this is different," Laitrech said. "It won't last. The others you see here have been glowing for hundreds of years."

The Monsignor's frown deepened. "I must say I hadn't expected to find the heretical practice of Patterning taking place in this holy of holies."

"Oh, they aren't Patterned," Laitrech said. "These are all still fully disruptable."

The Monsignor's eyebrows shot upward. "You know the distinction?"

"You aren't the only one who reads outside the lists. Let me be plain. What I'm trying to show you is that the Ordinals have long possessed arcane knowledge of their own and have been charged with using that knowledge in the service of the Church."

"I still don't see the difference between this and that for which we persecute heretics."

"Well, for one, unlike heretics, Ordinals undergo a vetting process before they are appointed." His smile turned sly, "well, *usually* anyway. Second, the Ordinal's Relic is key to the exercise of his abilities. Without it, nothing works. I presume you can see the wisdom of providing such a fail-safe in the unlikely event an Ordinal were to abuse his gifts."

"Ah, and this is why you suspect any old Relic won't do?"

"Precisely. We've been able to obtain results using only the original nine Relics."

The Monsignor had a seat at the table and propped his leg up. "But if an Ordinal had no interest in performing these parlor tricks, then wouldn't just any old Relic suffice?"

"In theory, perhaps, but in practical terms it would be a disaster. At best, an Ordinal carrying a counterfeit Relic would be viewed as a second-class citizen. More likely he'd be treated as an outright imposter. The psychology is strong even for the majority of Ordinals who make little or no use of the thing. They've even been known to jockey for status according to whose Martyr was considered to be more 'saintly.' That's why I've advised His Primacy that if your status as an Ordinal is to carry any weight, you'll need an authentic Relic. I have to say, though, I seriously doubt even that will be enough to overcome the stigma of adding an Ordinal by fiat."

"Perhaps you can convince him to reconsider?"

"I doubt it," Laitrech said. "I can sometimes influence him while he is in the process of making a decision, but I've had little luck once he's made up his mind."

The Monsignor sighed. "I've had that experience as well. It seems such a lot of trouble when I want no part of either the position or the parlor tricks. I can see absolutely no way to reconcile them with my well-known position against Phrendonic heresy. The hypocrisy is staggering."

"No one need know about the parlor tricks," Laitrech said. "And before you dismiss them out of hand, you may want to investigate them more fully. Unlike your heretics, Ordinals have the power to heal."

The Monsignor's voice gained an edge. "And yet, my brother has only months to live?"

Laitrech's eyes flashed. "I am only one man. You see the volumes of knowledge buried here. It would be one thing if any of the other Ordinals had any interest or ability at all, but as it is, I must first ferret out the knowledge and then I have to learn to apply it. And that's assuming I even understand their terminology, which often I do not. And that's in addition to my duties as Ordinal. Only a fraction of what we once had rests in this chamber, but it is still far more than one man can hope to master in so short a time."

"I'm sorry," the Monsignor said. "What I said was uncalled for. I'm just frustrated that there seems to be so little we can do."

"If it is meant to be, it will be. If not, it will not, regardless of what we do."

The Monsignor raised a dubious eyebrow. "I've rarely found such fatalism to be conducive to a productive work ethic."

"True," Laitrech replied. "But it is conducive to a healthy acceptance of the inevitable."

"Oh, I don't know. If I've learned anything during in all my years of service, it's that 'inevitable' is a relative term."

. . . . .

Thurman rose to his feet behind his cherrywood desk as the Ordinal's cavalcade made itself comfortable in his new office. Isrulian had an established a reputation for being opinionated, especially with respect to how to best fix all the terrible problems besetting his beloved Church…and how the Primal was going about it all wrong.

Thurman bowed. "I am honored, Your Ordinence."

Isrulian nodded in acknowledgement. "And how are we getting on here? I understand there were some issues relating to heresy?"

"Yes, Your Ordinence, but we have it under control. We have extracted a confession from the traitor and are working to discover the identities of the heretics who were paying him."

"The traitor didn't name his coconspirators? Strange, it almost makes one wonder why he bothered, if you take my meaning."

Thurman reddened. "The process has been made more challenging by the traitor's limited grasp of the language. He's a Shunese defector."

"Ah, I see the problem. It's not like you can get a reliable interpreter either. All those Shunese are shifty. I was worried you were just being too soft on him. Your father, as you know, has all sorts of radical notions about the supposed 'rights' of heretics. I say they give up those rights when they commit the heresy."

"I think he believes that they don't actually lose their rights until the heresy is proven."

"Ridiculous. You wouldn't be wasting your time investigating someone who was innocent. I've long maintained that your father could stand to have more faith in the system."

"Fortunately, since we have a confession, we don't even need to address the issue."

"True," Isrulian conceded, "which brings us to the next order of business." He clapped his hands twice. "Leave us."

Isrulian's retinue filed silently out of the room.

"Now," he said. "Can I see it?"

"Of course." Thurman removed a tiny ivory box from the drawer of his desk and tilted back the lid.

Isrulian peered intently into the container. "Is that a tooth?"

"It's one of the back teeth. A molar, I believe."

"And you've already paid for it?"

"I had little choice. My source was unwilling to wait for confirmation, and I wasn't willing to risk passing it by."

"I would have expected it to look older. You know, pitted or dingy or something."

Thurman shrugged. "Maybe they are more resilient than normal teeth. We won't know for certain until you test it."

"Yes, well I suppose so." Slowly, almost reluctantly, he

grasped his snake pendant. His voice wavered as he recited an ancient prayer.

"No, that's not right," he said. He took a deep breath and started over. The second time, he managed to get through it, and looked expectantly at the tooth.

Nothing happened.

"What does it mean?" Thurman asked. "Is it genuine?"

Isrulian snorted. "It means they shouldn't try to force feed old dogs like me new tricks. I'll try again."

Isrulian recited the prayer a third time. As he concluded, the yellow-white tooth darkened to a deep ebony.

"Did it work?"

"Yes!" Isrulian exclaimed. "I did it."

"So, is it genuine?"

"I don't know yet. For that, we'll have to wait."

CHAPTER FIFTEEN

ᴆᴇꜰɪɴɪɴɢ ᴍᴏᴍᴇɴᴛꜱ

Miss Connelly, if you could stay behind a few moments," Reston said. "Otherwise—class dismissed."

Miranda sighed as she shoved her history text back in her book bag. She'd been hoping Reston would forget about her request for an extra credit project. Things had gotten a little too complicated—she needed time to work out what was going on before involving anyone else.

"Miss Connelly," Reston said. "First I want to apologize for being distracted when we chatted yesterday."

"That's all right, Professor. I was a little distracted myself."

"You did seem to be a little unsettled. Is everything all right?"

Miranda fought down the urge to confide. She was now well aware the book she carried was heretical, and Miss Maxtine's insistence that Mathers had been the man with the pry bar did nothing to enhance her faith in authority. She had seen him only briefly, but she was certain she would have remembered Mathers's presence in her dormitory.

"Everything's fine, Professor. Thank you for asking."

"I couldn't help noticing that Miss Merinne was absent today."

Miranda didn't quite know how to field the implied question. While she was getting a bit worried that Dona hadn't been back to the dormitory for two straight nights, she was conscious that Dona and Alexi may have become an item, a conclusion strengthened by his absence from class as well. She had no desire to embarrass Dona by raising an alarm if the two of them had simply disappeared on a romantic getaway.

"I don't know where she's been hiding lately, but she has been known to spend long hours in the library."

"She's been in the library, then?"

"I'm not sure," Miranda said. "I just said that because it's something she does."

"So, she's not home sick?"

"I really don't know. I've been pretty busy with classes lately, and I haven't been back to the room much."

"She was fine this morning, though?"

"She was already gone before I woke up."

"So she spent the night in the dormitory?"

"I can't really say for certain. If she did, she got up early. Professor, why are you so concerned about Dona? Did she do something wrong?"

"I don't mean to be nosy, but it's so unusual for Dona to miss class."

"I'm sorry if I seem impertinent, Professor, but how could one absence seem unusual?"

"Unusual given her temperament, I mean."

"I grant you she's intense about classes."

"I was also expecting to talk with her about her project today."

"Oh yes," Miranda said. "I've been thinking about that, too, and I've decided I can probably do all right in the class without one."

"Very well, but don't let it get too close to the end of the semester if you think you might change your mind."

"I won't. I'll see you Friday, then."

"Oh, and Miss Connelly?"

"Yes, Professor?"

"If you happen to see Miss Merinne, could you tell her I'd like to see her as soon as possible?"

"I will."

. . . . .

Once Jonas was certain Tilly was stable atop her horse, he handed the reins to Alexi, who, with Dona's help, had gotten four horses saddled. The tendrils of smoke seeping into the old warehouse from around the door jamb were a potent reminder of the need to hurry. Jonas had already given up any hope of saving the wagon. Even had it been able to outdistance any pursuit, its distinctive appearance would be too great a liability. He did, however, take the a few minutes to skim some of his more precious items into his saddlebags.

"Alexi, crack the door," he said. "See how many more are out there."

Alexi peered out. Smoke from the burning brothel was attracting the attention of passers-by, but as far as he could tell, only one was in Church raiment. The man's attention was focused entirely on the brothel, his mouth agape.

"Only one, I think," Alexi said. "On foot."

"I hope you're right, or we might not enjoy our new destination."

"Speaking of which," Dona said. "Where are we going?"

"The Artists' Colony, at least for starters."

"Why there?"

"Mount up," Jonas said.

Although annoyed that Jonas had ignored her question, a loud crash from the brothel underscored the practicality of his suggestion.

Together, the four of them burst forth from the warehouse, nearly trampling the priest as they shot past the blazing brothel. They also passed two more armed ruffians lying in wait for any refugees trying to escape by the back door. They cried out in alarm as their quarry slipped through their fingers, but without mounts or ranged weapons, there was little else they could do.

Jonas led them on a circuitous jaunt through the city, taking at times narrow, little-used alleys through which they had to ride single-file. He also took them in directions opposite of their ultimate goal. After more than half an hour without incident, he finally relaxed a little and, satisfied they had of thrown off any pursuit, slowed his pace to a trot. Tilly was still sniffling. Jonas was ashen and grim.

Dona pulled her horse alongside his. "Why the Colony?"

"You have a better suggestion?"

"I was just curious about your reasons. It's not what I would have expected."

"Mainly because the Church is unwelcome there."

"It is?"

"Last I heard. Some years back, there was an exhibition by several prominent artists giving their interpretations of defining moments in Church history. Let's just say the Church was not amused by some of the liberties taken. They demanded the exhibition be destroyed and the artists punished."

"What happened?"

"Nothing. The Princess not only ignored the demands, but issued a proclamation reaffirming the Colony's devotion to

artistic freedom and specifically praising the exhibit as vi-
sionary."

"And the Church tolerated that?"

"Not with grace. They appealed to the Crown Prince—a
move I expect was intended to undercut the Princess's sov-
ereignty over the island. To his credit, despite substantial
Church pressure, the Crown Prince maintained he had no
jurisdiction in the matter, since he considered the island to
be its own separate nation."

"So the Church lost?"

"They excommunicated the Princess. And when that didn't
work, they placed the whole island under interdict."

"Did the Princess relent?"

"It seems she was never very religious to start with. She
lost a few artists who feared the Church's wrath, but over
time, her bold protection of their artistic expression has
brought in far more."

"Wasn't she afraid the Church would send troops?"

"Military might is not the Church's strong suit. Not only
that, but I doubt the Crown Prince would have been thrilled
by the idea of an armed force entering his city, regardless of
the reason. And he certainly wouldn't be inclined to allow
the Church to take the island by force, given its economic
importance."

"So the Church lost?"

"The exhibition was eventually destroyed at night by a
small group with sledgehammers. That inspired the Princess
to muster a security force to protect the artists. I once saw
them eject a priest bodily from the island, which I suppose is
not surprising given that the Princess is still excommunicated
and the island is still under interdict. I expect they'd think
twice before they pursued us there."

"But where will we stay?" Dona asked. "Do you intend to just camp out in the park?"

"Heavens no," Jonas said. "It just so happens that I recently came by a tidy sum. We'll be fine for money, at least for a while."

"In that case," Dona said. "I think I know just the place."

.   .   .   .   .

Ordinal Isrulian sighed. "Regrettably, I think we must conclude your so-called Relic is a fake."

"How tight is the timing?" Thurman asked. "Could it just be weak?"

"It's been two full hours, and your tooth is still black as midnight. A genuine Relic should have thrown off the effect within about an hour, or so I am told."

"So I was defrauded?"

"It would seem so. I must admit to being a tad put out that I was summoned here on such slender evidence. I'm sure I don't need to remind you of the countless responsibilities that burden even the least dedicated of Ordinals."

Thurman bowed his head. "Of course not, Your Ordinence."

"In fact, I would have been disinclined to make the journey at all, were it not for the gravitas of the Goodkin name."

"I offer my humblest apologies."

"Be that as it may, the Church is out a substantial sum of money, I am out six days' travel, and we are no closer to our goal."

"I will not rest until the thief is brought to justice."

"And we will still be no closer to our goal. It seems to me your time might be better spent tracking down a *bona fide* Relic rather than wasting additional resources on the merchant, who probably has no better way of determining a Relic's authenticity than you do."

"Let me reiterate my mortification, Your Ordinence."

There was an awkward pause.

"Well, as long as I'm here, I may as well make my rounds of the local churches. At least then it won't be a total loss. Would you be so kind as to call in my retinue?"

"Of course," Thurman said, striding toward the office door. "And I assure you I shall make every effort to solve this problem as quickly as possible."

"You'll permit me to doubt. It's not every day we happen across the remains of a martyr."

Thurman opened the door and beckoned. "Nevertheless," he said. "If I fail to deliver, it is only because it was not humanly possible."

Isrulian raised an eyebrow. "A word to the wise, young Goodkin. If you make a habit of promising the world, it is prudent to lay in a healthy supply. Once it's broken, even the most skillful repairs can't restore a promise's original luster."

Thurman stepped aside as the Ordinal's retinue appeared.

"Don't bother coming back in," Isrulian said. "We're making rounds."

Before Isrulian had even left the building, Thurman was already at his desk, writing furiously. Cartier burst in, agitated and out of breath.

Thurman didn't even look up. "You're late. I trust by now you have the spirits merchant in custody?"

Cartier winced. "It was a disaster. We finally tracked him to a brothel, but during the attempt to capture him, he escaped on horseback with three others."

"Don't tell me," Thurman said. "One of them was a young woman with dark hair."

Cartier blinked in surprise. "Why yes, how did you know?"

"A lucky guess. Are your men in pursuit?"

"No," Cartier said. "That's the disaster I was telling you about. Two Inquisitors and three of our mercenaries entered the brothel to apprehend the suspect, but they never came back out, and the brothel itself went up in flames. All five must have perished."

Thurman stopped writing and looked up. "Are you telling me that two of our Inquisitors gave their lives today in the line of duty?"

"I did everything I could, but the fire was so unexpected and everything happened so fast that by the time I realized something was amiss, it was already too late. Do you want me to gather more men and pursue them?"

"Yes, yes, I'm sure you did everything you could. But now our duty lies not with pursuing our enemies, but in seeing to the welfare of our fallen. We must recover their remains and ensure they receive a proper hero's burial."

Cartier nodded. "I'll see to the remains just as soon as the fire is out."

"Please do. After all, it's not every day we find ourselves in the solemn position of mourning the passage of even a single martyr, let alone two."

"Heroes, certainly," Cartier said. "But don't they have to die for the act of professing their faith to be true martyrs?"

Thurman frowned and his eyes narrowed. "Close enough."

. . . . .

Under the moonlight, the rectory garden projected an otherworldly serenity. The alien croaking of frogs dominated the night sounds, and the sculpted topiaries and planted beds seemed almost somber in monochrome. The sun-drenched version may have been more pleasing on the eyes, but the moonlit version calmed the soul. The Monsignor could easily understand why his brother spent so much time here.

"Laitrech tells me you should have been in bed an hour ago."

"Easy for him to say. He has all the time in the world."

"He seems to think you will have even less if you ignore his advice."

"Today, I've decided that quality trumps quantity. The weather could turn any day now—I may not get another opportunity to enjoy the garden like this. How go the preparations?"

"I think the tailor is finally finished taking the measurements. I shudder to think how long the actual fitting could take."

Darron took a deep breath. "Armand, I know you aren't comfortable with this whole business, and I know there's really no way I can thank you enough for your sacrifice, but if there is anything I can do to make up even a tiny fraction of what I owe you, promise you'll tell me."

"I appreciate the thought, but the Church has already given me everything I require."

"I'm sorry for putting you in this position. I know full well it may not be in your best interest, but as Primal, I have to think not of just what's best for my brother, but what's best for the Church."

"I know you always mean well. Where we disagree is that I am a firm believer that how you achieve something matters at least as much as what you achieve."

"Allow me to amend my offer. If there's anything I can do, short of submitting to a lecture…"

The Monsignor chuckled. "Speaking of lectures. Laitrech gave me a very interesting one today."

"Oh? What about?"

"It was mainly on the responsibilities of Ordinals."

"That's what I like about Laitrech—he's always been one to anticipate a need."

"I have to say I found it more than a little unsettling."

"In what way?"

"Well, it started out as a discussion about what you were planning to do about obtaining a Relic for the new Ordinal position."

"I hadn't considered that. Surely it shouldn't be a major issue. You aren't disturbed by the thought of carrying a Relic, are you?"

"No, that's not it at all—it's what they do with them that disturbs me."

"You mean the healing? I thought we'd talked about that."

"It still strikes me as more than a little heretical."

"Oh please," Darron said. "Don't you think you are taking this heresy fetish of yours just a little too far? Ordinals were using Relics to perform good works long before Phrendonic heresy even was heresy. You can't seriously be suggesting all the Ordinals over the ages have been heretics?"

"All I'm saying is that I am having a difficult time distinguishing between what the Ordinals do and what Phrendonics do."

"Heresy is often characterized by subtle distinctions."

"Your position is inconsistent," the Monsignor said. "People have been put to death for practicing Phrendonic heresy, but now I am to understand that the Church not only condones, but approves, similar behavior in the highest echelons of its leadership?"

Darron shook his head. "I just don't see a problem here. Ordinals are high-ranking officials, often with years of theological training, who report directly to the Primal. If anyone can be trusted with this knowledge, surely they can."

"Are you suggesting the Church should make exceptions for Phrendonic heretics on the basis of whether they are trustworthy or educated? Do we deny Ordinals their Relics if, by chance, they are neither?"

"If someone abuses his position, we can solve the problem by taking away his Relic. Can you say the same about Phrendonics?"

"When was the last time an Ordinal had his Relic taken?"

Darron grinned. "See how successful the selection process has been?"

The Monsignor blinked in incredulity. "You have the gall to say that after forcing me to accept an Ordinal position you had to invent for the sole purpose of mitigating your own admittedly poor choices?"

"What would you have me do? Take away all their Relics?"

"That would resolve the inconsistency."

"I can't do that, and you know it. They'd mutiny."

"So much for a successful selection process, eh?"

"They shouldn't have to anyway. A Relic is a relatively minor perk for a lifetime of dedicated service."

"If it's so minor, they probably wouldn't even miss it."

"Don't bait me. This is just not something I'm able to grant—the repercussions would be too damaging."

The Monsignor shook his head. "That puts me in a very uncomfortable position. I will be assuming an office that encourages me to do precisely the same sorts of things I've spent considerable effort working to prevent others from doing. Hypocrisy of that magnitude will destroy everything I've achieved in a lifetime of trying to atone for Father's abuses."

"Don't start that again. Father did what needed to be done under very dangerous and trying circumstances."

"We both know that doesn't excuse what he did. If I've accomplished nothing else, I've at least proven the same goals can be achieved using humane and rigorously fair methods."

"All you've proven is that *you* can do it, and under far less trying circumstances. When will you learn that not everyone is capable of what you are? Don't you get it? That's precisely why I want you to be an Ordinal. No one else can do what you do."

"That's ridiculous," the Monsignor said. "All it takes is commitment to standards of decency, a little patience, and a modest amount of insight. If we can find no one else in the entire Church who displays these traits, how can we hold ourselves out as having any moral authority at all?"

"Dismiss it all you like, but you know in your heart it's true."

"Well, if it is, then you have just made my case for me. If I'm the only one in all the Church with these traits, we certainly can't entrust anyone else with the dire responsibility of carrying a Relic."

"If you really feel that strongly about it, by all means get yourself elected Primal and take all their precious Relics away. I promise not to stand in your way for very much longer."

"And after you bestow upon me the enviable title of 'hypocrite' just how do you expect me to be able to garner any votes at all?"

"We all have our little challenges to bear," Darron said. "I'm sorry, but from my perspective, that one seems pretty minor."

"Then perhaps the Church should revisit its stance on Phrendonic heresy."

"You risk much to achieve your precious 'consistency.'

I certainly don't need to remind you, of all people, of the atrocities perpetrated by Phrendonic heretics, much less the societal inequities they fostered."

"There were actually not very many atrocities," the Monsignor said. "And most of those were committed defending themselves from over-zealous Inquisitors and their brutal methods. Surely such atrocities could be addressed on a case-by-case basis."

"And the societal inequities?"

The Monsignor shook his head. "I have no answer for that. They are the primary reason I have spent a lifetime supporting the prohibition, but I can't continue in good conscience if I am personally guilty of fostering those same inequities."

"Good news," Darron said. "As an Ordinal, you'll have all sorts of other responsibilities to keep you occupied. In fact, you'll be able to give up the Inquisition entirely."

Laitrech poked his head through the door. "I'm sorry to interrupt, but His Primacy really should be getting some sleep."

"Yes, I should be heading to bed," Darron said, attempting to rise from his bench. He only made it part way up, before he sat heavily back down.

The Monsignor reached out to steady him. "Are you all right?"

"I'll be fine, but I wouldn't mind a little assistance."

Laitrech took his arm. "I'm right here," he said. As the three men entered the rectory, the Monsignor noticed that Darron was even paler than when he had last seen him, a fact that had been hidden by the moonlight. He hoped their conversation had not taken too much of a toll.

"I'm sorry if I was too argumentative."

Darron flashed him a weak smile. "You wouldn't be you if you weren't. Sleep well, brother."

"You too. Perhaps I'll see you tomorrow?"

"Are you all right to take the stairs?" Laitrech asked, "Or will you be sleeping in the guest room tonight?"

"With help, I'm sure I can manage the stairs. Besides, Armand will need the guest room. Did he tell you he came up with a way of solving the problem with the Relics?"

Although already at the guestroom door, the Monsignor could still hear their conversation. His stomach clenched as he realized that what he thought had been a private conversation was about to become painfully public.

"He didn't," Laitrech said.

"He suggested we simply take them away from everyone."

"Did he now?"

"Of course I told him that wasn't an option."

"I'm glad to hear it."

The Monsignor turned back toward his brother in shock. He just barely caught sight of the two men as they topped the stairs. For a brief moment, he felt the heat of Laitrech's gaze. And then they disappeared into the Primal's private chambers.

CHAPTER SIXTEEN

REUNION

Verone Nevinander nodded to the guard as he secured the wrought-iron gates behind her. She so rarely passed through them of late she was surprised he even recognized her. While she had once toyed with boycotting these festivities, and was now suffering pangs of regret for her change of heart, she never truly had a choice—for although she managed to steel herself against a great many of the vicissitudes of her life, she still couldn't stand to see her mother beg.

The long walk up to her father's villa would have been a delight for anyone else. The drive was flanked by stately elms, which swayed in the breezy warmth of the autumn sun. Songbirds of every description voiced their unabashed enthusiasm for generations of hospitality in an endless musical barrage. To the left, the well-tended orchards were laden with the spoils of summer, and to the right, the pond teamed with lush water lilies and exotic goldfish. But these idyllic scenes held no joy for Verone, to whom they represented merely a grim reminder of a life she had been all too eager to escape.

Her mother Nathalie was waiting for her on the veranda. Slender and graceful, she carried herself with a subtle air of surrender that only the distraction of frenetic social activity had any power to banish. It was yet another item on Verone's long list of things for which she held her father accountable.

Nathalie extended her arms. "Veronique," she said, "I'm so glad you could come."

"Thanks for inviting me, Mum."

After a quick hug, Nathalie led her inside.

The glass panels lining the back of the foyer opened to the courtyard beyond, which was where her mother favored entertaining, weather permitting. As they passed, she waved at an enormous round table smothered in gifts. "You can leave the package there."

"Don't mind if I do," Verone said. "How is father doing? He's not in one of his moods, is he?"

"I think he's genuinely looking forward to this. You know how he loves to be the center of attention."

"How could I forget? Who else's arms were twisted, or am I the only guest?"

As usual, her mother ignored the barb. "Oh, everyone's here. It's going to be such a wonderful day."

"Everyone?"

"Well, a number of your father's business associates, as well as your aunt Olivia. Oh, and your brothers, of course."

"Even Thad?"

"Thaddeus arrived early this morning."

"That must have taken some serious persuasion."

"I did stress how important this occasion would be to your father."

"And he still came?"

"And Reginald and Jedidiah arrived with their families yesterday. And Damien's family has been visiting the entire week. He's been taking your father out hunting, and they've had such a good time together."

"He always was the biggest suck-up."

Nathalie slid open a glass panel. "Why don't you come back and see the courtyard? We've been working on it for weeks."

"I'm sure it's lovely. You always did have a flair for such things. Thad is convinced he gets it from you."

Verone had to admit the courtyard was charming. A quaint gazebo had been erected near the back for a band of musicians who were just starting to assemble. A series of long tables had been draped with white linen tablecloths, which were in turn festooned with white ribbons and strings of freshwater pearls. Fresh-cut flowers decorated the center of each table in elaborate centerpieces, each resembling one of the many songbirds her mother was so fond of. A small dais dominated the center of the courtyard near the fountain. It held a single table with the most elaborate of the centerpieces: a proud pheasant—her father's favorite game bird. A small army of servants presented tasteful appetizers to the many guests already milling about. Banners in red-and-white linen hung from the courtyard walls, decorated with wishes for a happy 65th birthday. As she surveyed the decorations, Verone couldn't help feeling that they were somehow more reminiscent of a wedding than a birthday party. She wondered whether her mother was subconsciously using this event as an opportunity to deliver another of her little hints.

"I was right, Mum. It's stunning."

Nathalie gave her a shy smile. "Thank you. The boys all mumbled nice things, but I don't think they really appreciate it."

"Hey, Verone."

"Thad?" She turned to face her younger brother, whose fair hair was similarly blessed with a touch a ginger. But there the resemblance ended. Unlike Verone, Thad was long-legged and lank. His angular face lit up as she greeted him. "Fancy meeting you here," she said.

He delivered a brotherly hug. "I was just going to say the same thing about you."

"I thought you said you'd never set foot in this house again."

"Mum applied the thumbscrews."

"I got the same treatment."

"Oh you two," Nathalie said. "Why don't we get a closer look at the courtyard?"

She'd just begun herding them when an older guest called out to her. "Nathalie, you've outdone yourself."

Nathalie's face lit up. "Oh, excuse me for just a moment," she said, bustling off.

"Tell the truth, Thad," Verone said. "He's going to make the announcement today, isn't he?"

"Mum didn't say."

"Then who did? Face it—nothing else, short of wild horses, could have dragged you back through that front door."

"It's not like I'm on any kind of terms with anyone who's likely to know."

"Don't be coy with me. I changed your diapers."

"Honestly, I don't *know* anything, but I do happen to remember that Grandpa made his announcement on his 65th birthday."

"That's it?" Verone asked skeptically. "That's all it took to get you here?"

"That and the thumbscrews. Mum seemed to want this so badly I could hardly say no."

"So we're both in the same boat. We just couldn't bring ourselves to pass up the opportunity to see how he plans to abuse us this time."

"I sort of hope he outright disinherits me," Thad said. "A nice clean break would be so much healthier than this purgatory of uncertainty."

Verone helped herself to a drink from the tray of a passing waiter. "Nothing's stopping you from cutting the ties yourself, you know."

"And wonder for the rest of my life if I might have ended up rich? As tempting as that sounds, I've managed to resist."

Verone started down the steps into the courtyard. "Clearly you should be spending more time with your mother."

"I see her from time to time. Hey—wait up."

Verone browsed the placemats until she found one with her name on it, and had a seat. Thad, whose name had appeared several place settings away, switched his tag so that it was next to Verone's.

"All right," he said. "What did Mum tell you?"

Before she could reply, a fanfare of trumpets signaled the official start of the festivities. Dancers in exotic costumes cavorted through the courtyard. Confetti showered the guests from above. Although the band in the gazebo had not yet finished their setup, the dancers came equipped with castanets, cymbals, and other forms of percussion. Together, they created a primal rhythm that was already seducing some of the less inhibited guests into participating.

Thad gawked. "She spared no expense this time, did she?"

"Mum always did love a party."

A tall ruddy guest who had been swirling through the crowd with two of the dancers paused in front of Verone's table.

"As I live and breathe. If it isn't my long-lost little sister."

"Hello Damien," Verone said.

Damien eyed Verone's ample figure. "I see exile agrees with you. And here I spent all that time worrying you were going to starve to death after you walked out on us."

Verone fluttered her eyelashes. "And miss any chance I might have had to wrest my share of the estate from your hot little hands? Don't be silly."

Damien's expression was that of a predator toying with hapless prey. "Well, you never know. I guess it's possible the return of the prodigal daughter might prove to be a more compelling strategy than life-long loyalty of the doting son. We'll just have to see how that plays out, won't we?"

"I wasn't aware strategies had anything to do with it," Thad said. "The tradition is to split things equally. After all, that's what Grandpa did. Dad talks a good talk, but that's never been a very good indicator of what he's actually going to do."

"Isn't that cute. It's little Thad, still clutching after Verone's apron strings, just like he always used to. So, how is our little *artiste*, anyway? Is it really better looking *for* a patron instead of looking to *be* one?"

Thad's face reddened. "I like it just fine, thank you."

"Still living in that shanty on the island, or have you upgraded to a barn?"

"I've lived in more unpleasant places."

"Oh really?"

Nathalie chose that moment to rejoin them. "I see you three have had a chance to get reacquainted. What do you think of the party so far?"

Damien gave his mother a peck on the cheek. "Awesome, Mum. No one throws a party like you." He waved as he allowed himself to be pulled away by the dancing girls.

"Everything is perfect, Mum," Verone said, "When are we expecting the guest of honor?"

"I can schedule the dancers, I can schedule the hors d'oeuvres, and I can schedule the music, but I've never once managed to schedule your father."

"But he's going to miss half the party." Thad said. "It seems such a shame."

Nathalie beamed at the implicit compliment. "Don't worry. There's plenty more where this came from. Oh, it's almost time." As quickly as she'd come, she was off again.

Verone noticed that Thad's nose was still wrinkled, as if he'd just caught a whiff of something that had been sitting out in the sun too long. "What's the matter? Surely you weren't expecting our darling Damien to improve with age?"

"I guess not. After all, no matter how old they are, dregs are still dregs. I suppose the same is true for the twins?"

"Doubly so."

Thad's groan was interrupted by another round of blaring trumpets. The man of the hour stood blinking in the sunlight. Spotty applause erupted as guests began to realize just what it was the trumpets had heralded. It quickly grew to an ovation.

"He looks old," Thad said in Verone's ear.

Verone noticed it too. Her father had always been a large man, but he had carried it well. Since she had last seen him, however, his jowls had achieved wattle status, seeming to arrive just a few seconds behind his chin, quivering there in momentary uncertainty until dragged unceremoniously to their next destination. His once-reddish hair, which had long ago retreated from the crown of his head, was now silver, as were the two great brow thickets perched above his eyes. But the eyes themselves had not changed—they were still confident, sharp, and utterly devoid of empathy. As they passed over her, they paused briefly in recognition, and the corner of his mouth pulled itself up in a little half-smile. Verone shuddered at the sight of it.

On Nathalie's cue, exuberant strains of birthday music rang out from the gazebo. Slowly she made her way through the crowd and up the steps to the railing where her husband still stood taking in the well-wishers and merriment with a self-satisfied smile. She threw her arms around him. The crowd waited expectantly for her to address them, but when their kiss lingered, thunderous applause erupted again.

She led him by the hand down the steps and through the crowd to the dais and had him take his seat. Then she smoothed her dress, caught her breath, and turned to face the crowd. A drum roll from the band quieted both the leftover applause and the hushed voices of several guests still trying to sneak in that last little gossipy tidbit.

"My goodness, aren't you all in a good mood tonight?" she said, eliciting a round of cheers. "Alistair and I want to thank you all for making this the most memorable Nevinander gathering yet…and it's only just getting started."

A hearty "hear, hear" erupted from Damien and the twins, who were seated with their families at a long table just down from the dais.

"As of today," Nathalie continued, "my Alistair has finally achieved that watershed year when Nevinanders have traditionally retired from public life, and I'm sure you'll agree few are more deserving. Please join with me in wishing him the happiest birthday imaginable."

Cheers, whistles, and deafening applause drowned out the band, which had begun another vigorous round of birthday music. During the ovation, Mum delivered one last kiss and took the seat next to Alistair's. As the applause died down, Alistair rose to his feet.

He gestured for Nathalie to stand again. "If there exists a luckier man, I surely don't know who he is."

Reluctant and blushing, Nathalie curtseyed and took her seat again.

Alistair continued. "Forty-four years ago, I made the best decision of my life when I asked pretty little Nathalie Fesseldown to be my wife. Now it didn't exactly seem that way at the time, of course. As with any life-altering decision, people are prone to second-guess themselves, and I was no exception. Yes, I had my doubts, and I suspect Nathalie must have as well, though you never would have known it. No sir, her voice was just as clear, steady, and decisive as could be, when exactly two weeks, three days, twenty hours and thirty-three minutes later, she finally said yes."

Scattered laughter flickered through the crowd.

"As you can imagine, at the time I viewed the delay to be cause for some concern. I wondered what she could possibly be thinking that would result in *any* delay, much less such a long one. At first, I thought she must just not want to appear to be too eager. Then I started to wonder whether she needed extra time to gently break the bad news to all the lesser suitors. I admit there was even a moment or two where I wondered whether she might be under the misapprehension that somewhere out there, there might actually be a better choice. I have always been a great admirer of optimism, but there are limits.

"So I asked her 'why the delay?' And you know what she told me? She said 'for a decision as important as this, I can't just "think so." I have to be as sure as I can possibly be, and that's not something one does overnight.'"

"My little Nathalie taught me a valuable lesson that day, though I admit it took a few years for the full truth of it to sink in. You see, because she waited until she was as sure as she could possibly be, she was able to devote herself whole-heartedly to her choice, and I believe that has made all the difference."

The audience made an attempt at applause, but Alistair held up his hands.

"That brings us to another important decision—one where I daresay a mere 'I think so' would not be good enough either. In fact, if you had not expected this decision to be announced today, despite your obvious and incontrovertible affection, fully half of you would have probably sent your regrets."

At that, Verone noticed Damien smirking at her across the courtyard. She met his gaze, but deliberately kept her own look unreadable.

"We all know," Alistair continued, "that there has been a long tradition for the Nevinanders to retire and pass on their estate to their designated heirs. Indeed, when he turned 65, my father stood on this very spot and made what was no doubt one of the most difficult decisions of his life. Bowing to the pressure of generations of tradition, he did what my little Nathalie refused to do: He settled for a choice he thought *might* work, instead of taking the time to be as sure as he could possibly be. In a misguided attempt to be fair, he split his estate down the middle, giving half to me and half to my sister. Had he taken the time to be sure, he would certainly have realized that by so doing, he not only crippled his estate, he destroyed his family as well. It took me years to repair the financial damage. The rest remains beyond repair.

"It's no secret that I have vowed to keep my own estate intact, but there is still the question of which heir. Who from among my many children would be best suited for steward-ship? For something this important, I cannot permit myself the luxury to choose solely on the basis of charisma, loyalty, or cleverness, any more than one would choose a spouse based on any single one of those factors. Therefore, after much thought, I have decided only that I am not yet as sure as I can possibly be. Until I am, any reports of my retirement will undoubtedly be greatly exaggerated. In the meantime, I give my heartfelt thanks to you all for your attendance and your attention. I am told dinner will be served momentarily. Enjoy."

Although the pronouncement surprised Verone not in the least, it warmed the cockles of her heart to observe Damien's look of horror. She shook her head in puzzlement. Even as a child, she had wondered why her brothers were so quick to dismiss their mother as a resource when it was perfectly obvious that no one had greater access to the inner workings of their father's mind.

Next to her, Thad groaned. "What have I done to deserve this?"

Verone chuckled. "Hoping for something a little more decisive?"

"I was hoping either to be rich or to never have to set foot in this pit of despair again."

Verone couldn't help noticing that his despair did not seem to interfere with his appetite. "Your expectations were unrealistic. Since when has he ever made anything that painless?"

Thad chewed intently. "My fault for being perversely optimistic. At least the food is good."

"Which obviously makes it Mum's doing."

"Good point. Are you going to eat that roll?"

"Help yourself." She was obliged to repeat that phrase several times throughout the meal, not without some resentment. By the time dinner was over, she felt her brother must have consumed fully twice what she had, including the lion's share of her rum-soaked birthday trifle, which he had seized in the throes of his feeding frenzy without even bothering to ask. Yet, she knew that after all was said and done, he'd arrive home tipping the scales a pound or two lighter, whereas she would have gained five just for having had the audacity to sit at the same table with something claiming to be rum-soaked.

She distracted herself from the injustice of having failed to inherit her mother's metabolism by scanning the courtyard for signs of the after-dinner entertainment. She was expecting the troupe Nathalie had commissioned to show up any time now, and the sooner the better. She'd really rather have them out of the way before the arrival of her own modest contribution to the evening's line-up. She didn't have to wait long.

A clash of cymbals announced the performers, who slid down ropes all around the courtyard, carrying lighted torches in their teeth. A series of choreographed back flips brought them front and center, where, as one, they bowed to the man of the hour, who was still in the midst of an especially large helping of trifle. Within moments, the jugglers drafted Alistair into their routine. He stood trapped among three of them as they cheerily juggled the lighted torches around him. Alistair tried his best to convey nonchalance, but much to the amusement of the crowd, his discomfort was plain. The look in his eyes gave him away, as did the unnatural way he held himself erect, and the involuntary gulp that escaped him every time a torch came close. It turned out to be such a crowd pleaser that the jugglers dragged it on and on, bantering among themselves as though they'd completely forgotten Alistair was there. Finally, Alistair closed his eyes entirely, as though he couldn't bear to watch any longer. Abruptly, all the torches went out, even the ones in mid-flight. The jugglers exchanged shocked glances, wrapped up their routine, and took a hasty bow to hearty applause. Alistair tentatively opened one eye, then the other, and when he determined the coast was clear, he took a bow as well.

Alistair's self-satisfied smirk was not lost on Verone, who leaned over to Thad. "Still clearly fixated on always being in control, I see."

The sun was setting by the time her Mum's pre-planned entertainments had run their course and the tables had been cleared away to free up the courtyard for dancing. Verone spent some of that time catching up with family friends she had not seen in years. She had hoped to leave much sooner, and she was finding it tiring to mingle while maneuvering to keep her father at a safe distance, but she dared not leave until she knew whether her efforts had borne fruit. Finally convinced there was no point in staying any longer, she found her mother to say her goodbyes. Since some of the other guests had also decided to call it a night, Nathalie and her sister Olivia had planted themselves strategically at a small table by the glass panels that now separated the villa from the courtyard once more.

"Well, Mum, I had a lovely evening."

Nathalie was horrorstruck. "You aren't leaving, are you? The dancing has only just started. I'm sure there are a multitude of nice young gentlemen down there who could use an accomplished partner."

"Subtle, Mum,"

"I just meant that it would be sad for all those lessons we got for you to go to waste."

"Mum, I was six. Most of these dances didn't even exist then."

Olivia, as was her wont after a few toddies, saw fit to intervene. "Oh leave the girl be, Nathalie. She's onto you anyway, and headstrong like her father—if she thinks for one minute she's being led, she'll run full speed in the opposite direction, regardless of whether it takes her anyplace she wants to be."

"I don't know what you're talking about," Nathalie sniffed. "I just like to make sure my guests are well-cared-for, and providing accomplished dance partners when you host a dance is one way to do that."

"Fine, ignore my advice," Olivia said, "but don't blame me when the girl sees fit to insulate herself from your meddling by putting on even more weight."

"*Olivia!*" Mum said.

The comment stung. Verone knew that Olivia was fond of her and just trying in her own way to keep her mother from becoming overbearing, and she knew she never would have put it that way if she'd been toddie-free. But despite those truths, Verone suddenly found herself struggling to hold back tears.

"I'm sorry hon," Olivia said, clearly appalled at what had just blurted out of her. "All I meant to say was that your mum should give you a little more space."

Verone winked. "Yes, more space will come in handy once I gain all that extra weight." The gentle riposte helped her regain her composure. She leaned down to give Olivia a goodbye hug.

"Oh, give your old drunk Aunty a break. And don't be such a stranger. If I have to wait another five years to see you, you might find me spewing nonsense even without benefit of a nice warm toddie."

As Verone straightened up, she bumped someone who hadn't been there before. Turning, she saw a short substantial woman with a large package topped by a prodigious red bow. She was wearing an expansive floral hat that must have been at least twenty years out of fashion, and a gown to match. The unmistakable scent of roses permeated the area, and this woman seemed to be the epicenter.

"Oh, how clumsy of me," Verone said.

"The fault was mine," the woman replied. "My apologies."

Verone made to hug her mother goodbye, but then stopped short. Nathalie was staring at the rose-drenched woman with saucer eyes, her expression warring between dismay and disbelief. Olivia, by contrast, registered only surprise and maybe a hint of amusement, as though she thought the party might finally start to get interesting.

"Marguerite? Is that you?"

"Good evening, Nathalie," Marguerite said. "How have you been?"

"I've been, uh, just fine," she replied. "And yourself?"

"Quite well, thank you. I was heartened to receive the invitation. I was beginning to think after all these years that Alistair would never get over his childishness. Was that your doing, or is he letting his grudge pass with his estate?"

"I certainly can't take credit for that."

"You're looking good, Olivia," Marguerite said. And, finally recognizing Verone, she added: "And this must be little Veronique."

"Welcome home, Aunt Marguerite. Can I take your wrap?"

"Thank you, dear." She allowed Verone to unwrap her while she switched the package from one arm to the other.

"Would you like me to take the gift as well?"

"Thank you, but I would just as soon deliver this myself. I'm sorry I wasn't able to make it sooner, but as you could probably guess, I had a previous engagement."

"Oh, of course," Verone said. "Happy birthday."

Marguerite nodded. "Now, would you be so kind as to direct me to Alistair? This package is getting heavy."

"I think you'll find him with the boys down by the makeshift fire pit," Verone said. "At least that's where I last saw him."

As the overpowering scent of roses trailed Marguerite down the steps and into the courtyard, Mum fixed her sister with an incredulous look.

"What's she doing here?"

Olivia grinned. "Delivering a package?"

"But he's been drinking."

"It's his birthday. You had to know he'd be drinking when you invited her."

"You don't understand," Nathalie hissed. "I didn't invite her."

. . . . .

Alistair sat enshrined by the fire pit like some ancient pharaoh indulgently accepting tribute from the subjugated masses. His three eldest sons gathered around him like jealous counselors, each vying to be the favorite. Furthering the illusion, the structured music of the afternoon had given way to wilder, rhapsodic melodies, and the dancing, fueled by rhythm, firelight, and the free flow of spirits, had followed suit. Surveying the scene, Marguerite's visceral reaction nearly forced a change of heart as she recalled the insatiable lust for approval and control that had driven what had seemed an insurmountable wedge between them.

No, she told herself firmly. He was man enough to make the first overture. You can at least have the grace to give it a chance.

Ignoring the churning in her stomach, she did her best to project a cheery tone. "Happy Birthday, Alistair."

Alistair froze mid-sentence. After a long pause, his head slowly swiveled toward the sound of Marguerite's voice, his face a mask of loathing. The brothers fell silent.

"What are *you* doing on *my* property?"

For the first time it occurred to Marguerite that Alistair might not have been aware she'd been invited.

"I received an invitation to celebrate your birthday, and I accepted. I was delighted to be given the chance to put our differences behind us."

"You refer to theft of half my birthright as *differences?*"

"Whatever the wrongs you perceive that I have done you, I would like to try to make amends."

"Ah, yes, there's the sister I remember. Ever so talented, so tolerant, so reasonable so…condescending. Clearly just because I perceive them as wrongs doesn't mean they actually are, and you are so very patient to overlook my mistaken perceptions to achieve the greater good."

"I'm sorry. I'm certainly not here to offend you. I'm doing my best here. Can we at least *try* to work things out?"

Alistair laughed incredulously. "And why on earth would I want to do that?"

Marguerite's voice dropped to a hoarse whisper. "Because…I miss you."

Alistair stopped short and blinked, as though that was the last thing he'd expected. Then his eyes narrowed. "And why else?"

"What do you mean?"

"Don't toy with me. You could have 'missed me' hundreds of times over the past few decades. Why now?"

"I'd thought you'd made an overture with your invitation."

"If you had really wanted this so badly, we both know you wouldn't wait for my overture. Try again."

"I also thought maybe handing off your estate would have given you some perspective."

"Aside from the fact that I haven't, it's well known that when I do, the bulk will go to one heir and one heir only. Clearly there's been no change in my perspective. We know far too many people in common for you to expect me to believe you weren't aware of that. I'm running out of patience. Why now?"

Marguerite met his gaze, her jaw working. Finally, she looked away.

"Oh, very well. There's an Inquisition gaining steam at Exidgeon. We're trying to stay on top of it, but I can't make any guarantees. I thought you should know."

"You came here to tell me that? You must have really let it get out of hand, then."

Marguerite bristled. "It's not my sole responsibility to manage it."

"No?" I'd have sworn it was precisely for such situations that father saw fit to bestow upon you, and you alone, among many other things, his precious set of wands. You remember the ones, yes?"

"I was more responsible. You gave him little choice."

"Yes, well apparently responsible is not always the same as effective, is it? I'm surprised though, that the great and powerful Marguerite would choose to abase herself to me, her lowly brother, when she allows things to fester beyond her ability to rectify."

"Look, I'm only here to inform you. I'm not asking for your help."

"Well, then, if it's not your sole responsibility, and you aren't asking me, who else did you have in mind? Or were you just highlighting my irresponsibility and dereliction of duty as some of those endearing qualities that make you miss me so?"

Marguerite held out the package. "I can see my coming here was a mistake. I'd thought this gift might be a good start for healing the rift between us, but no doubt you'll just view it as another of the many things you were entitled to in the first place. Please take it, since looking at it now would only make me sad."

Alistair made no move to accept it.

Marguerite finally set the package on one of the chairs. "I hope someday you find peace." And then she turned to leave.

"I hope one day you hurt at least half as much as you hurt me," Alistair called after her.

Marguerite shuddered, collected herself, and then resumed her departure. She swept up the stairs and out through the villa in a swirl of rose-scented petticoats, her chin high, her expression, desolate.

Once she was gone, Alistair stood and picked up the package she had left behind. After considering it a few moments, but without opening it, he dropped it into the fire pit. Shaking his head, he trudged up the steps and into the villa.

Meanwhile, the ribbon smoked and shriveled, and the plain white wrapping paper ignited, peeling away in flaming brown strips that crumpled and turned black as the updraft carried them high into the air. The peeling paper revealed for a few moments the skilled portrait of a proud and accomplished man who bore a striking resemblance, in different particulars, to both his son and his daughter. And then that too succumbed to the flames.

CHAPTER SEVENTEEN

SOUL SEARCHING

Jonas insisted they leave the city. To throw off pursuit, they spent the night in a rough camp and returned by a different route the next morning. It was noon by the time they finally arrived at the Expatriate Hotel. Jonas tried for a suite of rooms on the first floor but was told no such rooms existed. He settled for a small apartment above a carriage house on the hotel grounds, hoping the window wouldn't be too high to escape from should the need arise. During the negotiations, Dona, who had fallen a few paces back from the counter, put a finger to her lips. She had to give the clerk credit for taking the hint—short of a brief instant of recognition, he gave no sign they had met before. Jonas didn't seem to notice, and although Tilly was no longer weeping openly, she was still too distraught to be aware.

Jonas and Alexi stabled the horses in the carriage house, while Dona escorted Tilly up to the suite—two small bedrooms connected by a common area. Tilly collapsed on a bed, and Dona took a seat in the common room, crossed her arms, and waited for the men to show up. Jonas strode in, pipe smoke trailing behind him, Alexi in tow. He immediately began inspecting the lock.

Alexi sank into the chair across from Dona. "You think they'll follow us here?"

"Perhaps not openly," Jonas said. "But remember what happened to the art exhibit." After a few moments he stopped fiddling with the mechanism and tried improvising a bar across the door.

Dona cleared her throat. Jonas had played them long enough—it was high time he came clean. "Don't you think it's time you told us just what kind of trouble you've gotten us into?"

"Me?" Jonas asked. "I thought you were the heretic."

"Don't change the subject. "What is that medallion, and why did you want it so badly?"

"It's unimportant now, and really, none of your business. Actually, you are probably better off not knowing."

Tilly appeared in the bedroom doorway. "Tell *me* then." Despite the bags beneath her eyes and the tremor in her hands, her voice was firm. "Help me understand why Nanna had to die."

"Tilly, you're exhausted." Jonas said. "Get some rest. We can talk about this tomorrow."

"I'm not asking again. Either you start explaining, or I walk out that door, find that Inquisitor, and ask him myself. You decide."

Jonas stopped work on the door to meet his sister's gaze. He sighed, set down the board, and dropped into a chair.

"It was a polished piece of bone," he said simply.

"Go on."

"The Inquisitor wanted to buy it."

"Why would the Monsignor's son want to buy an old piece of bone?" Dona asked.

"Jonas," Tilly said. "I'm too tired to play twenty questions and too impatient to let Dona do it for me. Out with it."

"I'm coming to that. Give me a chance."

Tilly shifted a little but let him continue.

"Dona, do you remember my cart?"

"Who could forget?"

"So what did I sell?"

"I'm not exactly sure. I presume medicines, tonics, and potions?"

"That's how it started, but the more I traveled, the more I discovered that people were fascinated with the brews of other lands. So I started buying up the alcohol of one place and selling it for a tidy sum in the next. Over time, that became the bulk of my business, and I changed the signs on my cart accordingly—by adding the term 'spirits.'"

Tilly sighed and took a seat.

"I'm not following," Dona said.

"It's the sign that got me into trouble. After a few months making pretty good returns on my brew exchange, I got an odd customer. He asked if I had any spirits in stock. I asked him what kind he fancied, and he said 'the kind that bind the soul.' Now I didn't know what to make of that exactly, but I suspected he wanted the distilled stuff and started showing him some of those, but he just shook his head. So I showed him some of the ales and wines, but he didn't want those either. I finally asked him if he was looking for some specialty spirit. 'Oh, yes,' he told me, 'the kind that doesn't come in a bottle.'"

"Now if he'd said that to any other merchant, it would probably have ended the conversation."

Dona's brow creased. "What did he mean?"

"I wasn't sure, but I had enough of the right kind of esoteric education to speculate. So I played a hunch: I told him there are 'grave' consequences for peddling that kind of spirit. He smiled at that, saying he could likely make it worth the risk."

"You've lost me," Dona said. "What did he want?"

"Exactly what he said he did."

Dona stared at him blankly.

Jonas tried another tack. "Do you believe in the soul?"

"You mean in the religious sense?"

"Sure."

"I haven't seen any evidence to support the idea one way or another. I know the Church has a bunch of theories about it, but I never found them particularly convincing."

"Perhaps you haven't had access to the right tools—tools only available to a certain kind of heretic."

Tilly snorted. "This is getting a little far afield from an explanation."

"On the contrary."

Tilly sighed.

"All right," Dona said. "What would I think if I had the right tools?"

Alexi's eyes lit up. "Oh, I get it. You're talking about the difference in duration between a decay sorcel cast on an object as opposed to a person."

"Exactly," Jonas said.

Dona huffed. "Alexi, don't give him any ideas. He's creative enough without your help."

"No, listen," Alexi said. "What he's saying is that you can use a spell as a tool to detect the existence of a soul."

"Look," Dona said, "I'm not even sure I buy the whole spell thing yet."

"It makes sense, though. Phrendonian suggested in the book that spells cast on people had a dramatically shortened duration because a person's soul puts up some sort of resistance."

"Idle speculation," Dona said. "There could any number of reasons for spells to last less long on people. Flesh might just not be as stable as a rock."

"Ah," Jonas said, "but what would you say if the resistance persisted after death on something with similar stability, like say a bone?"

"Maybe there's just some special property of things that were once alive."

"Even if it only persists in one bone and not the rest?"

Dona began to suspect Jonas was spinning these distractions solely to divert her from the truth. To her dismay, it seemed to be working—she heard herself ask the obvious follow-up question. "Are you trying to tell me this medallion of yours contains a *soul?*"

"I tested it myself."

"Really? And just how does a nouncer test such a thing?"

Jonas reached into his pocket and held up a carved wooden rod with a tiny jewel tip. "He uses the right tool, of course."

Tilly's mouth fell open. "You told me you lost that."

Jonas shrugged. "So I found it again."

"You were supposed to destroy it."

"How could I? It was the last thing Dad ever gave me."

"He only let you play with it, then he put it back. He didn't give it to you—you stole it."

"Under the circumstances, do you really think he'd begrudge me?"

"That's not the point. It puts us all at risk."

"I don't see how. No one ever knew about it but you."

"What is it?" Dona asked. Tilly's reaction made it clear the object was more than a mere distraction.

"It's a minor thing, really. I always called it a Color Wand. I touch the tip to something and it vests a Color spell on it. This is just the red one, but Dad had a whole set. Using it, I could tell if something had a soul on it based on how long the color lasted—and it only lasted on the medallion for an hour. On nearly anything else, it would have lasted a whole day."

Jonas pocketed the wand again. "Anyway, this guy offered to set me up with a sweet deal if I could sell him something with spirit on it. He'd apparently heard rumors of people who sold such things by advertising themselves as spirit merchants."

"You aren't suggesting the Monsignor's son wanted to buy a soul from you?"

Tilly was on the verge of tears. "How could you? How could you work with the Inquisition?"

"I didn't even know that's who it was until later. And by then it was too late to pull out."

"I don't understand," Alexi said. "Even with a wand to detect such a thing, where did you end up finding one? I wouldn't even know where to begin."

"I have my sources," Jonas said.

Tilly shuddered. "Oh, Jonas. You didn't."

"It's not what you think. I had very strict instructions that it couldn't come from consecrated ground."

Dona blinked in shock. "You mean you robbed graves?"

"No-no-no," Jonas said. "No consecrated ground, remember? I simply took a side trip into the edge of Drewor territory. The barbarians there expose their dead to the wind on wooden platforms. No digging required, and the Drewors are more animal than human anyway. With the wand, it was a simple matter to grab what I needed and get out."

Dona's nose wrinkled. "I don't even want to think about that."

"Why?" Tilly asked. "You were doing fine with your business, and even if you weren't, you could always have come to me."

"Doing fine? I was subsisting at best, and it was hard work. And what would have happened if I'd gotten hurt, or when I got too old to drive the cart? We were rich once, and it was all taken from us. I saw an opportunity to reclaim some of what we lost from the very people who took it, and I jumped at it."

"But grave robbing?"

"Oh, you should talk. At least I wait to sell a soul until after it's dead."

Tilly's voice shook. "Not precisely. You were still very much alive when you sold yours to the Inquisition, and you took Nanna's down with you."

She retreated into the bedroom and slammed the door.

Jonas sighed and pounded on the door. "Tilly, open up. I didn't mean it."

Dona felt the warmth of Alexi's hand on hers. "We should give them some privacy. Let's take a walk."

"Good idea."

Wandering the sculpture gardens near the hotel was beautiful but frustrating, since it was too easy to be overheard by passers-by to have a meaningful discussion. At last, they came upon a lily pond near a massive willow. The tree's languid branches caressed the water's surface, but just beyond the pool they also concealed a patch of grass. Dona took Alexi's arm and led him deep beneath the boughs until she was satisfied they could no longer be seen. "So, now what?"

"What do you mean?"

"I mean, what are we going to do? I'm not sure I'd feel safe sneaking back to school and pretending nothing happened, but I doubt we want to spend the rest of our lives with Tilly and Jonas playing hide and seek with the Inquisition either."

"We don't have any idea how long this thing is going to last—everything might be back to normal in a couple weeks."

"And it might not. I don't know about you, but I can't afford to abandon school until we find out. What if there's a full-blown Inquisition again, like the one in Caprian?"

"Then we might be better off leaving town entirely."

"And end up like Tilly and Jonas?"

"So, what do you suggest?"

Dona set her jaw. "We can either be pawns or players. I'd rather be a player."

"You mean oppose the Inquisition? That's crazy."

"Didn't you hear Jonas in there? The Monsignor's son paid him to rob graves to steal souls. I can't imagine that's a Church-approved practice. If people found out, they'd be outraged."

"Yes, they would—at anyone with the temerity to accuse a respected Church official of such a heinous act. Who are you going to believe—the Inquisitor, or the supposed nouncer who sells potions and totems out of a donkey cart in his spare time? The nouncer, right? He can even prove it, using a little bit of the selfsame Phrendonic Heresy he supposedly renounced. And if that's not good enough, his sister, the madam, will attest to his pristine character."

"I'm not saying it would be easy."

"You have quite the knack for understatement."

"Look. I have no intention of sitting passively by while external events determine my fate. I can at least try, can't I? Even if I can't win, maybe I can lose less."

"And just how are you proposing to 'win' this situation?"

"The first thing we should do is decide whether to involve Michlos. Do you think we can trust him?"

"Depends on what you mean by trust. He did go out of his way to help, but there is no doubt he has his own agenda. Without knowing what that is, your trust would be blind."

"True, but he defeated Everson when Reston's whole gang couldn't. He's clearly a heretic, and that makes it pretty unlikely he'd want the Inquisition to succeed. He's been helpful in the past, and now we have knowledge he wants. I'm inclined to trust him. Maybe he can do something with this information that we can't."

"It's risky—he seems influential enough that a wrong choice could be a real catastrophe." Alexi took her hand. "But then again, you took quite a risk trusting me. The least I can do is return the favor."

Dona clambered to her feet. "Great. Let's go send a message before I lose my nerve."

. . . . .

"*Gone?*" Thurman asked.

Cartier licked his lips. It's a bit of a puzzle, Father. When I left the brothel, it was in flames, clearly destined to burn to the ground. Yet, when I returned to the site, the structure was heavily damaged by smoke, with some of the upstairs rooms gutted, but intact. There was no sign of any remains."

"Are you suggesting our martyrs may have survived?"

"Either that, or someone else got to them first."

"Who would have wanted to remove the bodies?"

"According to witnesses, the Constable and some of his people were on the scene shortly after the alarm was raised. They cordoned off the area for several hours after the fire."

"You think the Constable's men took the bodies?"

"I'm not familiar with their protocols, but I wouldn't be surprised. I'd have pursued the matter, but I understand the relationship between an Inquisition and the local authorities can be…delicate."

"This isn't a delicate situation," Thurman said. "We are well within our rights to demand the remains of our fallen brethren."

"True, unless, of course, they did survive and there are no remains, in which case questions might be raised about what two Inquisitors were doing in a local brothel."

"That would be none of their business."

"Do you really want to encourage such speculation?"

Thurman paused for a moment. "It doesn't look so good, does it? And we have the same problem even if the Constable does have the remains."

Cartier nodded. "It raises the same questions, except if the Constable has the remains we can't deny they were ever there."

Thurman dragged his hands down his face and groaned. "Why does this have to be so complicated?"

"The righteous path is often steep."

"So what do you suggest?"

Cartier shrugged. "I'm not sure there are that many options. If the Constable has the remains, we can't afford to let that start any scandalous rumors. Maybe you should take charge of the situation and announce that the brothel was harboring heretics."

Thurman shook his head. "It's one thing to declare an Inquisition at a small University. It's another thing entirely to declare one in a major city. After Caprian, the Crown will almost certainly move to quash us, and we are still painfully low on manpower."

"Perhaps, but this isn't really about starting a full-scale Inquisition—it's about maintaining your image. You might try using our lack of manpower to your advantage, say, as an excuse to ask the Crown for assistance. It doesn't really matter whether they grant it or not, since either way, the request justifies the presence of the Inquisitors at the brothel. People will be outraged by the heinous murder of Church officials by these dangerous heretics. It's a much better story than 'the bodies of two Inquisitors were discovered at a local brothel.'"

"I don't suppose there's any chance they were burned beyond recognition?"

"Can you really afford to rely on that?"

Thurman rubbed his temples. He had a sickening feeling his authority was slipping through his fingers.

CHAPTER EIGHTEEN

ÐAMAGE CONTROL

The Monsignor collapsed in one of the high-backed chairs lining the balcony. The seat afforded a panoramic view of the west quarter of the Holy City, where the Square of St. Xara stretched out beneath him, a gigantic maze of cobbles and shrubbery. With effort, he propped his throbbing leg up on the chair next to him. He'd pay for the arduous trip up the stairs, but sometimes the pain was worth it. After hours of relentless badgering by administrators demanding signatures, protocol coaches instructing him in the fine points of ceremonial trivia, and tailors expecting him to try the umpteenth vestment for fit, he'd earned a break. When he found himself momentarily alone, he'd seized the opportunity and hobbled up the stairs to this balcony, which served as his brother's pulpit to the city.

The gentle breeze, the crisp morning sunlight, and the drone of everyday hustle and bustle conspired to sooth his frayed nerves. He closed his eyes and leaned back, fully intending to sneak in a short nap before his tormentors tracked him down.

A rumble like thunder brought him back to his senses. A battalion of men on horseback pranced into the central square below. As far as he could recall, this wasn't a holy day, and he wasn't expecting any celebrations or parades. The last thing he wanted was a surprise public display in his honor. He leaned over the railing for a better view. These men had the look of Inquisitors arrayed not for pageantry, but travel. Upon reaching the center of the square, the column turned and headed away from the balcony toward the city's west gate.

His pulse quickened. *What on earth is Darron up to?*

The Monsignor found his brother in the rectory, beset by his own swarm of administrative gadflies.

"I think we need to talk."

"Good morning to you too," Darron said. "What will we be talking about?"

"Privately."

He shrugged and signaled them all to leave. Despite harried expressions, they still managed to clear the room in seconds.

"I've wanted to do that for hours. Now, what seems to be the problem?"

"Where are you sending a battalion of Inquisitors, and why wasn't I informed?"

"I have no idea," Darron said. "Surely you don't think I attend personally to everything that happens in this city?"

"Do you have any idea how much political damage a force that large could do?"

"I suspect I'm about to find out."

"Darron, please. Don't let this erupt into a full-fledged disaster. I need to know who ordered it and for what purpose."

The rectory door creaked slowly open.

"I hope I'm not interrupting," Laitrech said. "I couldn't help noticing the exodus. Is everything all right in here?"

"Ahh, just the man," Darron said. "Armand has concerns about a bunch of Inquisitors leaving the city this morning. Do you know anything about that?"

"A little. Apparently there's been a bit of a disturbance, and Inquisitors were requested to remedy the problem."

"What kind of disturbance?" the Monsignor asked.

Laitrech shrugged. "Heresy, I expect."

The Monsignor huffed. "Why I wasn't I informed?"

"I suppose they thought you already knew."

"And why on earth would they think that?"

"Because your son Thurman placed the request. You mean he didn't tell you?"

The Monsignor paled. *"Thurman?"*

Laitrech shrugged again. "I'm sure they thought you'd approved it."

The Monsignor placed his hand on his brother's shoulder. "I know how much this new Ordinal position means to you, but Thurman may have gotten himself in over his head. I have to go."

Darron gaped. "You can't leave now. The ceremony is only a few days away. Important guests are already *en route.*"

"He's my son. I'm sorry."

Darron's jaw worked in agitation. "Whatever he's involved in, I'm sure a battalion of Inquisitors can get him out of it just fine."

"Or in so deep I won't be able to repair the damage."

What little color Darron had drained away. "We may not get another chance at this."

"I'll come right back just as soon as I am sure he's not in trouble. In the meantime, I'll need a carriage to take me to Trifienne."

Darron trembled. "You planned this all along, didn't you? Placate the feeble old man and then duck out at the last minute."

"I admit I never approved of the idea, but for Thurman's sake, I gave my word, and I fully intend to keep it."

"Of course you do. And if I'm still well enough to insist on it when you get back, what will your excuse be then?"

"I'm really very sorry, but I don't have time to play your little games. Something has gone terribly wrong in Trifienne, and there's no telling how many lives are at stake. Now, are you going to call me a carriage, or must I commission one myself?"

Anger flickered in Darron's eyes, but he mastered it. He turned to Laitrech. "See to it, please."

Laitrech bowed. "As you wish, Your Primacy."

"Thank you," the Monsignor said. "If you'll excuse me, I'll gather my things."

"One moment."

"Yes?"

"Has it occurred to you that Thurman may be better off without you?"

"What do you mean?"

"How old is Thurman now? "Forty-five? Forty-six?"

"What's your point?"

"In all those years, has he ever done anything to distinguish himself?"

"He has been a great help to me."

"I'm sure he has. But you must be aware that his contributions as your assistant, regardless of how exemplary, will only serve to bolster your own reputation. You, my friend, cast a very long, very dark shadow. How much longer do you suppose Thurman's reputation can remain planted in such deep shade without withering?"

"Thurman is doing just fine, thank you. He's traveled in circles that would be inaccessible to other junior clergy."

"Yes, as your carriage driver. Imagine the respect that engenders."

"He's far more than that, and you know it."

"If he's so talented," Darron said, "why hasn't he struck out on his own instead of serving all this time as your assistant. Don't you trust him?"

"Of course I do."

"Oh really? Then why do you feel this sudden urge to run off to Trifienne? Are you *trying* to steal his thunder?"

"Of course not. But an Inquisition can be a nuanced and dangerous matter."

"And you don't trust Thurman to be nuanced?"

"I didn't say that."

"Not in words, anyway. Look at it this way—if Thurman can resolve the situation by himself, you're only hurting his reputation by swooping in at the last minute to 'rescue' him. It could be a very long time before he has another opportunity like this one, and he's not getting any younger."

"An Inquisition is not an 'opportunity.' There's too much at stake."

"How about this, then. If Thurman effectively manages a difficult situation in Trifienne without your interference, I'll grant him a bishopric. If you intervene and handle it for him, I'll withdraw the opportunity. Imagine how thrilled he'll be when he finds out."

The Monsignor shook his head. "No wonder your legacy is suffering. Did you vet your Ordinals with similar care?"

Darron's smile was weak, but smug. "So I take it you'll be staying?"

"On the contrary. You've just helped me appreciate how even the noblest of intentions cannot make a wrong into a right. Regardless of what you do, I'm sure Thurman will understand that. I have faith that, when you think about it, you will too."

A tremor shook Darron. "Don't leave me."

The Monsignor embraced him. "I'll be back as soon as I can. I swear."

Darron stared vacantly after his brother as the door closed behind him.

"By then," he said, "it will be too late."

. . . . .

Perhaps unsurprisingly, the Crown had not seen fit to designate a specific minister to process requests for Inquisitional assistance. Cartier had hoped this oversight might play to his advantage by allowing him some leeway to approach one with strong religious leanings and a sincere desire to help him, but in the end, it had merely wasted his time. Hours of patient waiting in the offices of numerous petty officials had yielded him little but discomfited side-long glances and nimble administrative evasions. In the end, his hot-potato request had landed him squarely in the place he'd wanted most to avoid—the office of Constable Connelly.

It's not that the Constable was impious or corrupt. To the contrary, he was known for a strong work ethic and well-developed sense of fairness. Unfortunately, he was also known for his keen investigative mind and a most inconvenient perception that the Church plays no legitimate role in the investigation of criminal matters. Despite his reservations, however, Cartier had little choice but to proceed.

The Constable looked up from his notebook. "And just what exactly does Inquisitor Goodkin mean by 'our assistance?'"

Cartier licked his lips. "Inquisitor Goodkin is sensitive to the fact that the situation has moved beyond simple heresy

into a realm that would justify the involvement and cooperation of secular authorities."

"If by 'involvement and cooperation' you mean that we
are welcome to investigate the brothel for evidence of murder
and arson, let me assure you—that investigation is already
underway."

"I am heartened to hear it is in such capable hands. I trust
we can rely upon you to release the remains of our departed
Inquisitors into Church custody at the timely conclusion of
this investigation?"

"Thank you for your vote of confidence, Father. Speaking
of the deceased, could you perhaps be more specific regarding
their purpose for being at the brothel?"

"Certainly, Constable. As I said, they were investigating
allegations of heresy."

"Allegations by whom?"

"I'm sure you can appreciate the sensitive nature of that
information, given that suspects may still be at large,"

"Indeed I can. If people out there are in need of our protection, I find we are quite a lot better at it if we know who
they are."

"A compelling point. I'll recommend to Inquisitor Goodkin that he release that information to you in my report."

"I would appreciate it, Father. And what can you tell us
about the suspects? Is it your position that they had motive
to murder your Inquisitors out of fear their heresies would
be discovered?"

"We would have had a far better handle on the answer to
that if the Inquisitors in question had survived to report back.
Under the circumstances, all we can say for certain is that
they were there investigating allegations of heresy."

"What kind of heresy?"

"You'll be discreet?"

"You have my word."

"Very well, then, they were allegations of *Phrendonic Heresy*. I'm sure I don't need to tell you of the potential for disaster if this outbreak has spread beyond the University and into the city proper."

"You think the situation at Exidgeon may be related?"

"It's hard to say. I don't think we can rule it out."

"I see," the Constable said. "In that case, I'll apply for emergency jurisdiction to investigate the University as well. If, as you say, the city is under threat of Inquisition, I'm sure it will be granted."

Cartier paused.

"Is there a problem, Father?"

"Well, no. It's just that I expect Inquisitor Goodkin has things well in hand there. An additional investigation could cause a panic."

The Constable shrugged. "As I understand it, Father, the Inquisition already has a visible presence there. Compared to them, we'll be lucky to get noticed at all. Not only that, but for reasons of public safety, it would be prudent to have militia already on the scene if, as you suggest, there is any possibility of a panic. Don't you agree?"

"I hate to see you go to that trouble, but if you are convinced, then of course I defer to your superior expertise. If we can be of any assistance, please let me know."

"Thank you, Father," the Constable said. "We'll definitely be in touch."

CHAPTER NINETEEN

TWISTS OF FATE

After several attempts to make sense of them, Verone concluded that she wasn't misinterpreting her directions, they were outright wrong. At least that infernal heat wave had finally broken. It was a huge relief to walk somewhere without constantly having to mop the sweat from her brow. Oh well, there was nothing for it but to try again. Nearby she spied a dapper gentleman who appeared to be waiting for someone, his coat over one arm, walking stick in hand.

"Pardon me, sir, could you direct me to the infirmary?"

He gazed on her with intense blue eyes that didn't look so much at her, as through her. The effect was so disconcerting that she turned to see who he was looking at. There was no one else there.

After a long moment, his eyes focused and he smiled welcomingly, as though greeting a dear friend.

"Well, I'll be," he said. "No matter how many times you've seen something, it never actually looks quite the same as when you live it, does it?"

Verone blinked. "I beg your pardon?"

"Ach, forgive me. I do tend to forget myself, but then, who could blame me? I am Rayen the Magnificent, but please, my dear, radiant lady, call me Rayen. Do you believe in fate?"

She took a deliberate step back. "Um, I really haven't given it much thought."

Rayen stroked his chin. "No, I suppose you wouldn't have yet, would you? I have always found it amazing that the more accomplished the individual, the more likely she is to fall prey to the illusion that mere force of will can master the reins of destiny. I never cease to marvel how people can ignore the overwhelming influence of fate on their daily lives. In my experience, far more turns on the 'chance meeting' or the 'accident of birth' than on all the best-laid plans ever devised."

The 'accident of birth' comment struck a nerve. "Nonsense," Verone replied. "Choices clearly matter. For example, they can neutralize the advantage of an 'accident of birth,' as you call it, by getting you disinherited."

"You speak as though getting disinherited were some sort of choice. Was it for you?"

An exasperated voice exploded from the doorway behind Rayen. "*There* you are. I've been looking all over for you. You had me worried sick."

The woman resembled Rayen—she shared his blue eyes and fine features. However, whereas Rayen's face was smooth and ageless, the woman's was lined and gaunt. In contrast to Rayen's rich, dark hair, hers was touched with gray.

"I'm really feeling much better now," Rayen said.

"So I see. Let's try not to have any more episodes, shall we? Dona's still missing and I don't have time for this. Now come along."

"Wait," Rayen said. "This is the lady I've been telling you about."

The woman paused, closed her eyes, and sighed. Then she turned to Verone.

"I apologize if he's been bothering you."

Verone extended her hand. "Not at all. In fact, he's been most charming. I'm Verone."

"Well that's a relief. I'm Amanda, the sister of 'Mr. Magnificent,' here. I try my best to keep an eye on him, but there's only so much I can do."

"Think nothing of it. Say, I couldn't help overhearing that someone was missing?"

"Yes, I'm told my daughter hasn't been attending classes for some time now, and that's most unlike her."

"How dreadful. Do they have any leads?"

"I'm not sure yet. Getting a straight answer from an academic is a bit like lancing a boil—the harder you squeeze, the more you get, but the less stomach you have for the process."

"I know just what you mean," Verone said. "To whom have you been speaking?"

"A Professor Reston. He sent a message asking if my Dona happened to be at home. Said he was wondering because she had missed several classes. I knew right then it had to be serious. My Dona would never miss a class on purpose. And now he acts all surprised when I show up on his doorstep looking for answers."

"He wasn't helpful at all?"

"He was polite but guarded. Told me it was probably nothing to worry about, that it's not unusual for students to treat themselves to a few days off after a major presentation, and that he'd notify campus authorities to be on the lookout just in case."

"If it's so common, why did he write to you in the first place?"

"I was just asking him that when Mr. Magnificent here had another one of his little episodes."

Rayen drew himself up and cleared his throat. "I'll have you know it was a vision, not an episode. You speak as though the Sight were some sort of dread affliction. I am a seer, not a leper."

Amanda sighed. "Yes, of course it was. What was it this time? A plague of locusts? A breech birth? Or perhaps a conspiracy among the goats to poison the cheese?"

"Madam, that is unduly harsh. You know as well as I the Sight frequently manifests metaphorically."

"And with much writhing and frothing. Believe me, I am all too familiar."

"A small price to pay for a glimpse into the mysteries of the infinite."

Amanda shook her head. "Why do I even bother?"

Rayen put his arm around his sister. "I'm sorry I'm such a burden. I don't mean to be."

Amanda wiped her eyes.

"Don't cry, Mandy. We'll find her. She's fine, you know... I *saw* it."

"Don't," Amanda said, pulling away.

"It's true." He cleared his throat dramatically and recited:

> *Through the maelstrom's fury, assailed by sacred vice,*
> *The Tainted soars on wings of fate to love not once, but twice.*
> *Embracing a birthright unlooked for, guided by vengeance and spite,*
> *Unwittingly gaining a purpose from one of bewitching delight.*

"Stop it."

"But it tells us she's all right."

"It tells us nothing."

"What about Henry then?"

"Don't start with me."

"Perhaps I can be of some help," Verone said. "Why don't I round up my church group? I'm sure they would be delighted to help search for your daughter."

Amanda brightened. "That would be so very kind of you."

"Think nothing of it. Let me go get the word out. Perhaps we could meet at St. Sophia's by three o'clock? It's right downtown. Just ask—anyone can point you right to it. We'll need a good description of the young lady and suggestions for likely places to look. If you happen to know what she was wearing or if she carried anything distinctive, that would help too."

"I don't know what to say."

"Say you'll be there."

"Oh, I'll be there, all right."

"As shall I," Rayen said. "You see what I was saying about how chance meetings can alter the course of fate?"

"Come along, Rayen." Amanda said. She wrenched his arm so fiercely he nearly lost his balance.

Verone chuckled under her breath as Amanda dragged him off. "Well, Mr. Magnificent, I must admit, you do have a point."

. . . . .

Professor Hepplewhite leaned back in his office chair. "We've missed you in class."

Dona settled into the chair across from him. "I've missed being there. How have the presentations been going?"

"They vary, as you might expect. I'd like to thank you again for being such a good sport about presenting for the Monsignor. He seemed quite taken by your choice of topic."

"I'm glad to hear that. I was mortified to find out I was speaking about his mother."

"I could see where that might be uncomfortable. I'd like to say I could have warned you had you been more forthcoming about your topic, but I had no idea either. I suppose you are curious about your grade?"

"I have been sort of wondering."

"I'm pleased to tell you your presentation received a passing grade. I do wish you'd been present for the class comments. I think you would have found them helpful."

Dona's jaw dropped. "You mean I didn't get a high pass?"

"It was a solid and thought-provoking performance delivered under trying circumstances. I would even go so far as to say it passed with flying colors, but I'm afraid it didn't quite rise to the level of a high pass."

"I don't understand," Dona said, a storm brewing in her eyes. "Adam Deargard got a passing grade for his talk, and pretty much all he did was stammer. The only thing he managed to convince anyone of was that the word 'um' can be tragically overused. I'm glad to know my work was at least on a par with that."

Hepplewhite cleared his throat. "I'm not at liberty to discuss the grades of other students. What I can say is that to receive a high pass from me, a student must push the very limits of his abilities."

"Which is, of course, impossible if that student should happen to be a 'she.'"

Hepplewhite raised an eyebrow. "That argument suffers from one of the same weaknesses you displayed during your presentation."

"Which is?"

"By playing the role of the martyr, you risk polarizing your audience. A manifest injustice can be a powerful motivating force, but only if the vast majority of your audience is on board about the injustice. Absent that, portraying yourself as a member of the aggrieved class only wins you the status of unsympathetic whiner. In that case, those who will stand with you are merely those who agreed with you in the first place. The rest, while perhaps neutral initially, may well now stand firmly against. In my judgment, that is not the goal of good rhetoric."

Dona snorted. "Perhaps if I'd made more liberal use of the word 'um'?"

Hepplewhite sighed. "I admit that if your goal was to obtain a high pass, you may be at a disadvantage, but not for the reason you might think."

"If you seriously expect me to believe this mysterious reason is not that you go way easy on the men, I'm all ears."

"Miss Merinne, I've taught rhetoric to hundreds of students over the years, and I think I've become a fair judge of ability. Of course, you are still early in your training, but you may be the most gifted student I've ever encountered, perhaps, save one. If I were to give you a high pass for your performance last Friday, solid as it was, I would be doing you a disservice. After all, the goal of higher education is not merely to achieve the lowest common denominator—it's to encourage students to recognize and maximize their potential. That means a student with vast potential may find herself faced with commensurately high expectations. In short, if you were to actually push your limits, your presentation would be nothing short of amazing. Amaze me, Miss Merinne, and you shall have your high pass. Surely you don't think you aren't up to it?"

This was not the reason Dona had expected, and it took a moment to sink in.

"So," she finally asked, "who did you think was more gifted?"

Hepplewhite's eyes twinkled. "As I said, I'm not at liberty to discuss other students."

"As I recall, you said the grades of other students, not their inherent abilities."

"Maybe you can tell me, since this other student, by some strange quirk of fate, happens also to be in your class."

"You don't mean Alexi, do you?"

Hepplewhite held up his hand. "I've already said too much."

"Did you have a chance to discuss my presentation with the Monsignor?"

"Briefly. He seemed quite favorably impressed, although he may have been a little biased by the subject matter. It's been quite some time since he's had to deconstruct a speech in an academic setting, though he was quite expert at one time."

"Do you think he'd be willing to meet sometime to talk about it? After all, if I'm going to amaze you, I'll need all the help I can get. Unless, of course, you think he's too involved with this new Inquisition to have time."

"I think he'd have been delighted to meet with you, if he were still in town."

"He's not in town? I thought he was staying with you."

"He did, but he left in a rush some time ago."

"But then who is running the Inquisition?"

"His son Thurman is running things here. With the Monsignor gone, I'm not exactly in the loop, but from what little I hear, Thurman has been ruffling a few feathers. I hope he knows what he's doing. In all our years of friendship, I never once saw the Monsignor generate this much controversy."

"Does the Monsignor even know what Thurman's doing?"

"I don't know, but I had thought the Monsignor was trying to keep the Inquisition low-key. Clearly Thurman has other ideas."

"What could have pulled the Monsignor away?"

"He didn't say, although he did intimate it was a family matter. I didn't pry and he didn't offer."

"Thank you for your help, Professor."

Hepplewhite stood. "I trust we will be seeing more of you during class time?"

"I have some personal issues at the moment, but I'll be back just as soon as I can."

"Is there anything I can do?"

Dona shook her head. "I think I can manage."

"Well let me know if something arises."

"I will. And Professor?"

"Yes?"

"Thank you for being so patient."

Hepplewhite smiled. "It goes with the territory."

Dona emerged from Hepplewhite's office building, drew her coat in close against the chill, and started off at a brisk pace. A trim figure in a long dark coat slipped smoothly from an alley and into step beside her. The black leather of his gloves concealed his swarm of jewelry, and his hair, once shot with gray, was now uniformly black—almost startlingly so. Except for the faint suggestion of crow's feet that bracketed the smoky green glint of his eyes, he blended remarkably well into unfamiliar territory peopled overwhelmingly by beings indigenous to a wholly different generation.

"You were right," Dona said. "The Monsignor left town some time ago. Thurman's in charge."

Michlos nodded. "Did he mention why he left?"

Dona's mouth tightened. "He didn't know, or he wasn't saying—I couldn't tell which. All I could get out of him was that it was a family matter. Oh, he also mentioned Thurman might not be handling things as the Monsignor would have preferred."

Michlos smiled. "Well that is hopeful, at least."

"So you agree that we should move on to step two, then?"

"I agree it's worth a shot. I reiterate that we absolutely must work out the details of a viable plan B, first. Plan A is fraught with too many uncertainties."

"Agreed. Well, this is my turn. I'll see you later, and thanks for your help."

Michlos gave a short nod. "See you then."

Dona veered to the left, while Michlos kept moving forward. Neither looked back.

Moments later, Reston answered her knock on his office door.

"Michlos has agreed to help," she said, trailing off as he put his finger to his lips.

He motioned for her enter and closed the door behind her.

He spoke softly. "There has been a small…complication."

"What now?"

"Shhh," Reston said. "Not so loud."

"Sorry," Dona whispered. "What's happened?"

"Your mother is on campus looking for you. She pummeled me with questions this morning until your uncle had a seizure. I had to cancel class to see him to the infirmary."

Dona's mind raced. "Did they say why they are here? They aren't given to surprise visits."

"That's probably my fault. When you went missing after the brothel fire, I sent your mother a message asking if by chance you had ended up there. I told her I was a little concerned that you had missed some classes."

"You did *what?*"

"Shhh. It may look foolish in hindsight, but in my defense, I was worried sick."

Dona gaped at him. "But this could ruin everything."

"Why don't you just assure them that everything is fine and urge them to head home to attend to your uncle's condition. He seemed quite ill."

"The seizure, you mean? Oh, he does that all the time."

"Even so," Reston said. "Once they see you are in one piece, you should be able to send them safely out of harm's way."

"You clearly don't know my mother."

As if on cue, the voice of Amanda Merinne echoed down the hallway, increasing in volume as she approached. Dona threw Reston a wild-eyed look, but he only shrugged.

. . . . .

"Rayen," Amanda said, "I don't have time for any more of your foolishness."

"But Mandy…"

"Don't you 'but Mandy' me."

"But she's the one I've been telling you about."

"Enough!"

Rayen fell silent as Amanda knocked solidly on Reston's office door.

After a long pause, she knocked again.

"Professor?" she called out. "Are you in there?"

Muffled sounds of movement emanated from within the room. With a perplexed glance at Rayen, Amanda bent closer to listen until her ear was nearly pressed against the door.

When the door finally flew open, she was so startled she dropped her reticule. She scooped it up, hoping to use the movement to conceal her mortification at being caught eavesdropping. There was no hiding the color in her cheeks, however.

"Mrs. Merinne," Reston said. "such a relief to see your brother has recovered so quickly."

"Thank you, Professor. I wonder if we might take a few more moments of your time?"

Reston hesitated. "I'm afraid I was just leaving for a meeting."

She brushed past Reston into his office. "We'll make this brief, then. Come along Rayen."

Rayen shrugged sympathetically at Reston and did as he was told.

Once inside, she shivered, and rubbed her shoulders. "Gracious, it's freezing in here. Then she noticed the fluttering curtains. "Ah, here's the culprit." She strode to the window and slammed it shut. "That's more like it. Honestly, Professor, you should be more mindful of your surroundings. You'll catch your death."

. . . . .

Dona crouched close to the wall of the building and headed north. It would take her close to the Exidgeon gates, but heading south would take her toward the entrance of Reston's building, and she had no way of knowing when her mother and uncle might emerge. She planned to cross the road that ran through the gates as quickly as possible and make a wide loop back to Alexi's fraternity. She couldn't be sure the fraternity was safe, since she didn't know whether her mother had gotten to Miranda or Helena yet. To buy time, she had directed Reston to suggest her mother have a chat with Hepplewhite. That would let her mother know she was alive and well, and provide a distraction while Dona found Alexi and retrieved Jonas's medallion.

She forced her way through the shrubbery far enough from the gate to avoid arousing any suspicion. A carriage was parked outside the building across the street, and she hoped it would provide some measure of cover. Satisfied she had crossed without being seen, she straightened up and did her best to look like any other student. Intent on gaining the alleyway between Dexter and Canasty Halls, she sidled past the horses hitched to the carriage, noting with surprise how heavily lathered they were.

Heading around in front of the horses, she found herself in full view of the man standing on the opposite side before she realized it. Her heart skipped a beat, until she saw he was merely the groom. A study in nonchalance, she started once more for the alley. She hadn't gone two more steps before panic seized her once more, this time in the form of the Monsignor's voice.

"Miss Merinne, is that you?"

She fought down the urge to run for it. Instead, she swallowed, forced a smile, and faced the carriage.

"Monsignor, how wonderful to see you again."

With assistance from the groom, the Monsignor climbed out of the carriage. "The pleasure is all mine. I'm sorry I never had a chance to ask you what you thought of the opera, but by the time I finished my delightful chat with the Princess, you and the Delauren boy were already gone. It was my fault, of course. I do have a tendency to go on. I—"

"Father? What are you doing here?"

Thurman had appeared in the doorway across from the carriage. He stepped fully into the sunlight.

"It's good to see you too, son."

Thurman really couldn't avoid seeing Dona now. His eyes widened and then darted several times between her and his father.

Time seemed to grind to a standstill. In her mind's eye she saw Thurman's arm rise, that awful accusatory finger stretch out, and his lips form the single damning word 'heretic,' but to her amazement, history failed to repeat itself. Instead, Thurman inclined his head in her direction and said simply, "friend of yours?"

"Miss Merinne," the Monsignor said, "I'd like you to meet my son Thurman."

Though doubtful her luck could hold much longer, Dona felt compelled to continue the charade. "Delighted to meet you, Father."

Thurman's narrowed sidelong look left little doubt that he had recognized her. "Likewise," he said.

Why didn't he act?

"Wonderful to see you again Miss Merinne," the Monsignor said, "but, if you would be so kind as to excuse us, my son and I have urgent business."

"Of course, Monsignor. Another time, perhaps? I'd be fascinated to hear your views on the opera."

"And I yours," the Monsignor said. "Until then."

Dona turned to Thurman and nodded. "It was a pleasure, Father."

Thurman nodded in return. As he and the Monsignor headed for the doorway, she strolled serenely away. Once the coast was clear, she ducked into the first available alley and ran as fast as her legs would carry her.

CHAPTER TWENTY

AMBUShEδ

I came as soon as I heard you'd requested a battalion," the Monsignor said, "What happened?"

Thurman seated himself behind his cherrywood desk. "We have established that the traitor Shoruga was selling military secrets to Phrendonic heretics. Since he resisted all our attempts to persuade him to identify his co-conspirators, we couldn't afford to take any chances. Until we know how many we're up against, we're better off safe than sorry."

"How did you establish Shoruga's guilt?"

"We got a signed confession."

"He was willing to confess, but unwilling to identify his conspirators? Doesn't that strike you as odd?"

Thurman shrugged. "The Shunese are a superstitious lot. He was probably more afraid of Phrendonic retribution than he was of Church justice. It's not unheard of."

"Did you find out just what these military secrets were?"

"He never revealed those either, but once we had the confession, we didn't need that to proceed."

"It might have been useful for deciding how much backup to request, no? Where is Shoruga now? I think it's time we had another chat."

"You've had a long trip," Thurman said. "You should get some rest and a good meal in you before you trouble yourself. We have the Inquisition well in hand."

"I beg to differ. A battalion of Inquisitors will be showing up any second. No doubt the instant they do, a certain Crown Prince will be demanding to know our justification for bringing so many armed men into his jurisdiction. When that happens, I will need to give him more than the signed confession of a single Shunese traitor. The nap and snack will have to wait."

"I said I can handle it."

The Monsignor shook his head. "I know I left you in charge on very short notice, and I appreciate your efforts on my behalf, but this situation has become incredibly volatile."

"You don't trust me."

"It's not a matter of trust. Everyone needs help once in a while."

"Except you, of course."

The Monsignor laughed. "In case you hadn't noticed, I need help just to climb a flight of stairs."

"How kind of you to remind me just exactly what type of task you feel you can trust me with."

The Monsignor sighed. "I can see we have some very important issues to address—and there's nothing I'd like more than to have that conversation right this minute, but I'm afraid the urgency of this situation makes that impossible. I need to see Shoruga *now*."

A third voice chimed in: "You're out of luck, I'm afraid."

Ordinal Isrulian glided into the room, attended by several members of his retinue. "How nice to see you again, Monsignor." He made the honorific seem an insult.

The Monsignor struggled to his feet. "Ordinal Isrulian. What an interesting surprise."

Isrulian peeled off his gloves and handed them to a hovering assistant. "I could say the same about you. According to an invitation I recently declined, you are within minutes of being late to your own Ascendency."

Thurman stared as his father in shock.

"The ceremony has been postponed," the Monsignor said.

Isrulian idly examined an inkwell from Thurman's desk. "Obviously. I'm curious, though. What explanation will you offer those who lacked the foresight to decline?"

"Your Ordinence, we have a potentially dangerous situation brewing here. There really isn't time to—"

Isrulian slammed the inkwell on the desktop. "I asked you a question, *Monsignor*."

The Monsignor took a step back. "I…I suppose that my services were required to assist with a difficult Inquisition."

"So in effect," Isrulian said, "you'll be proclaiming to the entire Church that your son couldn't be trusted with handling the situation for just three more days? How proud you must be. He'll be forever known as the son who denied his father the Ascendancy."

Thurman grew pale.

"May I remind you my Ascendancy is merely postponed, not cancelled."

"Perhaps."

"Now if you'll excuse me, Ordinence, I have evidence to gather."

Isrulian waved Thurman away and seated himself in his chair. "I take it he hasn't told you then?"

The Monsignor faced his son, eyebrow raised. "Told me what?"

Thurman looked away.

"Thurman, what is it?"

"Shoruga, he…he didn't make it."

"What do you mean?"

"He hanged himself."

The Monsignor stared at his son in disbelief. "How?"

"It wasn't my fault," Thurman said. "How could I have known?"

"Well, that complicates matters. Without a witness, I suppose my only option is to reexamine the physical evidence. Maybe there's something I overlooked."

"I can think of something," Isrulian said.

The Monsignor eyed Isrulian dubiously. "Such as?"

"Well, for one, your connection to Chancellor Wiggins."

"No offense, Your Ordinence, but I was referring to facts that are relevant to the current investigation."

"You don't think a conspiracy to conceal an enclave of heresy is relevant?"

"Oh for crying out loud, I don't have time for this nonsense."

Isrulian flashed him a crooked smile. "Nonsense?" He produced a document from inside his cloak and tossed it on the desk before the Monsignor. "I have here a signed confession from Chancellor Wiggins detailing a conspiracy between the two of you to conceal the very existence of this Inquisition, right down to creating and disseminating false reasons to justify your presence on campus. What reason, I wonder, could our acclaimed Inquisitor General possibly have to conceal rather than expose this pernicious heresy?" Rising from his seat, Isrulian leaned forward, bracing himself on Thurman's desk. "*What did they offer you?*"

The Monsignor laughed. "Isrulian, you missed your calling. They could use a talent like yours over at the opera house. As for your silly little conspiracy theory, it's been common practice for years now to downplay an Inquisition during an initial investigation. Your charge will never stick."

"Perhaps not. But until a Special Inquisitor can be appointed to investigate these charges, I'm afraid we'll have to take you into custody. Thurman, arrest this man."

"Don't be ridiculous," Thurman said. "I can't arrest my own father."

Isrulian pursed his lips. "You can, and will, unless you prefer to share his fate. I'm sure his cell could easily accommodate another co-conspirator."

The Monsignor held out his hands for Thurman to bind. "Just do as he says. I don't know why he wants to ruin his career like this. It will only last as long as it takes for Darron to get wind of it."

Isrulian studied his fingernails. "Assuming, of course, he lives that long."

. . . . .

Alexi was still amazed that Dona had managed to convince Jonas and Tilly to accompany him to the fraternity, particularly after Jonas had scoffed at the idea as idiotic. Jonas's objections had become decidedly less strenuous, however, after he'd pointed out that, once there, they could retrieve the medallion. When Tilly finally declared in favor of Dona's plan, Jonas shook his head, but didn't argue further. Alexi guessed that Dona had won her over while he and Jonas slept, knowing it would be difficult for Jonas to deny her pretty much anything at the moment. Women, it seemed, had ways of winning arguments that had very little to do with the merits.

Getting onto campus hadn't been all that difficult. Jonas and Tilly simply approached the Inquisitors as the parents of a bright young student interested in exploring Exidgeon as a possibility. Once at the fraternity, Alexi had taken them directly to the basement meeting hall before heading upstairs to fetch the medallion. It only took him a few minutes to find it in a pile of laundry. Then, instead of waiting for Dona in the in the meeting hall with the others, he grabbed a textbook and headed out to the front stoop. He was getting woefully behind, and the escalating tension between Jonas and Tilly was not conducive to studying.

Lost in his attempts to decipher Driessen's tortured didacticism, Alexi's first clue that he was no longer alone was the blade leveled at his throat.

"Give me one good reason why I should let you live, knave."

Alexi gently pushed the blade away. "Because if you kill me, they'll probably assign you a fencing partner who actually has a chance of beating you."

Alphonse sheathed his practice saber. "Your argument has merit. I shall spare your miserable life."

"Gee, thanks."

"Where were you last week? Helena and I were going to ask you and Dona out dancing, but both of you had gone missing. You didn't elope or anything crazy like that, did you?"

Alexi eyed Alphonse dubiously. "Helena?"

He sat beside Alexi on the stoop. "You remember her, don't you? She's Dona's roommate?"

"Oh, I remember."

"You know, I think she might be the one."

"Helena? Are you sure you don't mean Miranda?"

"Ah, Miranda," Alphonse said. "Now there is a lovely creature. But she's a bit too delicate for my taste. I prefer the company of someone who feels genuinely fortunate to have me by her side to that of someone who feels *I* should feel fortunate. Marriage should be a mutually beneficial collaboration of complementary skills, not an endless struggle to prove superiority. Oh—no offense."

Alexi laughed. "You don't find an accomplished woman attractive?"

"Of course I do. Among other things, Helena is an accomplished dancer, seamstress, and cook."

"I see your point. I'm glad things are working out so well for you two."

Alphonse slapped Alexi on the shoulder. "And I have you to thank. We're going dancing again tonight, if you and Dona care to join us."

"I'll ask, but I suspect tonight won't be good."

Alphonse hopped to his feet. "Perhaps later this week, then. In the meantime, I may as well get some studying done. Once Dona gets here you won't have any more time for me anyway."

"How did you know I was waiting for her?"

Alphonse grinned. "Aside from the stoop being a really uncomfortable place to work math problems, the fact that she's running up the drive was a pretty good clue. I'll see you later."

Alphonse ducked into the fraternity moments before Dona arrived, flushed and frantic, to seize Alexi's arm.

"We've got to get out of here. The Monsignor's son knows I'm here."

"Oh no—at the fraternity?"

"No, on campus. I just talked to him, and I'm sure he recognized me."

"And he let you go? Why?"

Dona glared at him. "Oh, *my* fault. I guess I didn't think to ask."

"I mean, do you think he had you followed?"

"How should I know?"

"He didn't," Michlos said, following in Dona's footsteps, "but it would be good to get inside anyway."

"Michlos!" Dona said. "What did you find out?"

"Inside, please."

Alexi led Dona and Michlos down into the basement.

"Any problems getting past the gate?" Dona asked.

Alexi grinned. "None, though it was a lot less fun than the time we did it."

Dona flashed him a smile. "We do make a good team, don't we?"

"The best!"

His grin faded when he tried to open the meeting-hall door, and it didn't budge. "That's odd."

Tilly's muffled voice seeped out to them. "Who is it?"

"It's me, Alexi."

"One second."

After some soft scratching sounds and a click, the door swung slowly open. Alexi stepped inside.

"Where were you?" Jonas asked. "We were starting to worry."

"I was waiting outside for Dona to get here."

"You might have mentioned that."

"Dona's back?" Tilly asked.

"Right here," Dona said, following on Alexi's heels.

Michlos was right behind her. "Permit me to introduce myself—"

The pupils of Jonas's eyes dilated to twice their normal size. "Tilly, *run!*" Pulling a knife, he launched himself at Michlos.

"Jonas, no!" Dona cried.

Michlos raised his hand, but his jewelry was still covered by his gloves. Instead he deflected most of the initial thrust with his forearm. The two men tumbled to the floor under the force of Jonas's assault, struggling for control of the knife.

Tilly screamed. Dona grabbed for Jonas's foot, hoping to pull him off Michlos before he could do any more damage.

"Alexi," she cried, "don't just stand there."

Fighting the urge to throw himself between Dona and Jonas, Alexi instead retreated into himself, striving for focus.

Jonas's boot hit Dona in the shoulder, knocking her backward.

"Alexi, help me!"

Jonas's knife crept closer and closer to Michlos's face.

"Tilly," Jonas cried, *"get out!"* But Tilly stood transfixed.

And then Jonas went limp. His knife clattered on the floor. Dona snatched it up.

Alexi wiped the sweat from his brow with his sleeve. "That was close."

Her eyes huge, Tilly leaned over her prostrate brother. "Jonas?"

"He's fine," Michlos said. He heaved Jonas to one side, scrambled to his feet, and brushed himself off. "Sleeping, unless I'm mistaken."

"He's sleeping," Alexi confirmed. "And just for the record, I *was* helping."

"So I see," Dona said flatly.

"You have my thanks, Alexi." Michlos said. "Without your help, I have a feeling that would have gone much worse."

Tilly bent down, checking Jonas for injuries. "You old fool."

Dona caught sight of a trickle of red through a gash in Michlos's sleeve. "You're bleeding!"

Michlos removed his gloves and coat and pulled up his sleeve. He shook out a handkerchief. Dona helped him tie it over the wound.

"It could use a stitch or two," he said. "But that can wait until after the meeting. So, I take it he wasn't briefed I would be attending?"

Dona reddened. "It was difficult enough to get him to meet with Professor Reston. I was still working on a way to get him to agree to meet with you."

Reston's voice filtered through the door. "Nothing to see here. Everyone please just go back to what you were doing."

Only once the footfalls on the stairs had finally receded, did Reston pop his head in. "Sorry I'm late. Did I miss anything?"

CHAPTER TWENTY-ONE

A WO(DAN'S TOUCh

The Venerable Assembly of Church Mothers convened in the basement of St. Sophia's without delay upon hearing their services were desperately required. The ladies sat primly in a hodgepodge of cast-off chairs drawn up before an ancient blackboard.

Although technically required to wear them only during actual services, several of the ladies were clearly using the gathering as an opportunity to model their newest veils. Under the impression they were planning to hold a bake sale, several others had arrived bearing pies, cakes, and cookies. Polite but sustained chewing made it perfectly clear that these ladies were not the sort to allow such bounty go to waste, at least, not so long as there were starving children in the world.

Using a crooked pointer, Verone enumerated the facts. "The victim's name is Dona Merinne. She disappeared from Exidgeon and has been missing approximately a week. She has dark brown hair and blue eyes."

Mrs. Muscany raised a hand. Despite a valiant attempt to brace her arm at the elbow, she still failed to conceal a slight tremor.

"Yes, Mrs. Muscany?"

"Has the child run away from home before?"

"Mrs. Muscany, we've already established Dona is a University student—she no longer lives at home."

"Well no wonder she ran away then. A child's place is with her parents."

Verone blinked once, and then twice. "Yes, well, thank you for that. Now, in case I failed to mention it, Dona is twenty years old, is about five foot seven and weighs—what is it now, Mum?"

"Are we sure it's a good idea to go into all these details? We all know how sensitive young women can be about their measurements."

Verone swallowed hard and smiled.

"Thanks, Mum—and she is of *slim build*. She was last seen in a white blouse and a dark blue skirt, carrying an oversized satchel of the type students frequently use for books. Mrs. Merinne, did you have anything else you'd like to add?"

Dona's mother stood in the back row. Heads craned for a glimpse of the new speaker. "Only to say bless you all. Oh, and there are some who say Dona greatly favors me."

"Very well, then," Verone said. "We could search either the University or the city, but given the University is a more manageable size, I suggest we focus our efforts there first. I propose we divide it into quadrants and split up into four groups. Since it is centrally located, we can set up a command center at the Chapel. You have a question, Mrs. Caldor?"

"Is it possible Dona was abducted? If so, shouldn't we tell the Constable? I'm sure he'd take it seriously, since his daughter is a student at the University too."

"An excellent suggestion. I'll see to it personally right after we are done here."

Mrs. Caldor beamed. "So glad to help."

"I *said*," Mrs. Curtsik said in a loud voice, "I bet those hands have never washed a dish."

All heads turned.

"Oh, I'm so sorry," Mrs. Curtsik said, blushing furiously. "It's just that Mrs. Temrich is a wee bit hard of hearing."

"What?" Mrs. Temrich said.

Mrs. Curtsik practically shouted. "I told them you are hard of hearing."

"I hear just fine. I can't help it if you insist on mumbling."

The church's pipe organ suddenly heaved out discordant hymn fragments.

Verone covered her ears. "Who's playing the organ?"

"Oh, that's probably Mrs. Tibbleman," Mrs. Temrich said. "She went out to use the privy some time ago. Sometimes she forgets she's not the organist anymore."

With great relief, Verone noticed Father Cartier had arrived. He was standing in the back, arms folded, wearing an amused grin.

The organ music stopped as mysteriously as it had begun.

"Right," Verone said. "Let's open our envelopes to see what teams we are on. Once you know your number, report to your team leader. She'll handle your directions from there. And thank you all for coming out to help."

Rayen intercepted Verone on her way to greet Father Cartier. "Dear lady, I wanted to tell you how grateful we are for your efforts on Dona's behalf."

"Think nothing of it. We're all delighted to help."

Rayen nodded, as if confirming something he'd long suspected. "Ah yes, selfless as well as beautiful."

Unused to this kind of attention, Verone tried to discern his motive, but when nothing came to mind, she moved instinctively to deflect instead.

"I thought you were convinced that Dona was alive and well, and that we were all just wasting our time?"

"Oh, she is, but I also firmly believe that a kindness is never wasted. History may never recognize you for your contributions, but I want you to know that I do. You see, I know a thing or two about underappreciation."

Amanda's voice echoed across the basement. "Rayen, it's time to go."

Blushing, he presented Verone with an envelope. "This is for you."

She accepted it just as Amanda descended on them.

"Rayen, didn't you hear me? And stop annoying Miss Nevinander—she doesn't have time for your shenanigans."

"I'm ready. Does this mean we're off to see Professor Hepplewhite?"

It's too late for that. By the time we got there, he'd be gone for the day. We'll have to do it tomorrow."

And as quickly as Amanda had appeared, the two of them were gone.

Father Cartier was looking impatient. Verone tucked Rayen's envelope in her case and strode over to meet him.

. . . . .

"That should do it," Michlos said.

Jonas's eyes fluttered open. He tried to move, but could not. He struggled briefly, testing the strength of his restraints, but gave up when it became clear they would hold. With few other options, he devoted himself to assessing the situation. He was still in the basement chamber, tied securely to a chair. Tilly hovered nearby. Dona, Alexi, the Enforcer, and someone he presumed to be Professor Reston were all gathered around.

"I'm sorry about having to tie you up," Dona said. "But you gave us no choice."

"They promised to untie you just as soon as you promise to behave," Tilly said. "Do you think you can do that?"

"And I would like to apologize for springing myself on you," Michlos said. "I had thought you'd be expecting me."

Jonas glared at him. His companions had not the slightest appreciation for the danger this man posed. "Oh, you *are* good. So low-key, so soft-spoken. How could these fine folk have any idea what they are up against?"

"Well," Dona said, "I got a pretty good idea at the Sultan's Respite. Clearly, he's not without resources, but he's been more than helpful with them so far."

Jonas shook his head. Dona and Alexi seemed bright enough. Perhaps there was a chance he could still get through to them. "Have you asked yourself why? Why would an Enforcer of his caliber spend his time helping a young college student? What does he get out of it?"

"What do you mean by Enforcer?" Dona asked.

"Ask your buddy. I'm sure he'd be happy to tell you all about it."

"All right," Dona said, turning to Michlos. "What's he talking about?"

Michlos hesitated.

"Um, Michlos?"

"You'll understand, I hope, that there are some things I'm just not at liberty to divulge."

Jonas's expression was simultaneously grim and smug.

"All right then," Dona said. "What *are* you at liberty to divulge? Are you one of these Enforcers, or not, and what do they do?"

Again, Michlos paused.

Alexi broke the silence. "They protect the heretical descendants of Phrendonian's apprentices from being discovered by the Inquisition."

"Perfect," Dona said. "Isn't that exactly what we are here to discuss?"

"And why would he need your help to do that?" Jonas asked.

"Because every little bit helps?"

Jonas fought to master a rising sense of panic. Obviously, he would need to try harder. "Ah, the naïvete of youth. Did it ever occur to you that any heretic who isn't a member of their exclusive little club poses a security risk? You, my dear, are just another potential loose end—a fact you made abundantly clear to your Enforcer buddy at the Respite with that pretty little locket of yours."

Dona shook her head. "If that's true, he could have disposed of me at any time."

"And miss the opportunity to eliminate the entire infestation? He's using you. You fell for it hook, line, and sinker, and now you've dragged the good Professor into his trap as well. You can't say I didn't try."

All eyes turned to Michlos.

He took a step back. "Jonas is correct that I have a vested interest in blocking the Inquisition. It's a fact I have in no way hidden from any of you. Think about it this way: I have studied the ways of the Inquisition in some detail—if I were the monster he accuses me of being, why would I not simply extract what I needed to know using the same methods they use?"

Yes! Now he was getting somewhere. "Even beheaded, the serpent twists. You could have tortured Dona to your heart's content, but you could never gain what she doesn't know. You needed someone higher up in the organization to be sure you didn't miss anyone."

Dona eyed Michlos suspiciously. "All right then, what are you hiding?"

"I can't reveal the identities of my clients," Michlos said. "If any of you should fall prey to the Inquisition, then all would be lost. The rest I have told you."

"What were you doing at the Respite?" Dona asked. "I don't believe you ever mentioned that."

"Ironically, I was attempting the converse of your Plan A. We had been watching the Monsignor and his son for some time. When Thurman started meeting with Jonas here, and the Monsignor was always absent, I became curious as to why. Imagine my surprise when I found out our spirits vendor really was a 'spirits' vendor. Based on what we knew of the Monsignor, we thought it a good bet that he might not be involved. I was hoping that by catching Thurman red-handed transacting business with our jaunty grave robber here, we would gain enough leverage to convince Thurman to sabotage the Inquisition. Unfortunately, things didn't go quite as expected."

"Professor?" Dona asked. "Alexi? Any ideas?"

"Hmm," Reston said. "If you are asking me to choose between the grave robber and the extortionist, I admit to being a bit conflicted."

Alexi touched Reston's shoulder. "I don't think she's asking you to choose, Professor. I think she's looking for a way to resolve the impasse. Plan A needs both of them."

Tilly stepped forward. "Let me help, then. The Inquisition has destroyed my life. It has taken both of my parents, my inheritance, and now it has destroyed what little livelihood I was able to cobble together out of the rubble. Michlos, you could be Chervil incarnate for all I care, but if you are against the Inquisition in any way—any way at all, then I am with you." She turned to Jonas. "And you. Since you are more than a little to blame for this, you are going to help, and help to the best of your ability. If you should hesitate at all, for any reason, I'll turn you over to the Inquisition myself. Is that clear?"

Jonas paled—she was ruining any chance he might have had of saving them. "But Tilly—"

"Don't make me do it now."

It was over. There was no reasoning with Tilly when she was like this. He slowly nodded.

Satisfied, she began working open the knots holding Jonas to his chair.

Michlos regarded Tilly for a long moment. "Thank you," he said at last.

"Don't mention it."

"I should tell you that all is not lost if we succeed."

"Is that so?"

"The brothel still stands—I arrived in time to save it. Parts of the upstairs are burned, of course, and there is some smoke damage throughout, but the structure is salvageable."

"Then you have my thanks."

With a heavy heart, Jonas noticed that even this news couldn't bring a smile to Tilly's face. Fitting, seeing as how they were all surely doomed.

. . . . .

Cartier took the liberty of ordering Verone's meal for her. Although she viewed the attempt at chivalry to be patriarchal and outdated, she had to admit his taste in food was impeccable. The restaurant, named Tabalaria for reasons no one could quite remember, was a Trifienne institution. It had survived in Cartier's family on the same spot for over 100 years. During their short walk over from the Church, Cartier had described some of his experiences as a lad working in the kitchen. During those years, Church had been a welcome escape from restaurant drudgery. Little had he realized that later in his life, the roles played by Church and restaurant would be reversed.

"The ladies seem quite excited about this new project," Cartier said.

"They do seem genuinely eager to help, don't they? Bless their hearts."

"Who was this lost young lady again?" His tone made it clear he was just being polite and wasn't really interested. Fortunately, that was just the way Verone wanted it.

"Oh, just the truant daughter of someone I happened to meet this morning. I'm sure she's not in any real danger, but her mother seemed so devastated, I couldn't resist trying to help in some way."

"You have a good heart."

Verone chuckled at that. "Yes, well, I'm a pushover for a damsel in distress."

"Don't minimize it. It's a rare gift these days. Speaking of which, I wanted to thank you again for your helpful suggestions regarding the Monsignor and his son. By simply trying to help them feel welcome in Trifienne and volunteering my services, as you suggested, I've secured a position as Thurman's private secretary. And seeing as he's taken over the Inquisition here, my role is becoming increasingly visible. Given their access to the Primal, I think it's pretty clear my star is rising."

"I'm so pleased. It's gratifying to hear that virtue doesn't always have to be its own reward. What kinds of things do they have you doing up there at the College?"

"Any and everything. Thurman seems to view my role as a mix of adviser and problem-solver. For example, the other day, I took it upon myself to point out that finding dead Inquisitors in a brothel could be damaging to the Inquisition's position. I suggested they ask the Crown to assist in rooting out the heretics as a way of taking the emphasis off a potential embarrassment and placing it firmly on the notion that there are heretics among us."

"Have the heretics fled the University and gone into town then?"

"It's possible. Thurman had us follow a particular suspect, and, after a long and ugly chase, he led us to that brothel. I don't know if the man had any specific ties there or was merely stopping in to avail himself of the services. What I can say, though, is that he escaped in the company of three others. Meanwhile, two Inquisitors and several mercenaries burned to death in the brothel fire. Yet, the brothel itself suffered only minor fire damage. It looks pretty suspicious to me."

Verone sampled the roast lamb. "And these other three were heretics too?"

"Two women and a young man. We haven't been able to discover their identities. We were told another woman's remains were recovered at the scene, but the Constable has yet to give us access to the bodies. We are working under the assumption the dead woman was the madam."

"Do you really think there will be all that much speculation about the purpose of the Inquisitors there?"

"We'll see. I've already spoken with the Constable about it."

"How did that go?"

"He seems less friendly to the Church than I would have liked. And there's a risk he might station militia up at Exidgeon, but once the battalion of Inquisitors we requested shows up, I expect that should be little more than a nuisance."

"A whole battalion?"

"Phrendonic heretics can be dangerous. What happened at the brothel only underscores that. We don't want to take any chances, particularly since we don't know their numbers or what their goals are."

"I guess that makes sense. You said that Father Thurman had taken over the Inquisition here? I hope nothing untoward has happened to the Monsignor?"

"Called away on urgent business. Apparently it's top secret—I'm not sure even Thurman knows what it is."

A young man suddenly appeared at Cartier's side. "Can I interest you in dessert, Father?"

"I'll have my usual, Jamie. What do you suggest for the lady?"

Jamie turned to Verone. "Apples are in season, and the cobbler is delicious."

Verone's mouth watered. "That sounds wonderful." Although under other circumstances she might have felt obliged to decline, she was still feeling deprived in the dessert department as a result of her brother's shameless theft of her rum-soaked birthday trifle.

Cartier smiled. "You heard the lady."

"Very good, Father," Jamie said. He disappeared as instantaneously as he had appeared.

"They're *so* good here," Verone said.

"They're putting on a show for the Father. I wouldn't expect them to be quite so attentive to someone who just wandered in off the street, but even then, they do a pretty respectable job. It's a matter of pride with us."

Verone sipped her wine. "I have to say I'm a little unnerved by the possibility of heretics here in town. Do you have any idea yet who they are or what they want?"

"Thurman may have some suspects in mind, but if he does, he hasn't been forthcoming. And, wouldn't you know it, our one lead in the case had to go and kill himself."

"How dreadful."

"It wasn't a pretty sight. One of the newer Inquisitors fainted dead away."

"And he was your only link to the heretics? What about the heretics at the brothel?"

"Now wait—I only said one of them was a suspect. Thurman never said he was connected to the heresy. Still, the deaths of the Inquisitors make it pretty likely they were concealing something they didn't want discovered."

"Did you find anything there?"

Cartier shifted uncomfortably. "We haven't been able to get in to do a decent search," he said. "The constable has it cordoned off as a crime scene and is not giving us access."

"Can they do that?"

"At this stage, we are still picking our battles."

"But it seems so odd. After all, you are both on the same side, aren't you? Why would they want to turn down your help?"

"It's not uncommon for local law enforcement to get proprietary."

"Even in a matter that lies so squarely within Church jurisdiction? If I didn't know better, I'd think there might be something fishy going on."

Cartier's forehead creased. "With the Constable, you mean? There's no evidence to suggest he's doing anything other than protecting his turf."

"Well, he must be getting his orders from somewhere. Didn't you tell me once that the Professor who killed himself was getting money from some sort of special fund?"

"He was a Hathaway Scholar. They apparently get research money directly from the Crown, and they tend to work on projects related to the military."

"Oh," Verone said. "I suppose that doesn't make sense, then. After all, what possible interest could the military have in some obscure form of heresy?"

Cartier blanched. "Well, this isn't just any heresy."

Verone reached for her fork as Jamie presented her with a steaming cobbler. "It isn't?"

"I hadn't really considered it before, but I suppose Phrendonic Heresy could have significant military applications. And I suppose the Constable does ultimately take his orders from the Crown."

Verone laughed. "You're not suggesting the Crown Prince is a heretic, are you?"

Cartier did not seem amused.

"What's wrong?"

Before he could answer, Jamie presented Cartier with a bread pudding nestled in a cloud of cinnamon and whiskey vapors.

"Jamie, the check, please?" The young man bowed and disappeared.

"I'm so sorry," Verone said. "I didn't mean to upset you."

"No, it's not you. I just realized how late it's getting."

"Well every minute has been fascinating. I hope we can do it again very soon."

"I'd like nothing better," Cartier said.

Jamie reappeared.

"By the way, the cobbler is fantastic," Verone said.

Cartier paid without bothering to read the bill. "I'm very sorry to have to leave in such a rush."

Verone rose to her feet as well. "Think nothing of it, Father. And thank you. Now, off with you—you don't want to be late."

"We'll talk soon." He gave her a brief hug and headed for the door.

After a quick glance about, she sat back down. Satisfied no one was looking, she swapped Cartier's untouched dessert plate for her empty one.

She took a bite and sighed contentedly. "Timing really is everything, isn't it?"

. . . . .

"It'll never work," Jonas said.

"I've heard just about enough out of you," Tilly snapped.

Dona touched Tilly's arm. "Let him speak. If he thinks it won't work, I want to know why." Since ostensibly rejoining their ranks, Jonas had become exasperatingly taciturn. Now that he'd finally expressed an opinion, Dona didn't want anything to discourage him. She trusted compulsory alliances about as far as she did most of Jonas's potions.

Tilly frowned, but backed off.

"You can't just bribe the Inquisition to go away," Jonas said.

"We aren't exactly bribing them," Dona said. "It's more like an agreement to keep their dirty little secret in return for their cooperation."

"And what's to keep them from breaking the pact? It seems to me it would be a whole lot easier for them to just accuse the whole lot of us of being heretics. Once they do that, nothing we say is going to matter."

Dona sighed. "I just don't believe the Monsignor is a party to this."

Jonas eyed her dubiously. "Why on earth would you think that?"

"When I ran into the two of them by the carriage today, Thurman obviously recognized me but didn't say a word. Why would he stay silent like that unless he was afraid of what I could tell the Monsignor?"

"Same reason your Enforcer here didn't off you as soon as he had the chance," Jonas said. "He needs all the co-conspirators."

"The Monsignor isn't that type of person."

"Then that's another reason your plan doesn't make sense. If he's the fine upstanding Church Father you believe him to be, how do you know he won't simply turn his son in, and *then* take the heretics into custody?"

"Wait a minute," Dona said. "Who said anything about heretics?"

"Won't it be obvious when you ask him to leave town without finishing his business? Besides, as you pointed out, Thurman already thinks you're a heretic."

"So obviously, I can't be the one to make the deal."

"Who else is going to do it? The Enforcer, here?"

Tilly growled. "Jonas…"

Michlos merely chuckled. "Actually, I kind of like it: 'The Enforcer.' It makes me sound all interesting and mysterious. Anyway, Dona and I discussed that point at length. We felt it might be best if I prevailed upon the Constable to make the deal—the Inquisition could then just bow out of Trifienne and let the Constable investigate the heresies instead. That way, the Monsignor need not feel like he's sacrificing his integrity, and it gives the impression the Constable's motive is simply to get the Inquisition out of his hair."

Jonas eyed Michlos sidelong. "And just why do you think the Constable would agree to do this?"

"I suspect he'd agree to quite a lot if it got the Inquisition out of his jurisdiction. And, of course, we 'Enforcers' are not without our subtle means of persuasion."

Jonas snorted. "Oh yes. After a little bit of that chair-bondage technique, he'd no doubt be putty in your hands."

Michlos shrugged. "It's served us well so far."

"All right then, say the Constable agrees. Why would the Monsignor believe my story when his son denies our deal, which he undoubtedly will?"

"You have a point," Dona said, "which is why you aren't going to accuse him."

"Then why do you need me?"

"You're going to give Thurman the rope he'll use to hang himself."

"What? And miss the fun of tying him to his chair?"

"If all goes well, no persuasion should be necessary. All you have to do is complete the original deal you made with him. As far as we know, that should be something he will still be eager to do and, with the Monsignor back in town, something he will want to do in secret."

"How is that going to help?" Jonas asked. "It's not like once the deal is complete he's going to go running to his father and confess. And the Monsignor still isn't going to believe me."

"That's the tricky part. We have to make sure the Monsignor is present to witness the whole thing without Thurman knowing it."

"And just how do you plan to manage that?"

Dona was beginning to regret encouraging Jonas's participation. "I'm still working on it."

Reston chuckled. "I know a certain garden shed that would be perfect."

Michlos raised an eyebrow. "You'd like me to persuade the Constable to ask the Monsignor to spend quality time in a garden shed? I like a challenge, but I do have limits."

"What about a box at the opera?" Dona asked. "We know he likes that."

Reston shook his head. "Didn't you say he's already seen *Amoretorium?* And since it just opened, it may be quite a while before there's a new show for him to see."

Dona frowned. "Well, *I'd* see it again."

"It really ought to be the Artists' Colony," Alexi said. "The Church isn't welcome there."

Jonas snorted. "In which case, your goody-two-shoes Monsignor would never go there."

Michlos inspected his bandage. "Oh, I don't know about that. He might find an invitation difficult to refuse, assuming it comes from the right person."

Jonas huffed. "The whole place is under interdict, and the Princess herself has banned the clergy from setting foot there. How do you fake an invitation to get around that?"

"You are probably right…" Michlos said.

Jonas permitted himself a self-satisfied grin, but Michlos continued.

"…which means the invitation will have to be genuine."

Jonas buried his face in his hand. "This is getting us nowhere."

Reston sighed. "He has a point. Michlos, could we at least try to keep suggestions within the realm of possibility."

Michlos smiled. "Ironic, isn't it. Of all people, a Phrendonic is the one questioning what's within the realm of possibility. Very well. If we are agreed that the Monsignor requires an invitation to visit the Artist's Colony, I shall procure one."

"You're not getting it." Jonas said. "The Monsignor is not going to violate the Princess's edict, regardless of who invites him."

"Unless," Michlos said, his jade eyes twinkling, "that invitation should happen to come directly from the Princess herself. You see? I do get it."

CHAPTER TWENTY-TWO

AUDIENCE

It didn't take long to work out the rest of the plan. Jonas, however, remained skeptical that Michlos could deliver on his promise, insisting on some sort of proof before he would commit. Michlos bid them to work out some way of satisfying Jonas's concerns while he went to get his wound stitched. Jonas shot down each suggestion until Reston proposed having an eyewitness accompany Michlos to procure the invitation. Dona immediately volunteered, in part because she was eager to demonstrate her trust in Michlos, and in part because she was thrilled by the prospect of meeting the Princess. In the end, they agreed she was the best choice, if for no other reason than staying on campus had become more dangerous for her than for the others.

As a result, Dona found herself hanging on for dear life as Michlos's steed carried them through the gathering darkness. He made short work of the gate Inquisitors in much the same way that Reston had. They were about halfway down the ramp when he pulled off to the side.

"Hello," he said. "Do you see that?"

Dona peered out from beneath the hood of the cloak she had borrowed from Alexi. Squinting through the mists settling in the lowlands, she caught occasional flickers of light. As she watched longer, the mists stirred, and she glimpsed a multitude of them, laid out in a regular pattern.

"You mean the lights?"

"I do."

"What are they?"

"Unwelcome guests, I expect. They look like campfires to me."

"Oh, they can't be campfires. There must be a hundred of them."

"I hope you are right, but just in case, I think we'll have to make a detour."

Before Dona could ask where, the horse lurched into a full gallop, and she was obliged to cover her head with the hood once more to fend off the wind's vicious bite.

After what seemed an eternity, the twinkling lights of Trifienne came into view, and the horse slowed to a trot. Although the mazes of Trifienne were difficult to negotiate even during the day, Michlos picked his path with confidence, pulling to a stop before a quaint home in an affluent section of town.

"Stay here," he said. Dona geared up to argue, but he was already off his horse and pounding on the door.

"Hold on to your britches. I'm coming."

The voice sounded vaguely familiar, but Dona couldn't quite place it.

Finally, the door flew open, revealing the round face of Constable Connelly.

"Michlos?" he said. "I take it there's an emergency."

Dona's jaw dropped. "Constable?"

"Dona, is that you?"

It was Michlos's turn to be surprised. "You two know each other?"

"He's my roommate's father."

"What are you doing here?" the Constable asked. "And whatever it is, Miranda isn't mixed up in it, is she?"

"It's a long story," Michlos said. "Suffice it to say that on the way here from Exidgeon, we spotted a large number of regularly spaced campfires on the plain to the east. Whoever they are, they could be here by as early as midday tomorrow."

The Constable gave a low whistle. "Any idea who they might be?"

"Only guesses, and they're no substitute for good scouting."

The Constable nodded. "I'll get on it." He turned to face Dona. "If for some reason you need to stay here, you know you're welcome, right?"

"That's very kind of you, Constable, but I'm fine, if a little chilly."

"All right, I won't delay you two any more, then. I'm going to be plenty busy myself tonight."

Michlos nodded and hopped back into the saddle. "I'll be in touch."

As he urged the horse into a trot, Dona flipped back the hood. The wind was less harsh in the city, and she hoped to prod Michlos into answering some questions.

"You never mentioned that you knew the Constable personally," she said.

"Neither did you."

"So how do you know him?"

"We've worked together on a number of projects."

"Does he know you're a…an Enforcer?"

"He doesn't ask, and I don't tell."

"If he asked, and you told, would he still work with you?"

"I hope never to find that out."

"And the Princess? I suppose you two are old friends as well?"

"I try not to promise things I can't deliver."

"Who *are* you, anyway?"

"I thought we went over that."

"Are all of the Phrendonic families so well connected?"

"It varies, depending on the person and the family."

"So who else do you know?"

"I'd love to share a rundown of my social calendar, but during an Inquisition, I believe such matters are best divulged on a need-to-know basis. Surely you understand."

Dona sighed. "I suppose so. But you realize I'm not going to be the only one with questions."

"Our friend Jonas has already made that abundantly clear."

"Well, you have to admit, the whole idea did seem a little far-fetched."

"And this, coming from the man who claims to rob graves for the Primal's nephew? I think it's more likely he just doesn't like me."

"Wait, you mean the Monsignor is—"

"The Primal's brother? Didn't you know?"

"I had no idea."

"That's part of what makes our plan so attractive. There's more at stake here than just the individual reputations of Thurman and the Monsignor. What Thurman is doing could prove ruinous to his uncle as well."

Dona shuddered. "But wouldn't that make it more likely the Church would try to silence anyone who knew?"

"That is a possibility. I guess we'll just have to make sure it remains an unattractive one."

Dona grew silent. For the first time, she began to appreciate that her experiences of the last few days might forever deny her any chance of finishing her education. While she felt great sympathy for Jonas and Tilly, she had never truly believed she might actually end up like them. She pulled her hood back up and shivered as they galloped across the cold marble span and into the strange sanctuary that was the Artist's Colony.

On warmer evenings, the colony foregrounds played host to a festival of lights and colors where lesser-known artists ran booths to hawk their wares, and where grizzled carnies congregated in the hopes of enticing spare change from pockets of would-be patrons. But on nights like this, the fair-weather patrons migrated to warmer climes. With them went the camp followers. To Dona, their empty booths had all the charm of a ghost town, and she pulled the cloak around her even more tightly.

Passing the booths, they rode deeper into the heart of the colony. As they left the public areas behind, trees began to crowd the narrow road. When the encroaching darkness made it impossible to proceed, Michlos slowed their pace and removed a glove with his teeth. A moment later his head was engulfed by a brilliant yellow radiance. He stuffed the glove in a pocket and prodded the horse back up to speed. As her eyes adjusted, she determined the source of the light was the buckle on the front of his wide-brimmed hat.

"Aren't you afraid you'll be seen?"

"Not as afraid as I am of hitting my head on a low-hanging bough. We should be far enough in to be safe."

The trip grew even more eerie, since the light distorted the many sculptures interspersed among the trees, making them appear to writhe and twist, or sometimes, to leap out at them. Although she knew it was silly, she could feel her heart pounding harder with each grotesque revelation. She was so startled by the sound of Michlos's voice that she almost lost her grip.

"You may find the Princess to be…disconcerting. Be polite, speak when spoken to, but try not to reveal any unnecessary information."

"Is she dangerous?" Dona asked. That possibility hadn't occurred to her before.

"That depends on what you mean by dangerous. She holds a political position that's untenable by any measure and has not only survived, but prospered—and she's done it all on her terms. She's not someone to trifle with."

"Isn't that exactly what we are doing?"

"Let's hope she doesn't see it that way."

The trees gave way to a vast expanse of manicured grounds out of which rose an ancient stone edifice. Dona found the squat architecture jarring given the moonlit beauty that surrounded it.

"Here we are," Michlos said. "Ranselard Keep."

"Are we near the old prison, then?"

"It is the prison."

"Wait. The Princess lives in a prison?"

"It wasn't as hard to convert as you might expect. Many of the traitors it housed over the years were of royal blood and were treated as such. And it does have the advantage of being secure."

Michlos slowed the horse and dismounted, leading it by the reins to the portcullis that substituted for a front gate.

On the other side, a small light bobbed toward them. The elaborate sword at the belt of the man carrying it suggested he might be one of the keep guards, but he was otherwise so outlandishly dressed she couldn't be certain. From the patent leather boots, to the black-and-white striped doublet with its white starched collar, to the black velvet hat that was more plume than fabric, he looked every inch a dandy.

"Master Michlos?" he asked squinting against the light from Michlos's hat.

"Hello, Newcomb. How are you this evening?"

"The cold puts an ache in the knees, but can't complain otherwise."

"Do you think Her Highness would be amenable to receiving guests?"

"Is Her Highness expecting you?"

"Not this time, I'm afraid."

Newcomb sighed. "Well, if you were anyone else I'd tell you to look into making an appointment, but Her Highness seems favorably disposed to grant exceptions where you're concerned."

"I'm flattered."

"Whom shall I say is calling?"

"Oh, forgive me," Michlos said. "May I present Miss Dona Merinne?"

"Nature of business?"

"Personal."

Newcomb shook his head. "I don't know how you get away with that. I'll be back." He trudged off down the hallway.

"Remember," Michlos said quietly. "No unnecessary information."

"I'll remember," Dona said.

They waited less than ten minutes before the portcullis lifted. Newcomb reappeared in the company of another man in a similar outfit.

Newcomb offered his hand to assist Dona down from the horse. His fashion twin took the reins from Michlos.

"Her Highness will see you now," Newcomb said. "Come this way."

Although Michlos showed not the slightest reaction, Dona jumped at the rumble of the portcullis falling closed behind her.

The corridor was unlit save for his lantern and Michlos's hat, which he now carried at his side. As near as Dona could tell in the strange light, framed masterworks competed for every inch of wall space. Now and again they had to swerve to avoid the occasional art piece crafted in three dimensions.

"When will the new gallery open?" Michlos asked.

"Not soon enough," Newcomb said. "We have some rooms where the canvasses are stored three deep."

"Is this the new gallery uniform, then?"

"Alas, no. It's this year's winning design chosen by Her Highness from among the guard livery submissions at the Montmorency Festival. One can only hope that next year practicality will make a resurgence."

They came to a stop before a stairway leading up into one of the towers at the back of the keep. "Her Highness is in the studio," Newcomb said. "She's expecting you."

Michlos led the way up well-worn stone stairs. The door at the top was apparently a remnant of the keep's prison days, since it was constructed of thick wooden beams held together by heavy iron banding.

Michlos tapped three times.

"It's open."

Dona stepped back while Michlos tugged on the iron ring. Although the rough old hinges groaned a little, the door moved surprisingly easily. A great hall was revealed, dominated by a crystal chandelier. Devoid of candle or lamp, each of its pendant crystals emitted a gentle radiance. The aggregate effect was dazzling, and Dona had to shield her eyes to see anything else. Tall wooden easels were scattered about the hall, many of which contained canvasses in various stages of completion. The largest stood directly beneath the chandelier, its canvas receiving the devoted ministrations of the room's sole occupant.

The Princess didn't look up from her brushwork. "Michlos—what a lovely surprise."

"We are honored, Your Highness," Michlos said, bowing formally. "Thank you for seeing us."

The Princess finally seemed satisfied and dropped her brush in a nearby crock. Assuming her full height, she turned to face her guests. Dona couldn't recall the last time she'd seen a woman quite so tall. Her gown was simple, but elegant. It was certainly not the sort of thing Dona would have envisioned someone wearing while painting, and yet, there wasn't a speck of paint on it.

"Always so formal," she said. "If I didn't know better, I'd say stodgy was your middle name. Oh, and who have we here?"

Dona curtseyed low. "Dona Merinne, Your Majesty."

The Princess laughed. "Majesty, eh? While I would certainly welcome a promotion, the formality I can do without. You have no idea how tiresome it can be day in and day out. Michlos, you aren't contagious, are you?"

"She didn't get it from me, Your Highness."

The Princess held up her hand. "You're doing it again."

"My apologies, Highness."

"Oh, you're hopeless." She turned to Dona. "So, Miss Merinne, Michlos almost never brings any of his friends to come up and play. What's your secret?"

Michlos cleared his throat. "Miss Merinne is—"

"Perfectly capable of speaking for herself, I imagine."

Michlos fell silent.

Dona's mind raced. She hadn't expected to do any of the talking, and Michlos hadn't told her how he planned to obtain the Princess's cooperation.

"I'm just here in case he needs my help."

"Are you? Well, now you have me intrigued. What kind of help does he anticipate you might be providing?"

Michlos shifted uncomfortably. "Miss Merinne will be—"

"Michlos, since you had the foresight to bring that amazing hat of yours, would you be a dear and run downstairs and have Newcomb bring up a bottle of Anosti-Yarren from the cellars? There's one from 912 I've had my eye on, and I think your visit makes for the perfect occasion."

To his credit, Michlos's hesitation was almost imperceptible. "Of course, Your Highness. I'll be back momentarily."

"Take your time," the Princess called after him. "Now then, Miss Merinne, please, call me Celeste, and if you don't mind, I'll call you Dona."

"Oh, I couldn't possibly."

"Consider it an order then. Go ahead. Give it a try."

"Well, I guess if it's an order…Celeste."

The Princess put her arm around Dona's shoulder. "See, it's not so hard. Now, come tell me what you think of my painting."

The Princess guided Dona over to the canvas. It depicted a still life, perhaps three quarters complete. The design featured objects arranged on a tabletop, among them a model ship, a jeweled scepter, a textbook, a delicate vase with a single rose, a golden goblet engraved with serpents, a shock of wheat, a sword, and a small lacquered stick with a notch out of its center. The objects were arranged on a nearby table that had previously been obscured by the canvas. Dona was no judge of art, but even to her eye, the painting lacked the subtle artistry that would have made the objects seem realistic, and the saturated color palette made them unnaturally vibrant.

"I like it."

"What do you like about it?"

Dona was gripped by unease. How much could she safely say? On the one hand, the Princess seemed a little vain, but at the same time, she was clearly intelligent enough to know when she was being handed a platitude.

"The arrangement of the objects, for one. They give a nicely balanced composition."

"What else?"

"Well, the simplistic technique combined with the intense colors gives the objects an ethereal quality. It makes them feel less like objects and more like…symbols."

The Princess eyed Dona appraisingly. "Go on."

"For example, the goblet with the snakes could be considered symbolic of the Church, in which case the scepter probably is intended to be the Crown. If that's true, then the sword probably represents the militia."

"What about the vase?"

Dona only had to think a moment before it came to her. "Beauty," she said. "And that can only mean the Artists' Colony."

"Impressive," the Princess said. "And the textbook?"

"Easy," Dona said. "Exidgeon."

The Princess laughed. "I need a name for the piece. What would you suggest I call it?"

Dona considered the other items. "I'd call it 'Trifienne.' Almost all the major political factions are represented."

The Princess beamed. "'Trifienne' it shall be. You realize you are making it difficult for me to complain about how misunderstood I am as an artist."

"I have to say, though," Dona said, "I'm not sure what the lacquered stick represents."

"You mean the promise stick?"

"Promise stick?"

"You really don't know? Now that's unexpected."

Dona blushed. "Am I missing something obvious?"

The Princess retrieved the stick and handed it to Dona. "Notice the notch cut in the center? See how that makes it easy to snap in two?"

"Yes, of course. But why would someone make a stick like this?"

The Princess laughed. "Because like promises, these sticks are made to be broken."

Dona returned it to the table. "To what end?"

"Well, no doubt Michlos could explain it better than I, but the idea is that when you break the stick, you break the spell on it as well."

"Oh, so it represents the families, then?"

The Princess raised an eyebrow. "That's one interpretation. I'm getting tired of all this standing. Come sit with me in the gallery."

The gallery was precisely that. Portraits lined the walls, although unlike the artwork they'd seen on the first floor, these portraits were hung for display, not storage. Below each portrait, a brass plaque proclaimed the artist and the name of its subject. To Dona's delight, a glowing crystal suspended from a wire lit each one, and all were of women.

The Princess took a seat on a plush ottoman, one of several that decorated the space. "Welcome to my private collection." She patted the ottoman next to her, and Dona joined her.

"So, quickly now, before he gets back. What does Michlos want of me this time?"

Dona was a little taken aback by the directness of the question. "I'm sure he can put it better than I can."

"He'll get his chance. Right now, I'm interested in your version."

Dona glanced back toward the studio, but Michlos was nowhere in sight. "I'm sorry, Your Highness. If I had known you would want my version, I would have prepared something."

"It's *Celeste*, dear. And, if I were looking for a prepared statement, I would simply ask Michlos."

Dona felt trapped. Because she had no idea what Michlos was going to say, her only real choices were to deny she knew anything or to tell the truth and hope that Michlos would do the same. Any differences in their stories might lead the Princess to think one of them was lying, and she doubted that the Princess would suffer liars well. Since there was almost no chance the Princess would believe she didn't know anything, telling her that would jeopardize all the goodwill she had gained during the art discussion. There was no way she was going to do that."

"All right then, are you aware of the Inquisition taking place at Exidgeon?"

"I've heard the rumors."

"Well, we'd like to stop it before it gets out of hand, you know, like it did in Caprian."

"A laudable goal, but you must be aware that I have no influence whatsoever where the Church is concerned."

"We know," Dona said. Then she cringed as she realized agreement might be considered disrespectful. "I mean, we weren't going to ask you to influence them."

"I'm relieved to hear that."

"We think we might have a better way. Monsignor Goodkin and his son Thurman are in charge of this Inquisition. Do you know them?"

The Princess smiled.

"Oh, I suppose you wouldn't, would you? Anyway, the Monsignor is the Primal's brother, and it turns out that his son Thurman was paying our friend Jonas to rob graves."

The Princess blinked. "Your friend robs graves?"

Dona winced. She should have followed Michlos's advice. Now it was too late. "It's a long story. They weren't consecrated graves or anything, but Jonas is convinced what they wanted wasn't money, it was souls."

"Souls?"

"I know it seems far-fetched, and it probably doesn't really even matter if that part is true, but we don't think the Monsignor was involved. So, we thought that if the Monsignor were to find out what his son was up to, we might be able to use that to get him to call off the Inquisition."

"So where do I fit in?"

"Well, the problem is that we don't think the Monsignor is likely to view our friend the grave robber as a reliable source."

"I can see where that could be a problem."

"So we thought that if the Monsignor could actually witness his son completing the transaction with Jonas, then he'd have no choice but to believe us. And if the transaction were to take place somewhere in the Artists' Colony, then Thurman wouldn't be free to bring any other Inquisitors with him to back him up."

The Princess raised her eyebrows. "So you'd like my permission to allow this to take place on the island?"

"Well, it's more than that. We need a way to get the Monsignor to witness the transaction, and we were hoping you'd be willing to invite him here."

"Invite the Primal's brother *here?* Even assuming I could be convinced to do such a thing, why would you think he'd come?"

"I don't know how Michlos intended to convince you, but I think I know why the Monsignor might come. I've met him. He seems a genuinely thoughtful, caring man. From his perspective, I'm sure he'd view any chance of healing the rift between you and the Church as worth a shot."

"You've met him? Under what circumstances?"

"I'm a student at Exidgeon. He sat in on my rhetoric class the day I gave a talk about Antoinette Barget."

"You've heard of her?"

Dona laughed. "Well, I certainly didn't know during my talk, which was about how unfairly the Church had treated her, that the Monsignor would also happen to be her son."

"What an extraordinary coincidence. And he wasn't upset?"

"On the contrary, he was complimentary. He even went so far as to say he was embarrassed that he hadn't made more progress in redressing gender inequality in the Church."

The Princess stood suddenly. "I'd like to show you something." She strode along the gallery until she came to a full-length portrait of a doe-eyed young woman in a simple white gown clutching a bouquet of stargazer lilies.

"Welcome to my gallery of remarkable women. This piece has long been one of my favorites."

The caption on the brass plate read:

> *Antoinette Barget, oil on canvas, Urien Abel-roy, circa 871.*

From the hallway outside, she heard the faint sound of frantic footsteps. They slowed upon reaching the studio, and after a moment, Michlos sauntered into the gallery carrying a bottle and three glasses.

"We looked everywhere for a vintage 912," he said, "but 914 was the closest we could find."

The Princess's eyes glinted. "Oh, I'm terribly sorry. How could I have been so careless? Not to worry. I'm sure the 914 will do just fine, though you might want to let it settle before you open it."

Michlos set the bottle and glasses on an ottoman and removed his hat, tucking it into his belt. "I trust Miss Merinne's company was agreeable during my absence?"

"Completely. I had no idea she'd prove to be so fascinating."

Michlos's eyes darted to Dona. "Oh?"

"I must admit I was particularly captivated by the part about her friend robbing graves for souls to sell to the Church."

Michlos lost all color. "Yes, Miss Merinne has quite a vivid imagination."

"I was also deeply intrigued by the part where you were going to convince me, despite my being excommunicated, to invite the Primal's brother to tea."

"Your Highness, Miss Merinne is young and perhaps still a bit naïve. I'm sure she meant no disrespect."

"You aren't suggesting that inviting the Monsignor to tea would be naïve, are you?"

He paled even more. "Of course not, Your Highness."

"Good. What day do you think would be best?"

Michlos shook his head. "I'm sorry, best for what?"

"Really, Michlos, you should pay better attention. I'm asking what day would be best for inviting the Monsignor to tea, assuming, of course, you don't think it would be naïve."

"You'll actually do it?"

"Oh, don't sound so surprised. Would you have bothered to come all the way out here if you had really thought I wouldn't?"

Michlos started laughing. "Oh, all right. I admit it. You got me. Out of curiosity, what did she say to convince you?"

"Never you mind. Now open that bottle and let's get down to business, shall we?"

While Michlos fussed with the bottle, Dona scanned some of the other portraits in the gallery. A few of the subjects were immediately recognizable, but most were not. One in particular seemed familiar, but she couldn't put her finger on why. The plaque read only 'Dreamweaver' followed by a question mark. There was no reference either to an artist or a date. The subject was an attractive woman in her thirties, with long dark hair, arresting blue eyes, and an enigmatic expression that gave Dona a chill. The chill gave way to full-blown shock when she noticed the jewelry. Even on close examination, the necklace and earrings were indistinguishable from the ones she had stashed away in her hope chest.

"So why was this Dreamweaver person remarkable?" she asked.

Michlos and the Princess exchanged glances.

At last, the Princess spoke. "That one is a treasure, despite its subject, isn't it? Only five portraits of Dreamweaver are thought to still exist, all of them in private collections. I couldn't pass it up even though I couldn't determine the artist, or even verify with certainty that it actually was a Dreamweaver."

"It's lovely, but why did you decide to put her picture here, in this gallery?" Dona asked. "What did she do that was so remarkable?"

"Let's just say, that while many of the women featured here became famous for their achievements, a few of them chose infamy instead. Dreamweaver was one of those."

Michlos nodded his agreement. "Some aspects of the past

are best buried and forgotten, particularly during an Inquisition. Why do you ask?"

"No reason. I was just struck by her picture."

CHAPTER TWENTY-THREE

SEIZING OPPORTUNITY

Verone arrived at the Exidgeon University Chapel before the mists had lifted from the lowlands. Although she was eager to help the ladies get an early start, she drew the line at sleeping on a spare pallet on the floor of a drafty old building. They were just beginning to stir as she arrived.

She smiled brightly. "Good morning, ladies. I trust everyone slept well?"

A chorus of chipper good mornings greeted her.

Lesser beings would have bemoaned the less-than-ideal accommodations, but these were ladies on a mission. In no time, they had turned down their pallets, stoked the embers of the fireplace, and were cooking a simple, hearty breakfast.

Verone pulled Dona's mother aside. "I was wondering. Did you have a chance to check Dona's dormitory for clues?"

Amanda's eyes flashed. "I tried, but the house mother told me in no uncertain terms that she couldn't give me access to Dona's room without written permission from the Chancellor, as if the privacy of her roommates is somehow more important than my daughter's safety."

"How terribly unreasonable. Are you sure you were persistent enough?"

"I was, but she was adamant. She said she had just researched the policy last week. Apparently, the campus librarian had gotten just such a warrant to search her room for an overdue book. Can you imagine? She allowed a librarian to search her room for some musty old book but denied her own mother access to try to help locate her missing daughter."

"A book?" Verone asked. "Did she by any chance happen to say which book?"

"She didn't. I'm afraid at that point I became somewhat less than polite. Do you think it might be important?"

"Probably not. From your description, it doesn't sound like Dona would let a little thing like an overdue book interfere with her schooling."

"I didn't think so either, but then, I'm finding this whole situation baffling."

A shriek erupted from the sacristy at the back of the chapel. Verone arrived at the archway moments before Amanda did, just in time to hear Mrs. Caldor cry out once more.

Rayen lay sprawled and twitching on the sacristy floor near a makeshift pallet, his eyes bulging and his mouth frothing.

"My word!" Verone said. "Help me get him on the pallet."

Mrs. Caldor, her eyes haunted, kept her distance. "What's wrong with him? Is he dying?"

Amanda closed her eyes and sighed. "Oh, not again."

It took Verone and Amanda a few minutes to drag Rayen to a position where at least his head was on the pallet, but by that time, the twitching had mostly subsided.

"He'll want water," Amanda said. "I'll be right back."

Mrs. Caldor stared at Rayen, trembling. She hadn't moved since Verone arrived.

Verone sat on the pallet next to her patient. "He'll be fine, Mrs. Caldor," she said, checking Rayen's pulse as though trying to convince herself it was true. "He's apparently given to fits like this."

"How dreadful!"

"Why don't you get him a bowl of porridge? He'll probably be hungry too."

"Oh, good idea. I'll be right back." She pushed her way through the gathering gapers.

"Do you want me to get the undertaker?" Mrs. Muscany asked.

Verone smiled patiently "He's not dead, Mrs. Muscany, he doesn't need one."

"No, but if he does that again, *I* might."

Verone chuckled, and with the tension broken, the ladies began to disperse. Glancing back at Rayen, she was startled to see his deep blue eyes smiling up at her.

He spoke in a low, almost conspiratorial voice:

> *She braves a commotion of faith, she stirs up*
> *a cauldron of rage,*
> *Trifles with arts of perdition, and spatters her*
> *truths on the page,*
> *Mandates reversals of fortune, she wraps each*
> *success in a dare,*
> *Her whims can decimate empires, yet I wake*
> *and I find she is there.*

Verone blinked. Never before had she permitted herself to entertain the delusion that a man might wax poetic on her behalf. Men wanted vapid winsome creatures who cooed and swooned, and that was something she would never be. And then she remembered: this man believed these fits were the source of his powers as a seer, which could only mean that this performance was merely his latest feeble attempt at a prophecy. As quickly and unexpectedly as the little window in her heart had edged open, it slammed shut again. She colored faintly at her own naïveté and then assumed her customary mask of professionalism once more.

"You gave us quite a scare there, Mr. Magnificent."

Amanda appeared in the archway "Is he awake yet?"

He weakly propped himself up on his elbow. "I'm fine, Mandy. I'm sorry."

Amanda helped him take a few sips from a small crock. "Don't be silly. It's not your fault." And yet, it was clear from the tightness of her smile that she found the whole situation frustrating.

Verone moved back to give them space. And then Mrs. Caldor arrived to proffer the porridge, and Verone was edged out of the room entirely. As she turned to leave, Rayen's voice drifted out to her.

"Tell Verone to be careful with all those Inquisitors."

"You just lie back down and get some rest," Amanda said.

Verone shook her head. *As I thought, just another prophecy. Fitting, though—I'll be giving their faith a little commotion they won't soon forget.*

. . . . .

Thurman leaned forward, resting heavily on one elbow and drumming his fingers on his prized cherrywood desk. In the chair across from him, a tense and disbelieving Cartier was still prodding him to come up with some plan or stratagem to repair their damaged circumstances.

"Where is the Ordinal now?"

"Still sleeping," Thurman said. "Apparently destroying lives is exhausting business."

"But why would he want to destroy your father? He already outranks him."

"I've been wondering about that. Isrulian never did like my father, or my uncle for that matter, but he's never done anything like this before. Then again, these are unusual circumstances. It seems my uncle is seriously ill. All I can think is that Isrulian was afraid the other Ordinals might elect my father to replace him."

Cartier considered the implications. "That's a pretty risky move. What if he's wrong and your uncle survives?"

"He wouldn't even need to survive that long."

"Has Isrulian always been a big risk taker?"

"Not at all. In fact, he's always been one of the most conservative Ordinals."

"So why the sudden transformation?"

"Unless it isn't," Thurman said. "Maybe he doesn't see it as a risk."

"How could it not be? It's not like he could possibly know how long your uncle might linger."

"Oh, I can think of a way."

"How?"

Thurman eyed Cartier pointedly.

Cartier stiffened. "You can't mean that. Besides, Isrulian is here, and your uncle is three days' ride away."

"Obviously, he couldn't do it alone."

"A conspiracy?"

"Can you think of a better explanation?"

"No, but that doesn't mean there isn't one."

They fell silent, the only sound coming from Thurman's fingers thrumming the desktop.

"You have to go," Cartier said at last.

"What? You mean leave?"

"Yes," he said. "Get to your uncle while there's still time."

"What about my father? And what about the Inquisition? Someone's going to have to deal with the battalion when they finally arrive. My father's concerned that's going to end up being a very touchy matter with the Crown."

"Don't you see? You have to go. If you are right, Isrulian will do everything in his power to discredit your efforts here to make you, your father, and your uncle look bad. He's setting you up for failure."

"I can't just abandon my father."

"Saving your uncle is the best thing you can do for him. Isrulian didn't forbid you to leave, did he?"

"No, of course not, but then, I doubt the possibility occurred to him."

"Then you must hurry before it does."

Thurman hesitated. "What about the battalion of Inquisitors?"

Cartier shrugged. "I suppose you could always sign your authority over to me."

Thurman's jaw dropped. "You would willingly take my place in all this chaos?"

"I'd consider it my duty. Besides, once you are gone, I suspect his Ordinence will have far less interest in the goings-on at a small University out in the middle of nowhere."

"I'll go get the carriage."

"There's no time for that."

"Never mind. I'll just saddle up one of the horses."

"I think that would be best."

Cartier watched at the window as Thurman galloped out through the gates. Then he took a seat in the leather chair, put his feet up on the cherrywood desk, and laughed.

"Well then. I guess if anyone is going to get credit for exposing heresy in Trifienne at the very highest levels, it will have to be me."

. . . . .

Despite the early hour, Reston's basement meeting room was alive with activity. Tilly poured tea into the mugs of sleepy heretics, while Reston filled in Amberton and Tamry on the most recent developments. Jonas, for his part, had finally curled up in a corner and was snoring softly. Alexi had tried to focus on his geometry assignment, but Amberton's periodic outbursts made concentration difficult, and at last, he had given up.

"This is madness," Amberton cried, "pure and unadulterated. What makes you think the Princess would involve her island in an ongoing Inquisition? And even if she did, what makes you think it would have the slightest possibility of helping? Good lord, the odds against the timing working out are astronomical, and that's assuming Thurman even falls for it. The only viable solution is to shut down the entire project and burn anything that could incriminate us."

"Take a breath, there, Amberton," Tamry said. "Are you forgetting that the bulk of accusations in any Inquisition are by word of mouth? Burn all the evidence you like, but it only takes them finding one of us for the rest of us to fall. Even if it is far-fetched, creating incentive for them to abandon the Inquisition is a better idea than tucking our tails between our legs and hoping they happen not to notice us."

Reston's voice was firm. "Listen, I'm asking neither counsel nor permission—"

Spirited knocking echoed through the chamber. Alexi sprang up to answer it. The instant the door cracked open, Dona pushed her way in, chilled, but triumphant.

"She'll do it."

Alexi spun her in a congratulatory hug. "That's wonderful."

Reston favored her with a broad smile. "Well done. But where's Michlos?"

"He had to leave for the moment. There's some sort of force massing to the east of the city, and he's trying to help the Constable prepare."

"Force?" Amberton said. "What do you mean, force?"

"All I know is we saw campfires from the ramp last night as we were leaving to speak to the Princess."

Jonas sat up, suddenly alert. "How many?"

"I'm not sure. The mist was thick—a hundred, maybe?"

"A hundred men?" Alexi asked.

"No. A hundred fires."

Tilly shuddered and clutched the back of a chair for support. "Heaven help us—it's the first wave."

Jonas eyed each of them in turn. "Now would be a good time to say your prayers, gentlemen. The Inquisition is upon us."

Acknowledgements

Marilyn Gosz, whose serendipitous receipt of a misaddressed e-mail initiated this ten-year odyssey, and whose keen insights and constant encouragement nurtured it to maturity. Her involvement is a testament to the truth of Rayen's dictum: *Far more turns on the "chance meeting" or the "accident of birth" than on all the best-laid plans ever devised.*

Jean Jenkins, whose breathtaking editorial expertise has once again helped me produce a product of which I am immensely proud.

Mike Curdie, whose enviable artistic gifts made Trifienne leap from the page.

Adeela Syed, whose incisive feedback helped not just with the story, but with my whole perspective.

Brett Barbaro, whose interest in the manuscript ranged beyond mere text. I hope one day to oblige him with a game of Trumps of Doom.

Cindy Pury, whose thoughtful and meticulous suggestions on motivation and plot were absolutely indispensable.

Mary Vensel White, wordsmith extraordinaire and Author of *The Qualities of Wood*. Her keen eye ferreted out the dull spots and helped make them gleam.

Elspeth (Beth) Riley, editor par excellence, whose seemingly effortless facility with language informs not just my fiction, but my life.

Daniel Mendyke, whose keen ability to think several steps ahead helped lay a solid magical foundation and may even have won him a game or two of chess.

James Czarnik, who read despite all the other demands on his time—he taught me, once again, that "love is a verb."

Yergalem Meharenna, whose inexhaustible enthusiasm keeps me going even through the hard parts.

Marianne Smith, who believed enough in my writing and editing that she hired me to do it, and thereby changed everything.

Tam Czarnik: As did the Elves for the Ents, Tam gave me my voice.

Genelle Belmas: My inspiration and my love. I strive to make her proud in ways she does not expect, as she continues to do for me.

The Southern California Writers' Conference: who opened my eyes to the existence of publishing conventions and practices and made me appreciate their value. Their tireless efforts help me "suck less."

Nero: who warmed my feet throughout those long first-draft years. I shall miss him always.

Reshi: who after Nero left, decided I needed him and moved in. He was right.

The Pocket Watch used for the print-edition cover image was designed and crafted by **Lady Pirotessa** (at Blue Rose Creations). I *still* marvel at it.

GLOSSARY OF TERMS

Attunement: This property determines what constitutes a single object for purposes of vesting a spell—two or more objects attuned and in contact means a spell cast on one will spread to all of them. In general, items that remain in close contact for extended periods of time (about a year or so) become naturally attuned to each other. Thus, if a dagger blade is attached to a handle, and the two remain together for long enough, they become a single object for purposes of vesting spells (as long as they remain in contact as the spell vests) (see Vest). Certain Phrendonic spells from the Category of Enchantment can accelerate this process. In general, objects that are 95 percent attuned to each other behave as though they are 100 percent Attuned, while objects less than 95 percent Attuned behave as though they are not Attuned. Thus, once separated, Attuned items can lose their Attunement comparatively rapidly.

Category: Phrendonic spells can generally be grouped into one of seven categories based on how they function. Category dictates not only a spell's function, but places limits on spells that affect it. For example, a Dispel spell cannot generally affect more than one category. Thus, if two spells on the same object hail from different Categories, to dispel both, two different Dispels are required—one tailored to each of the Categories represented by the affected spells. The seven Phrendonic Categories are: Alteration Divination, Enchantment, Encryption, Evocation, Kinesis, and Summoning.

Charge: Some spells, referred to as Numeni (plural of Numenus), require an energy supply to maintain their effects. Charge spells collect and provide that energy—termed a 'charge.' A Numenus can only accept a new charge when it is empty of charge or very nearly so. A Reservoir spell can hold a charge until a Numenus vested on the same item is ready to receive one. Numeni, Charge spells and Reservoirs all possess a trait called Tolerance. A charge can flow from a Charge spell or Reservoir with a higher Tolerance to a Reservoir or Numenus with a lower Tolerance. If multiple receptive Numeni are available, the charge flows to the one with the lowest Tolerance. Once a Numenus receives a charge, it retains it until the charge is exhausted. Thus, if an Incinerate spell and a Light spell are both vested on the same item, casting a Charge spell on the item will have different results depending on the Tolerances of the three spells. If the Light spell has the lowest Tolerance of the three, the Light spell will receive the charge and the object will light up. If the Incinerate has the lowest Tolerance, the object will instead blow up. If the Charge spell has the lowest tolerance, the charge will have nowhere to go, and will dissipate without effect. Only the Tolerances of empty (or nearly-empty Numeni capable of accepting a charge) are considered for purposes of distributing charges.

Demon/Daemon: A soul displaced from its native body. The Church uses the term 'Demon,' Phrendonic practitioners prefer 'Daemon.'

Diffract: A type of Suppression spell that works on radiant effects (effects that extend beyond the target object in a radius, such as Darkness). Typically, a Diffraction spell is limited to affecting spells within a single category, e.g. Summoning. Since it only suppresses the effect without disturbing the spell's pattern, a Diffraction will not prevent a spell of the Diffracted Category from vesting within its radius. For that, one would use a Hedge, which is the corresponding radiant Dispel. See Dispel.

Dispel: A spell of the category of Alteration that disrupts the pattern of another spell vested on the same object causing it to dissipate. It is distinguished from a Suppression, which disrupts the effect of another spell, but leaves the pattern intact. If a Dispel is subsequently removed, the affected spell is still gone (provided it wasn't Patterned). By contrast, if a Suppression is removed, previously suppressed spells can often reassert themselves. A given Dispel is generally limited to Dispelling only spells within a single category. To be successful, the Dispel must be inherently stronger than the spell to be dispelled. Ordinals use the term Disrupt for essentially the same effect.

Evoke: To use a spell from the Phrendonic Category of Evocation. Evocation encompasses a Category of magic in which surrounding gasses are recruited into the pattern of a spell as it vests. Thus, solid objects may be created from air, although the spell itself must generally be cast upon an object to seed the effect. If the Evocation is dispelled or expires, the gas returns to its previous gaseous state.

See also Category.

Kinesis: The Phrendonic category of magic associated with spells that attract or repel.

Numenus: See Charge.

Ordinal: The nine Ordinals are appointed by the Primal, customarily for life terms. They rank just beneath the Primal, and upon a Primal's death, the Ordinals vote to determine his successor. Beneath the Ordinals are Archbishops, Bishops and Priests, in that order. The Inquisitor General is not technically part of that hierarchy—his role is to administer the Inquisition and he serves at the pleasure of the Primal. Thus, in his official capacity, the Inquisitor General reports only to the Primal, and his authority is as extensive or as limited as the Primal allows.

Passive Charge: Passive Charges are a special form of Charge Spell that collect energy over time, and when full (usually after about an hour) dump the accumulated charge into an available Reservoir or Numenus vested on the same item. Once emptied, they resume gathering energy, and the process repeats as long as the spell remains in effect. See also Charge.

Patterning: A Patterned spell is one that has undergone the process of Patterning to make the spell's pattern integral to that of the object on which it is vested. In essence, a Patterned spell becomes permanent, as long as the object it's vested on remains intact. Thus, a Color spell Patterned on a Promise Stick to turn it red would no longer have a duration—instead, the stick would remain red indefinitely. However, if the stick is broken in half, the spell dissipates like normal, except that if the stick is reassembled (provided the two halves remain attuned), the Patterned spell manifests once again and the red color returns. Patterned Numeni still require Charges to take effect. Like Attunement spells, Patterning spells reside in the Category of Enchantment.

Phrendonic Heresy: Practicing Phrendonic magic, as outlined in the work Practical Phrendonics, was officially declared heresy by the Edict of Caprian in the year 887. Some related practices, such as demonology, had been deemed heretical long before that. Prior to 887, a number of canon scholars viewed Phrendonic practices as already subject to those previous edicts. To them, the Edict of Caprian was little more than a clarification of existing canon.

Profanity: This term is used by the Church to denote an object upon which a Phrendonic spell is vested. Since Phrendonic spells generally don't last long unless they've been Patterned, it is usually presumed that a Profanity bears spells that have been Patterned.

Promise Stick: In its simplest form, a Promise Stick is a stick notched so that it may be easily snapped in two, usually to quickly break a spell without the bother of having to dispel it. In general, once a spell is vested on an object, at least 80 percent of the object must remain intact, or the spell is broken. Thus, if a Color spell is cast upon such a stick to turn it red, when the stick is broken, the spell is broken as well, and both pieces return to their normal color. However, if the stick is broken unevenly such that one piece retains at least 80 percent of its mass, the spell remains in effect on the larger piece, and dissipates from the smaller.

Reservoir: See Charge.

Sacrifice (Incinerate): Incinerate is a Summoning spell that instantaneously converts a Charge into light and heat in a radius around the targeted object. During the Caprian Inquisition, a number of Phrendonic heretic prisoners used this spell to immolate themselves rather than endure torture that might induce them to betray their compatriots. Inquisitors who got too close were often injured or killed as well. The Church's term for the practice, Infernal Sacrifice, gained traction at that time. Such a Sacrifice was an avenue of last-resort for a heretic, usually attempted after having been bound and masked or blinded. By casting the Sacrifice on themselves, they obviated the general requirement for the caster to see a spell's target to vest it. Since it's a Numenus, the Incinerate additionally requires a Charge to take effect.

Slept: Term of art used by Phrendonic practitioners to indicate that someone under the influence of a Sleep spell.

Sorcel: Phrendonic term for spell, specifically, one that has not been patterned and is therefore ephemeral.

Spell Radius: Radiant spells generally affect a 30-foot radius surrounding the targeted object. Skilled Phrendonic practitioners can modify radiant spells to have a smaller radius, but not a larger one. Spell Radius is to be distinguished from Casting distance, which is generally line-of-sight up to a maximum of 150 feet.

Spells vested on persons vs. Spells vested on objects: Spells vested on people or animals behave differently in some particulars than they do when vested on inanimate objects. For example, the maximum duration of a spell on a person is approximately an hour, whereas on an object, they can last up to a day. The difference is thought to result from an interaction between the spell and the person's soul.

Tag: A Phrendonic spell that creates a standard (though invisible) magical pattern, generally useful for interacting with other spells, such as Attractions or Repulsions. The term is also used to refer to spells that create non-standard patterns that are able thereby to avoid interaction with the standard spells.

Talis: Phrendonic term for a patterned spell effect.

Vest/vesting: The nearly instantaneous process whereby the pattern of a spell spreads across the target object. Once initiated by casting, a spell spreads to encompass all solid material that is both attuned to and touching the point at which the vesting initiated. Thus, if one were to cast a Color spell on the blade of a knife to turn it red, the spell would initiate at a point targeted by the caster and spread until it encompassed everything that was attuned to the blade. If the handle had been in association with the blade long enough, they would be Attuned, the spell would vest on the handle, and the handle would turn red as well. If the blade and handle were only recently assembled and therefore not Attuned, the Color spell would vest on the blade only, and the handle would not be affected.

About the Author

When Doug Bornemann was a boy, his mother would faithfully trundle her three sons into the family's candy-apple red Ford Galaxy 500 for bimonthly excursions from their home in rural Stockbridge to the Chilton public library—a tiny one-room affair tucked away in one of those solid brick public-service buildings so ubiquitous in small towns. To a more sophisticated observer, it might have appeared insignificant, institutional, perhaps even a bit dingy, but to a lad who didn't know any better, it was a room of hidden wonders and magic places, of unimaginable lives and exotic universes. Among its treasures—dog-eared copies of Charles Schulz's *Peanuts*, Roald Dahl's *Charlie and the Chocolate Factory*, and musty copies of James Blish's *Star Trek* novels, in hard cover. With his little pink card, he solved mysteries with the Hardy Boys and Jupiter Jones, took flight with Chitty Chitty Bang Bang, and wept for Margot when she missed her moment in the sun. He even learned to grok (or at least he imagined he did). Those seemingly innocent trips seduced him into becoming a reader, which had inevitable and profound repercussions on the rest of his life. His love of words propelled him through college, law school, and a doctorate in biology. In retrospect, he suspects that quite possibly may have been his mother's plan all along. Through his writing, he hopes someday to reach another young mind, and eventually, maybe even help to make a mother proud.

www.ingramcontent.com/pod-product-compliance
Lightning Source LLC
Chambersburg PA
CBHW030804260626
47169CB00001B/188